# Day of the Dead

## Andi Marquette

*Quest Books*
*by Regal Crest*

Texas

Copyright © 2013 by Andi Marquette

All rights reserved. No part of this publication may be reproduced, transmitted in any form or by any means, electronic or mechanical, including photocopy, recording, or any information storage and retrieval system, without permission in writing from the publisher. Parts of this work are fiction. Names, characters, places, and incidents either are the product of the author's imagination or are used fictitiously, and any resemblance to actual persons, living or dead, business establishments, or events is entirely coincidental.

ISBN 978-1-61929-146-1

First Printing 2013

9 8 7 6 5 4 3 2 1

Cover design by Mina Yamashita
Cover photo by Andi Marquette
Cover concept by Donna Pawlowski

Published by:

Regal Crest Enterprises, LLC
229 Sheridan Loop
Belton, TX 76513

Find us on the World Wide Web at
http://www.regalcrest.biz

Printed in the United States of America

## Acknowledgments

Many thanks to author R.G. Emanuelle, who talked me off many a writing ledge and gave me much love and support through the things life threw at me while working on this book; Albuquerque Police Department, whose quick responses to my questions helped push me toward what hopefully was a better path for this story; and Professor Elaine Carey, whose expertise on and conversations with me about the women who have run Mexican drug cartels provided lots of insight into my understanding of black markets, culture, and networks along the U.S./Mexico border. Thanks, also, to Regal Crest: author and editor Pat Cronin for her quick and efficient edit and to Trinka Kittle for her secondary edit and to publisher Cathy Bryerose for working to get this book to you, the reader, as quickly as possible. And thank you to the muses who offered inspiration at the times I really needed it.

And as always, many, many thanks to all of you — the readers — who have joined me and what I've dubbed "the New Mexico posse" throughout this series, and have been patiently waiting for the next installment. Here it is. May you never run out of green chile for the soul.

# Chapter One

CHRIS PUSHED THROUGH the knots of people gathered in the street to watch the aftermath of whatever tragedy had befallen the person in the house, now blocked from trespassing by crime scene tape and cops. Mostly neighbors, she figured, wearing jackets in the chill of a late October night. The neighborhoods just west of Albuquerque's Old Town were made up of family and friend networks, largely native Hispanic though newer transplants from Mexico and Central America also called this area home. Most of the houses were on the small side, built around World War II or slightly after, though some were older than that by a couple of decades. People knew each other here, whether by contact or sight, but they might not want to talk to the police because of a customary distrust of law enforcement.

Harper stood near the front door to the house, talking to one of the uniformed officers. He wore a department-issue jacket and jeans and work boots. Most of the time, Chris saw him in casual man-slacks and penny loafers. Tonight he looked like a truck driver originally from a state like Ohio.

She moved her jacket aside to show her badge – clipped to her belt – to a uniformed officer standing at the tape and the woman pulled it up a bit so Chris didn't have to stoop so low to get under it.

"Hey," Detective Dale Harper said in his flat Midwestern accent. "Glad you could join us."

"Yeah, well, not like people sleep at this hour on a Sunday or anything."

The cop next to him snorted.

"What've we got?" she asked.

Harper looked at his pocket notebook, mostly out of habit. He had probably already memorized what the cop had told him. "Our DB is a Hispanic male, late twenties, early thirties. Gunshot wounds to the chest, and groin."

"Anybody hear anything?"

"A Mrs. Marquez, next door." Harper gestured at a nearby house with his chin. The porch light was on.

"Is she outside?"

"Not anymore. But she did say she heard something after twelve-thirty. Doesn't speak much English."

That was almost an hour ago. Chris put her hands in her jacket pockets to warm them up. "Who talked to her?"

"Lauren."

She nodded, satisfied. Lauren's Spanish was good. "Okay." She looked at the uniformed cop. "Could you find Lauren and tell her I want to talk to her?"

"Sure thing. You got this?" He glanced at Harper, as if he was in charge. A guy thing, Chris knew. Unconscious, but it irked her.

"Yes," she said, reclaiming the lead. The cop shrugged and walked away. She took a pair of latex gloves out of a baggie-full she carried in her jacket pocket, and put the baggie back before she snapped the gloves on. Harper had his own, and he had already put his notebook and pen into his back pocket and was pulling his pair on. He handed her a pair of booties and she slipped them over her shoes while he did the same with his.

"Shall we?" he said, motioning at the door.

She stepped inside and stood for a few moments. The front door opened directly into a living room. A dark brown couch that sagged slightly in the middle stood against the opposite wall. A coffee table was upended in front of it, probably overturned by the now-dead man as he fell or was driven back from the force of the bullets that had killed him. He was sprawled on his back in front of the couch, arms spread, left knee slightly bent, right leg straight. He wore jeans, a white T-shirt now stained with blood, and black sneakers, the kind hip-hop artists sported.

"Was he found with that on him?" Chris gestured at the *Día de los Muertos* painted papier-mâché skeleton about a foot long that rested on his chest. It was female, dressed in a skirt and blouse. The figure wore a sombrero and held a guitar. Ammo belts criss-crossed her chest.

"I'll check." Harper left through the front door and Chris stared down at the dead man. It looked as if the figurine had been placed carefully on his chest, so it wouldn't fall off, its body positioned so it lay vertically on the victim's torso. A message, but to whom?

"Yeah," Harper said from the doorway. "Body was found with that on there, just like that. What do you make of it?" he asked when he rejoined her.

"It's a variation of *La Catrina*."

He looked at her with his "so?" expression.

Chris pulled her smartphone out of her pocket and did a search for the famous lithograph of Catrina, created by Mexican artist José Posada around 1910. In that image, Posada depicted a skeleton that was supposed to represent a once-elegant female figure from the shoulders up. A large feathered and flowered bonnet graced her grinning skull. Harper looked at it and nodded.

"Oh, yeah. I've seen this. Practically every Day of the Dead festival. What's the significance here?" He handed her phone back.

"I don't know. Posada did a lot of these *calavera* lithographs around the time of the Mexican Revolution. They were designed to poke fun at politicians and the class system without overtly naming anyone." She gestured at the figure on the dead man's chest. "Since then, she's represented as an elegant, wealthy woman, but other depictions of her have come up, like this one, in less formal dress, with different props."

"And that all means what, exactly?"

She shrugged. "She's become kind of a beloved folk image in Mexico. She represents death as the great equalizer. After all, she's a skeleton, and all her wealth didn't change the fact that being human means you'll die eventually."

Harper frowned and studied the body and gestured at the bullet holes in the dead man's chest. "Well, she was right. Looks like small caliber," he said. "I'd guess nine mil." He glanced around. "Not seeing any casings."

Chris looked around, as well. The killer might have taken those with him. If the killer took the casings, he probably took the gun, as well. Not an amateur, then.

Harper stood about three feet away from the dead man's head, looking down at him. The overhead light only offered a pale, washed-out kind of lighting reminiscent of cheap motels, so he had his flashlight out and moved its beam slowly up and down the dead man's face, then to his chest. Chris counted four bullet wounds in his chest and another in his crotch.

"You think there might be another shot in his chest but Catrina's hiding it?"

"Don't know. We'll find out when Sam gets here." He straightened. "I'd call this a hit, but he's shot in places other than the head. And then there's our little friend here."

"I'd think maybe drugs, but why leave that on his chest?" She shined her own flashlight across the man's face, then down his chest.

"That's generally where I'd go, but the chest wounds make it a little more personal. As does the groin shot. And the prop." The beam of his flashlight tracked down to the darker stain on the front of the man's pants, and the bullet hole that had caused it.

"Tats," she remarked as she shined her light on the vic's inner right forearm. *La Virgen de Guadalupe*, and she extended from his wrist to his elbow, in simple grays and blacks, entwined with roses and vines. Gangster script and skulls on his left forearm. "Nice work. You see any other ones that might indicate gang affiliation?"

"I like the way you think, Gucchi." He leaned a little closer and looked at the dead man's neck. He carefully pulled the collar of the man's tee down a little.

His nickname for her used to annoy her, but it had grown on her during the eight months they'd been working together. Besides, he could pronounce it better than her actual last name.

"Not seeing any in the usual places. Might be some on his back and chest. Sam'll find out. Jewelry?"

She scanned his hands. "No rings or bracelets. Necklace?"

"Nope."

She straightened and glanced around the room, looking for a phone or a wallet or something that might give them a clue about his identity.

"Might have ID in his pockets," Harper said, thinking along the same lines. He patted the vic's front pockets. "Feels like car keys on the right side, but I'm not feeling anything on the left. I'll wait for Sam to flip him."

"Okay. I'll check around, see what's here."

He grunted an affirmative and Chris moved through the living room into the kitchen. The overhead light was turned on and the same dingy effect spilled across the faded, 1970s-era scuffed linoleum. The cabinets were faded yellow, which helped give the whole room a sickly hue, though it looked and smelled clean. She looked through them and found a few mismatched plates and glasses, a couple of frying pans and pots, and a few eating and cooking utensils in a drawer. He didn't keep much by way of food. A bag of rice and a few cans of beans and soup were in one of the cabinets.

The refrigerator was just as bare. A six-pack of Mexican beer, tortillas, a to-go container with what looked like enchiladas, a bottle of orange juice and a carton of eggs. The stove and sink were clean, too, and a dish towel hung on a hook above the latter. She checked the small utility room just off the kitchen, where a stacked washer and dryer sat. They looked new. He'd been doing laundry, because the load in the washer was still damp. A plastic clothes basket on the floor was half-filled with jeans and T-shirts. She checked the back door, which was locked. The killer most likely came in the front and left that way, too, which meant the vic may have known his killer.

She left the utility room, crossed through the kitchen, and returned to the living room.

"Anything?" Harper asked.

"Go have a look. I'm thinking bachelor, and doesn't spend much time at home, though he was neat."

"He picked a bad night to be at home, then."

Chris chose not to respond. She knew Harper's flat, dark humor was his way of distancing himself from the shit they saw and dealt with, but sometimes, silence or simple yes or no answers went a hell of a lot further. Whoever the dead man was, he'd been somebody's son, maybe brother. He probably had friends somewhere who might be wondering why he didn't return their calls earlier that night.

She went to the side of the living room opposite the kitchen doorway to a short hallway. The first door on her left entered into a bathroom. Like the kitchen, it didn't contain much. The meds in the cabinet above the sink were all over-the-counter, for aches and pains and cold and flu. One toothbrush hung in the holder, and his personal hygiene items were all inexpensive, but placed neatly on the set of shelves above the commode and in a rack that hung on the shower head. She lifted the lid to the toilet tank, a place some people stashed drugs, but found nothing that wasn't supposed to be there.

A hall closet contained a few neatly folded towels and a couple sets of sheets as well as cleaning supplies. Chris checked the stacked fabrics and shined her flashlight around the shelves and corners, thinking that this was a guy whose mom had taught him how to clean, do his own laundry, and keep house, unless he had been in the military. That was another option. She pushed the door open into the one bedroom in this house and flipped the light switch. The bulb in the fixture was a high wattage, because it did a better job than in the other rooms.

His double bed was made, covered with a light blue comforter. Chris lifted one corner with her flashlight. No military-style sheet-tucking. Using her flashlight to hold the comforter up, she ran one hand carefully under the mattress on the three sides that weren't against the wall. She also checked under the bed, but found nothing. The shag carpet smelled musty, and she didn't want to be this close to it much longer. She stood and brushed her jeans off.

She looked at the top of the dresser for a while. A bottle of cologne and a gold bracelet sat on it, as well as a pile of change and a pair of black sunglasses. But that wasn't what drew her eye. Another papier-mâché figurine of a skeleton lay on its back next to the cologne. Skeletons like this one—a sort of generic *Día de los Muertos* painted figure—were relatively inexpensive, and easy to find this time of year, though they were more plentiful near the border. She nudged it with the butt-end of her flashlight, and its weight told her that it was probably empty, and not in use as a drug-smuggling device.

She studied it for another few moments, and wondered what its relationship might be to the one on the dead man's chest, then she went through the drawers of the well-worn dresser. Underwear, socks, tees, a couple pairs of jeans. He had preferred to ball his socks and just toss them in the drawer, but he folded his underwear, all bikini style. Finished there, she pushed the sliding door of the closet open. More jeans, hanging on hangers. A few more pairs of sneakers and a couple pairs of cowboy boots. He had a few button-down shirts, and favored black and white. His belts hung on a nail, but she didn't see any ties. A light leather jacket hung on a hook and a heavier black coat that looked like a working man's hung on another hook next to it.

"Sam's here," said Harper from the doorway.

"Okay. Will you back-check this room?"

"Yep. I already did the bathroom and the closet."

"Cool. Thanks."

She passed him and went back to the living room, where Sam Padilla, head of the Albuquerque crime lab was directing a couple of techs to take photos from different angles. He wore an APD baseball cap, but locks of his reddish hair stuck out from underneath. Sam always looked like he'd just gotten out of bed, and his sleepy, bemused expression had fooled many a criminal defense attorney in the court room.

"Hey," he said by way of greeting. "Anything I need to know about in the rest of the house? Medical Examiner will be here in a bit."

Chris shrugged. "No evidence of drugs, either product or cash stash. Guy was pretty neat. No evidence that a woman lived here or another man, for that matter."

"Love or money," Sam said. "Maybe love," he said half to himself as he shot a few photos from different angles of the body. He set the camera down and carefully picked up the figurine from the victim's chest. "Kinda personal, leaving a calling card," he said as he placed it in an evidence bag.

There were no other bullet holes under the figure, Chris noticed. "He might have an ID on him somewhere. And I think there's a phone underneath him. You can just see the corner of it, under his left hip."

Sam's flashlight beam worked its way down the dead man's chest to his crotch. "That's kind of personal, too." He looked up at her. "Does this feel like a hate crime?"

"Not anti-gay. Somebody clearly hated him, but I don't think it's because of that."

"Could you move that light closer?" Sam asked the other tech. They'd brought in a couple of portable lights and set them up near the body.

"Thanks," he said when the tech adjusted it. "We do have a phone. Good catch." He carefully extracted an iPhone from underneath the body. It may have been on the coffee table when the vic fell on it. The tech who had moved the light took it and placed it in a padded bag that Chris recognized as a Faraday, to shield electronic devices from wi-fi signals.

"You'd be surprised what we can get off these pups," he said. "If people really knew what their phones store, they'd probably freak."

"That's why I'm a flip-phone guy," Harper said. He looked at Chris. "Nothing that jumped out at me in there except another Day of the Dead thing on the dresser."

Sam glanced first at him, then Chris.

"That one was a basic decorative papier-mâché *calavera*, about a foot tall," she said.

"Huh. So I guess one of the questions you guys sort out is whether *La Catrina* was already in the house or whether the shooter brought her. What about drugs?" Sam asked.

"Nothing in the figure on the dresser, from what I could tell." She glanced at Harper for confirmation and he nodded.

"We'll bag that one too, and have a look at it," Sam said. He carefully ran his gloved fingers over the dead man's front pockets. "Feels like one of those thin wallets," he said as he pointed at the left side. He carefully reached into the pocket and slowly pulled it out.

"Let's see," he said as he opened it. "Two credit cards. And here's a driver's license. Victor Ramirez. Matches the cards."

"Don't make that official until we run it and make sure it's not fake and we match it definitively to John Doe, here," Chris said.

Sam nodded, closed the wallet and handed it to a tech, who bagged it.

"Let's have a look around outside," Harper said. "Back door's locked, so I'm thinking Mr. Ramirez here knew the perp." He pronounced it ram-EAR-ez, with a Midwestern drawl. The man was hopeless with Spanish.

"That's what I thought, too. Keep us posted," she said to Sam as she stood.

"Don't I always?" he said with a grin.

She kept her gloves on and followed Harper out the front door. Several people still stood on the other side of the crime tape, wrapped in jackets and robes, arms clutched around their bodies in the chilly October air. A few were talking to each other, but most simply stood and watched, expressions wary. She saw a couple of reporters she recognized from local news venues, here for the gory details in the morning shows. Like vultures, she thought with a tinge of disgust. A woman standing with the news crews caught her attention.

"Guess who's here," she said to Harper as they walked around the side of the house.

"Let's see," he responded without looking. "Our fave APD-hating bloggers."

"Bingo."

"Who'd they send?"

"Baca."

"And she's probably watching us like a freakin' hawk," he said.

"Yep."

"I'm sure we'll read all about it tomorrow. Can't wait," he added with a grunt.

Chris threw a last quick glance at the crowd then followed Harper and his flashlight into the back yard.

# Chapter Two

CRIME SCENE TAPE still fluttered in the late October breeze as Chris studied Victor Ramirez's house late Sunday morning. Things looked different in daylight, without the police lights flashing and the uniformed cops standing in the middle of the street, and without the crime scene RV blocking traffic, or the ambulance taking Victor Ramirez's body to the medical examiner's office. In the sunlight, it was just another Albuquerque neighborhood west of Old Town, where kids still played in the front yards of the small stucco houses, and men gathered on porches to talk and drink beer in the evenings and women cooked big pots of green chile and made tamales on weekends.

Would they still do that, she wondered, after what happened the night before? After someone shot a few holes in Ramirez? Would the people who lived in this neighborhood be able to carry on like they had before Victor died? Or would they mark time with a "before Victor" and an "after Victor" chronology, and lament the way it was, before violent crime came to their neighborhood?

Or would they even care? Maybe Ramirez wasn't well-liked or even well-known. Maybe the neighbors hadn't yet decided how to categorize him, and maybe some were relieved that he was gone, because they suspected he might bring trouble. She'd seen that many times, in areas of Albuquerque like this, where communities bound themselves together through a shared sense of ethnic identity and familiarity. Neighborhoods like this west and north of Old Town had raised generations of the same families, and bore the flavors of both *Nuevomexicano* and more recent Mexican or Central American residents. Some of whom, Chris knew, probably came here illegally.

Whoever had shot Ramirez went overboard, Chris thought as she leaned against the passenger side of her car. Whoever killed him wanted to be thorough. And whoever it was left a calling card, as Sam had said, but she still didn't know for whom. An execution-style hit was usually one shot to the head. A burglary interrupted might be a quick, panicked shot that may or may not find the target. Whoever had shot Victor Ramirez clearly wanted to make sure he was dead, and maybe didn't have the confidence of someone who was comfortable with guns. Or the shooter was really angry at the target and pulled the trigger more than once just because he felt Ramirez needed it.

She was inclined to go with the latter, but possibly the former. Someone who was not comfortable with guns but was really angry. Angry enough to pick up a weapon like that, go to Ramirez's house, and shoot him dead in his own living room. And then leave a calling card. Her gut told her the shooter had brought the figure of *La Catrina*, and that there was some kind of significance to that.

Chris pushed off her car and stood staring at the house, willing it to give up its secrets to her, but it remained stubbornly silent. She adjusted her blazer to make sure it hid the gun on her right hip. Chris had clipped her badge to her belt just to the left of her buckle, so it was easy to see up close, but not necessarily something anyone would notice from a distance. She carried a small digital recorder in the inside pocket of her blazer, along with a pen and a notepad, though in this neighborhood, she doubted anyone would allow themselves to be recorded. And she also doubted that anyone would want to do a sit-down interview with her, anyway. But maybe because her last name was Gutierrez, she'd have some play.

She turned at the sound of a car and watched as the older-model white Jeep Cherokee pulled up behind her vehicle. Harper unfolded his big frame from the driver's seat, got out, and shut the Jeep's door. He wore a navy blue windbreaker that she knew would be replaced by his usual trench coat once the daytime weather cooled enough. In Albuquerque, that was probably a few weeks away. He took his sunglasses off and slipped them into one of his jacket pockets.

"Solve the murder yet?" he asked as he approached, his expression as bland as his Midwestern features. Harper, though a big stereotypical Middle America corn-fed guy, could disappear in a crowd, behind his unassuming demeanor. Chris thought sometimes he affected that deliberately.

"Just about," she shot back. "After this, I'll check my crystal ball and get an address and phone number." *And then take another nap for a few hours.*

"I like that about you, Gucchi. Always willing to try new investigative techniques." He gave her a quick grin, which made him look boyish for a second. He gestured at the house to the right, next door to the one delineated with crime scene tape. "Let's see if we can scare up more info about Mr. Ramirez," he said, using the same awkward pronunciation he had the night before. He took his notebook out of his back pocket, and a pen from his shirt pocket.

Chris led the way to the front door, noting the Halloween decorations in the window. A cartoonish black cat, a ghost, and a skeleton. The kinds of decorations grade school kids put up in their classrooms. Mrs. Marquez probably had grandkids, or she gave out lots of candy to neighborhood kids. Harper joined her on the cramped porch, standing to her right, but in a way that anyone inside could see them both.

"*Buenas tardes,*" Chris said as she knocked on the screen door that separated her from the house's interior. "*¿Señora* Marquez?" She continued in Spanish. "It's Chris Gutierrez, with Albuquerque Police." She stood back from the door and moved her blazer so her badge was visible.

A woman appeared at the door, wiping her hands on a dish towel.

She wore a faded pink dress that didn't quite fit her ample frame. Her hair, mostly gray, was positioned in a loose bun on top of her head. She looked at Chris with mild suspicion. Harper got an even more wary look from her.

"Chris Gutierrez, Albuquerque Police," Chris said in Spanish again, pointing at her badge. "¿*Señora* Marquez?"

"Yes," Mrs. Marquez said in Spanish, in a voice filled with more suspicion than her eyes.

"I spoke with you on the phone earlier this morning, and said I would visit later with another detective. This is Dale Harper." She motioned toward him and he nodded respectfully, taking his badge out of his back pocket to show her.

"I don't know anything," she responded. "I told you and the other person with your department that."

"Yes, *Señora*, but sometimes things that people think are not important actually are important. May I please ask you a few more questions about Victor Ramirez?"

Mrs. Marquez studied her for a few moments, then grudgingly opened the screen door and joined them on the porch, barely big enough to accommodate them all. Harper was practically falling off the concrete step.

"Thank you," Chris said. "We just want to find out who killed Victor, and make sure that this person does not hurt anyone else. Please, could you tell me again what you remember?"

Mrs. Marquez seemed to relax a little bit, maybe because Chris spoke Spanish. She wiped her hands on her dishtowel again, perhaps collecting her thoughts. "It was very late," she started.

"Do you know what time it might have been?"

Mrs. Marquez hesitated, thinking. "A little after twelve-thirty. Julio on the other side—" she pointed at the house next door to her, the one without the crime scene tape, "comes home from work at twelve-thirty. I heard his car, so that is how I know."

Chris relayed the information to Harper in English in a low voice, giving Mrs. Marquez a moment to think. It was a routine they'd done many times with Spanish speakers. She'd translate and he'd take notes.

"And at one, Julio turns the light off in his back yard. That light shines into my window, so when it no longer shines, I know it is about one." She toyed with the dish towel and glanced around, as if worried that someone would see her talking to strangers. "I was having trouble getting back to sleep when I heard the shots. Julio had not turned his light off yet."

"More than one shot?" Chris was also writing things down, because she didn't want to interrupt Mrs. Marquez too much to translate.

"Yes. Maybe five or six. But I am not sure. Julio's dogs, they went crazy. Barking, barking. And then I heard a car start out front and it drove away very quickly."

"Did you see the car?"

"No." She looked as if she wanted to say something else, but stopped.

"Did you go outside?"

"No, not at first. Sometimes, in this neighborhood, you hear gunshots." She stopped, then continued, a harder edge to her voice. "It never used to be like that. Now the young men, they claim they have nothing to do, and they join gangs and get into trouble. Sometimes they play games with guns. I thought maybe that was what happened."

"Was he part of a gang?"

Mrs. Marquez pursed her lips and regarded Chris, debating, it seemed, what to tell her next. "He was new here," she finally said. "Nobody really knew him."

"New? In the neighborhood?"

"Yes."

Something occurred to Chris. "In the country?"

Mrs. Marquez shrugged, and Chris switched topics, knowing not to push that with her. Ramirez might have been in the country illegally, and regardless of what his neighbors thought of him, they would remain silent on that. Roots, after all, ran deep here, and often stretched across the shared border with Mexico.

"Did he associate with anyone in the neighborhood?"

"I don't think so. I never saw, and I am home during the day."

"Did he have a wife? Girlfriend?"

Mrs. Marquez stopped worrying the dish towel. "I saw a woman a few times, in the afternoon. But I do not think they were involved with each other, because she never stayed long."

"How long did Mr. Ramirez live there?"

"Not long. Three months, maybe."

"Did he work?"

She gave Chris a long, piercing look. "Not a good job like Julio has. Whatever he did, it was not legal."

"How do you know?"

She shrugged. "I have sons."

Grown sons, Chris figured, and no doubt Mrs. Marquez had known exactly what her sons were up to from the day they came into the world. Her own mother and grandmother were the same way with Chris and her brothers. Mrs. Marquez knew the ways of young Hispanic men, she was saying, and Ramirez, in her view, was up to no good.

"Do your sons visit you?" she asked.

"Yes. They come on Saturdays, but not Sundays," Mrs. Marquez said, anticipating Chris's next question. "They were not here when it happened."

Chris gave Harper the run-down in English. To Mrs. Marquez, she said, "What was Mr. Ramirez doing that made you think it was not legal?"

"He would leave in the mornings, sometimes, and other times he would be gone for a few days. He did not have regular hours, like men with legal jobs do."

"Drugs?"

Harper glanced up from his notebook, recognizing the Spanish word for what it was.

Mrs. Marquez shook her head. "Not here. Very few people came to the house."

Chris looked at her appreciatively. She was savvy, this Mrs. Marquez. "Can you describe this woman you saw who came to visit him?"

"Young. Maybe in her twenties. I only saw her from my window, so I cannot be sure." She paused. "She speaks Spanish," she added in a way that Chris deduced meant that Spanish might be the young woman's first language.

"Is she from the neighborhood?"

"No."

"Did she drive a car here?"

"Yes. And she would come sometimes with another woman."

"You are certain of that?"

"Oh, yes. She got out once, and leaned against the car while she waited. She is young, too."

"Could you describe these women to an artist?"

Mrs. Marquez frowned. "I only saw them through my window."

Chris calculated that the distance from Mrs. Marquez's window to a car parked in front of Ramirez's house was about eighty feet, and because her house sat a little bit forward of his, she would have lost sight of someone approaching his house about ten feet from his front door. Not an ideal observation point. Whether she was telling the truth about that was something Chris couldn't gauge. She provided Harper the information.

"Do you know what kind of car it might have been?" she asked Mrs. Marquez.

Mrs. Marquez shrugged. "I do not know cars, but it was gray."

"Four doors or two?"

"Four. I remember this because when the woman who waited got out the one time, she took her jacket off and opened the back door on her side to put it in the back seat."

Mrs. Marquez spent a lot more time at her window watching Ramirez's house than she let on. Chris wouldn't push it today, though. Neighborhoods like this required a delicate touch, especially where police were concerned.

"Did you ever see the license plate on the car?"

"New Mexico. I don't remember the numbers, but I saw the letters R, G, and F."

Chris wrote them down. "Do you remember the order of the letters?"

"I think the R was the first one. And I did not get a good look at the car last night," she added. "But it sounded very much like the gray car."

"How did it sound?"

"Like it has a hole in the muffler," she said, matter-of-factly. "Julio is good with cars." She nodded toward her neighbor's house. "My youngest son had a problem with his muffler and it sounded like the gray car. Julio helped him fix it."

"One more thing. Do you remember what time Mr. Ramirez got home yesterday?"

"Late, but before eleven." Her expression registered disapproval.

"Thank you, Mrs. Marquez. You have been very helpful. Please, if you think of anything else, would you call me?" Chris took a business card out of her inside blazer pocket and pointed out her phone numbers, circling her business cell number. "My cell phone number is better, because I always have that phone with me." She offered a smile and handed the card to her.

Mrs. Marquez looked at it then looked at Chris again. "Who is your family?"

"Gutierrez Construction. My father is *Nuevomexicano*," she responded. "My mother's family is from Chihuahua, originally, and my grandmother lives not far from here."

Mrs. Marquez's expression softened for the first time. "I will call you if I remember anything else."

"Thank you. And thank you for your time. *Buenos días*."

Harper clearly recognized the salutation and repeated after Chris, nodding at Mrs. Marquez respectfully. He was very good at being unobtrusively polite. Mrs. Marquez went back into her house and shut the screen door quietly behind her.

"What do you think?" Harper asked as they walked toward the street.

"I think Ramirez was doing something illegal. She didn't seem to know for sure if it was drugs, but his habits do send up a couple of red flags, if she's right about them." They had more houses to visit, more people to talk to. Chris sighed. They were in for a long day, after a long night. She craved sleep, but knew it wasn't in the stars for a while. "Let's run Ramirez's prints. I want to see if that's his real name."

"I was thinking the same thing," Harper concurred. "Beat Sam to the punch. Let me call those letters in, see if we can get a list of vehicles that match the description with those letters in the plate."

She waited while he did that and when he hung up, he slid the phone back into his pants pocket and looked at her. "Ready?"

She sighed. "As ready as I'll ever be for shit like this." They crossed the street toward the house directly across from the crime scene for the next interview.

BY TWO, THEY'D finished talking to everybody on Victor Ramirez's block that they hadn't spoken with the night before. Almost all said the same thing about him. Hadn't lived there long, few visitors, if any, and kept to himself. He was gone for stretches at a time, but nobody could pinpoint specific dates or blocks of time. No, nobody had seen any evidence of illegal activity, and no, they didn't know anybody who wanted him dead. A couple of people—both women—said similar things about the women who visited him, but they could add nothing beyond what Mrs. Marquez had already supplied.

"We need to find the women who visited him," Chris said as she and Harper compared notes at Harper's jeep. Late afternoon shadows stretched across the street, and the air had cooled, the tang of late fall settling in with it.

Harper mumbled an agreement and wrote something down. "First thing, let's run his prints, see if he comes up in this country. And maybe we'll get lucky with a hit on the vehicle."

"If he's not a citizen, we might have a problem." Chris rubbed her forehead as a headache brewed. They'd have to deal with the Mexican consulate then, and that would slow the investigation completely. Of course, if that happened, it was out of her hands, and she could move on to other cases, other families needing closure. If that happened, Ramirez would become somebody else's investigation.

"Diplomatic shit is a pain in the ass." Harper finished writing and put his notebook in his back pocket. "Go grab something to eat. I'll double-check the interview list and catch you at the station."

"Thanks."

"If anything happens before you get there, I'll call you." He climbed into the Cherokee, started it, and pulled away from the curb, tossing her a wave.

Chris remained outside her car a little longer and used the hood as a desk as she wrote the details of the interviews down while they were fresh on her mind, beneath the name of each person they'd talked to. Harper had gotten most of it, but she liked to make sure she had things written down, too, for her report.

A soft scuffing noise caught her attention and she looked up to see a little girl standing about ten feet away, watching her. Chris gauged her age at about seven or eight. She smiled at her in acknowledgment. "*Hola*," Chris said in greeting.

The girl didn't respond, and instead just continued to stare at her. Maybe she wasn't used to seeing a woman cop. Chris smiled again and went back to her notes. A couple of minutes later, she heard tentative footsteps approaching. The girl had decided to conduct her own investigation. She didn't look up, giving the child space to decide how she wanted to interact.

"What are you doing?" came her question in Spanish.

Chris looked at her, then, and answered, also in Spanish. "I'm writing things down so I don't forget them."

She seemed to consider this for a few moments, as she tugged on the hem of her faded blue shirt. A big yellow sunflower decorated the front, a match to her yellow pants. She wore pink tennis shoes and a pink barrette held her long dark hair out of her face.

"Are you writing what my mommy said?"

"I might be. Who is your mother?"

She pointed at a house across the street from Ramirez's, and two down on the left, if you stood looking at it. Elvira Guzman's residence. A large, smiling cardboard witch hung in the front window, and two uncarved pumpkins sat on the front stoop. She'd given her age as thirty, and Chris hadn't seen this little girl when she and Harper had spoken with her. No surprise there. She'd probably told her daughter not to come to the front door. Or her daughter hadn't gotten home from school yet. Chris hoped she was in school, at any rate. She glanced at her watch. About time for some to get out, so maybe that's where the girl had been.

"Yes, I am. I am writing down what your mother said." Chris never talked down to kids. She'd learned, after her oldest brother became a father, that kids were a lot smarter than most adults gave them credit for.

"Is my mommy in trouble?" she asked, her solemn dark eyes betraying a wariness nobody her age should have.

"No. I'm trying to find out who hurt Mr. Ramirez." Chris pointed at the house surrounded by crime scene tape. "I have to talk to people who live near him to find out if they know what happened to him."

The little girl pursed her lips, as if she was deciding whether to talk more. "What's your name?" she finally asked, in a tone beyond her years.

"Chris. And yours?"

She glanced at her house, then back at Chris. "Ana."

"I'm pleased to meet you, Ana."

"Are you police?"

Chris straightened. "Yes."

"You don't look like police," Ana said, skeptical.

"That's because I'm a detective." Chris put her notebook in her inner pocket and unhooked her badge from her belt and walked over to Ana. She handed it to her, and Ana studied it as if it were an archaeological find. "I don't have to wear a uniform all the time like other police," Chris elaborated. "My job is to find people who do bad things."

Ana handed her badge back. "Like the people that killed Victor?"

Chris raised an eyebrow as she clipped her badge back onto her belt. "Who told you that?"

She shrugged. "My mommy."

Chris considered Ana's statement. Elvira had said she watched the paramedics load Ramirez's body into an ambulance. "Did your mother say that Mr. Ramirez was dead?"

Ana nodded. "My mommy didn't like him."

"Why not?"

"He's a dirty coyote," Ana said matter-of-factly.

Chris stared at her. "Coyote? That's what your mother said?" That detail Elvira had neglected to share earlier.

"Yes. She told *Señora* Marquez that." Ana pointed at Mrs. Marquez's house. "My mommy helps *Señora* cook sometimes. *Señora* doesn't like him, either." Ana twisted the hem of her shirt around her fingers.

And Mrs. Marquez had left it out, too. "Why not?"

"I don't know."

"Do you remember when your mother called him that?"

"She called him that lots of times. But not to him."

That made sense. No reason for her to confront someone she suspected of smuggling people over the U.S. border. But not all coyotes had bad reputations. "Why did your mother call Victor that?"

Ana dug the toe of her tennis shoe against the sidewalk and stared at the ground. "I don't know." She looked up at Chris again. "I saw a coyote on the bosque. It looked like a dog. Victor didn't look like that."

Chris smiled. "You're right. He didn't. Did you ever talk to him?"

"A little. He always said hi to me and asked how I was doing in school."

Chris filed that away. Ramirez must have spoken Spanish. Unless Ana was bilingual. "Did you ever tell him what your mother said about him?" she asked, switching to English to test her.

Ana's eyes widened, like she couldn't imagine doing something like that. "No."

"Ana. Come here," came the command in Spanish, urgent, laced with suspicion. Chris turned and waved at Elvira.

"Time for you to go home," she said to Ana, switching back to Spanish. "Let's go." She walked her across the street and up to the porch where Ana's mother stood, watching Chris with suspicion. She beckoned Ana toward her and Ana complied, though she offered a little wave and a smile to Chris.

"Study hard," Chris said to Ana, still speaking Spanish, hoping Elvira would assume they'd just been talking about school things. Though chances were, she'd grill Ana as soon as Chris left.

"*Señora* Guzman," Chris greeted her. "Please, if you remember anything more, call me."

Elvira gave her one curt nod and pulled Ana closer. Chris took the signal for the dismissal it was and returned to her car. She heard the door of the Guzman house open then close with a finality that indicated she'd get no more information today. The chill hovering in the air had nothing to do with autumn. Chris unlocked her car with the key fob and got in, but she didn't drive away. Not yet. She studied Ramirez's house for what seemed like the hundredth time in the last day, noting how it looked in the late morning light.

Shabby. It needed a paint job and the mismatched curtains that hung in the windows looked designed to keep light out. And maybe to dissuade prying eyes. No Halloween decorations, or Day of the Dead cut-outs, which in this neighborhood were popular. Ramirez had clearly liked his privacy. Every window, she'd noticed initially, was covered with either curtains or blinds. In some cases, both. And all had been drawn to cover the glass. She thought then about what Ana had told her. Coyote. Human smuggler. If that was the case, Chris had a feeling it figured into his death. Whatever or whomever Victor Ramirez had brought over the border might have killed him. She started her car and pulled away from the curb.

# Chapter Three

YET ANOTHER CUP of coffee and a burrito from Garcia's restaurant helped take the edge off Chris's exhaustion. She'd bought a late lunch for Harper, too, and he ate at his desk while they talked.

"Still waiting on the vehicle list. That might be a good lead," he said between bites.

"When's the autopsy?"

"Sam said either tomorrow or Tuesday."

She nodded. "Let me know. I'll try to go with you."

"Will do. Let's see what our favorite anti-immigrant bloggers are up to." He set his burrito down and checked something on his computer. "Right on time," he muttered. He gestured at the screen and Chris leaned over his desk to look.

"Told you that was Baca last night," she said.

"Photos aren't very good. That's in our favor."

"What's the gist?" She sat back in her chair and reached for her coffee.

"Yet another murder," he read. "Blah blah blah, APD isn't keeping us safe from lawbreakers and in that neighborhood, there are lots of illegals." He glanced up at her. "Their term."

"At least they didn't use 'spic' or 'wetback'."

"Not yet. But I'm not done reading."

She took a sip of now lukewarm coffee. "Baca usually doesn't use those terms."

He grunted and continued reading. "And she didn't here. Nothing out of the ordinary otherwise, and like I said, the photos aren't that great." He clicked a couple more links on the site. "Huh."

"What?"

"Didn't realize they had a thing about gays, too."

She set her cup down and came around to his side of the desk. "When did they post this entry?"

"Three days ago." He pushed back a bit so she could get a better view of the screen.

"Jesus. So we have to close the borders to keep Mexicans out because you can never be sure that some aren't gay and bringing more AIDS into the country." She shook her head, disgusted.

"It's Burgess on this one," he pointed out. "When we have some time, let's see what we can find on him. Maybe find out why he started this blog."

She went back around to her chair across from him. "Because he has too much time on his hands and an axe to grind." But she knew he was right. The Legal Eyes bloggers had been dogging APD for months, and trying to pin every murder they could on undocumented immigrants, though they seemed to have an issue with legal immigrants and citizens, too, of the Hispanic variety.

Harper's desk phone rang. He picked up and had a brief conversation punctuated with several "uh-huhs" and "okays." He hung up and looked at her. "Be right back. We've got some data coming in."

She nodded, leaned back in her chair, and shut her eyes.

"Okay," Harper said after what seemed like barely seconds. She checked her watch. Nearly fifteen minutes.

"Good news and bad news," he said as he sat down with two manila folders.

"Let's have both."

"Good news is, Ramirez is his actual name. Bad news is, he's American, so we still have the case." Harper sighed in an "oh, well" tone. "So add him to your caseload, Gucchi. He's ours."

"Like the other thousand cases we're currently working will notice another one."

He shrugged. "Just trying to get you out of a thousand and one." He slid one of the folders toward her. "He's also got a record."

"What's up with it?" Chris started looking through the papers.

"Petty shit, mostly. All juvie. Stole a car with some buddies. Graffiti. Fighting at school. Nothing really scary. At least not that he got caught for."

"Where's he from?"

"El Paso."

Chris flipped through the pages. Right across the border from Juárez. That would certainly put him into contact with human trafficking networks. "Family in Mexico?"

"Don't know. His parents are U.S. citizens, though, both from El Paso, looks like."

She looked over at him. "Do we have a number?"

"Not yet. Can't find the parents. I've got a request in to see if they're still in El Paso or even alive. His file lists two sisters, but no current addresses for them. I thought it'd be easier to find the parents. I'm on it," he finished, letting her know that he'd notify them. And if he found family in El Paso, it meant one of them might have to go down there to talk to them. Chris knew it would probably be her because of her Spanish-speaking ability, which might be needed to conduct some of the interviews.

She looked back at Ramirez's file. "Lots of shit going on along that stretch of the border. Drugs. Human smuggling. Gun trafficking." And the murders that activities like that generally attracted. "Oh, talked to somebody else today after you left." She told Harper what Ana had revealed earlier that day.

He leaned back in his chair, hands behind his head. "Now that's interesting. What's your take?"

"I'm not sure, yet. Ana didn't know the human smuggling definition of 'coyote,' so I'm thinking her mom probably doesn't talk about it around the house. And she hasn't picked up on it yet at school."

"Mexican kids are savvy," he said. "Working narcotics in the South Valley showed me that. If there's anything like a coyote—" he said it with the flat American pronunciation, "in their neighborhoods or families, they don't say a word about it. Climate of fear keeps 'em quiet. Thing is, if they know about something, they just clam up. If they don't know something, they're shy, but they'll talk a little, like kids do."

"So you're saying Ana really doesn't know what a coyote is?"

"Not the human kind."

"That's what I was thinking, too."

"Doesn't sound like it. But it's a good angle. Mrs. Marquez sure didn't take a shine to him and she figured whatever he was up to was illegal. I'll buy human smuggling. Did you talk to Ana's mom again?"

"Not after I talked to Ana. I don't think she'd talk to me, anyway, about that. She didn't have much to say the first time we chatted. I doubt she'll admit to calling her neighbor a dirty coyote. Let's see where this human smuggling angle goes."

"It's that or drugs, but the drug angle doesn't really speak to me because he would be gone for days, which isn't typical for a local dealer. Can't be running around too much. The product comes to them. Unless he was a mule. That's another possibility. Though his house didn't have anything by way of drugs."

Chris nodded, running options through her head. "Plus there's the calling card thing. That meant something to the shooter, and it might have meant something to Ramirez."

"Yeah. Been thinking about that. Shooter probably brought the figure to the scene. It feels kind of personal."

She nodded. "Maybe he was a driver, making runs from Juárez or El Paso. Do you know anybody down there who might have a finger on that?"

"I'll check with Narc. Don't you have a contact there, too? Give him a ring. See what shakes out. I'll call some guys in Narc right now. See what we can see."

"Cool. Let me go over Ramirez's record and type up my interview notes. I'll check in with you in a few. Did he have a job in town?"

"Yeah. Jim's Paint and Body, in the South Valley. It's in the file. We need to take a trip down there ASAP."

"Tomorrow's going to be the better day for that. I doubt the place is open on a Sunday."

"It's not. I checked."

"What about his car?"

"It should be in impound. I'll check and see when we can go have a look."

"Sounds good. His phone?"

"We can check on it after we go to Jim's. Tony loves doing that shit and he'll probably have it all figured out by then."

She nodded and stood. As much as the department's tech wizard annoyed her, he did work fast. "See you in a few."

"Go home at a reasonable hour, would you?"

"You're one to talk." She picked up the file she'd been looking through. "Call me when you solve this, so I can get some sleep."

"You'll be the first to know," he said with a wry smile.

CHRIS HEADED SOUTH toward Central, thinking that maybe she'd just go to Old Town and have dinner at Monica's. The red chile was always good there. And she was damn tired. Too tired to cook. She sighed. It was also too early to call Dayna and see how things were going in San Diego. The irritation that came with a long day's end changed her mind about Monica's. She would much rather just be at home with a glass of iced tea and leftovers where she could talk to Dayna in peace. God, she missed her.

She turned left onto Central, which would branch into Lomas and take her to Albuquerque's near Northeast Heights, just east of Carlisle. Fake adobe houses—or "faux-dobes" as her best friend K.C. called them—predominated, though a few Craftsman-style bungalows and frame houses lined the streets as well. A mixture of retired people, middle-class, working-class, and college students plus young hipster-types had gravitated to this neighborhood. It was close to Albuquerque's Nob Hill, a funky artsy district along Central Avenue, a few blocks to the south. Central was best known as part of the original Route 66, and it split the city into north and south. Chris liked this part of Albuquerque, liked the variety of people, the quiet in the evenings, and how someone was always around to keep an eye on things.

She pulled into her carport, her headache already subsiding. She grabbed her briefcase as she exited her car and slammed the door shut with her foot before she locked it with her key fob. She turned to the security door that led from the carport into her kitchen and unlocked it and entered her kitchen, where she set her satchel on the island in the center of the room as a loud, insistent beep greeted her. She headed through the small dining room just off the kitchen, then into the living room, and entered her code on the alarm's keypad by the front door.

No mail on the floor beneath the slot. That was refreshing. She turned on her stereo—she was old school in that regard—and Etta James started belting out a blues tune from one of the CDs she'd left in the player. She turned the music down a little and returned to the kitchen, where she poured herself a glass of iced tea, then stared into the fridge for a while, sipping on the tea. Pizza, she thought. Definitely a pizza night. Her personal cell phone rang and she took it out of her pants pocket, her heart skipping a beat at the distinctive ringtone.

"Hey," she answered. "I was just trying to figure out what to do to kill time before I could call you."

Dayna laughed, low and throaty, in that way that made Chris tingle in certain places. "Guess what? We're done early. I'll be coming home tomorrow."

She grinned and shut the fridge. "That is the best news I've heard in a while. How'd it go?"

"Better than I thought. I'll tell you all about it tomorrow, when I see you. And I've got some really good news about it."

"Okay." She leaned against the island, her glass in one hand, phone in the other. "I miss you," she said after a few seconds. "A lot."

"Well, I miss you, too," Dayna said, and the warmth in her voice made Chris's day melt around her feet. "My flight gets in tomorrow night at seven. Any chance I might convince you to pick me up?"

"I think I could be talked into something like that." She ran through her schedule mentally. She'd go in early, try to finish by five, if nothing came up. She might be able to bail a little early, too. Hell, she'd go to the airport and sit there for three hours if she had to. Dayna inspired that kind of behavior in her.

"I heard that about you."

"Oh? What, specifically?" She took another sip of tea.

"That when it comes to me, you can be talked into anything," Dayna said, a smile behind her words.

"Mmm. I see K.C. has been spreading vicious untruths again."

"Not a chance. Sage said that."

"Damn her. I paid her to keep quiet." She laughed, thinking about her best friend K.C's partner, who K.C. had dubbed the "woo-woo cowgirl" during a visit to the state fair. "They're both right," she admitted, grinning. "I'm on record with that, Counselor."

"Duly noted. So have you eaten dinner?"

She took another swallow of tea before answering. "No. I just got in a few minutes ago."

"How about this? Order your pizza and call me back when you're ready. I'll be up for a while. I brought work along on this trip. I have to go through some briefs."

"Whose?" She quipped, smiling because Dayna knew that when she had had a long day and came home this tired, pizza was her comfort food.

"Ha, ha. Yours, I wish, but no such luck. Hold that thought, though. I'll talk to you in a bit. Bye, sweetie."

"Bye," Chris said. The connection clicked off and Chris whispered, "I love you," before she set the phone on the counter. She drummed her fingers on the island's tiled surface, staring at the phone. What was so hard about telling the truth? She sighed. She'd said it enough in euphemisms to Dayna. Why not the actual words? Gun shy, K.C. called it. But Chris hadn't known Dayna all that long. They'd only been seeing each other seriously for...what? Seven months? Could you really be in love with someone so soon? Sure, she'd told Dayna she was crazy about her. But love? Was that what this was? K.C. would say yes. So would Sage. She sighed again and picked up the phone to call for a pizza, extra green chile, then went to her bedroom and changed into sweats and a T-shirt. After that, she dialed K.C.'s number.

"Hey, *mujer*. Sage and I were just talking about you," K.C. said when she answered.

"Should I worry?"

"Well, yeah. Because you know we're always plotting shit."

Chris laughed. "*Chica*, truer words were never spoken."

"Detective Amusing over here," K.C. said, also laughing. "So what's up? How's Dayna?"

Chris took the pitcher of tea out of the fridge and filled her glass again. "She's fine and I need you." She took a drink.

"Damn, Chris. Must you say such things when you know I'm vulnerable to your feminine wiles?"

She almost spit tea across the kitchen and in the background, she heard Sage laughing.

"Wait. Have you ever had feminine wiles?" K.C. teased. "Nah. Just wiles. And a bad case of them. Have those looked at, will you? I'm sure Dayna can help you out there."

"And that's why I keep you around." She set her glass on the counter.

"I figured. Okay, for real. What's up? Got another wingnut group you need tracked? A militia check? Crazy apocalyptic bunker buddies in the East Mountains? I'm your gal."

Chris walked into the living room and lit the jar candles she kept on her coffee table. "Sorry, no. Though you are my favorite professor for that sort of thing. This is something else entirely. Remember that student you had last year? The one who did a project on illegal immigration that won that essay prize?"

"Yeah. Briana Lopez. Why?"

Chris returned to the kitchen and leaned on her island counter. "Didn't you find out that her mother came over the border with a coyote?"

"No, her aunt came over with a coyote. Briana's father was born in California and her mother is from Texas. But half of her dad's family still lives in Mexico. It was one of her dad's sisters."

"But she crossed into New Mexico, right? Not Arizona?"

"I think so. I can find out for sure, if you want."

"Yeah, actually. Let me know." Chris stared at the photo of Dayna she kept on the mantel and a dull ache settled in her chest, not entirely unpleasant.

"Can I ask what this is about or is it super-secret cop stuff?"

"Kinda super-secret. I'm just sort of looking at coyote networks. It might have a connection to a case I'm working on."

"Gotcha. Your secret is safe with me, *mujer*."

She smiled. "I know. Everything I am and everything I own is safe with you."

"And don't you forget it."

"Can't. You won't let me." Chris's front doorbell rang. "Hey, the pizza's here, *esa*. Gotta go. Let me know what you find out."

"Will do. Hi to Dayna from both of us. Bye."

"*Hasta*." She set the phone on the counter and went to her front door. Pizza paid for, Chris settled in for the evening, her candles throwing soft, warm light around her house and furnishings, a mixture of Mexico and the Southwest. By the time she'd finished eating two pieces of pizza, Ramirez was in a back file in her brain for the night. She ate one more piece, cleaned up, and dialed Dayna's number. The best kind of ending to any day.

# Chapter Four

SHE HAD JUST sat down at her desk the next morning when Harper appeared at the entrance to her cubicle.

"Morning, sunshine. You check your favorite blog?"

She groaned. "No. And hold on. Let me have my first sip of shitty department coffee." She took it. Yep. Shitty. But hot. "So what's the latest?"

"Burgess is ranting about another murder in our fine city, probably committed by illegals running roughshod over the border and bringing drugs and guns and you name it from Mexico."

"And?"

"He's talking about Ramirez, though he doesn't have his name yet. He claims he hit up the media talking heads to get the name of the poor man brutally dispatched near Old Town sometime in the wee hours of Sunday. I doubt they gave it to him, since he doesn't mention Ramirez by name."

Chris sighed. "So he thinks Ramirez is a fine, upstanding American just minding his own business and he gets randomly popped by somebody who crossed the border illegally?"

Harper shrugged. "That's about it. And APD is a bunch of sorry wetback lovers, because we're not doing anything to stop it."

"He used that term?"

"Yep. Nice guy."

"Christ. How is it he gets so many hits on that damn blog?"

"Lot of people looking for easy solutions to complex problems."

She frowned. "Does Jerry know?" She'd be surprised if the lieutenant didn't know, but Burgess's latest post was recent, so maybe Jerry hadn't seen it.

"Hell, everybody here knows. Except you, apparently. You ought to sign up for the damn thing, so you'll get the alerts. Anyway, careful. You know how this guy is. If he or anybody else from his little outfit calls, don't say anything you don't want showing up on the blog."

"Yeah. Thanks. See you in a few."

"Okay, then." He left, his head, shoulders, and part of his back visible over the cubicle wall as he walked back to his own workspace on the other side of the room. Chris's personal cell rang with a distinctive tone and she reached for it.

"*Buenos días*," she answered. When her grandmother called, Chris always spoke Spanish.

"*Mi'ja*, I am so glad I caught you. Peter called and he cannot bring my new shelves from the shop today after all. Can you do this?"

"I should be able to get there about five-thirty. I have something else to do later on." Of her three brothers, Peter tended to be the most flaky. He meant well. He just wasn't so great at organizing his time.

"Yes, yes. That is fine—" she stopped. "Ah. Dayna is returning today, then?"

Chris smiled. *Abuelita* always knew things. She didn't understand how, but some things in this world were just not meant to be understood, she'd decided. "Yes. Her flight arrives at seven."

"Oh, you mustn't interrupt that, *mi'ja*. Bring the shelves another time," she said, her voice filled with sly warmth.

Chris flushed, a little embarrassed at the jibe. "No, it's fine. I haven't seen you in a few days, anyway."

"Oh, your old grandmother knows how it is, when a loved one returns from a trip. But if you wish to bring the shelves today, I always love to see you."

"I'll bring them. Stay out of trouble," she ordered.

*Abuelita* laughed and they signed off, Chris's face still hot from her teasing. She put a call in to Carl Maestes, a detective in El Paso, and left a message on his cell to give her a call back. She then set to work poring over Ramirez's file.

Harper was right. Mostly stupid juvie stuff. Ramirez had managed to stay clean after the age of eighteen. That was interesting. Something obviously had influenced him. Or he just got better about not being caught. She suspected the latter.

Harper had scored a copy of his birth certificate. Victor Marcos Ramirez, born April 20, 1975. "4/20." The day that pot legalization advocates celebrated every year, usually by having dope-outs and hemp festivals, though 4/20 in police code had nothing to do with drugs. Still, the date was appropriate, if Ramirez was running drugs. And, because of K.C.'s research with regard to the right wing, Chris also knew that day was Hitler's birthday. She doubted Ramirez had known that, though.

A photo of him as a teenager getting booked for the car theft stared at her from the file. Typical sullen teen mug shot. No tattoos on his face, which was clean-shaven, and none on his neck, in this photo. She thought back to his body, lying on the floor of his house. She didn't recall any tats on his face or neck, and Harper had checked, but he did have them all over his arms. The juvie photos didn't include his arms, so she didn't know how long he'd had the tattoos.

She focused on his photo again. He hadn't been a bad-looking guy, but his eyes, even at that age, held a hard, calculating expression that Chris had seen in certain kinds of older men. The kinds of men who inflicted pain for sport. What kind of childhood set Ramirez on that path by the time he was in his teens? Or was he just one of the kids who ended up on the wrong side of his parents' expectations and then spent the rest of his life taking out his anger and frustration on others?

Chris looked through his work history. Mostly body shops,

including a three-year stint at a place in El Paso, but that was two years ago. She reached for her desk phone and dialed Harper's extension. They needed to make a visit to Jim's now, before Ramirez's identity was released to the press.

HARPER GUIDED THE Cherokee off Isleta Boulevard into the dirt parking lot of Jim's, a white rectangular building that looked a lot like most automotive repair centers. Four garage doors stood open, and one car was up on a rack inside one while two more were in various stages of repair in others. An interior wall divided the bay farthest from the main entrance from its neighbors. That was the painting room, and a guy was at work on the tailgate of a lowrider pickup. He looked up from his work as they rolled past, his gaze following Harper's vehicle.

He parked away from the main entrance, allowing room for actual customers. Chris unbuckled her seatbelt and got out of the Jeep, shutting the door behind her. She moved so she could look at the front of the building. A large chunk of stucco had fallen off the front above one of the garage doors, leaving what looked like a jagged reddish wound about two feet long. It had taken three painted letters from the word *Llantera*, leaving "Llant" in its wake. Enough letters to tell, however, that Jim's was also a tire shop.

Almost eleven in the morning, and warm enough to dispense with a jacket. Fall tended to linger in Albuquerque, easing its residents into winter gently. Chris opted to keep her lightweight black jacket on, a match in style to Harper's, though he preferred navy blue.

She waited for him to get his stuff together, and surveyed the immediate neighborhood. No sidewalks to worry about in this part of Albuquerque's South Valley, which reminded Chris of Mexico in some ways. Small, low-slung adobe and faux-dobe houses lined Isleta, which shot south off of Bridge Boulevard, the only border between front yards and ruts left by tires on rare muddy days. Here, people kept horses and chickens in their back yards, which often stretched for a half-acre or more, watered by the nearby Rio Grande as it wended its way toward the Gulf of Mexico. Huge willows and scraggly Chinese elms shaded front yards, their roots often buckling foundations laid in the early part of the twentieth century, if not before.

Signs in Spanish on nearby buildings advertised groceries and phone cards. Another indicated a bakery and next to that, a beauty salon. Shallow craters in Jim's parking lot signaled where the seasonal rain collected in puddles. Stacks of old tires stood guard along this side of the building. They'd been there a while, Chris deduced, from the undisturbed weed growth next to them.

"The owner's name is James Medina," Harper said as they approached the door. A flyer in the door's window advertised a Day of the Dead celebration at the South Broadway Cultural Center, taped next to an "open" sign that also advertised the shop's hours. Seven to six most days. Closed on Sundays.

She took her sunglasses off and put them in one of her jacket pockets. "All right. How about you take point on this?"

He nodded and reached for the door without questioning her statement. The place broadcast testosterone, and lots of it. Harper was good at getting information from the kinds of men who worked on cars and built things. He was ex-military, and carried himself like an understated tough guy—confident without needing to prove anything. The kind of guy other guys could talk to. And in this case, Chris figured that would score some points.

Harper opened the door into the customer area and a doorbell sounded as she followed him in. Clean enough, for a car repair and body work business. The usual car shop's accumulated grime along the windowsills, and scuffed linoleum that probably always looked dingy, no matter how many times it was mopped. The odors of oil, grease, tires, and bleach assailed her nostrils.

"Can I help you?" A wiry white man emerged from a back room, wiping his hands on a rag. He wore his blond hair in a crew cut, and sported a goatee. The name patch on his uniform shirt read "Alan." Chris guessed he was in his early thirties, and she noted the tattoo of a spider web that laced the left side of his neck, stretching from the collar of the tee he wore underneath his uniform shirt to his ear.

"I hope so." Harper removed his badge from his back pocket and placed it on the counter so Alan could see it. "We're with APD. I'm Detective Dale Harper and this is my colleague, Detective Chris Gutierrez. Is James Medina the owner here?"

Chris removed her badge from her belt and held it up for him. He gave it a cursory once-over, about the same kind of once-over he gave her.

"Yeah," Alan said to Harper. "But he's out of town. I'm the manager."

"We'd like to ask some questions about one of the employees."

His eyes narrowed at Harper's statement, and from the set of his jaw, he was about to become extremely stubborn. Chris clipped her badge back to her belt.

"About what?" he challenged.

"Would you be Alan Beck, then?" Harper continued, sounding both easygoing but professional at the same time as he picked up his own badge and put it into his back pocket. He always did his homework, something Chris appreciated about him. She took her notepad out of her back pocket and pulled the pen from its holder on the pad's case.

"Yeah." Alan switched his demeanor to cautious.

"Mr. Beck, we'd sure appreciate it if you'd help us out. Do you know this man?" He removed his notepad from his jacket pocket and took Ramirez's driver's license photo out. Harper placed it on the counter and Alan picked it up.

"That's Vic."

"Last name?"

"Ramirez." He pronounced it in a way that made Chris think he probably spoke some Spanish. Alan handed the photo back to Harper, and he put it in his notepad.

"Employee?"

"Off and on. Why?"

"Define 'off and on', please," Harper pushed. "Regular employee? Part-time? Sometimes? By contract?"

Alan set the rag on the counter. "His hours vary. He comes in as needed. We do some contract work, and we pay them by the job. What's this about?"

Harper paused just long enough to make Alan a little more nervous. "Mr. Beck, I'm sorry to have to inform you of this, but Mr. Ramirez is dead."

At first, Harper's words didn't seem to register, and Alan just stared at him, expressionless. He shook his head slowly after a few moments. "Dead? What happened?"

"Somebody killed him," Harper said, his statement softened by the empathetic tone he affected. "We're trying to figure out who he came into contact with before that happened."

"Killed? How?" Alan gripped the rag in his right hand so hard his knuckles whitened.

"I'm not at liberty to say. Was he here last week?" Harper moved closer to the counter.

"Yeah. Wednesday, I think. And then Saturday." He stopped and stared at the rag. "Jesus," he said softly. "He was working on a custom paint job for a longtime customer. He came in on Saturday and finished it."

"What time on Wednesday and Saturday was he here, by your recollection?"

"Got in around ten on Wednesday and stayed 'til six. He was here from noon 'til five on Saturday. He finished up the paint job and it looked great. He's good with custom painting. Damn. I can't believe it," he half-muttered, shock still lingering on his face.

"I'm sorry," Harper said again, and it sounded genuine. "How did he seem when he left on Saturday?"

Alan looked up at him, gaze unfocused at first, as if he was remembering. "Fine. I paid him for the paint job and asked if he wanted to go for beers but he said he had other stuff to do."

"Did he do or say anything that seemed out of the ordinary?" Harper wasn't giving Alan much of a chance to formulate responses, a tactic Chris knew he used to determine whether someone might know more than they let on. The less time for them to come up with stories, the better the chances of catching them in one.

"No. He was fine. He said he had to go out of town later this week but he'd be back Saturday night, so he could start another job next Monday I had lined up for him." Alan gripped the rag again. "Damn."

"Do you know if he had any friends or family in the area?"

Alan shook his head. "I don't know. He told me he was from El Paso, but that's all I really knew about him."

"Wife? Girlfriend?"

"He isn't married, I don't think. And he doesn't—didn't have a girlfriend. At least not a serious one."

Harper rocked forward slightly on the balls of his feet. "How long did he work for you?"

"About a year."

"Do you know where he lived?" Harper pushed another question at him.

"He said somewhere by Old Town. He moved a couple months ago to a house there."

"Any idea where he lived before that?"

"Over by Kirtland, but I don't know exactly where. It'll be in the files, though." Alan sighed and stared first at his hands and then up at Harper. He ignored Chris, which was fine by her. As she wrote, she observed him. If Harper hadn't run a check on him already, she wanted to. The spider web tat might indicate gang affiliation, but she didn't think he still ran in one. He might have ties, however, and Jim's could be a front for anything. Another angle to check.

"Anybody you can think of who'd want to kill him?" Harper asked, in a tone that Chris recognized as a particular guy-to-guy style of address. Not very emotive, but a recognition that it was a shitty situation.

"No, but then I only saw him here at the shop. Every once in a while he'd have a beer with us after work."

"What bar?"

"We'd usually just have a beer here. We have a fridge." Alan gestured toward the back of the room.

"I have to ask everybody this, Mr. Beck. Where were you Saturday night?"

"Santa Fe. My wife's family lives up there. We—me, her, and our kids—stayed the night with her parents and got back to Albuquerque Sunday around two."

"Did you go anywhere on Sunday after you got home?" Harper prodded.

"No. I was in bed around nine. I have to open in the mornings, so I'm up around five. Needed to get some sleep." A phone rang from the back, and Alan glanced over his shoulder then back at Harper. "I need to get that."

"Fine. Mind if we talk with your staff?"

"No." He left the rag on the counter and jogged to the back room.

Harper looked at Chris. "A few more chats for the road?"

"Definitely." She followed him out the main entrance and they walked to the first open bay. Thirty minutes later, they'd finished with four more interviews and all reacted the way Alan had. Shocked, didn't know much about Ramirez, but he seemed okay, and had beers every once in a while. Nothing that set off any alarms. They collected phone numbers and addresses of each one, just in case.

"Not getting any hits," Harper said as they walked back toward the shop's main entrance.

"Me, either." She reached for the door to the shop when a sleek lowrider pickup the color of emeralds pulled up next to Harper's blazer. Chris pulled her hand back from the door and she and Harper watched as a short Hispanic-looking guy got out. He closed the driver's side door and lit a cigarette that he took a drag on before he walked around the front of the truck to Jim's entrance. He wore mechanic's scrubs and black work boots that had seen a lot of use, from the looks of their beat-up toe caps. The boots gave him an extra half-inch, but Chris still had a good four inches on him in the height department and Harper seemed to tower over him. Another employee, she guessed, maybe in his mid- to late twenties. He wore his dark hair shaved close to his scalp, and a soul patch hung just under his lower lip. Harper nodded at him and he nodded back, took a last drag on his cigarette, then bent over and mashed it out in a nearby pail of sand next to the shop's door. Alan ran a tight ship, apparently.

"English?" Harper asked him and he nodded. Harper glanced at her, to see if she wanted this one. She did, and she wasted no time with it. Harper pulled his notebook and pen out of his jacket pocket.

"I'm Detective Chris Gutierrez and this is Detective Dale Harper. We're with APD. Do you work here?"

"Yeah," he said, looking first at Harper then at her.

"We'd like to ask you a few questions about one of your coworkers."

He shrugged, noncommittal. "Go ahead," he said in soft tenor with a slight trace of a Spanish-speaking accent.

"Could you give us your name, please?"

He half-smirked and pointed at the tag on his left pectoral, which said "Johnny."

She didn't take his bait. "Last name?"

"Griego. No 's'."

Harper spelled it out loud as he wrote it and Griego nodded.

"Victor Ramirez," Chris said, to see what his reaction might be.

"What about him?"

She kept her expression blank. Cocky. But that might prove beneficial because some people tripped on their arrogance. "Do you work with him?" She used present tense, to see whether that would mess him up.

He shrugged. "Yeah. When he comes in. Don't know him real good. He does nice work, though. Had beers with him a couple times." He slid his hands into his trouser pockets.

Griego used the present tense, too. Chris fired another question at him. "When did you see him last?"

For the first time, he hesitated, and looked from her to Harper then back again. "Saturday. He was here finishing up a job."

"Do you work on Saturdays?" Chris fired, testing his reactions.

"Yeah. Until four. Then home to get ready for dancing." He had regained some of his equilibrium and he gave her the kind of smile she figured he used on women at bars. Sadly, it probably worked on them. From her, however, it got him nothing.

"Do you have someone to verify that?"

"The bouncers at the Cooperage."

"What time did you get home?"

"Late. Maybe three."

"And Sunday?"

"Slept in. Then watched football with my neighbor most of the day." He looked at Harper like he was hoping for a guy cop ally through sports, but Harper remained granite-faced.

"How about your neighbor's name and address?" Chris shot another question at him.

"How about you tell me what this is about?" A touch of belligerence hardened his tone, and she relented.

"Mr. Griego," she said, softening her own tone, "Mr. Ramirez is dead."

He stared at her, clearly rattled. "How?"

"He was murdered."

"Shit." Griego ran one hand over his head. "Can I smoke?"

"Sure," Chris said.

He dug in his shirt pocket for his cigarettes, took one out, and returned the pack to its spot. With his right hand he took a lighter out of his front pants pocket and lit up. He took a drag and held the cigarette with his left hand, which looked like it was shaking.

"Any idea who might've wanted him dead?" she asked after he'd put his lighter away.

Griego shook his head.

"Was he seeing anyone?"

"You mean like a girlfriend?" Griego looked at her for confirmation and when she nodded, he answered. "No. Never married, either."

"Okay, Mr. Griego. Walk me through Sunday. When did you wake up?"

"Around noon."

"And then?"

He took a drag on his cigarette. "Got take out at Cervantes. Ate it at home. Then took a twelve-pack next door and watched two games with my neighbor. Went back to my place around seven. Watched TV for a while, then went to bed."

Chris held his gaze, pleased that he had to look up at her. "Where do you live?"

"Apartment complex near Gibson and San Mateo. I was with the neighbor in two-oh-five. Artie Padilla."

Chris mapped it in her head. Near the airport. Gibson ran east-west, a major thoroughfare that created a boundary between the city and Kirtland Air Force Base and the airport. Both the base and the airport lay south of the city proper. The residential areas there were a mixture of settled and not-so-settled, and sometimes crime from the latter slopped over into the former, disrupting the uneasy peace between them. She guessed Griego lived in a not-so-settled segment. Beck had said Ramirez lived near Kirtland for a while, too.

"Address and phone number?" she asked.

He provided both and out of the corner of her eye, she saw Harper writing the information down. He took another hit on his cigarette and turned his head to blow the smoke away from them.

"What did you think of Mr. Ramirez's work here?" Chris cast a wider net, to see what turned up.

He hesitated again. "It was good. I've worked cars for ten years, seen a lot of guys do bodywork. Vic was better than average, but not the best. Solid, though. If he worked full-time, he'd get more practice."

"What was his specialty?"

"He loves the lowriders," Griego said, using present tense. The finality of Ramirez's death hadn't hit him. "Those guys bring those in here, they want a cool paint job, so Vic could rock the skills he did have. He learned lowrider paint in El Paso."

So Ramirez had been proud of his work. Chris made a mental note of that. "What's different about lowrider paint?"

Griego relaxed. "Technique and look, mostly. Those guys want something slick, you know. Metallic sheen underneath, sometimes, so when the sun hits it, it sparkles. Vic could do a basic paint job on any car, but the lowriders were something he wanted to get really good at. Used to say he wanted to open his own custom car shop some day." Griego shrugged. "Lotta guys who work cars want their own place some day."

"What about you?" Chris dug around his edges a little.

"Nah. I like not having to deal with the overhead, you know. Pain in the ass."

Probably wouldn't leave much time for dancing, Chris thought. "Is this your only gig?"

"Mostly. I do some handyman shit around the complex." If it occurred to him that he was swearing in front of cops—and a woman cop at that—he didn't show it.

"Are you from here?"

"Cruces. But I'm New Mexico all the way." He injected his words with a little bit of *cholo*-style accent and gave her a rakish grin. When it didn't work on her, the grin faded.

"Did Mr. Ramirez have other jobs besides this one?"

"Don't know," he said, but the hesitation before he answered told her a different story.

"You and Mr. Ramirez hang out at all outside work?"

He shrugged. "A couple times. He came over to watch a game. Have a couple of beers. That's about it."

He sounded like he was forcing answers, like somebody who keeps coming up with excuses and only ends up sounding more suspicious. "That's it?" Chris asked. "Did he go dancing with you at the Cooperage?"

"Nah. He doesn't—" Griego hesitated and looked at his cigarette. "*Didn't* like crowds much," he corrected himself.

Chris registered that statement immediately. Griego knew a little more about Ramirez than he was trying to let on. "He have family in the area?" She changed direction again, but she kept her tone and expression bland.

"No. El Paso, and his parents are dead."

"Brothers or sisters?"

"Sisters, but I don't know where they are." He stubbed his cigarette out in the pail, rubbed his hands on the front of his pants, and glanced at the office door. Chris recognized that for what it was. He was late, and he didn't want to be.

"Did Mr. Ramirez mention anything to you on Saturday about going out of town after the weekend?"

"No," he said, but it sounded forced and he glanced away from her.

"Thank you, Mr. Griego," she said, releasing him. "You've been very helpful." She looked at Harper, who produced a business card from his jacket pocket and handed it to him. "If you think of anything else, please give us a call," he added.

Griego slipped the card into his back pocket. "Yeah." He nodded at them and went inside.

"Ready?" Harper put his notebook back into his pocket.

"Yeah. Let me check in with Beck one more time, see if we caught all the guys on staff."

"All right. See you at the car."

Chris nodded and entered the shop, passing Griego on his way out. He avoided her gaze and said nothing else to her. A man who claimed not to hang out with Ramirez too much, but who knew some family details and the fact that he didn't like crowds. Griego, she decided, needed some looking into.

# Chapter Five

"RAMIREZ WAS A private guy," Harper said as he and Chris exited the Barelas Coffee House just off lower Broadway. He had a toothpick in his mouth and he toyed with it as he walked toward his jeep. "Nobody knows shit about him but they all think he was a nice enough dude."

"People say the same stuff about serial killers." She put her sunglasses on and waited for Harper to unlock the passenger side door, idly scanning the surroundings. A woman standing outside the restaurant caught her attention. She was talking on a cell phone, turned slightly away from her. She looked familiar, but Chris didn't have a good view of her and Harper leaned in to unlock the door. The woman was probably a regular at the place, and Chris had seen her there a few times.

"What about Griego?" she asked.

He went around to the driver's seat and buckled up. He drummed his fingers on the leather cover of his steering wheel. As old as his Jeep was, he kept it squeaky clean. It smelled faintly of vanilla, probably from an air freshener though he hadn't put one anywhere obvious. Maybe he had a spray in the glove compartment. That thought amused her, Harper carefully spraying vanilla air freshener in his car.

"Knew a bit more about Ramirez than the others," he said as he started the engine.

"Even after saying he didn't, and that they didn't hang out much."

Harper grunted softly in acknowledgment. "What's the deal with the Cooperage?" He pulled away from the curb and headed back to Broadway.

"It's a steakhouse on Lomas, near the fairgrounds. The building that's shaped like half of a giant barrel. They do salsa nights on Fridays and Saturdays. Pretty popular for that."

"Never been. Good thing I have to check Griego's alibis. I'll find new places to hang out."

"I'm sure you'll love it." She stared out the window, thinking about Griego, watching the faux-dobe businesses and small houses that lined Broadway. They'd seen better days, but some were in nicer shape than others. A very few had been completely renovated and others had new paint, but the effect on them was like makeup on someone half-dead. The few tall buildings that marked Albuquerque's downtown stood to her left, and farther west than that, the tent-like series of long-dead volcanoes that looked like hills. "He's hiding something," she announced after a while. "I think he was closer to Ramirez than he wants us to know."

"You think he iced him?"

"Maybe. But I didn't get that read from him."

"He wasn't too broken up about it." Harper crossed Central and continued north, probably to avoid the slow-moving traffic on historic Route 66 into downtown.

"No, but he was surprised. So maybe they just ran together in terms of business, in whatever Ramirez had going on the side." That made sense. If Ramirez was running drugs or people from Mexico, he might've cut Griego in on it. The "why" of it eluded her, though. "I'll give the owner of Jim's a call," she continued. "Beck's probably already called him to tell him what happened, but you never know what else you can get out of people. What's your take on the place?"

Harper slowed to a stop at a light. "They look legit, but hell, even the mob ran fronts that were legit. You thinking drugs?"

Chris frowned. "Possibly. All Ramirez would have to do is drop a shipment there when he came in to work on a car. And maybe the cars he worked on were drop-off points." She envisioned the building's layout. It wouldn't be hard to do that, given the bay on the end was where he would've done the bodywork. "I'm not convinced it was drugs, though. Not feeling it. Don't know why yet."

"Good to be skeptical. But I think we should follow the drug angle for a while."

"Definitely. Let's check under every rock."

"See what crawls out," he concurred. "I'll check in with the ME and see if my Narc guys got back to me. You want me to run Griego?"

"Yeah, would you? I'll check death records on the parents and see if I can run down the sisters."

"Good plan." He pulled into his parking spot at the Medical Examiner's office on the UNM campus. "Let's get his phone, see what shakes out."

She nodded and unbuckled her seat belt and got out, thinking that she needed another cup of coffee.

CHRIS LEFT A message from her office phone for James Medina, the owner of Jim's, and hung up. She spent the next half-hour finishing up another report and organizing what she had on the Ramirez case and making a couple more calls. It seemed her phone was going to dictate her life, because ten minutes after her last call, it rang. "Gutierrez," she answered without looking at the caller ID.

"Detective?"

"Yes."

"Oh, good. I'm glad I caught you. This is Mary Baca, and I was wondering if I could ask you a few questions."

Chris clenched her teeth together then released them. "I'm sorry, Ms. Baca—"

"Mrs."

"Mrs. Baca," she corrected herself. "What is this regarding and what organization are you with?" She knew damn well who Baca ran with, but she didn't want Baca to know that.

"I'm a reporter," she said with a little bit of a huff, as if that should explain everything.

"I'm sorry, but you'll need to contact the APD media office. Let me transfer you." She reached toward the keypad on her phone.

"Just let me ask you one question," she pushed.

"Mrs. Baca—"

"When is APD going to do something about violent crime perpetrated by illegal immigrants?"

Chris frowned and bit back a retort. "I'm now transferring you to the APD media liaison."

"Detective—"

She didn't hear the rest of the statement because she pressed the transfer sequence on her keypad and hung up before anybody on the other end answered. She grimaced and noted the time and date in a call log she kept next to the phone. She then wrote, "Mary Baca, Legal Eyes New Mexico blog."

Her phone rang again and this time she checked the ID. She recognized it and answered it, with relief.

"*Hola*," said a familiar voice on the other end.

"Hey, Carl. Thanks for calling me back."

"You know I always help out a fellow badge-wearer. ¿*Como estás*?"

"Good, for the most part. You know how it goes. ¿*Y tú*?" Chris set her cup down, balanced the receiver on her shoulder, and grabbed a pen with one hand and a legal pad with the other.

"Same. This business—we never run out of bad guys." He sighed dramatically, and Chris pictured him sitting back in a chair, his feet up on a desk. For some reason, she always imagined him in cowboy boots, though they'd never met in person.

"Funny that. But if we did, you and I would be out of jobs."

"And then we'd have to take up golf with the *gringos*," he said, chuckling. "So, you chasing another crazy preacher?" he asked, referencing a case Chris had worked the preceding February.

"No. Something a lot different. Coyotes this time," she said, giving the word its Spanish pronunciation.

"*Esa*, you know finding those is like chasing a real one through the hills. If they don't want to be found, they won't be."

"Yeah, I know. But I've got a dead Hispanic male here who might have been smuggling people over the border."

"Huh," he said in a way that meant he was interested. "You know where he's from?"

"Your current city, *amigo*."

"What was his name?"

"Victor—Vic—Ramirez."

"Not ringing any bells, but that doesn't mean anything. Send me his photo and vitals. Does he have priors?"

"Juvie crap, all in El Paso."

"That makes it easy for me. Tell you what. Fax me what you can and I'll see what I can do."

"That would be a huge help."

He provided the fax number. "So what makes you think he was border-jumping?"

"A hunch. And a nosy neighbor."

Carl laughed, a gravelly sound that made Chris wonder if he smoked. "Best kind when you're working a case. Let me guess. Older woman, checking to see who was coming and going."

"Bingo," Chris said. Carl's mom was probably like Mrs. Marquez. "She said Ramirez would leave for days at a time. She suspected whatever he was doing was illegal."

"A trucker?"

"Nope. He worked an occasional contract at a local body shop. No record of other, full-time employment since he left El Paso."

"*Que extraño*," he mused aloud.

"I thought it was weird, too. And he was able to afford the rent on a house all by himself on a part-time contract here and there."

"Drugs, maybe."

"That's on the table. But there was no evidence at the house. No product, no equipment, no substantial cash. Trace is checking on some things, but I'm not seeing it."

"Check it anyway, *esa*. Nine times out of ten, that's what it is. But there is that one chance that it's something else."

"And that's why I'd appreciate it if you'd check around. I'm trying to cover every base I can."

"You got it. Can I give your number to fellow law enforcement if they've got some info?"

"Definitely. And let me know next time you're in Albuquerque. I'll buy you dinner."

He laughed. "That's a good trade. I'll see when I can get away and take you up on that."

"*Gracias*, Carl."

"*De nada*. Later."

She sat staring at her legal pad for a long moment, then wrote down the time and date and that she'd talked to Carl. A few minutes later, she faxed him the materials. When she came back, she saw that she had a voicemail message on her desk phone. She checked it and wrote down the details. James Medina, being extremely helpful. She called him back, but got his voicemail. She left another message thanking him and that she'd try to get in touch with him later. She had just hung up when her desk phone rang. She smiled at the ID for this one.

"Hey, Kase. What's up?"

"*Hola, mujer.* Got a little bit of info for you. Briana's aunt came into the country via Juárez. Neither New Mexico nor Arizona."

"Huh. So she ended up in El Paso then came into New Mexico?" Chris pulled her legal pad over and started writing.

"That's what Briana said. It was some years ago, though, but she said at the time, it was difficult to enter El Paso because the Border Patrol had ramped up its efforts in South Texas. Still, it's not as difficult to get in as people think. Before her aunt died, she told the family she'd come in east of the city, over the Río Grande. Her and several others."

Chris tapped the tip of her pen on the pad. "The aunt's dead?"

"Yeah, sadly. Cancer a few years back."

"Damn. How far back?"

"She died about three years ago, but she entered the country in 1999 or thereabouts. Briana wasn't sure if it was 1998 or 1999."

Before 9/11. Security tightened up after that. "Did Briana know who the coyote was?"

"No, but she said she'd check with her parents and get back to me. She doesn't think she'll get a real name, but she might be able to get a handle. You know. A nickname kind of thing."

"That might be useful. Even if he's not working there anymore, somebody might remember him." Chris stopped writing. "Did the aunt apply for citizenship?"

"Briana didn't say and I didn't ask. You know how screwed up that process is. Briana mentioned that the aunt was trying to escape an abusive marriage and drug violence."

"Where was she from originally?"

"I knew you'd ask that," K.C. said with a smile in her voice. "I think you're just as anal as I am. A town about thirty miles south of Juárez. Samalayuca." She spelled it out. "I looked it up. About a thousand people, and mostly ranching, though there's a big power plant, it looks like, that was built there in the late seventies. There're also some cool sand dunes that seem to be a tourist draw. I don't know what was going on in the Nineties there, but it probably did see a rise in violence with the cartels. And if you're getting beaten up by your husband, where do you go in a small town like that? Especially if his family's from there?"

Chris made a sympathetic noise. "No other family down there she could've lived with?"

"They do have other family, but Briana said that her aunt was very close to her — Briana's — dad. From what she understands, he told her aunt to come to the States because it would be harder for the husband to find her and, most likely, bring her back to Mexico."

"Did the aunt have kids?"

"No."

Chris finished writing and sat back, thinking. "What's your take on coyotes?"

"Mixed bag. Some are from the same villages as migrants. I mean, the people they agree to take over the border are people coyotes might know. Coyotes might even be friends of the family. Sure, there are some shady and violent coyotes, but there are also some in the local Mexican communities that have reputations to uphold. I did hear that some coyotes who are American citizens are making good money doing it. They generally demand cash and, as expected, some are assholes."

"So being a coyote is basically part of illicit border economies."

"Yeah. It's obviously still a shadow enterprise, but it's a good way to make a living for someone on the Mexican side. I read somewhere that a coyote bringing people into the States from Mexico can make twenty-five hundred dollars a person. That rate goes up exponentially for, say, people entering the U.S. from Ecuador. I also heard that American coyotes can make over a hundred grand a year smuggling people in."

"Jesus. Regardless, twenty-five hundred bucks a pop can go a long way in Mexico." Chris wrote the figure down.

"Hell, even if you're American and you bring, say, three people in from Mexico in a month at that price, that's almost ten grand. That can go a long way *here*. And if you have a good rep, people come to you. Coyotes operate differently now, *esa*. It's a business enterprise for some, and I've read that in some cases, coyotes and migrants work together to avoid the border patrol. The better you are as a coyote, the more customers you get."

"So basically, some of these *hombres* want to build a kinder, gentler rep for more customers."

"Exactly. But again, not all are that way. There are still terrible cases of abuse and rape and other violence perpetrated by coyotes on the people they're supposed to bring in. It depends."

Chris tapped the tip of her pen on her desk. "So what you're saying is that someone who crosses the border from Mexico and who has a good coyote probably isn't going to give him up to law enforcement."

"I'd say no. And even the bad ones are protected from that, if you think about it. If someone is brutalized by a coyote in the crossing, but they make it into the U.S. and enter the economy here, they're not going to tell anybody how they got in."

Chris frowned. No, they sure as hell wouldn't. They'd stay as far away from law enforcement as possible, no matter what happened to them before or after the crossing. Which meant that trying to figure out if Ramirez had, in fact, been a coyote was going to be a lot harder than she'd thought. Unless the women in his old neighborhood decided to talk about it. Chris sighed and tossed the pen onto her desk. Not likely.

"Damn," she said, frustrated. "How common are American citizens as coyotes?"

"Most research suggests that coyotes tend to be non-U.S. citizens or recent immigrants themselves. But some U.S. citizens do it, too, especially if they have the savvy and border knowledge and the language skills. It'd probably be an advantage, because he has legit documentation if anybody questions him. I'll check with my vast informational network," she finished with a laugh.

Chris smiled. "Excellent. And I've got kind of another little project for you."

"All right. Hit me."

"Randy Burgess. He runs—"

"Oh, yeah." She sighed. "The Legal Eyes New Mexico blog. I know his work." She said it with a special kind of K.C. sarcasm that came from years of researching far right extremism.

"You seen it recently?"

"Sadly, yes. Another APD bashing session, as well as the usual immigrant bashing."

"Can you look into Burgess? See what larger circles in your world he might run with? I'm trying to figure out where this guy's issues come from or if he's just the kind of guy who doesn't like brown people."

"Or cops, looks like. Unless they hate women, too. Hell, probably gays, too. I'll see what my vast network knows about Mr. Burgess and the crowd he's with. Is he bothering you?"

"I'm with APD. So yes, he is."

"I meant on a more personal level."

"Not yet, though Mary Baca, who blogs over there, just gave me a call and demanded to know when APD was going to do something about violent crime perpetrated by immigrants."

"Shit."

"Yeah. It is."

"Be careful with them, Chris. They have a tendency to record conversations and post them online. I have a feeling they also selectively edit those conservations."

"I know. All I told her was that I was going to transfer her to our media liaison."

"Good. And if they approach you on the street, be ready because they'll try to goad you into saying something incriminating."

"They sound delightful."

"They're people with a mission, and those kinds of people end up saying and doing crazy things to further it."

"Well, you'd know. That's why I keep you around."

"That and my fabulous sense of style."

She laughed. "That, too. Thanks, Kase. I hate that I sometimes send you into crap like this."

"Hey, I picked this line of work. Might as well put the info to good use."

"And changing the subject to more pleasant things, have you and Sage decided to do a Halloween get-together?"

"Yes. Sage doesn't have to go to Taos that weekend after all, so we're going to have an open-house kind of thing. You and Dayna are invited and no, you don't have to wear costumes," she said, laughing again. "Sage is also putting together another altar for Day of the Dead. You know how she digs that."

"She's more *Nuevomexicana* than I am," Chris said with a chuckle.

"Nah. She likes the artistic aspect of it, and the colors, and she's trying to get a grant to go to Oaxaca next year to cover it."

"She'd get some seriously beautiful photos there."

"That's her thinking on it."

"Sounds great. Send me an e-mail with the time and date for Halloween."

"Will do. And I'll let you know if Briana has any other info."

"Thanks, *esa*."

"Totally. Bye."

Chris put the phone back on the receiver just as Harper came in to her cubicle.

"Let's go hang out with Tony, see if he's been able to pull anything off Ramirez's phone."

"All right, but before we get to that, Medina called back."

"And?" He sat down.

"He left a message. He's in Chicago on business and he said that we could absolutely look at the personnel files on Ramirez and please, anything he can do to help is fine. He said he'd call Beck and let him know about the files."

"Huh." Harper scratched his chin. "Throwing us a bone? Or really innocent?"

"I'm not sure, honestly. If he's doing something illegal behind the scenes, he might already have Beck getting rid of stuff so when we go in there, everything's in order. But there's a chance that he doesn't know much about Ramirez and is truly trying to be helpful."

He exhaled and his cheeks puffed out. "We might never know. Beck's had all afternoon to clean up. Not tough to get rid of files."

"Not hardcopy," Chris concurred. "But if there's something not right over there, we can subpoena the computers."

He nodded. "That's doable. What else?"

"Finally talked to Ramirez's landlady. She's freaking out, to put it mildly."

"Well, yeah. Dead guy in your house is usually bad for business. She's probably not the shooter, since that only creates the mess. Killing your own tenants is also bad for business," he added.

"She wanted to know when she could get a crew over there to clean the house."

"What'd you tell her?"

"Not for a few days. I gave her my contact info and also info about local crime scene clean-up companies." Death wasn't pretty, no matter how it happened. She rubbed her eyes, as if she could rub away all the bad things she'd seen. The physical evidence of a violent death could be cleaned, but the emotional and psychological aspects of it—you couldn't scrub those away. "Still haven't located the sisters. I'm wondering if Ramirez had family in Mexico. Maybe that's where they are."

"That's possible." Harper fell silent, thinking. "Kind of weird, that we can't get a line on family."

"Maybe Ramirez was estranged from them."

Harper grunted, his "maybe, maybe not" noise. "The media released his name. Family might shake out with that."

"Parents won't. Both dead."

"At least we know to quit looking for them."

Chris shrugged, thinking that it sucked learning a family member was dead via a news report. Sometimes, though, that's how it happened. If that was the case here, Albuquerque Police would no doubt be criticized for not working hard enough to locate relatives. Chris rubbed her eyes again. "I love this job," she said, and Harper chuckled.

"Gets under your skin," he said. "What do you want to do about Jim's?"

"I'll go back, have a look at the files. If they're not in hardcopy, I'll have Beck print them out while I'm there. You want in on that?"

"Let's see what the phone shows. I've got all the records on order from the cell phone company, and they're being oh, so helpful this time around. I'm also trying to get any bank statements he had. But let's see if we can access anything before those come in. Speaking of—" he tossed a file onto her desk. "Mr. Johnny Griego."

She looked at it, then at him. "Anything juicy?"

"Nope. A couple of stupid juvie incidents, but he's kept his nose clean since then."

Or he didn't get caught, was the unspoken rejoinder to that statement. "Cruces?"

"Yep. Born and raised. Graduated from high school there, tried New Mexico State for a couple of years, but dropped out and started working at car detailing joints. Moved to Albuquerque four years ago."

"Any indication he knew Ramirez before he moved here?"

"Not that I could see. Maybe you'll pick something up, though."

Chris shrugged and set the file aside and picked up a legal pad and a pen. "Let's go see what Tony's up to."

He grunted an affirmative, stood, and followed her.

# Chapter Six

TONY DIXON WAS seated at his workspace, surrounded by computer monitors and various techie items that signaled his affinity for all things digital and computer. In keeping with his geek cred, he was also a comic book fanatic, which showed in the Ironman and Avengers toys he'd arranged into various poses on his shelves and file cabinets. Chris knew that his other love was baseball, and today he wore a Colorado Rockies tee. He looked up through his wire-rim glasses when they appeared in his open office door, a bottle of Mountain Dew poised at his lips.

"Hey," he said before he took a swallow and set the bottle down. "Got your boy's last text messages."

Harper took up a position behind him. "Did he use a password?"

"Yeah. Easy enough to crack." He looked at Harper critically. "Don't use your birthday. That's always the first thing I try."

"You're serious? That was it?"

"Yep. Probably figured nobody else would know it unless he told them. And he probably didn't tell anybody."

Like it mattered, Chris thought. Given enough time, a four-digit password could be figured out eventually.

"So what've we got?"

Tony pointed at the monitor directly in front of him. "Looks like the last text came in Sunday night at eleven thirty-seven PM."

Harper took his small notebook out of his back pocket and opened it. He repeated the day and time as he wrote it down. "What's it say?"

"It's in English and it says 'ready to go, meet you in EP Saturday, let me know if something comes up.' No name, but the message is from somebody he called 'G.' Here's the phone number." He read it off, then decided to put it up on screen.

"That sounds familiar," Harper said as he wrote it down. "Hold on." He went back through his notes. "Well, look at that. It's Griego's number."

Chris caught his eye. She had been writing on her legal pad, which she'd placed on a cluttered table behind Tony. "Interesting. 'G' for Griego?"

"Looks like it."

"That's just rude. He had a date with Ramirez and neglected to tell us."

"Must've slipped his mind."

Tony shifted in his seat, uncomfortable. He was weird about any gay reference and Chris figured it was because he protested too much about his internal feelings for guys.

"Okay," Tony interrupted. "The last outgoing message was at eleven forty-two. If your guy sent it, the last thing he texted was 'ok' then 'six'."

Harper wrote the information down. "So he was going to meet Griego somewhere this coming Saturday."

"EP. El Paso?"

"I like it," Harper said. "Probably at six. I wonder whatever for," he said sardonically.

"What about this?" Chris leaned against the wall behind Tony. "Maybe Ramirez was going to El Paso to pick up whatever he's transporting—assuming that's what he's up to—and Griego was going to meet him there. They'd make a transfer and Griego could go up through Carlsbad with whatever it was while Ramirez just went back through Cruces. He'd take I-25 so he'd be seen at the checkpoint south of Truth or Consequences without anything on him or anybody with him."

He nodded. "I like it. Keeps Ramirez in the clear and allows a transport to Albuquerque without hitting checkpoints."

She nodded, thinking. "There are three official ones. The one east of Las Cruces is between there and Alamogordo, so it wouldn't make sense for Griego to meet Ramirez in Cruces because he'd only have two options. Risk a checkpoint or take I-25 to the Hatch exit and then go southwest until Deming then shoot northwest. That's a hell of an inconvenience. He'd practically have to go to Arizona."

"Makes more sense, then, for him to go to El Paso and head east out of there then north into Carlsbad and up through Roswell."

"Much more sense. Not that border patrol wouldn't be watching, but if Griego drove his truck, it might actually work in his favor. Who in their right mind would use a truck like that to smuggle something or somebody from the border?" She wrote that down on her legal pad. "Did you run Griego?"

"Yep. Should have that in any minute now. I'll check when we're done here."

"Excellent. Anything in his other texts?" she asked Tony.

"Here." He scrolled through them as they appeared on his monitor. About twenty, she estimated. Nothing jumped out at her. All seemed innocuous, asking about meeting for beers or working on cars. She wrote down the three phone numbers that came up to cross-reference with the numbers she and Harper got from the employees at Jim's. The numbers that didn't match she'd call and when the cell phone records came in, she'd take a longer look.

"What about missed calls?"

Tony put that up, as well. Two, from the same local number. Ramirez had missed the calls on Saturday. Or he had chosen not to answer. One at 8:14 PM and the other at 11:22 PM. She and Harper both wrote it down.

"Let's see the numbers dialed."

Tony put that screen up and Chris nodded. "Uh-huh. He called that local number Saturday, at seven-sixteen PM."

Harper wrote it down. "There's no name or initial with it?"

"No." She picked up Tony's desk phone and dialed the number. It clicked right to voicemail and a greeting in Spanish in a woman's voice—she sounded as if she was in her twenties, maybe—asked the caller to leave a name and a number and she'd get back to whomever it was. Chris left a message in Spanish. "Hi, this is Detective Chris Gutierrez with the Albuquerque Police Department. Could you please give me a call regarding a man named Victor Ramirez? Thank you." She left both her office number and her work cell phone number and hung up. "I'm betting it's a cell phone and it's currently turned off." She was also betting that she wouldn't hear back. That was definitely an angle to follow up. What if the number belonged to the woman in the gray car that Mrs. Marquez had talked about?

"I'll run that sucker, too. So you want to call Griego or just show up?" Harper asked.

"Hell, I think it's better if we just show up. Let's catch him at work first thing tomorrow morning, before we go over Ramirez's car." She glanced at her watch. Three-thirty. "I have to run an errand at five and Jim's closes at six."

"Let's save it for tomorrow morning, first thing, and keep the element of surprise. I'll run these numbers, and check and see if anybody's come forward claiming to be family."

"Sounds good."

"Okay. Let me call Sam and give him the info about the texts. Tony, keep futzing with it. If you find anything else, let us know."

"All right."

"Maybe Deep Throat called him," Chris said. "Then all our questions will be answered."

"Uh, yeah. Whatever." Tony hunched over his keyboard.

"Thanks," she said as she and Harper left, but he didn't look at her again.

"You make him nervous," Harper said in the hallway.

"Why do you suppose that is?"

"You're scary."

She looked over at him and he gave her a grin. "Catch you in a bit," he said.

"The fun never ends." She returned to her cubicle and checked the phone numbers she'd pulled from Ramirez's text messages against the phone numbers of employees at Jim's. She sat back, thinking. All three numbers matched, and none of the text messages she'd seen had been sent over the weekend. In fact, all were at least a week old. The oldest was two weeks old. So Ramirez didn't have many people texting him and if he was doing something shady, he seemed to have ensured that those messages got erased. Until the cell phone company dredged them up. He'd left the last message, probably because he'd been shot before he had time to get rid of it.

She rubbed her temples, then typed "human smuggling" and "Mexico" into Google. Like K.C. said, sometimes a larger context helped you see a different perspective. Thirty minutes later Chris had a lot of different pieces but still nothing specific to Ramirez's death. She sighed and sat glaring at the screen for a few moments before she shut her computer down and placed her notepad in her satchel, ensured her typed version of her notes was locked in her file cabinet, grabbed her jacket, and headed out. She needed to pick up *Abuelita*'s shelves, catch up with her, and be at the airport by seven. Thinking about Dayna soothed her mood and by the time she left the parking lot, she was in a better frame of mind.


"HERE?" CHRIS ASKED in Spanish as she adjusted the shelves for at least the fifth time.

"More to the left."

Chris smiled and pushed the shelves about an inch in the direction *Abuelita* had requested.

"Yes. Very good." *Abuelita* inspected Chris's positioning and nodded, satisfied. Rudolfo, her small terrier mutt, sniffed the new furniture suspiciously. Since it didn't respond to his inspection, he returned to chewing on his rawhide near the doorway to the kitchen. Chris checked the stability of the shelves again, and the positioning of the arm of the couch to ensure that *Abuelita* had enough room to get between that and the shelves.

"Do you want me to attach them to the wall?"

"Oh, no. I may have you move them again."

Chris smiled.

"Have you time to visit with your old grandmother?" *Abuelita* gave her a wicked little grin and Chris laughed.

"Always. What sorts of news of the neighborhood do you have?" She followed her, noting the end table *Abuelita* had positioned in the corner near the arched entrance into the kitchen that held a framed photograph of her long-deceased grandfather and one of her uncle Luis, Jr., who had died in Vietnam. *Abuelita* had also placed Luis, Jr.'s GI dog tags on the table, along with his New Mexico driver's license, a pair of his father's cufflinks, and a few other unframed photos, including one of him with *Abuelita* when he was getting ready to ship out. The table also held a few jar candles. She smiled. *Abuelita* always put a few things out like that around *Día de los Muertos*, in remembrance of the two Luises in her life.

Chris sat at the table—the old 1950s-style that had been a constant here throughout her life—while *Abuelita* poured two glasses of iced herbal tea from the refrigerator. Chris knew it was herbal because *Abuelita* drank nothing with caffeine. She claimed it made her jumpy and she needed all her sensibilities when she mixed her traditional herbs to help alleviate the various aches and pains of the neighborhood residents.

"I thought perhaps my dear granddaughter would have news for me." She placed the glasses on the table and smoothed the apron over her dress. *Abuelita* never wore trousers. "Must I worry about what happened the other night?" She made a gesture with her lips in the direction of her front door.

She shook her head. "No, 'lita. That was something that was directed at a specific individual." She took a sip of the tea. Chamomile and blueberry. No doubt *Abuelita* had a couple different kinds in the refrigerator. She always managed to serve Chris chamomile, in an attempt to alleviate her stress. She never knew for sure if it worked, but she always felt better when she left *Abuelita*'s company. Whether that was the tea or *Abuelita* didn't matter.

"I have heard things about Mr. Ramirez," she said as she took the seat to Chris's right.

Chris looked at her, surprised. She never read the papers, and she didn't have a computer. Perhaps she'd caught his name on the news earlier.

"People talk, *mi'ja*," she said, smiling. "It is how we look out for each other." She wrapped both of her small hands around the glass and studied its contents for a few moments. Chris realized, looking at the veins in *Abuelita*'s hands, that her grandmother was aging. How much longer would she be able to live independently? Thank God she was still healthy, but how long would that last? *Abuelita* would not want to be a burden on anyone, though no one in the family thought that way. She had brushed off delicate overtures to discuss living arrangements for her if it came to that, so Chris and her brothers and parents had agreed that they'd all take turns staying with her and they'd hire a nurse if necessary. *Abuelita* would not want to leave her house. She would die in it, just as her husband had so many years ago. This was the way of things, she'd said once, and you might as well try to bring down a mountain by hand for all the good it did arguing with her.

"And what do they say?" Chris asked, burying her other thoughts.

"He was new to the neighborhood, and did not make attempts to learn its ways." She picked her glass up with both hands and sipped.

*Forastero* was the word she used. Chris sipped, too. Ramirez was definitely an outsider. He hadn't been there long and hadn't tried to fit in. Why did he move into the neighborhood, then? From what Mrs. Marquez said, he was gone more often than not, and didn't seem interested in layering himself into the community.

"Did you know him?"

"No. But I have treated people who lived down the street from him."

"Why do you suppose he was an outsider?" Chris asked, relieved that she hadn't known Ramirez.

"Perhaps he wanted to fit in, but ran out of time."

"Or?"

"Perhaps he was running away from something."

"Hiding?"

*Abuelita* shrugged again, in the way she did when she had thoughts on a matter but chose not to voice them yet.

"I don't think he brought crime to the neighborhood," Chris said. "It found him, because it seems he was involved in things that attracted it."

"These are my feelings, as well." *Abuelita* smiled at her. "If I hear anything else, I will let you know."

"Have you decided to start a new career as an investigator?" She teased.

"I only watch, *mi'ja*," she said with a mysterious half-smile. "And tell you what I see. It is amazing, really, what you learn if you keep your mouth shut and your eyes open." She winked and Chris laughed.

"Good advice."

"Now, before you go, I must show you something." She stood and left the kitchen. Chris finished her tea and set the glass on the counter next to the sink. *Abuelita* returned and handed her a piece of paper on which was a picture. Someone had printed out a photo. In it, a woman with long dark hair stood leaning against the passenger's side of a four-door nondescript gray car. She wore jeans, a feminine-cut blue T-shirt, and sunglasses. She was smiling.

"Who is this?" Chris looked up from the photo.

"Inez Morales. Her mother lives down the street."

Chris waited.

"Inez is missing."

"How long?" She followed her lead. *Abuelita* would tell her why she was showing her this photo soon enough.

"A week." She crossed her arms and pursed her lips.

"Has her mother gone to the police?"

"No." She gave Chris a hard stare. "She does not know that I have shown you this picture."

She frowned. Inez's mother, then, wanted to avoid contact with the police, which meant she, Inez, or both were in the country illegally. "I cannot do anything for Inez's mother if she won't talk to the police. You know that," she finished gently.

"Yes. But I am showing you this picture because I saw this car in the neighborhood."

"Oh?" She looked at the photo again. "Was Inez in it?"

"I am not sure. There were two women in it, and one looked like Inez."

A piece of the puzzle clicked into place. Two women. Gray car. Chris stared at her. "When did you see it?"

"The last time, Friday."

"Last time? How many times have you seen it?"

*Abuelita* thought for a moment. "Three over the past month."

"Did the car stop anywhere near your house?"

"No. But it drove past, from that direction—" she motioned with her right hand, toward the Rio Grande, about eight blocks west, "toward Old Town."

She nodded, thoughtful. "How old is Inez?"

"Twenty-five or twenty-six."

"Do you know when her birthday is?"

"I am sorry, *mi'ja*, I do not."

Chris smiled at her. "That's all right. Where was she born?"

"Las Cruces."

"May I have this?" Chris held the paper with the image up. "I'll make a copy and bring this one back."

*Abuelita* nodded. "Inez's mother gave it to me because she knows I watch. She is hoping I will see the car again."

Chris carefully folded the paper in half, so that the blank bottom part covered the image. Her next question she phrased delicately. "Is Inez involved in something she should not be?"

*Abuelita* shrugged, and this time the gesture indicated that she truly didn't know.

"If she's in the neighborhood, why hasn't she contacted her mother?"

*Abuelita* shook her head, expression troubled. "I have a very bad feeling about this, *mi'ja*. Inez was born in this country, but she has a cousin in Chihuahua. Inez wants to bring her and her cousin's daughter into this country, but the list for sponsorship is very long."

"Can Inez's mother be a sponsor?"

"I don't think so."

Chris nodded, thinking. *Abuelita*'s response told her that Inez's mother was probably in the country illegally. "How long has Inez's mother lived in the neighborhood?"

"Eight years. She told me she was in Las Cruces before that."

"Did she move into the neighborhood right away or did she live in other places before that?"

"No, she said she came to Albuquerque eight years ago."

"Is there other family in the U.S.?"

"I don't know. She has not mentioned any."

Rudolfo wiggled his way over to Chris and gazed up at her, adoringly. She bent down and scratched his head behind his ears, something he loved. "If one of the women in the car you saw was Inez, who was the other woman?"

"I don't know that, either. If one was Inez, the other couldn't be her cousin, because she is in Mexico."

So Inez's mother wants you to believe, Chris thought. She stood, leaving Rudolfo lying on the floor, his expression one of doggy disappointment. "Did Inez's mother ever mention Victor Ramirez?"

"No." She smoothed her apron. "She does not say much about her family or people she knows when she comes to visit. I only asked her last week how her daughter was and that was when she told me Inez had not contacted her, and she asked if I had heard or seen anything. She gave me that picture—" she pointed at the paper in Chris's hand, "and I told her I thought I had seen the car."

Chris looked down at *Abuelita*, trying to read what might be behind her words. "Did you ever meet Inez?"

"No."

"Do you know if she has a job?"

"No. Her mother does not talk of these things."

Chris chewed her lower lip. This was a delicate situation.

"I told you this because I am afraid that Inez may be someone crime follows." She smoothed the front of her apron again. "Her mother works hard, has always worked. She comes to me for medicines, and brings me food and herbs from Mexico that I cannot get so easily here. She watches over the children down the street when they are playing, and she cares for Mrs. Leyba when she is ill. And that is more often these days." She studied Chris's face, then. "I do not want whatever follows *Señor* Ramirez and perhaps Inez to move into the neighborhood. So I tell you these things."

"What does Inez's mother want?"

"To know that Inez is not hurt or in trouble."

Chris sighed. "*'Lita*, from what you have said, trouble could be the problem."

"I know. But if Inez's mother is to know for certain, then she will be able to decide what to do."

She wasn't sure what that meant. If Inez's mother was in the country illegally, she couldn't do much of anything to help her daughter if Inez ended up arrested. It would put her at risk. Or perhaps she would return to Mexico and seek help from family there. Immigration was not her purview, and it was an issue that had so many twists that Chris chose to remain non-judgmental about it, and instead address it as it pertained to victims of or suspects in a crime. She understood the need to escape the poverty and violence south of the border. She saw the results of both on rare trips to visit her own extended family in Chihuahua. "The only thing that will stop Mexicans from crossing the border," one of her distant cousins told her on one of those visits, "is if this country invests in its own citizens rather than feeding the cartels and government officials. Until that time, the border is a leaking dam."

"I can't make promises," Chris said, hoping *Abuelita* understood that it was bad enough if Inez's mother was in the country legally. If she was here illegally, that was a whole other issue.

"I know. I am hoping Inez went to Mexico, and that she will not return for a while, if at all." Her tone was hard, and Chris regarded her, understanding that Inez upset the neighborhood's balance, and sometimes it was best for people who did that to leave.

"Ah, enough of this," *Abuelita* announced. "I know you will do what you think is best and you will let me know if there is any information to be had." She made a motion with her hands as if she was washing them, adding a flourish to the end that indicated she was done with the matter for now.

Chris leaned down and kissed her on the top of her head. "Call me if you need anything before I see you on Sunday." It was Chris's turn to take her to church, and if there was time, she'd take her to a late breakfast afterward.

"Do not worry, *mi'ja*," she said with a soft laugh. "I am not so old that I cannot take care of myself." She held up her hand to stop her from saying anything to dispute that. "But if I need to, I will call. I always do."

"Thank you." She smiled, relieved, and gave her a hug, then bent to give Rudolfo another scratch. She returned to her car but waited for *Abuelita* to shut the door and wave through the window before she started the engine. She put the paper with Inez Morales's photo on it into her glove compartment. She'd show it to Mrs. Marquez tomorrow, after she'd visited Jim's. But right now, she needed to get into the right head space to be present for Dayna. Which, she discovered as she headed to the airport, was not hard at all.

# Chapter Seven

CHRIS PULLED UP in front of Dayna's condo in the North Valley, about three miles from downtown and a few blocks east of the Rio Grande. A mixture of pastoral and privileged, the North Valley kept one foot in its Spanish and Indian past and the other in a changing present, characterized by younger people with newer money looking for a slice of peace in an urban area.

Dayna's condo sat in a cul-de-sac just east of the north-south running Rio Grande Boulevard and just south of Candelaria, another major route that crossed Rio Grande and continued west a few blocks until it ended at the Nature Center, near the river. Chris turned off her engine and got out. She walked around to the passenger side and retrieved the plastic bag from Little Anita's New Mexican food, down near Old Town. She'd brought Dayna home from the airport and called in the order then drove down to get it while Dayna showered and "organized herself," as she called it, much to Chris's amusement.

She locked her car and walked through the wooden gate set into the six-foot faux-dobe wall that fronted the condo. She closed the gate behind her and moved into the interior courtyard and up the step to the front door, which echoed the gate in style. Chris used the house key Dayna had given her to unlock it and she stepped into the tiled foyer and shut and locked the door behind her. Beyond the foyer was what Dayna called her "front room," which was actually a formal dining room, since the kitchen, to the right, overlooked it above a low counter that doubled as a breakfast bar. The kitchen was accessible through a wide, arched entranceway. Dayna did keep a large mission-style table in the dining room, but she most often ate at the counter. Three wooden stools stood under the counter's overhang.

"Hi," Dayna called from the bedroom.

"Hey," She responded, her heart skipping a beat as it always did when she heard Dayna's voice. She entered the kitchen and set the bag of food on the island then took plates out of one of the cabinets. "Do you want wine?"

"Love some." Dayna entered the kitchen and came up behind Chris. She slid her arms around her waist and rested her head against her back. "There's a bottle of white in the fridge."

But Chris didn't move right away. She leaned back into Dayna, and covered her hands with her own. "Have I told you how much I missed you?"

"Mmm. I believe you mentioned it once or twice," she said with a chuckle. "But I love hearing it, so do tell." She released her and took a stemless wine glass from another cabinet. "I've got some lime Perrier in the pantry," she said as Chris filled her glass halfway with wine.

"Sounds good." She replaced the stopper in the bottle and returned it to the refrigerator, smiling because Dayna knew her habits, knew that she didn't drink alcohol if she was on duty early the next day. "Go sit down. I've got this."

She stopped opening food containers. "Yes ma'am, Detective." She placed a light kiss on her lips, and pulled away with a soft groan. "Don't want to start with that. I won't stop."

Chris grinned. "I'm counting on it."

Dayna arched an eyebrow. Even in baggy sweats and faded tee, with her hair hanging damp around her face, she made Chris ache in places she didn't know she had.

"You are some kind of beautiful," Chris said softly as she leaned in and kissed her not once but several times.

"What is it about you and kitchens?" Dayna murmured against her lips. "As if you're not already hot enough."

She laughed. "Seriously. You need to eat."

"Oh, I plan to." She grinned wickedly and lightly bit Chris's lower lip, which sent flares of delight down her spine.

"Wanton hussy."

"And?"

"Just pointing it out."

Dayna giggled and slowly pulled away, but she threw another one of her flirty little grins at her as she picked her wine glass up and went into the dining room. Chris stared after her, then jerked her attention back to dinner, which she dished out onto plates and carried to the table. She placed one at the head, near Dayna's glass, and the other at the seat next to it. Dayna wasn't in the room, but Chris heard music start playing through the speakers positioned in wall brackets on either side of the archway into the kitchen. She listened for a few seconds, and recognized Fleetwood Mac. Good choice, she thought as she returned to the kitchen and poured herself a glass of Perrier over ice.

Dayna was lighting the three pillar candles she kept on the table when Chris sat down. She blew the match out and set it on the closest ceramic candle-holder. She sat down then, and took a sip of wine. "Thank you. This is perfect."

"You're welcome. But anywhere with you is perfect." She reached over and clinked her glass against Dayna's.

She stared at Dayna for a moment, and the air between them seemed to still with things she wanted to say. Instead, Chris picked up her fork and started on her own enchiladas. After a few bites Dayna looked over at Chris. "Saying things like that only makes me want to stick around for more."

"So I hope." She held Dayna's gaze, and let herself get lost in her eyes, the color of an ocean, or the deep blue that Greek seaside villagers might paint their doorways. She reached for Dayna's left hand and brought it to her lips. "I really, really missed you."

She smiled. "I really, really missed you, too."

Chris released her hand so she could finish her dinner. Plus, she sensed that Dayna needed to process more. She'd gotten pretty good at reading her moods, and found that she enjoyed learning her layers. Dayna hadn't said much on the trip home from the airport, which was her way of unwinding before talking about deeper things. "Did you get what you needed out of the trip?"

Dayna glanced over at her. "Actually, yes," she said with what sounded like a little bit of relief that she brought it up.

"You want to talk about it now?" She took another bite and chewed, waiting. Dayna hadn't really gone into details over the phone about what went down in San Diego regarding the lawyers' meeting over the insurance policy her ex had left her. Dayna had to meet her sisters, too, and get some things done for her mom before she came back, and she preferred processing things in person, something Chris appreciated.

Dayna smiled at her. "You're getting good at this communication stuff."

"I'm taking lessons." She grinned back and squeezed her hand.

"They're working. Anyway, the attorney for Anne's family, as I told you, is still a very nice guy, and I think he gets why I didn't want the money. Hell, even if I had known before Anne died that she'd taken the policy out and put my name on it, I still wouldn't take it."

"How about her family?"

She sighed. "Assholes, as usual. They were assholes when Anne and I were together, assholes when she was in the accident after we broke up, and they're still assholes, even though she's been gone a while." She pushed the last bit of enchilada around on her plate. "Are they truly assholes like that all the time?"

"Probably."

Dayna set her fork down. "I don't understand that. Are they shitty because Anne was gay? Or because she was bipolar?"

"Maybe both. You told me how homophobic they are, but maybe they also feel that Anne being bipolar was something else to keep hidden."

Dayna made a disgusted noise in the back of her throat. "Do they honestly think I caused her to be gay?"

Chris shrugged. "You'd make me realize I was gay, if I hadn't."

Dayna smiled and kicked her lightly under the table.

"It's true." She winked at her.

"I doubt that. You already know who you are." She stroked the back of Chris's hand, and the sensation on her skin was a mixture of safety and sensuous. "I do sometimes wonder if Anne ever knew who she really was," Dayna continued. "But she never stayed on her meds long enough to find out." She took a sip of wine. "She told me once soon after we got together that being bipolar for her was like carrying pieces of herself in a box and she was always trying to figure out where the pieces went and sometimes, she almost had a complete picture but other times, she couldn't make them fit together." She lapsed into silence and stared into the flame of the nearest candle, still stroking Chris's hand.

"I thought about accepting the money from the policy," she said after a while. "You know that. And about signing it over to her family." Her fingers stopped moving for a moment, and then she clasped Chris's hand in her own. It gave her a little thrill, when Dayna did simple things like that. "But I don't think she would have wanted that. She took out the policy after we'd broken up. I still think she was trying to make amends for all the financial shit I had to clean up after she left."

"Sounds like she was." Chris moved her hand, and interlaced their fingers, thinking about what she'd felt when Dayna first told her about her ex, and the shopping sprees Anne had gone on in the throes of mania, how she'd stopped going to work, run up thousands of dollars in debt, and how she'd managed to keep it hidden for weeks. She'd wondered what Dayna was looking for, and why she was willing to take a chance after something like that, when she herself struggled with trust, and with losing control.

"I didn't want the money. Not for myself," Dayna said. "I know in my heart that Anne was trying to do the right thing, but accepting it didn't feel right. I was angry when I found out she'd been off her meds, and about the extent of the financial damage, but Anne wasn't malicious. She was ill." She sighed again. "I still don't want the money, and I still think it would be a disservice to her memory to accept it and sign it over to her family."

"I think you made a great decision. So how'd it go down?"

She sighed again, this time with relief. "That friend of mine from law school I told you about—the one whose brother is bipolar—did send me a list of five research centers and five treatment centers two days ago that he said were some of the best. It was the best timing, because I really didn't want to deal with this anymore. That made it really easy, because then I didn't have to go looking myself, and the money wasn't hanging over me." She grinned. "Every center on that list got some of the money." She caught Chris's eye. "I told the attorney to tell Anne's family where the money was going, and that each donation was in honor of her, in her name." She picked up her glass with her free hand. "I don't expect to hear back."

"Sounds like closure," She offered, cautious and hopeful. Dayna had kept her in the loop on this issue, but she'd wanted to deal with it herself, and Chris took a support role, imagining herself as the back-up player on the bench. Cheering Dayna on, keeping her spirits up, and ready to go in if necessary, but accepting her decisions about the matter.

Dayna took a sip and put her glass down. "It was. The best kind." She squeezed Chris's hand. "And then I got to come home to you." She pulled her hand away, but only to move her chair closer. She stroked

Chris's face. "You have no idea what that means to me. No idea how it feels that you were here, waiting for me, and that you've been so supportive." She smiled and Chris's heart nearly stopped at the expression in her eyes. Dayna traced her cheekbone with a fingertip, and it seemed that heat coursed down Chris's neck to her thighs.

"I know it's hard for you to talk about feelings," she added. "But I think you're doing better, and I want you to know I've noticed."

"That's part of the deal. Keeping me up on the game plan," Chris said with a smile.

"I expect you'll do the same with me. I'm not that great in the feelings department, either. The debacle with Anne probably had a hand in that, but there's other baggage, too. I'm the one in the family who's always had to be in control and deal with shit. My sisters, for all their worldly ways, suck at making decisions, and they're not great at organization. Don't know how all that fell to me, the youngest, but there it is. I basically raised myself, especially after Dad got sick and Mom didn't know what the hell she was doing."

"You did a great job of it."

"In some ways, yeah. In others...still figuring it out." She squeezed Chris's thigh. "I always wanted to be around people who made me feel calm, because I didn't have a lot of that growing up. Law school was really calming. It's rigid, after all. Structured. And a lot safer than the military. I needed those surroundings, because it helped ground me and it gave me skills and a sense of purpose. I don't know what would've happened if I'd met Anne in a different context and had to go through all that shit without my background in law school."

Chris grabbed her hand. "I think you would have figured it out, eventually. It might have taken you a lot longer and it might have fucked you up for a while, but I think at your core, you're a survivor."

Dayna stared at her for a long moment. "The first time I saw you at that conference in Santa Fe," she said, "I had a feeling I'd be safe with you. It was just a little thought, you know, because I didn't know you and we hadn't formally met. I figured we wouldn't, or if we did, it'd just be a 'hi, how are you' kind of thing. But I hoped I'd meet someone with your energy." She moved her fingers into Chris's hair. "And then there you were a little later, handing me a fresh beer."

"You looked like you might want one." She leaned into her touch, remembering that night, and how Dayna moved her, even from across the patio, at that reception. "No sense leaving a woman parched at an event like that, surrounded by adoring men."

She laughed. "So how come you took a chance? I might have had a boyfriend. Or been with one of those adoring men," she teased.

"That wasn't the vibe I got off you. Besides," she added, teasing back, "I caught you checking me out."

She pulled her hand back. "Oh, really?"

"Yep. You said you did later, but I did notice it that night." She brushed a piece of Dayna's hair away from her face.

"Oh, you did? And what went through your mind?"

"I didn't think I could be that lucky, and that maybe you thought I was someone else and you were just trying to place me in context."

She stared at her. "You seriously thought that?"

"The first couple of times I saw you looking my way, yes. But then you did it again, and at that point, I paid more attention. Not that it was hard." Not that she could have stopped, once she'd spotted her in the crowd. It was something almost visceral, she realized, the first time she saw Dayna Carson, the first time she heard her voice and her laugh, and the first time their skin met when Dayna shook her hand in introduction. Something visceral, and it punched a hole in her carefully constructed boundaries, and dared her to extend an invitation.

"I see. I became the subject of an investigation." She moved her chair closer, so that her legs were inches from Chris's. "Good thing you're trained in that sort of thing," she said, leaning in and brushing her lips along Chris's cheek.

She closed her eyes and bit back a groan. "That's right," she managed. "I'm a professional."

"What other investigative techniques do you use?" Dayna's teeth closed lightly on the skin of her neck and the jolt of pleasure went all the way to Chris's feet. She gasped.

"The kind I think you'll appreciate," she managed.

"I think so, too." And Dayna stood, her smile all the incentive Chris needed.

She stood, as well, but before she could move away from the table, Dayna pulled Chris's mouth to hers and Chris slid her arms around her instead, and it was a melding of more than lips, more than bodies, and much more than lust.

"You know," Dayna said after a few long, delicious minutes, "lest you think I'm terribly rude, as much as I'd like to talk more and get caught up on your end of things, I find myself wanting something else a lot more." She ran her thumb lightly along Chris's cheekbone.

"I can definitely oblige whatever you have in mind."

"I was hoping you'd say that."

Chris kissed her again, and almost lost all coherent thought. She pulled away. "I have to get up pretty early, though."

"Don't worry. I'll do all the investigating." Dayna lightly nipped her lower lip.

"Oh, you think so?"

"Wouldn't want you not to get enough rest."

"Thank you for your concern for my welfare." She glanced at the table and Dayna cocked an eyebrow.

"Leave the dishes, Gutierrez. There are other things that demand your attention. And I'm one of them." She fixed Chris with a deep, smoldering gaze and led her to the bedroom.

# Chapter Eight

HARPER CHECKED HIS watch again. "Almost nine. I don't think our boy's gonna show."

Chris looked out her passenger window at Jim's, across the street. "Beck said he was due in at eight." She tapped her fingers on the folder filled with personnel records. So much for catching Griego off guard.

Harper took out his cell phone and opened his notebook. He found the number he was looking for and dialed.

"Hi, Mr. Beck? This is Dale Harper with APD. Is Mr. Griego in?" He paused, listening. "And he hasn't called?" He glanced over at her and shook his head. "That's strange. If you hear from him, give us a call. Do you have my number?" He closed his notebook as he waited for Beck's response. "That's it. All right. Thanks." He ended the call.

She looked over at him. "So Griego's not going to show up."

"Beck's worried. Says Griego always calls if he's running late or sick." He looked through his notebook again and dialed another number. "Mr. Griego, this is Detective Harper with APD. We have a couple more questions we'd like to ask you, so please give me a call back." He provided his work cell phone number then ended the call. "What do you think?"

"Let's go see if he's at home."

"I'll be pretty upset if he is and he's just avoiding my calls," Harper snarked. He set his phone in one of the Cherokee's cup holders and started the engine. He backed out of the parking space near the shops that faced Jim's and pulled onto Isleta, headed south, toward Rio Bravo Boulevard. Chris looked through the personnel files as he drove. "Griego does have family listed in Las Cruces. Whether they're involved in whatever he was up to with Ramirez remains to be seen."

"More damn phone calls," Harper muttered as he turned left onto Rio Bravo.

"My sentiments exactly. Isn't police work great?"

"It'd be a lot easier if the bad guys just turned themselves in." They were headed over the bridge that spanned the Rio Grande, and Chris looked out at the parts of the bosque she could see. Rushes and willows lined the banks, and over the low concrete wall of the bridge, she caught a glimpse of one of the river's many sandbars. Dayna often went running along the trails that crisscrossed the bosque, some of them legal, some not. Heat raced down Chris's thighs as she thought about last night with Dayna, and this morning, when Dayna had gotten her up with a cup of coffee and a long kiss.

A great way to start the day, and an anchor, no matter what happened. That thought led her to another that had been coming up quite a bit the last few weeks. Where was this relationship going and where did she want it to go? She was in love with Dayna, that much she knew though she still had a hard time articulating it. Did that translate into further commitment or shacking up? She stared at the papers in the file, but they didn't register. She and Dayna needed to talk about it, but she wasn't sure whether she dreaded it because of what Dayna might say or what she wouldn't.

Harper exited onto I-25 northbound and accelerated. Chris put thoughts of Dayna in her "later" file and figured Harper would exit at Gibson, which would take them east, toward the airport. She concentrated again on Griego's file. "Not much else to go on here. He's been in Albuquerque, according to this, for the past ten years."

"Has he always worked at Jim's?"

"The past five years. Before that, he was at Pep Boys over on Central near San Mateo for three years. And before that, he worked at a detailing shop for a while. Looks like he just really likes cars."

Harper grunted and maneuvered into the exit lane for Gibson. "The stuff came in on him, but I haven't had a chance to check on what we got. I'm guessing stupid juvie stuff, if anything. Sounds like he kept his nose clean. Here, at least."

"Or never got caught."

Harper grunted in agreement and she closed the file. She doubted she'd find anything incriminating about the other employees, but she'd check later. Right now, her money was on Griego.

"Here it is," Harper said a few minutes later. He turned left into the parking lot of a two-story stucco apartment complex that at one time probably was a halfway decent place to live. Now, it broadcast its years in the paint peeling from the doors and the unkempt side lot, littered with empty bottles and cans. Probably built in the seventies, Chris guessed. A lot of chintzy shoebox structures went up in Albuquerque during those years. This one looked like a motel and sat across the street from the airport. The residents here probably timed their conversations around airplane noise.

"His truck's not here," she said as she got out of the Jeep.

"Just our luck." He locked up and they walked toward the outside stairs. She automatically scanned for evidence of drug use, but the parking lot and walkway in front of the lower level, at least, were litter-free. The residents apparently tried to make the best of what they had. A child's toy scooter stood near an open first-floor apartment door and she heard ranchera music emanating from the room within. She followed Harper up the stairs to the second floor.

The walkway on this level was clear, too, and the wrought iron railing to their right that kept people from falling into the parking lot below seemed intact. Strong enough to lean on, and she was sure it got a lot of that, especially in the summer. Guys talking, having a beer and watching the traffic on Gibson.

"Should be this way," Harper said. "Two oh seven."

Griego's apartment was the last one on the end. Harper knocked on the door and they both waited a few seconds. When nothing happened, he tried again.

"Mr. Griego, it's Dale Harper with APD. Open the door, please."

They waited a few moments more, but got no response from Griego's apartment. They did, however, get one from the neighbor in 205. The door opened and a short pudgy guy dressed in faded dirty jeans and a tight white T-shirt leaned out. She pegged him as Hispanic, around fifty. He eyed them suspiciously, beneath heavy black brows. Chris had a few inches in height on him.

"He's not here."

She moved her jacket to show him the badge clipped to her belt. He frowned even more.

"Thanks," she said. "Do you know where he went?"

He shrugged. "Saw him yesterday but not since."

"I'm Detective Gutierrez and this is Detective Harper. We're with APD. Mind if we ask you a few more questions?"

He looked from her to Harper and back again, and shifted uneasily. "Okay," he relented.

"About what time did you see Mr. Griego yesterday?" She didn't have to look to know that Harper had taken his notebook and pen out.

The guy shrugged. "Afternoon sometime. I get off work at three. His door was open so I went over to see if he wanted a beer." He shrugged. "He didn't. So I went back to my place and he left after that."

"Good to know. Could we get your name, please?"

"What for?"

She regarded him with one of her best stone-faced cop expressions, and waited him out.

"Artie Padilla," he said after a few uncomfortable seconds.

"Thank you, Mr. Padilla. About how long have you known Mr. Griego?"

He shrugged, which seemed to be one of his only gestures. "A year or so. When I moved in, he was living here."

"Do you know this man?" She took her own copy of Ramirez's driver's license photo out of her jacket pocket. Padilla took it from her and studied it.

"Guy named Vic. He'd come by once or twice a week, have beers with Johnny and watch football or basketball sometimes." He handed it back. "I hung out with him a couple times at Johnny's."

No surprise, she thought, as she pocketed the photo, that Griego had hedged those details, as well. "Did you ever see any women at Johnny's? Or with Vic?"

"You mean like a girlfriend?"

"Yes. Or female relatives or friends."

"I saw one, a few times. Some girl named Inez."

Score. Morales was another link between Griego and Ramirez. "About how old was she?" Chris asked.

"Don't know. Twenties, I guess." He shrugged again.

"Did you catch a last name for her?"

"Nope. Didn't ask, either," he added. "None of my business."

She didn't respond to that, since he seemed to make a lot his business, like checking to see who was banging on his neighbor's door. "Was she a relative of Mr. Griego?"

"Nah. They didn't act like it. They was never glad to see each other. Maybe they was exes or something." He laughed a little, and Chris suspected he had a few of those in his past, and that they were never glad to see him, either.

"Would she visit Mr. Griego with Vic, or did she come alone?"

"Sometimes alone. A few times with another girl, but she'd wait in the parking lot. A couple times Vic was at Johnny's when she came by. He never looked glad to see her, either."

"Define 'few'. Two? Three?"

"At least three. I wondered why she never came up, but whatever. Women." He rolled his eyes.

"Did you happen to see the car she came in?"

And again, he shrugged. "Some little gray thing. Didn't get a good look at it or the other girl."

Double score. "Do you know who the other woman might have been?"

"Nope. She never came upstairs."

"When was the last time you saw this Inez?" She kicked herself for not bringing the photo *Abuelita* had given her for a concrete identification.

"Yesterday."

Harper stopped writing and glanced first at Padilla then at Chris.

"When?" Chris asked.

"A couple hours after Johnny left."

"Did you talk to her?"

"Yeah. Told her the same thing I told you. He wasn't home." He shrugged.

"Was anyone with her?"

"Don't know. I didn't come out of my apartment, so I didn't see the parking lot. She looked mad." He shrugged for probably the fifth time. "But she always looked mad when she came around."

Chris filed that away. "Where do you work, Mr. Padilla?"

"Construction. Mostly houses. Just finished one up on the West Side, so I got a couple days off."

"Got a name for the company?" she asked.

"Stevenson."

Legit company, but she'd check his claim out, anyway. "Thanks for your time. If Mr. Griego shows up, we'd sure appreciate it if you'd give us a call." She handed him her business card. He looked at it, then back at her.

"What's this about?"

"Mr. Griego might know something about a case we're working on. We need to ask him a few questions," she said in a pleasant, vague tone.

He shrugged, this time in dismissal. He closed the door and she heard the lock click. Harper finished writing in his notebook and put it back into his jacket pocket. "You want to leave a calling card on Griego's door?"

"No. My guess is, Padilla will call him."

Harper grunted something and started walking down the gangway to the stairs. "All right. I want to check Griego's alibi at the Cooperage. Then let's have a look at Ramirez's car. I'll drop you off."

"Okay. I'll check on the phone records and see what I can find out about this Inez. How about at eleven we meet to check the car?"

"Sounds good." He put his sunglasses on and descended the stairs, Chris right behind him.

CHRIS KNOCKED ON Mrs. Marquez's door again, a little louder, and waited some more. She'd called her from the station after Harper dropped her off and asked if she could stop by to show her a photo and Mrs. Marquez had agreed, though grudgingly. Maybe she'd decided not to talk to her after all, even though she'd warmed up a bit toward the end of the interview on Monday. She started to knock one more time when Mrs. Marquez opened the interior door. She wore a light green house dress and big pink fuzzy slippers.

"*Buenas tardes, Señora Marquez*," Chris greeted her. "Thank you for agreeing to see me," she continued in Spanish.

Mrs. Marquez nodded brusquely and pushed the screen door open. Chris moved to her right so the door could open. She held it open with her left shoulder and handed Mrs. Marquez a copy of the photo *Abuelita* had given her. "Do you recognize this woman?"

Mrs. Marquez took the photo and studied it. "That is the car I told you about," she said after a while. "I cannot be sure about the woman, though. I did not see either of them up close." She continued to look at it. "It is possible that this is the woman who drove. She would also go into the house. She is not wearing her hair like the other one, the one who would wait." She handed the paper back to Chris.

"Are you sure about the car?"

"Yes. It had the tire like this one, here." She pointed at the back passenger side tire, which was missing a hubcap.

Still not much to go on. Lots of gray cars missing hubcaps, but at least she was sure that it was the right rear tire. "Thank you. Have you noticed anything else since Sunday?" she asked, staying away from words like "murder" and "killed."

Mrs. Marquez hesitated, as if she was trying to determine whether she should tell Chris anything. She glanced past Chris's right shoulder, toward Elvira Guzman's house, then back at Chris. "There was a man," she said, deciding to tell Chris something after all. "Yesterday afternoon."

"Oh? Walking?"

"No. He drove a truck that I have not seen in the neighborhood. A very pretty one, though I do not approve of those lowriders."

"What color?" she asked, though she had a strong feeling she already knew.

"Green. It sparkled."

"What did he do?"

Mrs. Marquez shot a quick glance at the Guzman house again. "He drove very slowly by *Señor* Ramirez's house."

"Did he stop?"

"Yes. Right in front, but he did not get out."

Chris nodded, encouraging.

"I could not see what he was doing, because the back window of his truck was darker than the others."

"How long did he stay?"

"Not long. A few minutes. And then he drove away, that way." She pointed west, toward the river. "He turned onto the next street and I don't know where he went from there."

So Johnny Griego had paid a little visit to the scene of the crime. He'd driven west, from Rio Grande Boulevard, parked in front of Ramirez's, then pulled away and turned right, probably on his way back to the boulevard. "Do you know about what time this happened?"

"Around three." She thought for a moment. "Yes, that was it, because one of my sons called me then, on his way to pick up my granddaughter at school."

"Thank you. Again, you have been very helpful. Has anyone else been in the neighborhood?"

"Just the reporters. I did not talk to them, though."

"Have you told anyone else about this man?"

"No. But I think you should know, since he is not from the neighborhood." She let that statement hover, and Chris suspected that she wanted to add something about Ramirez's suspected activities.

"*Señora*, what do you think Mr. Ramirez was doing for work?" Chris tried again, though Mrs. Marquez had not wanted to say anything in the first interview.

"Something bad," she said, lowering her voice though there was no way anyone outside of Chris would have heard her in her regular tone. "Something that might have hurt people."

"Drugs?"

"No. But something like that."

"Here?"

"No, but what he was doing followed him." She had lowered her voice even more.

"Where do you think he went, on those days he wasn't here?"

"I heard he went to the border." She said it with conspiratorial finality and Chris knew she wouldn't get anything more out of her.

"Thank you again." She handed her another business card, as a reminder. "Please call me if you see anything else or remember anything else."

Mrs. Marquez nodded as she took the card and Chris stepped back so she could close the door. She turned and headed down the walk to her car. Whatever Ramirez was doing had followed him. The same thing *Abuelita* had said. And maybe it followed Inez, too. She got into her car, thinking about what kind of trouble it was that Ramirez couldn't shake.

CHRIS PLACED A file on Harper's desk and sat down in the chair across from him. "Here, in case you wanted to go through the personnel files from Jim's, too."

"Did you find anything more interesting about Ramirez?"

"No. Current address, date of birth, social security number. Everything matches the official record. There are copies of his W-2 forms. Looks like he did a year of contract work for Jim's. The money varied, according to the job."

Harper looked through the papers. "So basically, Jim's is still on the up-and-up and we're still not sure what the heck Ramirez and Griego were doing outside of the car stuff."

"Yeah, basically. However, I did get something else." She handed him the copy of the printed-out photo she'd shown Mrs. Marquez.

Harper glanced at it, then at her.

"That's Inez Morales, and she's gone missing. Mrs. Marquez thinks that car is the one that she saw at Ramirez's, based on the missing hubcap on that right rear tire."

"You're thinking this is the Inez from Griego's place?"

"Yes."

"Huh. Okay. So who's Morales and where did you get this photo?"

"Inez is the daughter of an acquaintance of my grandmother."

Harper sat up straighter. "How long has she been missing?"

"According to Morales's mother, and via my grandmother, a week."

Harper frowned. "What's the story with the mother? Will she talk to us?"

She regarded him for a moment, appreciating the fact that he seemed to pick up on things she never would have credited him with at the beginning of the year. "Probably not. My grandmother thinks this Inez is bad news, and in some kind of trouble. She doesn't know if Morales knew Ramirez or not, but she has seen this car driving down her street three times in the past month. My grandmother is very sharp, and if she says this car has been in her neighborhood that many times in a month, chances are it has been."

Harper gazed at the photo for a while. "Gray car, like Padilla said. Kind of a weird coincidence, if the Inez from Griego's place is a whole different one." He looked up at her. "All right, how do you want to play this?" he asked, and once again, Chris appreciated his tact. Immigration was a touchy subject, and the borders between legal and undocumented weren't always physical.

"I have a feeling the mother is not documented. My grandmother doesn't seem to know for sure, and she's never asked. The mother has been in Albuquerque for eight years, but my grandmother says she will not go to the police. She just wants to know what her daughter is doing, so that she can make some decisions, my grandmother said."

"Like what?"

"I don't know. Maybe to wash her hands of the daughter, if she's running with the wrong crowd. Or maybe get her some help."

Harper leaned back in his chair. "Is the daughter legal?"

"My grandmother says she was born in this country."

He stared at the ceiling for a few moments. "Damn. All this immigration shit jacks things up. Nobody talks to anybody, we can't help anybody, we don't know which people coming over are good guys—" he stopped and sighed. "So let's run a check on Inez, see what comes up." He looked at her pointedly. "Is she a person of interest?"

"Let's call her an interesting person for now." Chris then told him what Mrs. Marquez had said about the green truck.

"Well, now. Our boy Griego knows a lot more than he told us. He was looking for something." He looked at her quizzically. "What do you suppose it was?"

"I'm guessing anything that pins him to Ramirez."

"You don't think he's the shooter?"

"No," she said. "But I do think he and Ramirez were engaged in illegal pursuits and Griego's trying to distance himself from that, now that his partner-in-crime is dead."

"Or he's looking for something Ramirez had that's worth money. Drugs is my first guess, but we've been over that house and nothing like that showed. Money's my next guess."

She nodded. In a crime like this, money was a good motivator, but where the hell was it? "Yeah, but we didn't find any of that, either, unless he's got it stashed in a wall or under the floorboards. That's old school, and time-consuming. Not something I see a guy like him doing."

Harper nodded, thoughtful. "I agree. Not seeing Griego as the shooter, either. You?"

"No. He was pretty rattled when we told him Ramirez was dead. I don't think he faked that. But I do think he has an idea who did it."

"Maybe that's why he went missing."

"Could be. Maybe he's scared. He's not the type to ditch work for no apparent reason other than that."

"This Morales—I'm liking that as a link," he said. "Good thing your grandma keeps an eye on things." He smiled at her. "Both my grandmothers died when I was in my twenties. You're lucky, Gucchi, to have one still around."

"I know," and Chris relaxed, because in his tone he had absolved *Abuelita* of responsibility for Inez Morales and her mother. In his mind, she was a tipster, and that's how he was going to approach the information. They were local cops, after all, and immigration enforcement was not in their purview, though it was an elephant in the room in a lot of ways. In certain neighborhoods, people didn't talk to the police, either because of their own undocumented status or the status of others.

The history of relationships between immigrant communities and local law enforcement wasn't the best, no matter where in the country they were. Loyalty to one's neighbors and ties south of the border generally kept mouths closed. Fear, too, silenced people, and not always the fear of deportation or law enforcement, but fear of providing information that would make someone a target of reprisal, especially if that person was undocumented. Chris sighed, glad she wasn't a border patrol agent or a federal immigration officer. Solving crimes was hard enough, without the added immigration issue.

"Did you run Morales?" he asked.

"Not yet. I'll put a call in."

"How about we go have some fun in the meantime and dig around in Ramirez's car?"

"Definitely. I'll be right there. You want coffee?"

"I'd love some fresh, hot, crappy department coffee, thanks," he said. "See you in a bit."

Chris stood and left his cubicle and went back to her own, where she checked her messages. Nothing that she needed to deal with yet. She wrote down a couple of notes to herself.

"Hey, *esa*."

Chris looked up at fellow detective Mark Aragon's tall, bulky frame as it filled the entrance to her cubicle. As usual, he was wearing cowboy boots, which only added to the imposing figure he cut. "What's up?"

"*El jefe* tells me you've got a dead dude who might've been doing some human smuggling," he said, using the Spanish term for "boss," something he did when he talked about Lieutenant Jerry Torrez.

"Not sure. It looks like a possibility, though. Jerry seemed to think it was something to follow up on, anyway. More interesting than the usual drug angle, at least."

"Well, if you're still looking at that, I've got a contact here who retired from the Border Patrol last year. He worked the South Texas line for a few years, including Juárez. He'd be willing to talk to you, give you some perspective on how coyotes work."

"I'd definitely appreciate that. Can you put me in touch with him? Give him my office and work cell numbers?"

"Will do." He braced his forearms on the top of her cubicle wall, one on either side of the entrance. The wall came up to his shirt pockets. "How's that crazy researcher of yours?"

Chris smiled. Mark always asked about K.C. "Fine. Busy with teaching."

"Tell her I'm sorry, but I don't have any wingnuts for her to chase around. I'll keep looking, though." He grinned. "As soon as I find some, she'll be the first call I make."

"And I'm sure she'll appreciate it, *ese*," Chris said with a laugh. "Thanks for the tip. What's your guy's name?"

"Dan Marshall. I'll give him a call, and hopefully you'll hear from him in the next day or so, unless he's out of town on one of his fishing trips."

"Sounds good. Thanks."

"*No hay problema.* Take it easy." He started walking away.

"You, too," Chris said after him. She was about to stand up but instead put a call in to the duty officer to see if someone could run a records check on Inez Morales. She dropped a copy of the photo off with the records guy, got two big Styrofoam cups of coffee from the department coffee station, and headed over to the crime lab across the parking lot.

# Chapter Nine

"NOT A WHOLE lot of interesting," Harper muttered as he looked through the few papers Terry had taken out of the glove compartment and left bagged on the folding table in the crime scene lab's garage. Chris liked working with this tech. Terry was always pleasant and mostly patient. She looked back at the car. Ramirez wasn't a flashy guy when it came to his own car. He had driven a basic blue Ford Taurus, probably around ten years old, four-door.

"He took care of the car, though," Harper continued. "Looks like Jim's did basic maintenance for him, too." He held up a couple of clear plastic evidence bags with pieces of paper that Chris surmised were auto repair invoices.

Terry was engaged in checking under the front passenger seat with a flashlight. "Got something," she said.

Chris leaned in just as the flashlight's beam glanced off something white. At first, it looked like a doll but a beat later, it registered with her as Terry pulled it out from under the seat and held it up.

"Huh," Harper said over Chris's shoulder. "So our guy really was into Day of the Dead."

"Maybe." Chris waited for Terry to bag the figure and hand it to her. She turned it over, looking for evidence that it had been slit open. "Carl told me that one case he worked had a guy running drugs out of Juárez in Day of the Dead skeletons like this. Those were bigger, though. About eighteen inches tall, different kinds. The drugs were stuffed in baggies and put into the body cavities before the paint went on." This skeleton was a match to the skeleton in Ramirez's house. It was painted to look like it wore a red jacket and blue jeans and a cowboy hat graced its skull. She couldn't see any evidence that it had been sliced open anywhere. She hefted it, but it felt empty.

"I don't think it's been used for drugs," Terry said, "but the lab'll find out for sure." She took it from Chris and set it on the folding table. Harper grunted a response and continued going through the papers Terry had found in the glove compartment.

Chris studied the figure. They were ubiquitous throughout Mexico and the Southwest, collected as folk art and used to grace memorial altars this time of year especially. Nothing unusual about Ramirez having one, since he had been from El Paso. But what was it doing underneath the seat of his car? If he wasn't using it for drugs, why was it in here? Didn't seem that he missed it, given where she'd found it. Like he'd tossed it in the back and forgot about it. And why did he have one just like it in his bedroom? And why did the shooter—and she was sure it was the shooter—leave a figurine on his body?

The crime lab's garage was roomy enough to provide space for a couple of counters and tables when going over a vehicle. She went back to the car and watched as Terry lifted the mats carefully by each corner to check underneath, but nothing showed.

"It looks pretty clean," Terry announced. "Way cleaner than a lot of cars I see."

Ramirez had kept the car clean, for the most part. No visible sign of blood or drugs that Chris could discern with just the naked eye. She looked at the back seat for tears that might indicate something hidden. Nothing.

"Hey, Terry," she said. "Could you open the trunk for a peek?"

"Sure." Terry went around to the front and popped it with the lever.

"Thanks." Chris stared into it, as clean and uninteresting as the rest of the vehicle. Maybe Terry could pick something up from it.

"Yo, Gucci. You ever hear of a *mercado* in El Paso?"

"That's the general Spanish term for market. Is this is a specific place?" She came around to where he stood at the table.

"Looks like it." He handed her a plastic baggie that protected a white flyer. It advertised upcoming Day of the Dead festivities in El Paso, at a place called Mercado Mayor. She turned the baggie over, but the backside was blank.

"Ramirez was supposed to meet someone in El Paso this Saturday, and I'm guessing at the Mercado." She put the baggie on the table, front side of the flyer up. "It's near downtown." And thus, near the border. "It's a collective of vendors and small businesses that also sponsor festivals. There's an outreach arm, too, if I remember correctly. One of my brothers went last year to some festival." She studied the flyer. "Maybe Ramirez was going to meet this someone at the Mercado."

"Could be."

Something hit Chris. She looked up at him. "Shit, Harper. It's been staring us in the face. It's still really easy to cross from Juárez into El Paso over the foot bridge near downtown. The Santa Fe Street Bridge. It might take a couple of hours because of the lines, but all it costs is basically a quarter and a reason to be going onto the American side. Otherwise, if you can prove you have employment in Juárez, which decreases the likelihood you'll stay in the U.S., and you have legitimate-looking documentation, there aren't many questions asked. Plus, people go shopping and clubbing in El Paso from the Juárez side all the time."

"Huh."

She picked the flyer up again. "Thousands of people cross that border at that bridge and the other bridges every damn day. A lot of them have family on both sides, and wealthy Mexican families often send their kids to El Paso private schools for a better, safer education. Others work in the States and live across the border. They cross into the United States in the morning, and then go back over in the late afternoon or evening, just like people who go shopping in the U.S. or who go over to visit family."

He rocked forward on the balls of his feet, something he did when he was thinking about something during a conversation. "Damn, you're right. I hadn't thought of that, either. It would have been easy for Ramirez to meet someone in El Paso at a store or a restaurant and then drive them to Las Cruces, if we're talking about human smuggling."

"We are talking about that. But probably not Cruces."

Harper frowned, puzzled. "Why not?"

"I doubt Ramirez would want to travel in his own car with whatever human cargo he had. Too easy to be remembered in Cruces, especially if he was meeting Griego and that truck of his. Griego's from there. Ramirez probably wouldn't have wanted to take the chance that they'd be seen together there."

"So they'd meet in El Paso. Then what?"

"Ramirez would turn the cargo over to Griego, who would have to get around checkpoints. There's one on I-10 west of there, one on Highway 70 to Alamogordo, and one on I-25 to the north. Remember, you can't avoid the one on northbound I-25 unless you exit south of there, toward Hatch, which actually takes you south and west again."

Harper rocked forward on the balls of his feet again. "Okay, so Griego meets Ramirez in El Paso and then Griego goes up to Alamogordo on whatever highway that's down there."

"Possibly. But I'd guess he'd go east out of El Paso past that and take the other highway north to Carlsbad. From there, the two-lane highway to Roswell. He could catch I-40 at Clines Corners. Easy forty-mile drive into Albuquerque then." She turned and looked at the car, running through various scenarios in her head. She hit one she liked.

"What about this? Ramirez meets Griego in El Paso after making his appointment. Then Ramirez heads back to Albuquerque via the usual route—I-25. He's stopped at the checkpoint north of Cruces, but that's okay. He wants to be stopped because it clears him if anything happens to Griego. Meanwhile, Griego drives east with the cargo, probably human, and heads up to Carlsbad. And what if he's driving his own truck? A vehicle that obvious might actually end up throwing suspicion off him. After all, who in the hell would smuggle people from the border in that thing?" She looked back at him.

He nodded. "I like it. But they could have switched cars, too."

"That's a possibility." She motioned at Ramirez's car. "The trunk's big enough for a person to lie in and it's cool enough now that putting someone in it probably wouldn't kill them on that long a drive."

"Still a lot of what ifs. We need something solid."

She put the flyer on the table again. "Let's assume that Griego hasn't let Ramirez's contact know that he's dead. Maybe he's going to try to make the haul himself."

"Maybe. But why would he risk it?"

"Money. Fear. Maybe both." She frowned. What if someone had something on Griego, and if he didn't make this run, he'd be in some serious shit? She stared at the flyer. Something had spooked him, and enough to make him disappear from his home and his job. "Let's put out a BOLO on his truck with locals and law enforcement between here and El Paso."

"You think he'd still be driving his truck?"

"Maybe to Cruces. He's from there. He probably has family or friends there and if so, it's a place to ditch the truck."

"Good call. I'll check in with his family down there, see if they've heard from him or seen him. What about that?" He gestured at the flyer.

"Not sure. We don't really know what's going on or who Ramirez was supposed to meet. I think our best bet is to find Griego, and hopefully before Saturday. If we don't, at least one of us will be going to El Paso."

"All right, then. Damn, I love police work."

"Hey, Terry," Chris said.

The tech popped her head up from the back seat.

"If you find anything you think we need to see, will you call?" Chris asked.

"Don't I always?" she smiled.

"Yes, you do. But Harper and I are insecure about that kind of thing."

Terry snorted a laugh. "Whatever." She went back to work and Chris followed Harper out of the garage.

CHRIS STOOD AND stretched. She'd been sitting at her desk for the past two hours trying to get caught up on a couple of other cases while she was waiting for Inez Morales's file and word from Harper about Ramirez's cell phone records and his bank statements. She glared at her computer, frustrated. Nearly four o'clock. She'd been working this case most of the day, and she still felt like they were getting nowhere. A flyer from a market in El Paso, three Day of the Dead figures, a missing man, and a missing woman who may or may not play a role in the death of Ramirez. What was she not seeing?

She looked through her note pad and found the local number that Ramirez had called before he died. She called it again, from her desk phone. Again, right to messages, and the female voice asking the caller in Spanish to leave a message. She did, and hung up, but picked the phone up again and dialed Harper's extension.

"Yo."

"Did you get a chance to run that number Tony pulled off Ramirez's phone yesterday?"

"Yeah...hold on. I just printed it out." He put the phone down and she waited for what was probably only a couple of seconds but felt like a minute or more. "Pay dirt, Gucchi. Inez E. Morales."

"Hot damn." Finally. A definitive tie between Inez Morales and Ramirez, which explained why the woman on the other end of that number wasn't returning her calls. "Okay, I'm going to see if I can chat with Morales's mother. No guarantees, but I'll give it a shot."

"Sounds good. I'll let you know if the BOLO turns anything up."

"Do we have Ramirez's bank statements?"

"In an hour or so. I'll let you know."

"Thanks."

Chris hung up and called *Abuelita*. She didn't answer, so she stood and grabbed her satchel and jacket. She'd stop by and see if *Abuelita* could run interference for her with Morales's mother. She was on her way through the lobby of the police station when someone called her name. She stopped and waited.

"Hey, got your info on the Morales woman."

"Thanks, Rick. Appreciate it." She took the file. "Did you look through it?"

"Not really. Figured you needed it ASAP."

"Thanks. I'll let you know if there's anything else interesting I need you to track down."

He grinned. "I'll be waiting." He tossed her a wave and retreated back down the hall. Chris slid the folder into her satchel, with the dozen other folders she needed to go through for other cases, then slung her jacket over her shoulder. Maybe Dayna wouldn't mind a quiet evening doing homework together. She smiled and headed to the parking lot, wondering why she was afraid to approach her with the future. Maybe it was because she wasn't very good with the future in some respects, because it generally never worked out the way you thought it should.

Her personal cell phone rang, and she smiled again. "Hey. I was just thinking about you."

"Something good, I hope." Dayna's voice caressed her ear.

"Always. What's up?"

"Dinner tonight?"

She leaned against her car. "I'd love to, but I also have some homework."

"Me, too. I'll take care of the food. You won't have to worry about it."

"Well, I have this really nice bottle of wine that is just dying for a beautiful woman like yourself to have a bit of it."

Dayna laughed. "Why, Detective Gutierrez. Are you asking me over to your house?"

She grinned. "Yes. Did it work?"

"Hmm. You know what happens after a homework party, don't you?"

Images of Dayna undressing flashed in Chris's head. "So I was hoping."

"Me, too. What time?"

"Six?"

"Done. See you then. Really looking forward to it."

"Same here. Bye." Chris hung up and stared up at the darkening sky and then over at the Sandia Mountains to the east. The glow of pinks and oranges was fading from their flanks with the setting sun, and the air held the nibble of autumn. She dialed K.C.'s cell, but she didn't pick up so she tried her at home.

"Hi," Sage answered.

"Hey, Sage. How are you?"

"Finer than frog's hair, as K.C.'s grandpa says."

Chris smiled. "Not an expression I ever thought I'd hear from you. Is K.C. around?"

"She had a late meeting at school. She should be home in an hour or so. Everything okay?"

"The usual. Cases that won't let me solve them."

Sage waited a couple of seconds. "And?"

Chris hesitated. Sage would invariably figure it out anyway, given her intuition and mystical vibe, but did she really want to talk about Dayna with her right then? "Not sure. Just sorting through some things."

"Good for you. If you want to talk, you know where to find me."

"Thanks. You know it takes me a bit longer than most to do that, though."

"I do. And just a reminder, you're family," she said, warmth in her voice. "Whatever you need, just let us know. I'll tell K.C. you called."

"Good deal. Catch you later. Bye." She hung up before she really did start spilling her guts to Sage. She got into her car, thinking that as scary as it was, she wanted some idea from Dayna about where this relationship thing was going. She buckled up, started the engine, and headed to *Abuelita's*.

CHRIS PULLED UP behind the white Chevy Tahoe parked in front of *Abuelita's* house, and sighed. She wasn't really in the mood to deal with her mother today, but it looked like she didn't have much of a choice. She debated pulling away from the curb and heading home, but one of the two women inside had no doubt realized she was there. The front curtains were open, after all. With another sigh, she unbuckled her seatbelt and got out.

The door opened before she got to the tidy front porch.

"*Mi'ja,*" *Abuelita* said with obvious relief. "What brings you here?"

"Questions," Chris said in Spanish. "But they can wait. Is everything all right?"

"Fine, fine." She waited until Chris bent down to peck her on the cheek. "But you know how your mother is," she whispered in her ear.

Chris choked back a laugh.

"Christina?" Rosa called from the kitchen. Chris winced, but she'd given up trying to get her mother to call her anything else.

"Yes," she responded. Rudolfo snuffled her feet and she bent down to give him some scratches behind his ears. "What's going on?" she asked in English before she stood and went into the kitchen, *Abuelita* and Rudolfo behind her. Her mother preferred English, since she'd been born in the U.S., and though Chris thought it was a weird hang-up, she didn't question it.

"I'm helping Mom with tamales," she said, also in English as she worked over a bowl of *masa* at the counter. She presented the right side of her face to Chris for a kiss. She had her dark hair pulled back in a tie, and she wore a pair of dark slacks and a loose-fitting feminine-cut T-shirt. She was a younger, more curvaceous version of *Abuelita*. Chris had gotten her father's height, but her temper, *Abuelita* teased, from her mother.

"For?" She pecked her on the cheek.

"Church. San Felipe is having a fall festival this weekend. How are you?"

"Fine. Busy." She stood watching her mother, feeling out of place in *Abuelita*'s kitchen, something that always happened around her mother.

"How is Dayna?" *Abuelita* asked pointedly in English for Rosa's benefit and Chris stifled another laugh. Her grandmother and her mother were at odds over Chris's love life. The latter because she considered homosexuality a sin, the former because she thought Rosa's views were outdated and ridiculous.

"Good." She left it at that, because she felt her mother's dark eyes, expression disapproving, on her. "So how many tamales?" she asked, deflecting the unspoken lecture.

"Fifty, I think. Can you have dinner with us this weekend?"

"Depends on work," she hedged.

"You have to eat sometime."

"Rosa, Chris has many things to do," *Abuelita* scolded. Chris glanced at her, glad for the support.

"I'm not sure," she said, "But I might be able to help take things over to San Felipe this weekend, if you need it."

Rosa made a noncommittal noise and worked the *masa* a little harder.

"How's Dad?"

"Fine. He's in Rio Rancho all week, working on houses up there."

"Good. Glad there's business." Chris caught *Abuelita*'s gaze, pleading through her expression for her to rescue her from this conversation.

*Abuelita* shrugged and picked up her apron from one of the chairs at the kitchen table.

"John called," she tried again. Mention of her youngest brother generally loosened her mom up. "He said he talked to you last week about Thanksgiving. So what do you think?"

"I don't know."

"It'll be fun," Chris pushed, gently. "John's really excited about cooking for you. And you won't have to do much work, or clean up afterward, since it'll be at my house. Maybe he'll try out some of those French recipes he's learning at school," she coaxed. "And give them a good New Mexican spin."

Rosa shrugged. "I'll have to talk to your father about it."

"And it would be great if you'd make your *posole*. Nobody can do it like you can."

Finally, she cracked a smile and looked up at her. "I do like the idea of not having to clean up. But your house isn't that big."

"We'll make room." Chris gave her a one-armed hug. "You can relax a little for Thanksgiving this year. Let John and me set it up."

"I'll talk to your father," she repeated, but she was smiling more broadly now. Chris had already talked with Pete and Mike, and both brothers loved the idea. They were going to put up a tent over her back yard ramada and set up some standing heaters. John had already talked to their father, as well, and because he was the youngest, he could pretty much convince any of the family to do whatever he wanted. Even though he had just come out as gay earlier that year. This was his way, she knew, of demonstrating that he was still a Gutierrez, and still cared about the family. In some ways, she knew, it was harder on her mother that he had come out than when she did. But for whatever reasons, the tension that had surfaced between Chris and her mother hadn't between her mother and John.

"*Mi'ja*," *Abuelita* said, "Could you check my sink again? I don't think it's working properly."

Silently thanking her, Chris released her mother and nodded. "What's it doing?"

"Come and see." She bustled out of the kitchen through the living room, Chris behind her. Once at the bathroom, she switched to Spanish

"Have you found Inez?"

"Not yet, but you were right. She may be mixed up in some trouble. Is there any way her mother would talk to me? Off the record. I'm just trying to figure out where she might be, and her mother might have a better sense of that."

She frowned. "I will find out. Perhaps she will tell me some things."

"Let me know, either way." She beckoned at the sink. "Is there really something wrong with it?" she asked, teasing.

She shrugged in her "there might have been" way. "Your mother loves you, in her way. She is just uncomfortable with the idea, you know." The idea of Dayna, was what she meant.

"I do know. But she needs to start getting comfortable with it."

"That is not for you to decide. Nor is it your concern."

Chris sighed. "It is my concern. She's family."

"So is Dayna." *Abuelita* smiled. "You do not have to choose between the two. You must live your life. What your mother chooses to do will be of her own making."

"It's not always so easy." Chris kissed the top of her head.

"No, it is not. But you are a woman grown, and you must do what makes you happy and feeds your soul." She grinned impishly. "And I know that Dayna makes you very happy."

A blush heated her face and she cleared her throat. "Okay, so is there anything wrong with your sink?"

"Of course not. Now leave us to our tamales. I will call you."

"*Ay yay yay*," Chris muttered. She returned to the kitchen and stood in the doorway. "Bye, Mom. I have to take care of a few more things today. Let me know about Thanksgiving."

"Okay." Rosa smiled at her and *Abuelita* squeezed past her into the kitchen, Rudolfo at her heels. She caught Chris's eye and winked, and Chris smiled back then turned and left the house, making sure the door clicked shut behind her.

Once home, she kicked her shoes off and opened the fridge, thinking a beer would be good, but she had to be up and working tomorrow, so she settled for decaf coffee instead and set to work getting the coffeemaker ready. Her personal cell phone rang with K.C.'s tone, and she clicked the "on" button on the coffeemaker and grabbed the phone before it went to voicemail.

"*Esa*," she answered.

"Hey. Sage said you called. What's up?"

"This and that."

Pause. "Uh-oh. What's going on? Are you okay? Is Dayna all right?"

She glanced at the clock on the wall by the back door. She still had forty-five minutes before Dayna arrived. "Yeah, she's fine. Everybody's fine."

"Okay, I'll just stand here waiting for you to tell me what's going on. Eventually, you'll get tired of the silence on the line and you'll give in. Starting now." She shut up, but Chris heard her breathing. K.C. would make good on her statement, she knew.

"It's nothing wrong. Just something I'm not sure about. And I saw my mom today."

K.C. exhaled softly. "Okay, first things first. Your mom pushed a couple of your buttons?"

"Not intentionally. I just don't know why she seems less tense around John since he came out than she is around me. I've been out to her around fifteen years, now."

"I think it's because you've got a pretty serious relationship in your life, now, and your mom's being forced into a position where she's going to have to acknowledge that. John's not seeing anybody seriously right now. So the gay thing is all back-burnered in her mind. Plus, he's the youngest boy. So he gets more special-ness than you do. Not to suggest you're not special," she finished with a grin in her voice.

"I'm just not the daughter she expected." And sometimes, it seemed her mother was never going to forget that.

"No. You're better."

Chris smiled. "Thanks."

"It's true. You're you. You know who you are, where you came from, and you appreciate every single day you're here. I love that about you. Your mom may never come around, but try to remember it's her stuff, not yours. Dayna knows about her, and she knows it's part of the package. And she's not running, from what I can see. And that brings us to the next issue. Is this something about Dayna?"

"Aren't you the psychoanalyst?"

"Sadly, I'm better with others than myself. And that's a whole other discussion. So. Dayna?"

"Yeah. And me."

"Spill it, *mujer*. Because you've got me worried." She was. Chris heard it in her voice.

She sighed. Did she want to talk about this now? Was it a good idea?

"Chris?"

"Yeah, I'm here. It's just the usual shit. What I'm doing, where I'm going. You know. That stuff."

"Oh, well, *that* I can handle. Let's see. Basically, you're wondering where you're going with Dayna, whether that's a good idea, and what she thinks about it."

"Have you and Sage been doing crystal ball shit?"

"No. I just know you that well. So am I right?"

She laughed. "Yes. You are."

"All right. I'm now going to make you even more uncomfortable. How do you feel about her?"

She leaned against the island in her kitchen. "Unbelievable. She's everything I could ever want in a partner."

"So explain to me what the problem is."

"I'm not sure. I guess I don't know what I'm supposed to do in terms of a future." The coffee pot finished its work and she got a cup out of the cabinet and set it on the counter.

"Whatever you and Dayna decide to do, is what. There are no set rules about how you go about doing that. You do what works for both of you. It doesn't mean you have to shack up together. That works for some people." She paused for a couple of seconds. "Not so much for others. And I'm guessing you haven't really talked to her about this."

"You're guessing right. You know I'm not the best when it comes to things like this."

"Wait a second. Before we go down that road, what are you afraid of?"

Chris poured coffee into her cup and put the pot back on the warmer. "I'm not sure. I don't know if I'm afraid she'll want more than I can give or if she won't want anything at all."

"Whoa. That's about the most honest statement I've heard from you with regard to a relationship," K.C. said with a note of sympathy in her voice. "Let's phrase it differently. What do *you* want?"

She poured half-and-half into her cup, thinking. "Her. Us. Something a little more substantial than just 'seeing' each other." She stirred the coffee, and realized that she wasn't freaking out about that pronouncement.

"That is great news."

"How so?"

"Because it means you're willing to work on a future, even though you're scared shitless. Chris, that's big for you. Huge. And it's amazing. It's amazing that you're seeing this as it pertains to one particular woman, and that you're looking past your patterns. Should we have a celebration? Because this is awesome."

Chris laughed. "How about just a dinner at some point?"

"I'll take it. So what do you envision happening?"

"Not sure about that, either. There's a lot going through my head, and I'm not sure I even want to talk about it right now."

"Okay, fair enough. Do I need to worry about you?"

Or, in other words, are you going to do something stupid like run away from Dayna? Chris silently finished for her. "No. And we'll talk later."

"Gotcha. And if you need to, you know you can call me any time, *esa*."

"Thanks. Hi to Sage."

"Will do. Hi to Dayna. Later."

Chris hung up and set the phone on the counter. What the hell? It wasn't like she wanted to ask Dayna to marry her. She just needed a conversation about where they were going and what each of them expected. Nothing weird about that. Couples did that all the time. So why was she so nervous? Probably because her mom always stressed her out about her personal life, always made her feel as if she was doing something wrong. Chris had long since stopped apologizing for who she was, and she'd long since stopped trying to talk to her mom about her life and what was going on. Rosa had met Dayna, but she didn't accord her the same recognition that she did her brother Mike's wife and that dug at her. She knew it was her mom's crap, but it still affected her, and that bothered her, too.

Chris poured more coffee into her cup. *Abuelita* was right, of course. Chris had to make her own decisions about her own life, but it still hurt, dealing with her mom's views. She'd just have to figure out a way to meet her mom on other levels. But why the hell did *she* have to try to meet her mom on other levels? Why couldn't her mom try to meet *her* on certain levels? Irritated, she rubbed her head and went to turn on some music. Dayna would be there any minute.

# Chapter Ten

"WHAT'S THE MATTER?"

Chris looked up from her plate. "What do you mean?"

"You seem distracted." Dayna regarded her, waiting.

"Sorry." She took another bite, and though it was from her favorite Indian restaurant, she didn't notice the taste. "I stopped by *Abuelita*'s today."

"How is she?"

"Fine. My mom was there."

"Oh." The word was laden with acknowledgement about Chris's relationship with Rosa. "How'd that go?" she asked, sympathetic.

"The usual." Chris put her fork down. "I never know what to do around her, or what to say. Not that that's a new thing."

"You want to talk about it?" Dayna put her fork down, as well, and sat back in her chair, across from her.

"No." She reached for her fork, picked it up, then put it down again. "Yes. Maybe." She sighed, frustrated. "Shit."

"Sweetie, what's going on?"

Chris leaned back in her chair and stared up at the ceiling. "I hate that my mom acknowledges my brother's wife and my other brother's girlfriend, but not mine. I hate that I'm the one who has to let that go, and accept that it's her baggage, not mine, and just get on with it." She met Dayna's gaze. "It might be her damn baggage, but somehow, she manages to put it on my foot. And yours."

"I see your point." Dayna pushed her plate aside and reached so she could cover one of Chris's hands with her own. "I do. But in the great scheme of things, it's easier to move your feet than it is to pick up the baggage."

Chris stared at her for a long moment, then half-laughed. "True." Maybe that's the perspective she was looking for. *Abuelita* had said the same thing, but Dayna couched it in a way that made it obvious why it was better not to buy into her mom's issues. "Have I told you lately how amazing I think you are?" she blurted after a few more moments.

She smiled. "Not since Sunday."

"That's terrible. I need to do that more often. You're amazing."

"I think the same of you. So we have that in common, too." She traced Chris's fingers with her own.

"We have all the right things in common," she said, watching Dayna's hand on her own. "All the things I've always wanted to have in common with someone." She looked up at her again. "What am I to you?"

Dayna's fingers stopped moving and she raised an eyebrow. "I'm going to assume you didn't mean that to sound as harsh as it did."

She groaned softly. "Good assumption. I didn't." She pulled her hand out from under Dayna's so she could cover it with her own this time. "I've had something on my mind for a while, and I'm not sure how to talk about it."

"How about just saying what it is?"

"I think I'm scared."

"Of?"

"What you might say."

"Try me."

Chris nodded, wondering why this topic made her so damn nervous. She cleared her throat. "Seeing my mom today made me realize something." She paused to buy herself a little time so she could pick the right words. "My mother thinks more of my brother Pete's latest girlfriend than she does of you." She squeezed Dayna's hand, gently. "Like she's hoping that if she sees you as more temporary than Pete's girlfriend, then maybe you'll go away." Chris caught and held Dayna's gaze. "And that hurts. That makes me feel like somehow, I'm less than my brothers, that you're less than the women in their lives. You're this wonderful, beautiful person, and you're so damn important to me, but my mother diminishes that."

"No, she doesn't." Dayna moved her hand so that she could intertwine their fingers on the table. "She might try to do it. She might not even realize how hurtful she's being. I doubt she wakes up and thinks about ways to invalidate her daughter's relationship. It just happens, because right now, she can't move beyond the restrictions she set for herself in her mind. Who knows exactly what they are or how they got there?" She lifted their hands and kissed Chris's fingers. "She doesn't diminish anything you do or anyone in your life unless you let it happen."

Chris sighed. "It's hard, not letting it get to me."

"Well, yeah. She's your mom. Lots of baggage there, beyond the gay thing. That's just part of all the layers."

Chris studied their hands, entwined on the table, and she liked how just that simple gesture helped ease some of her frustration. "So how come *Abuelita* is so different about it?" She thought about the day she'd come out to her parents, nearly fifteen years ago, and how her mother had carried on about sin and evil, and *Abuelita* had shown up suddenly, as if she somehow knew something was happening, and in dramatic Spanish, she took Rosa to task for saying those hurtful things about her own daughter, and who cared who she was attracted to, as long as she was happy and healthy?

"Because it's just different when it's a parent. And *Abuelita*'s a different person than your mom." Dayna smiled, expression sympathetic. "Other than that, I don't really know."

She smiled back, started to say what she really wanted to, but stopped, uncertain. Dayna didn't say anything, either, and Chris knew it was because she was giving her the space to talk or not, and she'd follow her lead, whether the conversation continued or not.

"Look," Chris tried again. "I'm not very good at things like this, because I have a hard time with expectations. I might even be a little fatalistic. I try not to expect anything, because who knows what'll happen?" She paused. "But I need to say these things to you." She looked down at their hands again, and then back at Dayna's face, where she saw worry in her eyes, and etched in the lines across her forehead. She stroked the back of Dayna's hand with her thumb, trying to dispel her concern.

"We set a rule a while back, that we'd talk about things as they came up." She studied Dayna's eyes for confirmation.

"We did. And something has clearly come up. So let's talk about it."

She nodded and dropped her gaze to their hands again. "It's hard for me, sometimes, to do that."

"I know. It's okay. I asked you once to talk to me before you freaked out about anything. It seems to me you're doing all right so far."

She smiled. "For me, anyway." She reached for Dayna's other hand, then. "So I've realized something, and yeah, it scared me, but the more I thought about it, the more it seemed I was just reacting to old stuff."

"We all do that." She gave Chris's hands a squeeze.

"Yeah, well, I'm really good at it. But that's not what I want to talk about. I want to talk about us."

Dayna's eyes widened, but Chris didn't stop. She couldn't, now. "I don't want 'temporary' with you," she said after a few more seconds. "I don't want to be just 'seeing' you, and I don't want to be just your 'girlfriend.' You mean much more to me than that." She stopped, not sure she'd actually said it aloud, but the expression on Dayna's face confirmed that she had. She pulled one of her hands free from Chris's.

"I don't expect us to move in together, or buy a house or make any big purchases to prove anything," she continued, trying to soften the blow should Dayna freak out and decide to pull away. "I know your last relationship didn't work out very well, and you might not want to think about what we're doing just yet, but I just wanted that out there—"

Dayna reached across the table and covered Chris's lips with her fingers. She pulled her other hand free and got up, and came around the table to the other side, and stood next to her chair, looking down at her. And then she took Chris's face in her hands, leaned down, and kissed her in a way that made her lose track of what she had been trying to say, and sent fireworks through her chest instead.

"That," Dayna said as she finally pulled her lips away, "is for talking about things as they come up."

"Damn. I should do that more often."

"And this—" she kissed her again, harder and deeper, her hands still cupping Chris's face, still warm and soft against her skin. Chris turned in her chair and gripped Dayna's hips, both because she wanted to touch her, and also to keep herself from sliding off the chair from the unbelievably sexy onslaught of Dayna's mouth on hers.

"Means yes," Dayna finished as she pulled away again, the smile on her lips the one that had nearly knocked Chris off her feet the first time she'd seen it, left her wanting more than just conversation and jokes, more than a first kiss and a first night. She released Chris's face, but her smile remained.

Chris stood, relief and a strange excitement chasing each other through her chest. She brushed a strand of Dayna's hair out of her face, and whatever fears she may have had, whatever old issues had been left hanging on the door of her heart, disintegrated at the look in Dayna's eyes. "Hell, Counselor, I'm crazy in love with you." *Oh, my god. She'd said it. The L-word.*

"So I figured." Dayna slid her arms around her waist and rested her head against Chris's shoulder.

"How's that?" Chris pulled her closer, surprised at how easy it had been, after all, and even more surprised at how much lighter she felt, like the admission of her feelings had freed her somehow, in ways she hadn't anticipated.

"Because you hadn't left yet," she said, a teasing undercurrent in her voice. She looked up at her. "And for the record," she continued as she locked her gaze on Chris's, "I'm completely in love with you, so it clearly works out."

Chris smiled, giddy.

"Is there anything else you wanted to discuss tonight?" she asked as she traced patterns on Chris's neck with the fingertips of one hand.

"I guess I'm wondering how you want to define this relationship."

She stopped caressing her neck. "Honey, you don't need to move in with me. We don't have to buy a house or a cat or a dog or anything like that to prove anything to me. As far as I'm concerned, this is a commitment, and I'm going to treat it as such. Did you want to talk about official partner kinds of things? Or is that another conversation for later?"

Chris almost stopped breathing. She forced herself to calm down. "That's a conversation for later, please."

Dayna gave her the smile again, the one that made it hard for Chris to remain upright. "Fine by me," she said. "Are you okay now? Everything still intact?"

She nodded. "I'm not sure why I thought talking about that would be so hard."

"Has it come up in your other relationships?"

"Sort of. Not in a good way."

"That's why."

Chris smiled. "You're pretty smart, for a lawyer."

She gave her an "oh, really?" look and Chris laughed.

"You're not so bad yourself, for a cop." Dayna kissed her again, before she could respond. After a few moments, she pulled away. "Homework first. Then we'll do some more processing."

"I'm not sure I want to talk about it anymore tonight."

"Who said anything about talking?" She leaned in again and nipped her earlobe. Chills shot down Chris's back. "There are other ways to process, Detective. And I plan to use as many as possible." She gave her a saucy little wink, and went back to her side of the table.

"YO." HARPER STOOD in the doorway of Chris's cubicle. "Boss man wants to see us."

Chris set her coffee cup and the Morales and Griego files down on her desk and took her jacket off and tossed it onto the chair she didn't use. "First thing?" She was still basking in the glow of the previous evening and night with Dayna.

"Yep." He studied her. "You haven't seen Burgess's latest." It wasn't a question.

She groaned. "No."

"Have a look. That's why boss-man's on us."

She logged into her desktop and clicked on her bookmark for Legal Eyes. "Oh, fuck," she muttered as a grainy, rather blurry photo of her walking into the substation appeared at the top of the day's entry. The photo beneath it was of her and Harper, standing by his Jeep outside the Barelas Coffeehouse two days before. It wasn't a very good photo of her, fortunately, and it was hard to make out her features. Or much else about her, except she knew it was her because that was Harper, and that was his jeep.

"Son of a bitch," she said, and her glow dispersed immediately. The blog's headline read, "APD's finest keep the police stations and restaurants safe." But not the streets of our fair city, Chris thought as she skimmed the blog. That was the gist: the cops twiddle their thumbs in the nice substation and eat out while illegal aliens create chaos in the streets. They'd named her, and Baca, who had posted this particular entry, noted that she had spoken with Detective Chris Gutierrez Tuesday afternoon, the "lead detective" assigned to find the killer of Victor Ramirez.

"You talked to Baca?" Harper asked.

"Yeah. Day before yesterday. She called my direct line. Didn't think to mention it, since she didn't get anything out of me."

"What'd she say?"

"That she was a reporter and wanted to ask me a few questions. I told her that the APD media liaison was who she needed to talk to. Then she tried to ask me when APD was going to do something about violent crime perpetrated by illegal immigrants. I told her again I was transferring her to our media liaison and then I did."

Harper smiled. "Good job. Let the fruitcake experts handle it."

She looked at the second photo again. "This was taken yesterday morning," she said. "When I came in. And the one at Barelas—shit."

"What?"

"I saw Baca. She was standing right out in front of the restaurant, talking on her phone. I thought she looked familiar, but I didn't get a good look at her. Had to be her."

"What time was the station photo taken?"

"About six forty-five."

"They staked out the parking lot. Did you see anyone?"

"Not beyond the usual. They might have been using a long lens." That didn't work very well, fortunately. She thought back to yesterday. Her usual cursory sweep of the parking lot hadn't picked anything up before she got out of her car. The substation sat in northwestern Albuquerque, near Second and Montaño, a busy intersection in a mixed industrial/residential area. Buildings sat back from the roadside this part of Second, leaving a lot of empty space between blacktop and structures. Legal Eyes stalkers could've been parked in one of the empty lots near the intersection, where people sometimes parked cars they were trying to sell. Or in any one of the surrounding overflow parking lots. There was one just south of the one she used, off Second. Damn.

"So how come they didn't post a photo of me going into the station?" Harper asked. "I got here right after you."

"Because I drew the short straw that day. Who knows?" She sighed and clicked back to the APD home page. "All right, let's go see *el jefe*. Maybe he'll give the case to someone else, now that Legal Eyes is convinced I'm the lead detective."

"Fat chance. He wants it solved."

"Damn, Harper. I think you just flattered me."

He cocked his head. "Was that what that was? Forgot myself." He gave her a little smile and waited for her to precede him out of her cubicle to lead the way to Lieutenant Jerry Torrez's office.

Thirty minutes later, she sank into one of the chairs that fronted Harper's desk, which looked a lot like Torrez's. Sparse but organized, with very few personal items. Harper's included a pint glass with a beer logo to hold his pens and pencils, a framed photo of his adult daughter on his desk, and a Navy coffee cup. Like Torrez, Harper was ex-military and like the lieutenant, he didn't talk much about it though it showed up through his neat-freak office and attention to detail on a case.

He came in, carrying two Styrofoam cups of coffee, both with plastic stir sticks in them. "Mmm mmm. Fresh. Which means it's slightly less crappy than usual." He set one down within Chris's reach and sat down behind his desk, across from her.

"Tell me more about this Griego-Morales link. Boss-man liked it, too."

"It's not a solid link yet, but it's interesting. They're about the same age, both born in Las Cruces, went to the same high school. Big high school, but doesn't mean they didn't know each other or keep in touch after."

He stirred his coffee. "I like it. Smells sordid."

She gave him a look, amused. "Drugs?"

"Don't know. But it feels kind of like a high school reality show. Drama like that can hang around for years."

She didn't respond. She instead picked up the cup of coffee Harper had brought her and stared into it for a long moment. Why hadn't she noticed that someone was watching her yesterday? Legal Eyes now probably knew what she drove, and that pissed her off.

"What else jumped out at you about Morales?" He sipped his coffee.

"Not much. No record, though that just might mean she wasn't caught. Or she tried to stay out of trouble because her mom might not be in the country legally. Her high school transcripts are good. Solid B's and A's. Her last known address was an apartment complex near Indian School and Girard and her last job was at the Smith's grocery on Constitution and Carlisle. Near her apartment. She quit a month ago."

"Have you checked them out?"

"On my list of exciting things to do today. You got time?"

"Yep. What about her father?"

"No mention of one."

"Is Morales on the birth certificate? Might not be the actual surname. If Morales's mom came here illegally, she might be using somebody else's vitals."

"It's on the certificate." Chris took a sip. "Or she managed to enter the country legally—maybe on a visitor's visa to see family—and then just overstayed. That happens, too."

"Okay, but what does any of this have to do with Ramirez?"

"Something. Not sure what. We've got Morales calling him the day before he died, and also twenty minutes before he sent his last text to Griego. And possibly at his house right around the time he died, if the car Mrs. Marquez heard is Morales's. Plus, she most likely went to his house a few times, according to Mrs. Marquez, and she hung out with Griego. Maybe Morales is in on the human smuggling."

"Hell, maybe she whacked Ramirez," he intoned as he brought his own coffee cup to his lips.

"The thought has crossed my mind. But we don't have a motive yet."

"It usually comes down to love or money."

"What about revenge?"

"That's part of love. You don't necessarily have to kill someone you loved. You can ice someone for screwing over someone else you loved. But love—" he wagged his index finger in the air for emphasis, "that's an underlying theme in a lot of situations like this. Or she dusted him for money. Speaking of which—" he opened the folder on his desk. "Bank statements." He slid the folder across to her.

"Anything interesting?"

"Jim's paid him by check, since he was a contract employee. There are other deposits, but nothing over a thousand. Could be other contract work or under the table work. Not like that doesn't go on anywhere."

"He didn't spend much from this," Chris said as she looked through the papers. "A thousand in checking, a thousand in savings. Where the hell's the rest of his money?"

"You're assuming he has some," Harper said wryly.

"Of course he does. If he's involved in trafficking, he's getting chunks of cash. And I doubt he deposited it in an account. Does he have a safety deposit box?"

"Hell. Don't know. I'll call the bank."

"Lots of people stash cash in a safety deposit box. Maybe that's what he did with his."

Harper nodded and leaned back. "Motive for murder?"

"Sure. But that still doesn't explain *La Catrina*."

"Then it has something to do with love. Either him or somebody else he screwed over. Mark my words, Gucchi. Love or money."

He was right. Most murders were crimes of passion, and a lot of them originated in love gone wrong or betrayal. If all the murderer wanted from Ramirez was money, he or she would have just shot him once—probably in the head—and taken it. If it was a hit, one shot to the head would have accomplished that, and it was usually done by someone experienced with guns, someone who wanted to take care of business and then leave before the police showed up. Ramirez had taken five bullets, all at close range, and the killer had left a calling card.

"Maybe Ramirez had a bunch of cash in his house and the killer already took it," she said.

"Possible. But after five shots, the perp better know where Ramirez stashed it to get it and get out. And put the doll thing on him."

"That might explain why we didn't find any cash in his house. The killer took it."

"Okay," he conceded. "Love *and* money. So what do you want to do about Morales? BOLO?"

"Not yet. Let's go check out her former apartment." She stood.

"Give me a few minutes. I'm going to run some checks on Burgess and Baca. Make sure we're not dealing with total nutcases."

"Yes, because dealing with extreme immigrant-haters is always better than total nutcases," she said, half-joking.

"Hey, they posted shit about us and got personal with you, which means I can run a check on them, to ensure your safety and the safety of your colleagues." He sounded flippant, but his expression was hard, like a boxer sizing up an opponent, looking for weaknesses. "Be careful."

She nodded and went back to her desk, thinking about ways to circumvent using her own car for a while. Burgess and Baca might only be bloggers, but after all the years she'd known K.C., it didn't hurt to exercise a little caution when dealing with people who didn't care much for police or certain types of people. You never knew what would set them off. She stood in her office, thinking. Jerry had just gone over the usual precautions, about not saying anything that could be incriminating and being more observant with regard to surroundings.

But what else might set someone like that off? They'd already targeted her as a cop. They might make insinuations about her ethnic background, whether she was legal or not... She sucked her breath in. Dayna. Fuck. Wouldn't that be a scoop for their damn blog? Big ol' lezzie cop's relationship with big ol' lezzie prosecuting attorney. They could spin the hell out of that, and make all kinds of trouble for both of them. She kicked herself for a few more moments because she hadn't picked up that someone might be following her. She'd gotten sloppy, and that pissed her off, too. Nothing she could do about that, now, except be more careful. She opened Morales's file for the apartment address. Maybe the property owner knew where she went.

# Chapter Eleven

HARPER LOOMED IN the doorway to her cubicle thirty minutes after she'd talked to him. "One of Ramirez's sisters just called. April Lancaster."

She looked up at him and nodded, giving him a "hold on" signal with her index finger. "Okay, Carl. I'll look for the fax. Gotta run. *Muchas gracias.*" She hung up. "Where is she?"

"Ohio."

"Why the hell couldn't we find her?" Chris turned the page on her legal pad and wrote some notes.

He shrugged. "Didn't want to be found, sounds like. She goes by her second married name, and they've moved a lot in the past few years. Husband's military. She hasn't talked to her brother since high school. One of her friends from El Paso saw the news report and let her know. She's not too broken up about it."

"Where's the other sister?"

"Florida. From what the Ohio sister said, neither one of them has had much to do with our guy for years."

"She give any reason?"

"Not really. Just said their family wasn't very close."

She wrote that down. "Didn't even see each other at the parents' funerals?"

"The father's, yes. They were still in high school then. The mother's, no. She said he was in Mexico when Mom died, which was about seven years ago."

Chris leaned back in her chair, not surprised that Harper would've asked those questions. He was thorough that way. "Doing what?"

"She doesn't know, but she told me she's sure it was bad, whatever it was. The guy was just not Mr. Popular with the sisters." He issued a frustrated sigh. "She said she'd do the requisite paperwork to get final arrangements made since she's next-of-kin, but other than that, I don't think that's a road we need to check out."

She tossed her pen onto the desk. "I guess that's good. Helps narrow it down. Speaking of El Paso, Carl's faxing me some stuff. Hold on." She stood and brushed past him to the alcove where the fax and copy machines resided. It was just finishing printing something out when she got there and she picked up the sheets of paper to make sure they were for her.

"All right," she said when she returned to her cubicle. "Carl did some legwork down there for us. One of Ramirez's juvie busts involved a guy who had a rep as a big-time coyote in Juárez. He's apparently something of a legend along the border, but Carl says the guy hasn't been active in a few years. He thinks he's probably dead." She handed Harper one of the papers that Carl had faxed. "Point is, when Ramirez was sixteen, he was arrested for car theft, but the charges didn't stick. They couldn't prove he had actually done the deed and he played innocent, that his friend claimed it was his car and he wanted it repainted."

"So this friend was the coyote guy." He looked over at her.

"No. The friend's uncle was. The coyote—a guy known around El Paso as Juan Montéz—stepped in and said it was all a big misunderstanding, that his nephew had borrowed the car and was going to get it repainted for him as a birthday gift."

Harper gave her a sarcastic "really?" look.

"Whatever evidence Montéz produced, it worked. Ramirez got off." She gave him an equally sarcastic look.

"And maybe this Montéz guy taught him everything he knows about human smuggling," Harper finished for her.

"That's what I'm thinking."

"Probably not a chance we'll find him, either."

"Carl doesn't think so. Montéz isn't his real name. On the Juárez side of the border, he's known as *el fantasma*. The ghost."

"Great," Harper muttered. "We've got dead coyotes, ghosts, missing persons, and no freaking idea how any of it fits together." He handed the paper back to her.

"How about this? Carl says that one of the things Montéz would do is walk his pickups over the border from Juárez. He was Mexican, but he had relatives on this side. So he came and went quite a bit, no big deal. Carl thinks he was paying off at least one of the border guards, which made checking the paperwork easier. Then he'd walk whoever it was into El Paso and meet a ride at a public place."

"Huh. Nice job, Gucchi. That's the scenario you figured earlier. I'd buy it."

She placed the paper back on her desk. "So maybe Ramirez learned a thing or two from the ghost."

He nodded. "Except Ramirez has to work this side of the border, because otherwise it'd look suspicious, an American going into Juárez and coming back into El Paso with extra people. Maybe he can't work the border guards like Montéz could, or maybe 9/11 screwed him up a little so he has a new system." He sucked air between his teeth. "But what the hell is it?"

Chris stared at the papers from Carl. Public place. Easy to get lost in a crowd. Especially a crowd with lots of Latinos. "The bridge," she said, bringing her gaze back up to Harper. "It's perfect. Crowded, loud, lots of people in and out all the time. It's open twenty-four hours."

"What about the Mercado?"

"Possibly, but it's not very close to the bridge. Maybe Ramirez would meet his target at the bridge, then drive him or her to the

Mercado and hang out for a bit and then Griego would come along and take the cargo."

"I'm liking this." He rocked forward onto the balls of his feet, arms crossed. "Liking it a lot."

"Have we gotten anything from the BOLO on Griego?"

"Nope."

"Clarify it. Maybe he's on his way to El Paso to do whatever he and Ramirez were scheduled to do. I'd like to know what that is."

"In other words, don't pick him up."

"No. But I want Cruces and El Paso on it ASAP, because I think Griego is going to the bridge and maybe Mercado Mayor on Saturday and I want to know what for. What about his family?"

"Didn't tip 'em. Cruces police have been doing some extra drive-bys. No sign of him or his truck. Unless they're lying."

"That's possible, too."

He grunted noncommittally.

She checked her watch. "Give me a bit to make a couple calls and then we'll go check out Morales's former digs."

"Sounds good. We'll take one of the unmarked cars."

She was about to ask why, then thought about Burgess. Driving her own car was probably a bad idea. And getting into Harper's car might put him in a bad situation, too. Damn. She exhaled in frustration. "Shit."

"Yeah, kinda like having paparazzi on your butt," he said, droll. "Let me go see what all came up with either of those two. Oh—Sam called. Ramirez's autopsy is this afternoon. You want in on that, after we check out Morales's roommate?"

"Can you handle this one? I've got this other shit to check."

"Yep. I'll tell you all the juicy details."

"Can't wait."

He left and Chris glared at the files on her desk. She checked her watch again. K.C. might be in her office on campus right now, so she dialed the number on her desk phone. K.C. picked up on the second ring.

"Fontero."

"Damn, you sound like a detective or something, answering like that."

"Hey, *mujer*. I was just going to call you. I'm assuming you've seen Legal Eyes today."

"Unfortunately."

"When were those photos taken?" She was all business, but concern colored her tone.

"Early morning yesterday when I showed up at work and Monday lunch with Harper at Barelas."

Pause. "You're sure?"

"Yes. Whoever it was probably staked out the station from across

Second, in one of those areas where people park their cars off the road. Or maybe one of the parking lots south of the entrance. And I think I saw Mary Baca outside Barelas."

K.C. muttered something that sounded like a curse.

"Yeah, I know. Didn't see that coming. I'm probably going to leave my car here for a couple of days, at least."

"Good idea." She lapsed into silence, but Chris heard something unspoken in it, something tense.

"What?"

"I think you need to be extra careful with Burgess, Chris. He slams immigrants, but I cruised through the blog, and he's not a fan of gays, either. I don't think he'd be adverse to outing someone. Especially if that someone was a cop. Or a prosecuting attorney."

"Yeah, I've already gone there. I'll be calling Dayna later today."

"Good. And maybe you'd better stay with us for a few days. Kara won't be back for a couple more weeks, and I know she wouldn't mind you crashing at her place."

Chris pinched the bridge of her nose and closed her eyes, frustrated. It would be easy, though, staying at the mother-in-law house that sat just behind K.C. and Sage's place. K.C.'s youngest sister currently rented it and, by extension, she was family, too.

"When it rains, it pours, *amiga*," K.C. said. "Even in the damn desert. And Burgess might not be the type to come bang on your door, but you don't know what kind of people read his blog."

"I don't want to bring this asshole and his baggage to your place, Kase. If they're staking me out at the station, they'll probably try to do it wherever I am."

"Only if they find you. Ditch your car and don't go home or to Dayna's for a few days. By that time, you might have a suspect in custody for the Ramirez murder and they'll move on to the next target. Unless whoever killed the guy is undocumented, in which case they'll shift focus to the evils of bad border control."

She leaned back in her chair and put her feet on her desk. "Let me think about it."

"The Sage and K.C. bed and breakfast is officially open starting now. You've got a key. Just show up. I can drive you to work."

"It might not come to that. I'll let you know later. Do you have anything on Burgess?"

"Some, but I'll have more by the end of the day."

"Okay. I'll touch base later, *esa*."

"Excellent. Later." She hung up and Chris moved her feet off her desk so she could lean forward and return the receiver to its base. She scowled. K.C. had a point. Legal Eyes couldn't stake out her house if she didn't go home for a while. At this point, they probably didn't know where she lived. Chris was very careful about keeping that information under wraps. And she sure as hell wouldn't stay at Dayna's, even if she drove a different car. She could not be seen anywhere near a prosecutor's house while Legal Eyes had her under their scope. Maybe a hotel was the best solution. She stood and retrieved her jacket from the top of the file cabinet. No, because if she drove either her own car or a department vehicle, they'd track her to the hotel and then blog about how the city was paying to put her up while illegal immigrants ran wild in the streets. And the last thing she needed was to add to bad press, no matter where it came from.

Her business cell rang and she took it out of her jacket pocket. She didn't recognize the number, but she answered.

"Gutierrez."

"Hi. Detective Chris Gutierrez?" said a male voice, slightly nasal with a dry west Texas twang. In spite of that, he pronounced her name properly.

"Speaking."

"Dan Marshall. Marc Aragon asked me to give you a call, said you might need some insight into a few things along the border." He put a special emphasis on "insight."

"Hey, thanks for calling. I was actually hoping to talk to you. Is there a time and place that works for you?"

"Tell you what. I have to be on that side of town tomorrow morning and I can swing by the station. Nine sound good?"

Finally. Some decent luck. Maybe an ex-border patrol agent could open some more doors. "That would be excellent, Mr. Marshall. And I'll be sure to have a fresh pot of our excellent department coffee on hand."

He laughed at her sarcasm, a sort of bark-chuckle. "Hey, better than anything I got workin' the roads. You got my cell phone number in your phone, there?"

"Sure do. Thanks. See you tomorrow."

He signed off and she then called the front reception area to let them know Marshall would be coming by the next day. She made a note of the call, put her jacket on, and put her phone back in the pocket. A headache brewed but it was low-grade enough that she could ignore it for a while. She made sure her notebook and pen were in her other pocket, and she left her cubicle. All the cubicles were arranged in the middle of the room. A corridor around the outside took her to the other side, and Harper's work space. He looked up at her when she came in.

"Got something," she said. "The property owner of Morales's apartment says that she had a roommate, who's still living there. Britney Luna. I ran her. She works at the same Smith's Morales did. She's twenty-five. Maybe she'll have some info about where Morales is. Or where she went."

"Boy, I love police work," Harper said as he stood. "Let's see what shakes out."

INEZ MORALES'S LAST known address was listed in a complex that looked a bit like Johnny Griego's, though it was in a much nicer area. North of the UNM campus, the complex hugged a boundary between an area of smaller middle-class New Mexico-style homes and larger, ritzier ones along this part of Indian School Road. Built in 1960s boxy style, the grounds were nice and some of the units faced a central common area, reached via a breezeway. All the apartments opened to the outside. Morales's had been on the first floor. One of the neighbors on one side remembered her and her roommate. Nice girls, quiet. Chris thanked the neighbor and she and Harper walked to the door of what had been Morales's apartment. She knocked.

"Who is it?" asked a feminine voice from the interior.

"Albuquerque Police." Chris held her badge up to the peephole for a second then stepped back. "Could you please open the door?"

Chris heard a deadbolt and then a chain being slid back. The door opened, and the young woman who appeared wore a tight red V-neck T-shirt, feminine cut, and low-slung jeans that showed part of her stomach. A wide white belt was cinched around her waist, but it was clearly just for looks because the jeans fit too snugly to need it. Her dark hair fell around her face in ways that probably got her lots of attention from guys.

"Hi. I'm Detective Gutierrez and this is Detective Harper." Chris gestured at him. "Britney Luna?"

"Yes. What's this about?"

"We're looking for Inez Morales. We understand she was your roommate?"

Her expression went from wary to fearful. "She moved out last month. I don't know where she is."

"You sure about that?" Chris asked, and Britney's gaze moved from her face to the gun at her hip then back to her face.

"Why do you want to talk to her?"

"She may have seen something related to a murder investigation. We need to ask her a few questions."

"I don't know where she is."

"How about this gentleman?" Chris held up Johnny Griego's driver's license photo, blown up. Britney's eyes widened.

"I don't know him."

Chris raised an eyebrow. "You're sure?"

"Yes," she said, but she had dropped her eyes to her sneakers, which, Chris noticed, were a color reminiscent of Pepto-Bismol.

"So you're saying you never went with your roommate to meet this man?"

That caught her off guard, and she hesitated. "Yes," she admitted.

"We've got witnesses who say Inez was at this man's apartment building, within the past couple of weeks." She held the photo up again. "So you did go with her on some of these visits?"

Harper had his notebook out, and he was writing something down in it. Britney looked at the photo of Griego again, but not like she was trying to remember. She was buying time.

"Oh, that guy," she said after a few more seconds of silence. "I did go with her to his place a couple of times, but she didn't stay long."

"Do you know his name?"

"No."

She was lying. Harper stopped writing.

"How about this gentleman?" Chris held up Victor Ramirez's driver's license photo. "Witnesses say you were with Inez at his house a few times over the past few weeks."

Britney glanced at the photo, then at Chris's gun, then back at the photo. Definitely nervous.

Chris went a little harder. "This man is dead, Ms. Luna." She held up Ramirez's photo again. "Inez might know something about how he ended up that way. You can make this a lot easier on yourself if you tell us what you know and where Inez might be. Or you can talk with us at the station."

That got to her. One of her hands fidgeted with a strand of hair near her ear. She opened the door wider and leaned against the jamb. "He's dead?"

"Yes. So you'll be doing yourself a favor talking to us."

She considered the statement, and chewed on her lower lip. "Okay. Yes. I went with her to both Johnny and Vic's a couple of times. But only a couple. I didn't like either of them."

Harper started to write again.

"Why did you go, then?"

She shrugged. "She said she just wanted someone to come with her. Buddy system."

"Was she worried about something?"

"She didn't say specifically."

"When did you go with her?"

She thought for a bit. "Oh, I don't know. I think the last time I went with her to Vic's was about three weeks ago and to Johnny's a little before that. It was about the time she moved out of here."

"You're sure you only went a couple of times?"

"Yeah. I know it was twice to Vic's and once to Johnny's."

"Where has she been staying since she moved out?" Chris didn't want to push her too hard, but she wanted to draw more information out of her.

"She went back to Cruces. She said she got a good job down there and could make way more money than here."

"Do you know what job that is?"

"No. She said she was working for a friend who had his own business." It sounded like she was telling the truth with that statement. Inez might not have revealed much about whatever this "business" was.

"Did anybody help her move?"

"Johnny did. He has a really nice truck, but he borrowed one from his cousin or something down there and used that to move her stuff."

So Johnny and Inez might have been a bit closer than Johnny's neighbor supposed. "And this was about a month ago?"

"Yeah. But she came back a couple of times and she'd crash with me for a few days."

"Doing what?"

Britney shrugged. "She said she had to do some things here for her new job."

Strange thing to do, if you were based in Las Cruces. Unless she was working for Ramirez and he needed her to run something up from Cruces or El Paso for him. Or vice versa. "Did she say anything about what kind of work she was doing?"

"Not really. Just that it was pretty good money."

Chris studied her. She didn't seem to be lying about what little she knew about Morales's new job. "How did you meet her?" She folded the print-outs of the photos and slipped them into her jacket pocket.

"We both worked at Smith's." She shrugged. "We got along. She needed a place to live last year, and we found this place together."

"How well did you know Johnny and Vic?"

"I only met them a couple of times. Inez would ask me to wait in the car when she had to talk to either of them."

Chris heard Harper's pen on his notepad paper. "Why didn't you go inside with her?"

"She didn't want me to. I didn't mind Johnny too much. Kind of a player, but so are most guys." She threw a glance at Harper that Chris knew would just bounce off him. "Vic, though... I was always ready to call nine-one-one when Inez had to talk to him."

"Why was that?" Chris had adopted her easy-going chat style. It usually put people at ease and it seemed to be working on Britney.

She shook her head. "He had this look. I can't explain it. I don't think he liked women all that much. Not that he was gay or anything, but he was just one of those guys who has a real problem with women."

"So how did Inez meet him?"

"Through Johnny. He and Johnny worked on cars together at some shop down in the South Valley. And no, Inez wasn't with Johnny. At least not in a permanent sense. I think Vic and Johnny got her the job in Cruces."

Or, Chris thought, Inez went to work for Ramirez helping run people over the border. She may not have liked him much, but the money was probably good. Where, though, would she stay in Cruces? With Johnny's relatives or friends? In her own place? Nothing had come up in her file about a current address in Cruces. "How did she get along with Vic?"

"I don't know. She didn't talk about him, and I was only with her a couple of times when she talked to him. She didn't seem to care about him one way or the other, but she did say he wasn't the nicest guy ever."

"Did she ever have a problem paying her rent?"

Britney cocked her head, puzzling that one out. "No. Always paid the bills, too. Never late."

"Is she getting any mail here?"

"Not really. Coupons and stuff."

"Did she leave a forwarding address?"

"No. She just said to send important stuff to her mom."

Someone who was planning a legitimate move usually made better arrangements than that. Whatever Inez was doing, it didn't feel like it was completely legit. "How did she pay her bills?"

Britney brushed her hair away from her face. Her nails were also pink, but in a more muted tone than her sneakers. "She'd pay me cash for the rent and I'd write one big check to the landlord. She'd either give me cash or checks for the other bills."

So Morales had some cash around in addition to a bank account. If she was involved in running people over the border, that would explain the cash. They'd need to check her bank records, see if she was depositing any suspicious amounts of cash.

"Does she have any family in Albuquerque besides her mom?" Chris asked.

"I don't think so. She never mentioned anybody."

"Any family anywhere that you know of?"

"She has a couple of cousins in Juárez that she's really close to. They're sisters. Basically, her cousins grew up with her because their parents couldn't take care of them or something."

"Did these cousins ever come and visit her?"

"Not to Albuquerque, that I know of. Inez would go to El Paso and meet them there or go into Juárez. She speaks Spanish. I think she was trying to figure out a way to help one of her cousins immigrate."

"Have you met either of these cousins?"

"No. I never went with Inez to El Paso. Something happened to one of them a few months ago, and Inez was on the phone with her a lot. More than usual."

Harper's pen had paused.

"Oh? Do you know what?" Chris asked.

"Not really. Some kind of assault. Her cousin had to go to the hospital."

"Do you know this cousin's name?"

"Her first name's Marta. I don't know her last name."

"When was the last time you saw Inez?"

Britney tensed and looked down at her sneakers. "Two weeks ago. She drove up from Cruces and crashed here then left the next day."

Chris gave her a skeptical cop look. "You've been really helpful,

Ms. Luna. Don't screw that up now. Try again. When was the last time you saw her?" She enunciated each word in her question with extra cop emphasis.

Britney bit her lower lip and her gaze moved from Chris to Harper then back again. She'd get nothing from Harper except his blank expression. "All right," she said, half-exasperated and half-nervous. "She was here last weekend. She stopped by Sunday night. She asked if there was any mail."

"About what time did she come by?"

"I don't know. Maybe around eight."

"When did she leave?"

"Ten-thirty or so. I had to work the next day."

"Did she call ahead of time, to tell you she was coming by?"

She shook her head. "No big deal. She probably saw my car in the parking lot."

"So she spent at least two hours with you. What did she talk about?" Chris hardened her tone a little.

"Nothing much. We mostly talked about people we both knew here, and what everybody was doing."

"How did she seem?"

"Fine. She said she was tired from driving. I asked her why she was in town and she said somebody owed her some money, and that person couldn't go to Cruces, so she had to come up to get it."

"Do you know who this somebody was?"

"She didn't say. Just said she had to go by somebody's house to get money."

"And you haven't heard from her since?"

"No."

"Did you try to contact her?"

"I texted her a couple of times, to see how she was, but never heard back. I figured maybe she went to Mexico to help Marta or something."

Chris glanced at Harper, who was studiously jotting notes. She looked at Britney again. "So she just shows up Sunday night?"

Britney shrugged in a way that suggested that socializing could go on at any hour of any day and what of it.

"Okay. Does the name 'Catrina' mean anything to you?" Chris asked.

She shook her head, and her expression was clearly puzzled.

"All right. Do yourself a favor, Ms. Luna, and don't go anywhere for a while. In the meantime, if Inez or Johnny contact you, let us know immediately." Chris handed her a business card. "Whatever time it is. Call."

She took the card, glanced at it, then back up at Chris. "Am I in trouble?"

"Probably not. But I do recommend you let us get your fingerprints so we can rule you out of a couple of things."

"Oh, my God." Her eyes widened. "Do I have to go to the station for that?"

"No, we can do it right now, if you'd like. We've got a kit in the car."

"Okay." She left the door open a few inches and moved away. When she returned, she was wearing a black hooded sweatshirt. She shut the door behind her and followed Chris to the parking lot. Harper brought up the rear. He had yet to say a word, but she'd turn this show over to him because he had a really good dad way about him and Britney might respond well to that while undergoing a police procedure. Within ten minutes, he had her laughing as he wiped her fingertips off. He handed her his card, as well.

"Thanks, Ms. Luna," he said. "Please let us know if Inez contacts you. Or Johnny."

"Okay." She took his card and another tissue he handed her. "Bye," she said to both Harper and Chris before she walked away.

"Maybe I should've let you take that one," Chris said. "Your dad mode might've worked better."

"Nah. But thanks for making me feel like a grandpa," he said as he put the materials back in the kit. He placed the small sheet of her prints right on top so nothing would potentially smudge them. "What's your take?"

"She's scared."

"Shooter?"

"Don't think so. You?"

He stood and pulled his notebook out of his pocket. "No. But it's looking more and more like Morales might have herself in a bit of trouble."

"And if Luna's telling the truth about how many visits she went on with Morales, and Griego's neighbor is also telling the truth, that means there's a third woman involved who went with Inez to Griego's, at least."

"Huh."

She frowned. "And if Luna's telling the truth, Morales could easily have made it to Ramirez's in time to shoot him."

Harper grunted. "We don't really have probable yet. Let's try to get a definite tie between her, the car, and Ramirez the night of the murder. We need somebody to place her and her car at his house at the time he got popped. You think Griego knows more than he let on?"

"Not unless he's a hell of an actor." Chris recalled his reaction at the body shop when she told him Ramirez was dead. Hard to fake that kind of shock. Took the cocky right out of him. "I don't think he knew," she said. "And we still don't have any evidence that Morales killed Ramirez."

"Maybe not, but we've now got her in Albuquerque telling someone she had to meet somebody for money that person owed her.

She knew Ramirez and she'd been to his house. I say we BOLO her, too. We've got enough to bring her in for questioning, at least."

"Yeah. Here, Cruces, El Paso. And alert the Highway Patrol. For all we know, she's with Griego, driving around somewhere."

He emitted one of his noncommittal grunts. "Let's subpoena Griego's phone records. If Morales called him or texted him to come and get her, that'll show up."

Chris didn't respond for a few moments, thinking about Inez Morales. "This feels too personal. Ramirez got shot in the crotch and the killer left a calling card."

"Seems that way." He paused and rocked forward on the balls of his feet. "There's a Clint Eastwood movie, made in the early seventies. It's about this woman who starts hunting down men in a group of guys who raped her and her sister some years back. The film where Eastwood says 'Make my day'."

"I think I saw that one," she said, remembering it. "She shoots them in the groin and then the head." A woman seeking vengeance for a rape. Had whoever shot Ramirez done so out of retaliation for a rape?

He gave her one of his shrugs. "Something to think about. Maybe Ramirez was into more than running people across the border." He went around to the driver's side and got in while she took shotgun. The car—a nondescript blue Buick—smelled faintly of cigarettes, coffee, and fast food. Must've been on a stakeout. She buckled the seatbelt and knew, with a sense of unease, that she'd have to talk to Inez Morales's mother. She took her personal cell out and called *Abuelita* while Harper steered onto Indian School and drove west.

# Chapter Twelve

CHRIS USED THE hour she would've taken for lunch and worked out in the station gym instead. She showered and then sat at her desk and ate the salad she'd bought at a health food store. Harper hadn't said anything either for or against it when he parked in the lot outside and waited for her, but he didn't ask her to get him anything, either. Plus, he was on his way to watch an autopsy and he generally didn't like to eat anything before those. Probably for the best.

The workout cleared her head a little, both of the low-grade headache she'd had and the thoughts of the case. She texted Dayna to see if she was available to talk then called Harper's desk phone. He wasn't back yet, so she spent the next couple of hours organizing her notes and finishing some things on a different case. Her desk phone rang and Harper's extension appeared in the caller ID window.

"Yeah," she answered.

"Yo. Back from the meat locker and got some stuff on our buddies Burgess and Baca. Come on over, have a look."

She hung up and walked around to his side of the room. "Is it good?" She sank into the chair that fronted his desk.

"Juicy. Burgess has a bit of a record. Baca doesn't, but you never know what people are into. Just because it doesn't show up doesn't mean she hasn't been busy." He looked up from the file at her, a little smile on his lips, the kind of smile that Harper used when he was satisfied with the results of something but didn't want to broadcast. "He's got three past DUIs, one in California and two in Arizona. And he got himself in trouble for an assault in Phoenix a couple years ago." He pushed a file at her.

"Oh?" Chris opened it. "This is interesting. Arrested in Phoenix." She skimmed it. He pulled a gun three years ago on a group of Latino workers standing outside a Home Depot. "Was he drinking during that incident?"

"Doesn't say, but I'm guessing yes. He's also been arrested for refusing to leave public property. Protests." Harper made a "whatever" gesture with his hand. "Nothing that wouldn't get somebody on the other side arrested, too."

"Why'd he pull the gun?" She read more carefully.

"I'd say he was probably drinking. He told them to get out of his country and to quit taking jobs. All the guys, however, were American or legal residents."

"Sounds like a delightful man. What happened with the case?"

"Apparently had a great lawyer. Got the charges reduced to drunk and disorderly. Had to pay a fine, but got out of the jail time if he attended anger management classes and rehab."

"Did he?"

"Doesn't say here, but I'll make a couple of calls, see if he did. Because if he hasn't fulfilled the terms of the sentence..." Harper shrugged, an air of innocence in the gesture. "Might be of interest to the courts there."

And also might stir him up. "What about Baca?"

"Straight and narrow, at least on paper. She's formerly Mary Davidson, from Dallas. She married Phil Baca, who works as a high-level accountant at a firm here in town." He looked up at her. "What's that about? She's anti-immigrant and she hooks up with a guy whose last name is Baca?"

"No accounting for people's beliefs. You'll find Hispanics and Latinos involved in anti-immigrant movements and policies. Some might have parents or grandparents who immigrated legally, so they make sure to talk about how their families are legal and all these other people are screwing it up for everybody else. I've run into a few of those. Some, like her, marry somebody Hispanic or Latino who's legal and who claims legal family roots and that person decides that if his or her spouse is legal, then that should go for everybody else. Others—well, anybody can be anti-immigrant."

"Whatever floats your boat," he said, but with a little sarcasm. "She works as an administrative assistant at hubby's firm. So she's got a day job."

"What about Burgess?"

"Guy has a hard time with steady, traditional employment, according to this. He's worked construction on and off, and worked in a few different retail establishments for one- and two-year stints. Legal Eyes takes donations, so he's probably making some money there. He's divorced, no kids. Addresses are in there. Nowhere near your place or the station." He handed her the file. She took it and got up from the chair.

"Which means any money he makes probably goes mostly to him, depending on the divorce."

He gave her his agreement grunt. "You still going to leave your car here for a couple of days?"

"Yeah. I took the plate off and stashed it under the seat. Though it might be too late. They might already have my plate number."

"It wasn't on the blog this morning, so maybe not. Good idea, though. Just keep an eye out."

"Damn. What the hell put this guy on this path?"

He shrugged. "Now I think we know why he seems to be focused on you rather than me, if that station photo's any indication. Maybe he figures you're going to be an ally to all those illegal immigrants, and you won't arrest them because of your last name."

"I thought about that."

He leaned forward, then, his flat Midwestern expression harder and flatter than usual. "Here's the deal. This guy has some anger issues and a chip on his shoulder when it comes to immigrants. Or anybody who might look like 'em. Guys like this can do a lot of damage with soapboxes like blogs. So you need to watch your back. Watch where you go, watch what you say, watch who you hang out with. They've already followed you to work and taken a photo. That means they'll try for more. If you give them material, they'll feed on it. And it could be anything. You might just be out to dinner with friends or talking with somebody at the store. But in their hands, that becomes ammo and they'll use it against you, your friends, and the department."

"Yeah, I've been thinking about that, too."

"Good. We can't nail him for anything unless he starts saying anything libelous or threatens you. Or shows up and threatens you. Right now, he's exercising his First Amendment rights. Don't give him anything else to exercise over."

"Suggestions?"

"Keep a lower profile than you already do. Maybe stay with family or friends for a few days. Or stay here. But not Dayna's. That's a giant clusterfuck waiting to happen, if they find out who you're seeing. Tell her not to go near your house for a while, either, and do not go out in public with her. Once we get more concrete info about Ramirez, we can release that and maybe Burgess'll go looking for some other illegal immigrant crime. There's plenty of other brown people in this state to mess with. I'll drive you around for the next few days. Just let me know where you'll be and where you're staying."

She smiled. "You really are a dad, Harper. But thanks. Anything I need to know about Ramirez's autopsy?"

He slid a folder over his desk to her. "Photos of the body show a couple of other tats, but nothing that indicate gang affiliation. At least not any that I know of."

She opened it and looked through, noting the designs on Ramirez's back. Nothing on his chest or legs. The bullets that had killed him were 9 mils. Effective at short range if you got lucky or put more than one in the person coming for you.

"Standard ammo," he said, as if reading her thoughts. "Gangs like the nine mils, too."

"You still thinking this is gang-related? Because that's a caliber practically everybody uses."

He shrugged. "It doesn't feel like it. But it'd be pretty easy to get that kind of gun. If you're not that familiar with guns, that one would probably be okay. It took more than one shot, though. Ramirez might've tried to get the gun away from the shooter, and got a few more bullets for his trouble."

"So the crotch shot may not have been intentional."

"I don't know. At this point, it's tough to say. Take the folder with you. See if anything jumps out."

She did, and looked at her watch. "I've got a meeting with Dan Marshall, the retired border patrol officer, tomorrow morning. If you want to sit in, do."

"I'll let you know. What time?"

"Nine."

He nodded. "Might have something else to do. I'll let you know. Take that Burgess file, too. I've got one."

She reached for it just as Harper's desk phone rang. "Hold up," he said as he answered it. "It's Sam."

Chris sat back and waited, and listened to Harper's side of the convo. Sounded like Sam had some success with fingerprints. Harper hung up.

"Got bunches of prints off the doll left on Ramirez."

"It's not a doll."

He shrugged. "None of 'em panned out to anything."

She exhaled. "Shit."

"Yeah. All kinds of info, just not leading anywhere."

"We need to find Morales."

"Yep." He gestured at the file and she picked it up and stood.

"Thanks, Harper.

"I've got your back," he said.

"I know." She gave a little salute with the files and returned to her office, where she checked her personal cell phone. Dayna had texted her back telling her to call. Chris stared at the message, thinking about Legal Eyes. Sorry, honey, but I can't see you for a while. Crazy anti-immigrant bloggers on my ass. Just another day in cop-land. She dialed Dayna's cell number.

Twenty minutes later, she hung up and sat staring at her computer screen. Damn bloggers. Her personal cell phone rang with a tone that indicated the caller was not in her personal contacts list. She didn't recognize the number, but it was local.

"Hello?" she answered.

"Hi, Chris," said a voice she hadn't heard in over two years.

She tensed, and for a second, her brain was on complete lockdown.

"Chris?"

"Hey, Trish," she finally said, hoping she didn't sound as startled as she felt. "Been a while. And I'm guessing this probably isn't a social call. What's up?" Always good to keep things low-key but on point when an ex called. Especially one she hadn't spoken with since the break-up.

"I—okay, this is weird, calling you like this. I know it is. But I have a legit reason." She sounded as uncomfortable as Chris felt.

"It's okay. What's going on?" She kept the conversation moving, so neither of them would have to think too hard about anything beyond this phone call.

"We have a client who saw a news report about Victor Ramirez, the man who was killed near Old Town, and she recognized him."

"Okay..." she acknowledged, not sure where Trish was going. She was a social worker, whose primary demographic was low-income. Many of her clients were immigrants.

"I mean, she recognized him from a while back. She says he was in El Paso."

She sat up straight and reached for a pen. The New Mexico news reports hadn't included the fact that Ramirez was originally from there. "How far back?"

"A few years."

"So she knew him?"

She hesitated before answering. "He raped her."

Chris stared at the legal pad in front of her. "Jesus. Did she report it to anyone?"

"No. She had just arrived from Mexico."

Probably undocumented. "How did the assault happen?"

"He was the coyote who was supposed to take her from El Paso to Albuquerque."

"Which side of the border did she meet him on?"

"This side, at the Santa Fe Street Bridge."

"About how many years ago was this?"

"Four."

Chris wrote it down. She could hear Trish breathing. "Do you think your client would be willing to talk to me a bit about where exactly she met Ramirez and when?"

"I don't know. I'll ask." She sounded dubious.

"I'll treat it as an anonymous tip."

"Let me check with her," she said, with a little bit of relief. "I'll call you back and let you know either way. If that's okay."

"Of course it's okay."

"Well, you know, things didn't—it wasn't the best of terms between us. Just wanted to make it clear that I'm not trying to step on your toes or anything. Or stalk you."

Chris heard a smile in her tone and she chuckled. "I don't think you're stalking me. If you are, you're either doing a really good job because I haven't seen any evidence of it, or you're the laziest damn stalker in Albuquerque because you waited this long to start."

She laughed, and the tension in Chris's shoulders eased.

"I'll let you know probably by tomorrow," Trish said.

"Great. If I don't answer, leave a message. I'll get back to you as soon as I can."

"Okay. You can reach me on this number. It's my personal cell."

"Will do. Let me know what your client decides." She hesitated. "And thanks for calling."

"Chris—"

She waited.

"Oh, never mind."

"No hard feelings. I never had any. It was just...sad. It'll be good to see you. Hope things are going well."

Trish didn't respond for a few moments. When she did, her relief was apparent in her voice. "Same here. Maybe we can grab coffee or something, get caught up."

"Okay. In the meantime, I'll wait to hear from you. Later."

"Bye."

Chris clicked the phone off and stared at it. K.C. was going to love to hear about this. She pulled up her call log on her phone, added Trish's number to her contact list, then dialed Harper's cell on her desk phone. After she hung up with Harper, it occurred to her that Trish still had her cell phone number.

# Chapter Thirteen

CHRIS PARKED DOWN the block from her house, in front of a neighbor she knew was out of town for a few days. She'd taken one of the unmarked department vehicles that needed some routine maintenance. As long as she didn't do active pursuits or stakeouts with it, she could drive it for a couple of days.

One of the nice things about this block was that everybody knew each other and kept an eye on things. And because she was a cop, they'd come to her if something looked really suspicious. She walked once around the block, looking for vehicles or pedestrians who might be tailing her. She'd screwed up once. It would be much harder to catch her off guard now.

Satisfied, she let herself into her house and checked the back yard. It'd be a bitch to scale the six-foot stuccoed cinderblock wall, but paparazzi had done worse. Depending on the size of the chip on either Burgess's or Baca's shoulder, she wouldn't be surprised if they'd try something like that. Strong feelings cause strong actions, K.C. had told her once. A sentiment that could apply to police work, too. She took a Diet Coke out of the refrigerator and went to her back patio where she turned her grill on. K.C. would be there in a bit, and Chris wanted to have dinner well under way.

Twenty minutes later, she heard K.C. knock at the door that entered the kitchen from the carport.

"It's open," Chris called.

"Hey, tall, dark, and handsome," K.C. said as she came in, carrying a bowl covered with tinfoil and a file folder under her arm. "Sage's potato salad. And you can use this for a hat, to stop the evil Legal Eyes rays from penetrating your brain." She gestured at the tinfoil.

"Is there enough for both of us?" She gave her a quick one-armed hug, as she grasped a spatula in her other hand.

"I've got extra." K.C. set the bowl on the butcher block island in the center of the kitchen next to the condiments Chris had already put out. "You can never have too much tinfoil."

Chris laughed. "There's beer in the fridge, *esa*, if you want it. Burgers are almost done. Be right back." She returned with burgers and put one on K.C.'s plate.

K.C. finished dressing her burger and spooned potato salad onto her plate. She went into the dining room and Chris followed her and took the seat to her left.

"So what've you got?"

She finished chewing and took a sip from her beer bottle. "So, Dr. Fontero, how was your day? My day was busy. Hope you like dinner.

Thanks for coming over."

"All right, all right. How was your day and I'm so glad you could come over for dinner."

"That's better. You've got to earn that tinfoil hat, dammit." She grinned. "My day was busy, too. And Detective Gutierrez, this burger is divine. The green chile is particularly excellent." She took another bite. "You should totally give me your recipe for this."

"Fine. You're right. Dinner first. How's Sage?"

"Good. All that shit that went down in August with her dad seems to be settling a little more."

"It's only been a couple months, Kase. Give it time."

"Yeah. I'm not the most patient person." She toyed with her fork. "As I've been told," she added, sheepish.

"You're working on it. So where's Kara? I thought she was going to stick around for a while."

"She is. But she took a temporary contract that came up suddenly with some non-profit group in Seattle. She likes that, because it gives her a chance to see what other parts of the country she might want to settle down in."

Chris looked at her in surprise. "Wait a sec. Your younger sister is talking about settling?"

"I know. Swear to god, pigs are flying somewhere. She did handle all that crazy shit with Sage and River's dad well. And it's actually kind of cool having her around. Sage tells me it's good for my chi." She grinned.

"Of course it is. And your chakras and ju-ju and whatever the hell else Sage says it's good for." She reached for her soda. "Seems you cut her a little more slack, too." Not easy for K.C., given that she, both parents, and her older sister were high-achieving academics, compared to free-wheeling nature-girl Kara.

"I hope so. Whatever. We both managed to get through that."

"And she helped you stay present for Sage when she needed you." Chris took another bite of her burger.

"Yeah." K.C. sat for a moment, staring at the table. "She did. Never would've thought she'd be the grown-up in any situation, but she was in that one."

"You do a good job yourself, getting through stuff." A lot better, in some ways, than she herself did.

"Oh, here's some gossip. Sage thinks Kara might be in pursuit of River."

Chris stared at her. "Seriously? River?"

She shrugged, a "could be" gesture.

"I thought she was still seeing Shoshana."

"Off and on. They're more fuck-buddies, seems to me."

She laughed and almost choked on her burger. "So how are you taking that, Doc? First you find out your younger sister is bi, then she dates some art chick who put the moves on you first, and now she's possibly after your partner's brother."

"Right? The past couple of months have been crazy." She shook her head. "I'm not sure how I feel about Kara and River. I mean, when he was here during that whole freaky scene, I guess I did pick up that they have a rapport on some levels. They're both younger siblings, and both have kind of a rebellious outlook, though River's makes him more of a loner."

"But they're also very loyal to their respective families. Though in Kara's case, she hasn't voiced that." Chris cocked an eyebrow at her. "River. Huh. I assume Sage knows."

"Are you kidding? She knew the first time Kara saw River."

"How does she feel about it?"

She shrugged. "You know how she is. If it's going to happen, there's nothing anybody can do about it and the universe will find a way to get them together."

"Okay, that's the existential take. What about on a personal level?"

"She thinks it's 'interesting,' is the word she used. She's not sure anything between them could last, because River has a lot of baggage Sage doesn't think he's dealt with yet, but on the other hand, she thinks Kara might be the type of person who could draw him out into sorting through some things."

"Oh?"

"Kara's not really judgmental about people—unless it's family." K.C. grinned. "As so many of us are. But Sage thinks Kara could be the kind of woman who would give River the space he needs to figure some things out, without putting conditions on it."

"So how do *you* feel about it?"

K.C. pushed the remnants of her potato salad around. "Weird. I mean, he's Sage's brother. I guess that's a little too 'all in the family' for me. So I'm hoping nothing comes of it."

"But if something does?"

"What can I do? Tell her no, you can't see him? I'll just have to suck it up."

But she wouldn't be happy about it, Chris could tell. "You'll get through it."

"Says you. Speaking of getting through things, what's up with you and Dayna?" She gave Chris the kind of look Harper did when he was in Dad mode.

Chris smiled and told her the short version of the conversation they'd had the night before. When she finished, K.C. stared at her.

"Holy shit. You said that to her? All of that?"

"I did."

"Oh, my god. Huge. That's huge. Whoa. Congratulations. How do you feel?"

"Excellent. And then I had to tell her today that I can't see her for a while because I have crazy bloggers all up in my business."

"How'd she take it?"

"She's worried. And pissed." She shrugged. "It's not the first time APD has been targeted for bad publicity. I'm just pissed that I didn't pick up that somebody was taking my damn picture."

K.C. finished her potato salad and took another swallow of beer. "Why would you think somebody was stalking you?"

"I'm a cop. I dropped the ball."

"You were going to work. Like every other time you have in the past. And having lunch." She shrugged. "Okay. Let's talk about Burgess."

"Hold up. Here's some more gossip. Trish called me today."

K.C. stared at her. "What for?"

"Peripheral connection to a case. One of her clients might know something."

She frowned. "So she just calls you up out of the blue? After...what? Two years?"

"She's a social worker. She's trying to be helpful."

"Whatever. How'd the conversation go?"

"Civil. She admitted it was weird, calling me, but that she had a legit reason."

K.C.'s expression remained skeptical. "So what else did she say?"

"She'll call me and let me know if her client's willing to talk to me or not."

"Do you think Trish saw you on Legal Eyes and decided she missed your ultimate hotness or something and used that as an excuse to call you? See what you're up to?"

Chris laughed. "You're more paranoid than I am. It was kind of weird, hearing her voice, but it does sound like an interesting lead, if her client wants to talk."

"I thought you hadn't talked to her since the break-up."

"I haven't."

"So she follows your career and all and then suddenly decides that this time, she's going to call?" She crossed her arms and gave her a disapproving look. "What phone did she call you on?"

"Personal cell."

"Uh-huh. Did you know it was her calling?"

"No. Didn't recognize the number. I think she has a new cell phone."

"Uh-huh. And she transferred your personal cell phone number into it, even though you guys went through a not-so-great break-up."

"Since when is a break-up any other way?"

"Whatever. Why did she still have your phone number?"

"Why does anybody have anybody's phone number? Some people don't clean out their contact lists after a break-up."

"And she hasn't tried to contact you before this?"

She laughed. "Kase, chill. No, she hasn't tried to contact me before this. She was doing her civic duty and figured she could call me directly since she knows me and she knows that I won't pressure her client to talk if she doesn't want to."

"Ah. The client may not be documented," she said, getting it.

"Exactly. And you know how touchy this shit is, and how screwed up the system is."

"Gotcha. Okay, I won't assume nefarious motives behind one of your exes deciding to call you out of the blue. Speaking of nefarious motives, back to Burgess." She wiped her hands on her napkin and waited for Chris to finish her hamburger before she picked the plates up and put them in the kitchen. She settled into her chair again and reached for the folder.

"From what I could determine, he's got a history in anti-immigration. Guy's originally from Phoenix, and he spent some time doing one of those makeshift 'border patrols'." She slid a page across the table to Chris. "Burgess is the guy in the middle with the cowboy hat on."

Chris studied the photo, which was taken outside. She saw a saguaro in the background amidst the mixed desert brush. Probably southern Arizona. A rag-tag bunch of wanna-be military, is what the ten people in the photo looked like. Two women in the bunch. All dressed in desert camo pants and combat boots, though everybody had T-shirts on. They were all standing, some holding pistols against their chests. Burgess didn't have a gun. Instead, he stood looking directly at the camera, though he had sunglasses on, arms crossed, as if he was daring an immigrant to sneak across the border and take him on. He looked about average height compared to the other guys standing around. He wasn't heavy but not super-toned, either, from his bare arms. Clean-shaven, weak chin, dirty blond hair sticking out from underneath the brim of his hat. Basically, the kind of guy you might see at the mall. Nothing striking about him, nothing that might make you remember him.

"When was this taken?"

"Three years ago. There's one of those Websites that you make for free, with the schedule of patrols on it. It hasn't been updated in two years, so chances are, this group is defunct or the members hooked up with other groups or they founded a whole new group under a new name."

"He's got a record, too." Chris outlined what Harper had dug up and K.C. pulled another piece of paper from her file.

"Somebody posted about his arrest on this anti-immigration forum about that time. The usual conspiracies about being framed by the government. I checked a few of these boards, and Burgess was active on them before he came to New Mexico and started Legal Eyes. I've got more print-outs in here with his comments. He actually used his own name to post." She slid the file to her.

"Props to him," Chris muttered as she looked through the folder.

"Yeah. Not ashamed of his views, which include lots of shitty terms about Mexicans. He'll try to say he's only against the ones who cross the border illegally, but he's commented about 'Spics' on some of these boards, and talked about how everybody should be suspicious of all people who speak Spanish."

Chris read a few of the comments. "Major ax to grind with brown people, *esa*. The background Harper got is the nuts and bolts. Where he's lived, where he's worked. Did you find anything that might explain why he's got this hang-up?"

"Nothing that jumped out at me. He's been engaged in anti-immigrant sentiment for a few years, at least. Maybe he grew up in that kind of household, saw a few things that fit the stereotypes, and boom. He's in this movement, finds others that think like him, and goes on his crusade. I see it all the time, *mujer*."

Chris sighed. "Looks like he flames other people, too."

"That's one of his other fave things to do. He'll flame the shit out of anybody who even moderately disagrees with him. And you don't see any comments on Legal Eyes that aren't pro-Burgess or what he's doing, which tells me he's probably not allowing different views." She picked up her beer bottle.

"I spot-checked a few of the blogs," K.C. continued. "And as I suspected, he selectively edits what people say and distorts legitimate information. He gets his stats from a couple of the big anti-immigrant think tanks in the U.S. that get lots of play from the mainstream media. But if you dig around a bit, you'll find that some of those movers and shakers in the big groups have some ties to less savory groups and, in a couple of cases, to white nationalists."

Chris looked up at her. "White nationalists? Are you serious?"

"Yeah, sadly. It's documented. They'll post on lesser-known white nationalist sites and other hardline anti-immigrant blogs. One of the higher-up guys has a record of long-time correspondence with people in the white nationalist movement."

"Shit. Not that I'm overly surprised, I guess. I've heard comments on the street that would probably go over well with some of the people you research."

"Yeah. Sometimes anti-immigration sentiment crosses its own borders and ends up causing more trouble than helping the situation or reforming anything. And what starts out as legitimate concern about streamlining processes or making sure criminals don't cross the border or whatever slops over into 'all people from Latin American countries are bad.' Or whoever happens to be on the sociopolitical shitlist. Lots of flare-ups throughout American history where people flipped out and went after people they perceived as 'not American enough' or whatever the hell. It's usually in conjunction with economic downturns.

Extremism always finds a more willing audience when people are concerned about where their next meal's coming from or whether they'll have a job in the morning. So what Burgess is doing is nothing new in this country."

Chris slid the papers back into the file. "Yeah, well, it doesn't make my job of catching the bad guys any easier when some asshole with a blog starts going after APD and posting photos of us online, creating all kinds of bad publicity. Who the hell wants to talk to the cops if they're portrayed as a bunch of jerk-offs running around?" She leaned back, frustrated. "What about Mary Baca? I know I didn't ask you to see what you could find on her, but..." she trailed off, hopeful.

K.C. grinned. "Of course I followed up. I am the research goddess, after all."

"No argument here." She laughed and finished her Diet Coke.

"Interesting case. Originally from Texas and married to an accountant named Phil Baca. She's one of those who isn't anti-immigrant as much as she's anti-anybody who's illegal. She seems, from her posts at Legal Eyes, to be pushing a slightly more moderate vision than Burgess's. I'm thinking he keeps her around to appeal to a less hardcore crowd than the one he gets."

"Or he owes her something. Or her husband," Chris mused.

"I thought of that, too. So I checked for their 990 tax forms but Legal Eyes doesn't have any on record just yet. They're only a couple of years old, and there's always a lag-time before the info becomes available for the public. Or they're not non-profit. I didn't have time to check for other tax filings, but I'll let you know what I find out, if anything. Burgess maybe should've just stayed a blog instead of creating an organization. You can still take donations as a blog, after all, but you don't have the overhead."

She smiled. "Which means you're subject to greater scrutiny if you're up to something. Thanks, *esa*."

"You're welcome. Oh, and before I forget, Briana called me to say that no, nobody remembers the name of the coyote who brought her aunt over."

"No shocker there." She was quiet for a few moments. "So would you be okay with Kara and River as fuck-buddies?"

K.C. didn't say "what the hell" but her expression broadcast it.

"C'mon, Kase. The idea of Kara and River is still bothering you. You and I worked as that for a while. And we came through okay."

K.C. smiled, and Chris saw her over a decade ago, at the party where they first met, with the cute little grin and the twinkle in her eyes. K.C. sighed. "I guess I just don't want them to get too involved with each other because if it doesn't work out, the fallout could be shitty."

She shrugged. "They're adults. And it's their business. If they get heavily involved and it ends, they'll have to negotiate their own boundaries, and accept that most people are not going to tiptoe around them. River'll probably just go back up into the mountains and continue with his mountain man self."

"There. Right there," K.C. announced. "That's the reason it'll never work out between them. Because Kara's all nature-lover and animal rights and shit and River is Mr. Montana hunter man. It's an ideological divide."

"Sage has her Libertarian gun-rights and hunter side. And you've never even tried target shooting, let alone gone out in the woods and shot game. And you seem to work out just fine." Chris leaned her chair back, triumphant. "I think you're still thinking of her as your younger sister who fucks up and you feel like you know what's best."

K.C. mock-glared at her. "I hate it when you think you're right."

Chris smiled. "I *am* right."

"Fine. I hate that, too." She pretended to pout.

"Look, Sage is right. There's nothing you can do. So quit thinking about it."

"Yeah, yeah. Moving along, Detective Know-It-All." She made a dismissive gesture with her hand. "Please be careful. Burgess doesn't seem to be a nice guy, and he might get fixated on you personally."

Chris let her chair's front legs lower to the floor with a soft clunk. "What is it with weird men and me?"

"It's your sexy, independent cop vibe." K.C. made kissing noises and gave her a fake little growl.

"Yeah, well, the last time that happened, I got knocked around the bosque."

"Which scared the shit out of me, but you took him off the street, didn't you?" She leaned forward. "I worry about you almost every day because of the work you do. But I also know you're damn good at your job, and you won't take unnecessary chances or do anything stupid. In this case, I think Burgess will focus more on discrediting you and the department than on actively chasing you around the city. But he's willing to say anything to get attention, so just be careful who you're out with, and don't give him any ammo. Guys like that seem to go after women, especially. So maybe his ax isn't just with immigrants, but with women, too. And those of us of the gay persuasion."

"Lucky me."

"Seriously. Stay at Kara's for a few days."

"Not sure that's necessary. But if it changes, I'll let you know."

"Screw that. Just show up."

"We'll see. Between Harper and you and Sage, I think Burgess is the one who needs to be careful."

"Damn right. Okay, *mujer*. I've gotta go." She stood. "I'll leave that file for you, since I've got my own and I'll see if I can run down a connection between Burgess and Phil Baca. Not that it'll mean anything, but it provides a bigger picture."

Chris stood as well and walked K.C. to the side door, where she gave her a hug. "Thanks, *esa*."

"Always. Catch you later." K.C. pecked her on the cheek, gave her a grin, and left. Chris watched as she backed her car out of the carport to the street and answered her wave. She shut the door, thinking about Inez Morales, Victor Ramirez, and what might have brought her to show up at his house and possibly shoot him dead. Inez was an American citizen, but if she'd killed Ramirez, guys like Burgess wouldn't change their tune. He had a problem with everybody who even looked like they were from south of the border, so he'd no doubt find some way to spin it to blame more immigrants. In this case, he'd probably say that if Inez's mother hadn't come illegally to the country, then Ramirez would still be alive.

She reached for her land line to see if *Abuelita* had convinced Inez's mother to speak with her.

# Chapter Fourteen

FORMER BORDER PATROL agent Dan Marshall was about how Chris had pictured him. Not too tall, but solid and compact, like a steel box on legs. He moved like he still worked out, and he hadn't developed the paunch that so many men did once they hit their fifties. Or maybe he just worked to keep it off. He kept his blond hair in a buzz cut, and she wondered if he was ex-military. He wore faded jeans and a blue plaid flannel shirt tucked neatly into them, beneath a well-worn and probably well-loved bomber jacket. Harper would've liked him, if he had been able to make it this morning, but he had something else to run down.

"Hi, Mr. Marshall. I'm Chris Gutierrez."

"Detective." He shook her hand in a warm, strong grip, which scored him points. She tended to like guys who just shook her hand and didn't get weird about it because she was a woman.

"My office is this way." She gestured toward the locked double doors behind her. "Care for some coffee first?"

"Love some."

She led him to the communal coffee station and poured him a cup. "Accessories," she said, pointing at the sugar and powdered creamers.

"No, thanks. Black's fine." He took the Styrofoam cup and sniffed. "Smells better than what we got down on the border."

"Taste it first, before you praise." She poured about a teaspoon of sugar into hers and stirred it, then led him through the double doors to her cubicle.

"Have a seat," she said.

"Okay if I put this here?" He motioned at her desk.

"Sure."

He set his coffee cup on the edge of her desk, took his jacket off, and draped it over the back of the chair before he sat down.

"Thanks for coming by," she said as she pulled a legal pad over and reached for a pen.

"No problem." He settled into the chair and gave a quick look around. Cursory, but he probably didn't miss much. "So what's going on? Mark mentioned you had a case that might involve coyotes." He pronounced the word like a native Spanish speaker would.

"Maybe. I can't tell you much about the specifics, but I was hoping you could maybe enlighten me a bit about how a coyote might go about bringing someone over the border. Let's say for the sake of argument that it's a guy and he's based on the American side."

He nodded, thinking, and picked up his coffee cup. "Depends. Before 9/11, there was a lot more traffic over the Rio Grande than now in Texas. But in Arizona, the situation's different because of the topography." He took a swallow of coffee and smiled. "I gotta tell you, this is better than what we got on the border."

"You have my sympathies, sir."

He grinned. "Anyway, I worked the Texas line, mostly down along Juárez. Coyotes on either side used the public bridges to bring people over. I'm not proud to say that some of my fellow patrol may have been on the take, and let a few slide in. Not to suggest they didn't use the river, because they did. But the sheer volume of foot traffic between Juárez and El Paso—" he shrugged. "If someone had proper-looking documents, they could go into El Paso and overstay."

She made a few notes. "Did you work those bridges?"

"Yep. And you do get a sense of people. Students coming and going, women coming to shop and visit family. You figure out after a while the patterns of regulars, at certain times of the day. And if you really pay attention, you'll notice the daily shoppers versus the weekly versus the ones who don't cross all that often, but you don't know everybody because they don't always cross during your shift." He sipped. "I was down there a few years, so I got to know a few people. And after a bit, you kind of pick up on what to look for when it's someone who's not planning to go back to Mexico at the end of the day."

"So you'd pick up on coyotes, too."

"Oh, heck yes. Some were pretty slick and we couldn't nail 'em with anything. Others didn't know their asses from a toilet in a Mexican bar. Newbies, most of those. Busted quite a few of them, sent their cargo back home."

"How would they do it? The good ones?" She leaned back in her chair, assessing him. He had crossed one leg over the other and had settled into his own chair. Relaxed but coiled, like he could launch to a standing position in a heartbeat.

He set his coffee down on her desk, careful to place it away from her papers. "Even if the coyote is based on the American side—and even if he's American—he's got contacts in Mexico. Maybe family. He comes and goes. Easier to do that with an American passport, but if he's Mexican, he'll have proper documentation and probably family on the American side."

"Citizens on the American side?"

"Probably. The best ones build a reputation with networks on the Mexican side. They're known, but maybe not trusted completely, because he can screw you as soon as look at you and make off with your money. If there are family ties on the Mexican side that gives him some legitimacy." He made a couple of gestures. He had a habit of talking with his hands.

"So does he have to be on the Mexican side to walk somebody into Juárez?"

"Nah. One thing he might do is meet with the people or person he's bringing over a few weeks in advance, make sure they've got papers in order. He might have already charged 'em a fee to get documents made. Then he tells them when to go to El Paso, and that he'll meet 'em there. Pre-arranged. Or he might not meet anybody at all, face-to-face. He might just work with 'em over the phone or through one of his contacts, who sets everything up." He picked up his coffee again. "The less a client knows about a coyote, the better for him."

"How does the client know where to find him?"

"It's arranged via phone. Most likely through a personal contact who comes and goes over the border. That keeps things from being traceable. A meeting place is arranged, a time, and a signal. And the coyote always gets paid ahead of time."

Chris leaned forward and made a few more notes. "What kind of signal?"

"Depends. He might wear a certain color of shirt or some particular type of clothing like a hat of some sort with a particular slogan. Or he might be carrying something, like a stuffed toy. Especially if there are kids in the party. Then he can pretend to be a relative with a present for the kid." He took a swallow from the cup and smiled. "Takes me right back to my border days, coffee like this. I put away many a cup down there."

"Glad to oblige." She smiled back.

He thought for a moment. "There were a few coyotes who were major kingpins while I was there. And you also hear stories about coyotes before your time that were hard to catch. Some never do get caught. There was this one, even when I was working—Mexicans called him *el fantasma*—guy really was a ghost."

She stopped writing. "Juan Montéz?"

He gave her an appreciative look. "Yeah. Not his real name. To this day, we don't know what his real name is. Or was. Might be dead. Guy was slicker'n oil on ice. Ran people, drugs, and whatever else he could across the border. And he used kids as couriers and contacts. Like Fabian in *Oliver*. Little band of delinquents."

"Was he training them?"

"No doubt. Some of 'em he mentored in the fine art of human smuggling. Others were drug mules. We caught a couple. But that was rare, if they were Montéz's kids. He trained 'em well and he was picky about who could be a part of his posse." He shook his head, maybe in regret. "I will hand it to him, the guy was good at what he did, but I sure would've liked to nail him myself."

"Drugs?"

"Partially. I suspected he was doing some human trafficking, too."

She stopped writing and gave him a hard stare. "Sex trafficking?"

"Yep. Teenage girls. Probably younger. Couldn't prove it. We tried everything. Worked with the FBI for a while, but everybody's more worried about terrorism than what happens to young women. Lack of resources," he said, sarcastic. "So I tried to catch him at it myself. Put him under my own private surveillance. He always seemed to know when I was doing it, though. Because he ran squeaky clean until I got loaded up with other duties. Every time."

Maybe Montéz had a source in the Patrol, Chris thought.

"I'm pretty sure he had a mole," Marshall said, voicing what she was thinking. "Still makes me angry, thinking about it." He was silent for a few long moments. "He had a couple of signals that I figured out, though, and I'm pretty sure I had a hand in busting up a few of his drops. I'd like to think so, anyway."

She waited for him to elaborate.

"This time of year, he'd meet either mules or human cargo — sometimes both — from the Mexican side near the Santa Fe bridge. Sometimes he'd take the person to the Mercado Mayor, and hand him or her off to somebody else for further transport. That person might then hand off to someone else. Montéz had a hell of a network." He paused, thinking.

"His signal was a Day of the Dead figure," he said after a few moments. "You know what I'm talking about? The cheap paper ones that you can get just about anywhere in October and early November. Easy to purchase down there, and easy to wave around in a particular way. Lightweight."

Her instincts went on hyper drive. She opened one of the files on her desk and looked through the photographs that Sam had provided. She found the one she wanted, of the figure from Ramirez's dresser, and handed it to him. "Like this?"

"Just like that. About a foot tall." He studied the photo for a while. "Yeah." He handed it back to her. "Lots of vendors sell 'em, this time of year. That part of your case?"

She gave him a circumspect look and he smiled in understanding. "Gotcha," he said.

"How about this guy? You ever seen him hanging around Montéz?" She showed him Victor Ramirez's driver's license photo.

He picked it up and studied it like he had the photo of the figurine. "I can't be sure."

"How about this guy?" She showed him the mug shot of Ramirez when he was a teen.

"It's the same as the other one, but younger." He compared the two. "No, sorry. Can't say I saw him, but that doesn't mean he wasn't one of Montéz's guys. And if he was one of the better-trained ones, he'd be careful."

She put the photos back into the bunch in the file. Then, on a hunch, she opened the file on Burgess and showed him the photo of Burgess with his motley border patrol. "Recognize anybody?"

He leaned closer to the desk. "Yeah. This guy, this guy, and this woman ran with a wacko outfit in Texas for a while." He pointed at Burgess, the man standing to his right, and a woman on the end. "Texas Border Hawks, the group was called."

"How long?"

He frowned, thinking. "A couple of months. Must've been a good six years ago or so. They'd run their own patrols outside city limits, using ATVs. All camo'ed up like they were going to war." He rolled his eyes. "They'd call us if they came across any illegals, as they called 'em. Most of the time, they claimed they were helping put a stop to drug runners and possible terrorists. But usually, it was just some sad border jumper practically dying of exposure." He picked the photo up and stared hard at it. "I remember the taller guy—name was Burger or something."

"Burgess?"

"Yeah, that's it. Randy, I think." He looked at her for confirmation and she nodded, hardly believing her good luck. "A Patrol buddy of mine in Arizona knew him," he continued, "because he ran with the group in the picture there. That Burgess guy applied for the Border Patrol in Arizona, but was denied."

"Oh? Do you know when or why?" She wrote that down.

"No, but I could find out."

"I'd really appreciate that, Mr. Marshall."

"No problem. And call me Dan. Always glad to help out fellow law enforcement."

"Anything else you remember about Burgess or his buddies?" She picked up the edge of the photo then released it.

"Just that they were amateurs. Oh, in terms of weapons, there are people in those ragtag patrols that are ex-military or law enforcement who do know what they're doing to a certain extent, but—" he stopped and looked down into his coffee cup then back up at her. "Here's the thing. I was in the military myself, and I'm proud of my service. I'm also proud of my service with the Border Patrol. I grew up in Texas and spent a lot of time in the southern part of the state. I know how complicated things can be down there in terms of race and all that. But laws are laws, Detective. And it was my job to enforce them to the best of my abilities. I understand why people want to come to this country. I see the poverty on the other side of the border, and the economic instability. And the violence. Hell, if I was Mexican in that area, I'd probably make a try for it myself. I get that. But that's not how things are, and I worked to enforce the laws of this country, while trying to treat the people we caught entering illegally with decency and respect."

She nodded, not envying him the job.

"But guys like this—" he gestured at the photo, "made our job harder in a lot of ways. Some of them have real chips on their shoulders about undocumented folks. My buddy in Arizona says he's had armed neo-Nazis running around along the border doing God knows what. I hate to even think about it. And then there are the Patrol guys who chit-chat and make nice with groups like this, which only makes things even murkier in terms of law enforcement." He shook his head. "Policy is one thing. Being on the ground and seeing what some of these people go through just for the chance to have what you and I have—I gotta tell you, it changed my views a bit. But the law's the law." He finished his coffee and looked around her office. She took his cup and put it in her trash can.

"Burgess is here in Albuquerque, now," she said.

He frowned.

"He runs a blog called Legal Eyes, New Mexico. Two words. Legal and eyes."

He snorted. "Give him points for being kind of clever. Let me guess. Anti-illegal alien?"

"Pretty much. But he uses not-so-nice terms for Latinos in general."

"Figures. He struck me as just plain racist, and I only talked to him a couple of times when he was with the Border Hawks. Sure doesn't help anything with views like that. Probably got into trouble in Arizona."

"Why would you say that?"

He gave her a knowing expression, as if he was confirming what she already knew. "Hot head. I might have only dealt with him a couple of times, but you get a sense of people, in my line of work. Only a matter of time before he took a swing at somebody."

"A bit worse than that. He pulled a gun on somebody in Phoenix."

He shrugged, a "what did I tell you" motion. "Is he part of your case?"

"Peripherally. Part of the whole milieu." She organized the files she'd opened then closed them. "I really appreciate you coming in to talk, Mr.—Dan. Would it be okay if I contacted you if I have further questions?"

"Absolutely. Anything you need, just call. Always glad to help out." He stood and picked up his jacket and placed it in the crook of his left arm. She stood as well and he shook her hand again. "I'll see what I can find out about Burgess and his Border Patrol application."

"Thanks. And I have to walk you out. They don't want wayward strangers such as yourself wandering around back here."

He chuckled and followed her to the double doors that led to the lobby.

"Help yourself to more coffee if you'd like," she said as she buzzed him out.

"Thanks. Take care, Detective."

"You, too. And it's Chris." She gave him a smile and he waved at her as she let the door close. A productive discussion. She decided she did want to talk to Ramirez's sister after all. Because if Ramirez was one of Montéz's runners—and she had a strong feeling he had been, after talking to Marshall—he may have been involved in sex trafficking, as well. Which might be a motive for murder.

CHRIS TYPED UP the notes she had taken during Dan Marshall's visit and printed out two copies. One she put in her Burgess file and the other in her Ramirez file. She still hadn't heard back from Ramirez's sister in Ohio, and she'd left the message before she worked out and showered. She called Harper's cell and left him a message to call her back or check in when he got in.

She then spent the next thirty minutes creating a chronology from Ramirez's estimated time of death to Griego's disappearance. If Britney Luna was telling the truth, Inez Morales had plenty of time to drive over to his house and kill him. And if she did, why? She tapped the tip of her pen idly on the paper. Love or money. Which was it?

Her personal cell phone rang. She checked the ID. Trish.

"Hey," she answered.

"Hi. Sorry to bug you at work again."

"Don't worry about it. What's up?"

"My client is willing to talk to you, but not at the police station."

She'd figured that. "Okay. Where?"

"Can you come to my office?"

"Sure. When?" She prepared to write the information down on a piece of paper.

"Actually, she'll be here in an hour, and said I could call you to let you know."

Chris put her pen down. "Okay. I'll see you then."

"Thanks. Bye."

She hung up just as Harper appeared at the entrance to her cubicle.

"Our guy had no safety deposit box. At least not here in Albuquerque. I've got someone trying to find out if he had one in El Paso."

"You think it's a possibility he had cash in the house and the shooter took it?"

He shrugged. "Anything's a possibility. Freakin' Bigfoot could've gone in there and done the job, for all we know." He lowered himself into the chair Dan Marshall had used.

"Shit, if Bigfoot knocked Ramirez off, we'll have to move this to our weird occurrences division."

"Good. Then we won't have to worry about it anymore. You got anything else?"

She told him about her conversation with Marshall.

"That's some good background stuff on both our current difficulties. But we still don't have a damn shooter."

"Oh, got a call from a contact at Faith Social Services. I'm heading over there in about a half-hour. She's got a client who claims Ramirez raped her a few years ago in El Paso."

Harper's eyes widened slightly. "Proof?"

"Don't know. My contact says her client recognized him from news reports. Said Ramirez was supposed to be her coyote, but he raped her on the El Paso side."

He rubbed his jaw. "Huh. What's the deal with the client?"

"Talking off the record. Anonymous tip."

He sighed. "Hopefully it'll lead us to something we can use that's admissible."

Chris tapped her pen on her legal pad. "We may have to go to El Paso."

"Yep."

"I'm trying to call Ramirez's Ohio sister. I want to see if there's anything weird about him when he was growing up."

"Like sexual predator proclivities?"

She nodded.

"Good angle. Might explain the crotch shot."

She had been thinking that. But what *La Catrina* had to do with any of that she still didn't know. Maybe she should've asked Marshall about that. She'd give him a call later. "I'll let you know how this little meeting goes," she said to Harper.

"Okay, then." He stood and left her cubicle. She put her blazer on and slid a notebook and pen into the interior pocket, along with two folded-up print-outs. One had Ramirez's driver's license and the other Griego's. Just in case. She left out the back entrance and did a careful scan of the surroundings before she got into the unmarked cruiser she'd been using. Kind of weird, to go and meet her past like this, she thought as she turned right out of the parking lot onto Second Street then turned right again onto Montaño and headed east, toward the Sandias. Montaño would soon become Montgomery, and she'd take that up into the Northeast Heights and then cut over to Lomas.

Trish never liked seeing her with her gun and badge, she remembered as she drove. Dayna, on the other hand, loved it. She smiled, and thoughts of Dayna accompanied her on the ride, though she continued to check the rearview mirror and detoured onto side streets. Damn bloggers. Maybe something else would come along to distract them. She could only hope.

# Chapter Fifteen

CHRIS PULLED INTO the parking lot at Faith Social Services and chose a spot toward the back, next to a van that blocked the view from the street. Like a lot of buildings in Albuquerque, this one was light tan brick and looked like some of the newer buildings on the UNM campus. Low-slung, but not necessarily institutional. This structure, like those, didn't look bureaucratic or unwelcoming.

She stood next to the van and watched the street for a few moments, but nothing caught her attention. Lomas was a major thoroughfare, which might work in her favor if someone had managed to follow her. Three lanes of traffic, each side. On the other side, a shopping center with a Petco and a Target ensured more traffic. Satisfied, she walked to the front of the building, but a couple of other people were also going in, an older Hispanic woman and a younger man who Chris guessed was her son. She held the door for them and followed, as if she was part of their group.

The two people checked in at the window then went to sit down. Chris hesitated before approaching. A little nervous, maybe, about seeing her ex. The ex who had gotten closest, before Dayna. She shook it off and went to the window. A woman who looked to be in her twenties smiled at her. She had a wholesome, just-off-the-farm-in-Kansas vibe.

"Hi. Can I help you?"

"I'm Chris Gutierrez, here to see Trish Lucero. She's expecting me."

"I'll let her know you're here."

"Thanks." She stepped back and glanced around the waiting area, which reminded her of a doctor's office. Chairs had been set in groups of three or four, buttressed by small end tables piled neatly with various magazines. A flat-screen TV hung in the corner of the room, tuned to Univision, and a couple of large plants stood in other corners. A lot of natural light, she thought. If she was a client who knew she had to sit here for a while, she'd bring her sketchbook and work on a few drawings.

"Hi, Chris."

She turned at Trish's voice, a little bit of anxiety in her chest. "Hey."

A few seconds passed as they appraised each other in that way people do who haven't seen each other for a while and whose last meeting wasn't the best. Trish had lost a little weight, and she was dressed in a bright blue skirt and white blouse that made her seem younger than when they were together. She also wore a pair of stylish clogs that were popular with a lot of women. They gave Trish an extra couple of inches, but she was still shorter than Chris.

"You look good," Trish said with a little smile. Her long, dark hair was pulled back, and her brown eyes sparked with cautious warmth.

"So do you," Chris responded with an answering smile, anxiety decreasing as they passed this first hurdle. K.C. had told her once that if an ex said that to you, it was generally the truth. If an ex didn't say anything about your appearance, then you really needed to get your shit together.

"Is your client here?"

"In my office. Come on back."

Chris followed her down a wide, bright corridor through a door on the left into a narrower one. Trish stopped at a door about halfway down that was partially open. She went in and motioned for Chris to follow her.

"Graciela," Trish said in Spanish, "this is Chris, who I told you about."

Chris smiled, nodded, and offered a greeting, also in Spanish. Graciela didn't smile back, but she wasn't overtly hostile, either. Instead, she assessed Chris, a bit of resigned wariness in her eyes. She looked to be in her early twenties, but her expression and attitude were years older. She wore her hair shoulder-length and teased a bit in front and she was dressed in olive slacks, plain black flats, and a beige sweater. Professional. Chris wondered if she had an office job or if perhaps she was working a project for Trish.

"Would you like some coffee?" Trish asked them both, still speaking Spanish.

"Sure," Chris said. Graciela shook her head but murmured a thank you.

"We have actual cream here," Trish said to Chris in English. "Want a splash?"

"That'd be great."

"Be right back." She left, and Chris figured she was giving Graciela a chance to really size her up.

"Trish has told me you are a police officer," she said in Spanish, not wasting any time.

"I am. I'm a homicide detective." She took the chair next to Graciela, so that she was on eye level with her. She also made sure her blazer hid her gun and badge from Graciela's view. Those might set her off.

Graciela nodded, and seemed to ponder this. "Trish gave me assurances about anonymity."

"Yes. I understand. Whatever information you give me I will treat anonymously unless you wish otherwise."

She gave Chris a hard look then, satisfied, sat back in her chair.

Trish returned, closed the door behind her, and handed Chris a Styrofoam cup.

"Thanks." She sniffed. It smelled better than the department coffee.

Trish brushed past her and sat down in her chair, on the other side of her desk. Graciela relaxed a little more and Chris didn't say anything, letting her take her time. She glanced at Trish, who gave her a barely perceptible nod of approval. While she waited, she sipped her coffee — much better than the police brew — and glanced around Trish's office. Photos of Mexico and Central America hung on the walls, splashes of color against the white.

She'd put a rug down over the doctor's office-style carpet, which added some warmth and intimacy to the room. Wooden bookshelves stood behind her desk, filled with what looked like social services procedures manuals as well as some random titles that dealt with the cultures south of the border. Trish had always been into art. That was how they'd met, actually. She'd seen Chris sketching outside the courthouse four years ago and struck up a conversation with her. Had Trish known she was in law enforcement right then, Chris doubted she would have provided her number.

Graciela broke the silence. "The man I saw on the news — I did not know his name until then," she said in heavily accented English. Her voice was soft.

Chris glanced at Trish, who nodded again, then back at Graciela. "Did he use a different name in El Paso?" She switched to English, too.

She nodded, slowly. "We knew him as *el viento*."

Spanish for "the wind." Chris set her coffee carefully on the edge of the desk and took her notepad and pen out of her blazer pocket. She wrote that down, then looked up again. Graciela's expression was guarded now, and worried.

"It's not an official record," Chris said in Spanish. "I just don't want to forget the details."

Graciela looked over at Trish, who gave her a smile and nod of encouragement.

"How were you introduced to him?" Chris asked, still speaking in Spanish.

"A network," she responded in Spanish. "They only used first names or nicknames."

"And this network operates in Juárez?"

"Yes. And El Paso." She shrugged. "Maybe other places along the border. I don't know. One of my relatives brought me to meet someone in Juárez, and then the network notified *el viento*."

Chris asked another question, still writing. "How did this network take people over the border?"

Again, Graciela hesitated.

"I ask so that I can understand how *el viento* preyed on people."

"The contact on the Juárez side would supply some paperwork that proved employment in Mexico. It was for show, though, because we would cross with the crowds on the Paso del Norte Bridge in the evenings, dressed as if we were planning to go dancing. Someone in the network would come with us. A man went with me, pretending to be my date. On the American side of the bridge, the man took me to another man who was waiting. That man was *el viento*. He carried a *Día de los Muertos* figure to help the man with me know who he was. Not many people in the network have met in person." It came out in a rush, as if she was relieved to be talking about it.

"How long ago was this?" Chris asked, noting that Graciela referred to the Santa Fe Street Bridge with its other nomenclature.

"Four years."

"And this network—it was specifically coyotes?"

"Yes. To help people cross the border."

Chris stopped writing and looked up at her. "Graciela, I have to ask some difficult questions, now. If you do not want to answer, tell me."

She nodded and cleared her throat, nervous.

"When the man you were with left you with *el viento*, where did he take you?"

"Mercado Mayor. We met another man there."

"American or Mexican?"

"American. He and *el viento* spoke English to each other." She toyed with the hem of her sweater.

"Do you know what this other man's name was?"

"No. I did not speak much English then, but I don't think *el viento* ever used his name." She paused, and took a couple of deep breaths, calming herself.

Chris glanced at Trish again, who intervened, in Spanish.

"Graciela, if this is too painful—"

"It will always be painful. The only good thing is that the man who did it is now dead and I will not wake up from my dreams thinking he might find me again." She looked at Chris again. "*El viento* made sure to drive me out of the city limits, and into New Mexico before he did anything."

"Where was the other man?"

"I do not know. He and *el viento* exchanged keys and *el viento* told me I was to go with him the rest of the way to Albuquerque. I never saw the other man again."

"What kind of vehicle?"

"An old truck." She stopped, and waited for Chris to finish writing that. Then she continued, "I do not know where in New Mexico we were, but I know we had crossed into this state, because I saw the sign in the headlights. *El viento* drove about an hour longer, then turned onto an even smaller road. That's where it happened." Her tone went flat and empty and Chris waited a few moments.

"He was strong," Graciela said. "And he hit me a few times." She looked into Chris's eyes. "Even if I did get away, where was I going to go, out there? Who could I turn to? I was trapped," she added, years of old anger and grief palpable even in her soft tones. "When he was finished, he told me that there were men who would pay him a lot of money for me, and if I said anything to anyone about what had happened, he would make sure to tell them where to find me. So I said nothing."

Chris clenched her jaw. Sex trafficking. If Ramirez had been involved in that, it would definitely provide a motive for his murder.

"Did you see the other man again?"

"No. But I started to worry that *el viento* would take me to these other men that he mentioned. When we arrived in Albuquerque, he went to an apartment building."

"Do you know where?"

"I found out later. It is on Montgomery, just east of San Pedro."

Chris knew the place. She'd been called there a few times in the past. "What did he do there?"

"He told me he had to speak to someone, and he left me in the truck. I waited a while, and then I left."

She looked up from her notepad, surprised. "That was very brave of you. Where did you go?"

"I found a gas station and I called a number that a friend had given me in Mexico, in case something went wrong. I had a pre-paid calling card, too." She smiled, but there was no warmth in it. "Something had obviously gone very wrong."

"Whose number was it?"

"I don't know. A woman my friend's network called *La Catrina*."

Chris's gut clenched and she stopped writing. "How did this woman help you?"

"She sent someone to pick me up."

"Who?"

"A woman. An American, but she spoke Spanish." Graciela stared into space for a moment, as if remembering. "I do not know her name. She was young, though. Like me. She took me to her apartment for the night and then the next morning, got me into the system, as they say. That's how I met Trish." She gave her a smile.

"What did this young woman look like?" Chris asked.

"Latina. Long hair. Pretty. I did not see her again after that first night."

"And *La Catrina*? Do you know where she was?"

"No. It was a Mexican phone number, though. I don't remember it, but I do remember it was Mexico because of the country code. My friend who gave me the number told me that it changes."

Smart, Chris thought. Probably used burn phones, too. "How did she sound? Young? Old?"

Graciela thought for a few moments. "Not old. Not like my mother's age. But not young, either."

Which could mean almost anything. Chris wrote "30s?" in her notepad next to the name *La Catrina*. "What did she say to you?"

"She asked who had given me her number. I told her, and then she asked where I was. I told her, and she asked what had happened." She paused and cleared her throat. "I told her that, too."

"Did you tell her what the man called himself?"

"Yes. Then she said to wait inside the gas station, away from the windows, and she would have someone come within an hour. She said it would be a woman." She closed her eyes momentarily, then opened them.

"What kind of network is she part of?"

"I don't know. My friend, who arranged passage, said that *La Catrina* helps people. Especially women, and that people who worked the coyotes in certain parts of Juárez knew to give her number to women going north. But it was a number to be used only if something was very, very wrong. She would not help if *la migra* was involved." She used the border slang for immigration officials.

"Is she a coyote?"

"I don't know. Maybe sometimes. Many coyotes know of her."

"Did you know of her, before you came to Juárez to go north?"

"No. My friend told me about her, and said if something happened to me on the trip that I could call her for help."

Chris wrote "coyote" and "Juárez" next to *La Catrina*. "Did your friend tell you when it was okay to call her?"

"He told me never if the problem was related to *la migra*, and never if it was related to police. But if somebody hurt me or threatened to hurt me or sell me, to call her."

"Sell you? Your friend used those words?"

"Yes."

Human trafficking of the worst kind. Chris wrote that down and underlined it. "You have been very helpful, Graciela. I'm now going to show you photographs of two men." She set her notepad on the edge of Trish's desk and took the folded-up pieces of paper out. She unfolded Griego's first and held it up for Graciela.

"Do you recognize him?"

"Yes. That is the man *el viento* met at Mercado Mayor the night I came over the border."

"And this man?" She held the paper with Ramirez's photo up.

Graciela made a little noise. Her jaw muscles clenched, then relaxed. "That is *el viento*," she said in a colorless tone.

Chris re-folded the papers and put them back into her blazer pocket. So Griego and Ramirez had known each other for at least four years. She took her wallet out of her back pocket and removed one of her business cards and handed it to Graciela. "I appreciate the time you have taken with me. I know it was difficult, but it was also very brave of you to help me. If you think of anyone else or if perhaps you need anything, call me. The second phone number is my cell phone. If you are not comfortable calling my office, call me there. And Trish knows how to contact me, as well."

Graciela gave her a little nod and slid the card into her purse. She stood, and Trish and Chris did, as well.

"I'll walk you out," Trish said in Spanish. She picked up a ceramic mug with bright Mesoamerican designs from her desk. In English, she said to Chris, "Would you mind waiting here for a few minutes? I'll be right back."

"Sure, I'll wait." In Spanish, she said, "Thank you again, Graciela."

Graciela nodded at her, gathered her coat and purse and moved to the door. Trish followed, and Chris reached for her coffee. Lukewarm, but still better than the department's. She sat back down and looked over the notes she had taken.

Trish returned and closed the door behind her. She carried her mug, and Chris smelled coffee as she walked back to the chair behind her desk.

"Thanks," she said as she set the mug on a wooden coaster on her desk.

"For?"

"Not freaking her out."

Chris half-laughed. "You mean thanks for not playing cop?"

She shrugged and reached for her mug. "I guess I remembered you a little differently. The cop thing when we were together seemed...I don't know. Ever-present."

"It still is."

"Maybe you wear it differently, now."

"Or maybe you just see it differently." She took another sip. "I really appreciate that you called me about Graciela," she said, opting for a new conversational direction. "And I'm really glad she talked to me. Thanks on both counts."

"You're welcome. What do you think?"

"What she told me has definitely opened some possibilities in the case, but I can't really discuss those." She set the cup back on the desk and picked up her notepad. "What do you know about human trafficking along the border?"

"You mean just crossing? Or the kind that puts women in danger of sexual exploitation?"

"The latter."

She sighed and leaned back in her chair, cradling the mug between her hands. Her bright red nail polish almost matched the red around the rim of her cup. Trish had always favored red on her nails.

"I have a couple of clients who did run into that along the border. One lost a sister to sex trafficking."

"Did she ever see her again?"

"No." She lifted her mug to her lips.

"How does it work?"

"It depends. Some women are assaulted by the coyotes they pay to bring them across the border. Some of those coyotes take the money, then rape the women and abandon them in the desert. It's not like those women will go to authorities on the American side for help. And if they went back to Mexico, there's no guarantee anyone in law enforcement there would help them, either."

Chris thought about all the horrible things women faced, and the things that drove some to try to cross the border. She thought, too, about all the women who had been found dead in and around Juárez. Hundreds since the early 1990s. Maybe more, because it was difficult to get accurate counts. No, the sexual assault of a woman by a coyote would not be something Mexican authorities would deal with or even care about, especially with the rampant corruption and incompetence of law enforcement in that country over the years.

"And some women are brought over after paying coyotes and then turned over to someone else involved in sex trafficking. A situation like what almost happened to Graciela," Trish said.

"Have you ever heard of this *La Catrina*?

"Outside of *Día de los Muertos* references, no. I could ask around. I have some contacts in El Paso and Juárez."

"I'd really appreciate it if you would. And if they'll talk to me, you can give them my work cell. I'm not always in my office." Chris retrieved another card from her wallet and leaned over the desk and placed it next to the coaster.

Trish looked at the card for a few moments, then back up at Chris. "So how are you?"

"I'm good. Busy as usual." She gave her a smile.

"Are you still drawing?"

"Yes. I haven't as much in the past couple of months, but I do get a bit in here and there."

"Good. I always liked that about you."

Chris laughed. "Just that, huh?"

She smiled. "That and your cooking. How's your family?"

"John came out a few months ago."

Her eyes widened. "No. There's two of you in one family?"

She smiled. "I know, right? Yes. Two. But I seriously doubt Mike or Pete will join me and John."

"And how did it go with John?"

"*Abuelita* and I already knew, of course, as did Mike and Pete, for the most part. My mother is in denial, and my dad...well, he said as long as John doesn't screw everything that moves, then it'll be okay." She shrugged. "He said that about Mike and Pete, too."

She laughed. "How is he?"

"Culinary school in Los Angeles. Adjusting to life out of the closet *en la familia*."

"So he got the cooking gene, too." She sipped from her cup.

"Apparently so."

"How's K.C.? Is she still in Texas?"

"No, actually. She's back here, teaching at UNM and doing some law enforcement consulting. She met someone here, and they're very happy."

"I'm glad to hear that. I always liked her." She hesitated, and Chris knew she wanted to ask whether she was seeing anyone. She stopped that line of inquiry with a question of her own.

"And you? How is everything?"

"Things are good. My dad's health is a bit better, and he is better about following the doctor's instructions. Jen got married last year to a nice guy who works construction."

"Your wild-child sister?"

She laughed. "I know. We never thought we'd see the day, but this guy is very grounded and very sweet, and managed to convince her that she needed that in her life. She seems pretty happy."

"That's good to hear."

Another silence descended between them. Chris slid her notepad and pen back into her pocket. "Well, thanks again." She stood. "And if you ever just want to grab some coffee or something, give me a call."

Trish smiled, relief in her eyes. "I'd really like that." She stood and came around the desk. "Thanks," she said, and pulled her into a hug. Startled, Chris hesitated, then hugged her back. She'd definitely lost weight since she'd seen her last. And she was using a different shampoo. Funny, the things you noticed after a break-up.

"For not being an asshole ex?" Chris gently extricated herself and stepped back. "I think I was, at least at first."

"So was I."

"It's not like break-ups bring out the best in people."

Trish studied her for a moment. "I don't really want to talk about that with you. I think I just want to see you as you are, not rehash things that were."

"Same here." She held Trish's gaze a little longer. "Thanks again."

"You're welcome. Talk to you later."

Chris adjusted her blazer to make sure her gun and badge weren't readily visible so as not to worry anyone in the waiting area before she opened the door and let herself out. She closed it quietly behind her, and headed to the building's exit.

# Chapter Sixteen

CHRIS CHECKED HER messages when she got back to her office, but Ramirez's sister hadn't returned her call yet. She'd leave a message again tomorrow if she didn't hear back by then. She took her blazer off and placed it on top of her file cabinets then sat down and dialed Carl Maestes's office number. Hopefully, she'd catch him.

"Maestes," he answered.

"Hey, Carl. It's Chris."

"*Esa*. What's up?"

"You ever hear of a woman called *La Catrina* involved in border trafficking in your area?"

"Hold on." He had obviously set the phone down because she heard a soft clunk. A few moments later, he picked up again. "Okay. Got a file here. Short answer, yeah. Long answer, she's kind of got her own sort of legend. I'm assuming we're not talking about Posada's *Catrina*."

"I don't know. Maybe the border *Catrina* uses the folklore to her own advantage."

"In a way, she does. Here's what I know. And you won't find much of anything online. Whoever this is keeps things low-tech in that respect."

"Nothing?"

"Not really. Any kind of search brings up Posada's *Catrina* and all kinds of references to *Día de los Muertos*. Maybe that's another reason she chose that name. Anyway, there's been somebody calling herself *La Catrina* who works some of the cross-border networks. From what we can tell, she's strictly involved with getting women and kids across, and she comes down hard on anybody who messes either with her or the women she helps."

"Sounds like *La Llorona* in reverse. She's actually helping people cross the river rather than drowning them in it."

He barked a laugh. "Hadn't thought of it that way, but yeah. The first mentions of her we've got on record are in the early nineties. I wasn't here yet, but a few of my buddies who were told me about it and wanted me to keep my ears and eyes open in the Cruces area, in case she turned up."

She leaned back and propped her feet on her desk. "What exactly does she do?"

"Nobody really knows. She's very good at covering her tracks. Can't link her to drugs or any other portable contraband. Nobody knows who she really is, but we've got a lot of women who've said she helped them in some way when things got dicey for them."

"What kind of help?"

"Money. Food. Medicine. Someone to pick them up and take them somewhere. But it's never her. She sends others to take care of it. From what we can tell, she's got Mexicans and Americans working for her, both sides of the border. And she stays pretty localized, around El Paso and Juárez. But she's helped people farther away than that through her network."

"How do people contact her?"

He made a grunt, like he was reaching for something. "Phone. Kind of a 'use as a last resort' number that changes quite a bit. She's probably using burn phones, too."

She'd figured that. No chance of tracing anything.

"This have anything to do with the Ramirez case?" he asked.

"Maybe." She looked at the ceiling, thinking. "Does she use any kind of symbol? Sort of a '*La Catrina* was here' kind of thing?"

"We've had a few anecdotes. Some people claimed they've seen her and she has Posada's *Catrina* tattooed on her somewhere. Last year we found a guy dead on this side of the Rio Grande—still a John Doe. We think he may have been a coyote from the Mexican side. Early twenties, no ID, prints not in anybody's system. And you know how hard it can be to get anything from Mexican authorities. Kind of weird, though. A *Catrina* figure was next to him. One of those cheapie ones you can pick up easy. I figured it probably was a calling card from her network, but we couldn't prove it. The figure was clean. No prints. Nothing."

Chris took her feet off her desk, instincts practically tingling. K.C. called it her Spidey sense. "How'd he die?"

"Shot to the head. He took one in the crotch, too."

She wrote furiously on her legal pad. "Do you have any other cases like that?"

"Hell, lots of people die along the border, especially on the Mexican side, unfortunately. We both know what a mess it can be over there. But this one stuck out at us because it was different. I'll check, see if anything else turns up."

"Cold cases, too. And do you have a photo of the figure found with the body?"

"Yep. I'll fax it up to you, probably tomorrow."

"Thanks, Carl. I'll let you know what's up when we've got a better handle on things up here. Oh, and Harper and I will most likely be in your neck of the woods Saturday, following a hunch."

"Give me a call when you come to town. Do you need resources?"

"I'll check with Harper, see what he thinks. We're basically doing surveillance, probably at the Santa Fe Street Bridge. One or both of our BOLOs may show up. I'll keep in touch."

"*Muy bien.* Keep me posted, *esa.* I like running with your special ops." He chuckled.

"*Gracias,* Carl. *Hasta.*"

She hung up and picked up her business cell phone then dialed another number.

"Yeah. Dan Marshall."

"Hi, Dan. Chris Gutierrez here."

"Oh, hey. I was going to give you a buzz. I talked to my contact in Arizona about Burgess."

"Thanks. I appreciate that. Anything interesting?"

"He crapped out on the exam and apparently didn't feel driven enough to take it again. My contact there says he was glad he washed out because he didn't like Burgess's attitude. Guys like that tend to give the whole place a bad smell, was how he put it."

"How did your contact know Burgess?"

"He was running his little makeshift patrols down there, getting in the way and pissing agents like my contact off. So my contact would check around every once in a while to see if any of the makeshift folks applied for the Border Patrol. Burgess must've been on somebody else's radar too, because word got around that he had failed the exam."

"Did he continue to run his own patrols after that?"

"Yeah. And he apparently didn't really go public with not making the cut for the real deal. Maybe it pissed him off."

"Seems to me he was already pissed," she said dryly.

He chuckled. "Good point."

"Thanks. Also, when you were down in Texas, you ever hear of a network of coyotes run by a woman calling herself *La Catrina*?"

"Yeah, actually. El Paso and Juárez. She was a ghost, too. More than Juan Montéz because nobody I talked to claimed to have ever seen her."

"What do you know about her?"

"Not a whole lot. Cropped up in the nineties, and had a soft spot for women and kids, especially. So the stories go. I met a couple of Mexican women in the early two-thousands who said she'd helped them out when their coyotes failed to deliver. One of those told me she'd been assaulted by a coyote after she'd been brought into the States. *La Catrina* got her medical attention and a place to stay."

Chris wrote that down. "Did the woman know who *La Catrina* was?"

"No. She didn't operate that way. She never meets anyone who calls for help. She just sends it."

She sat back, frustrated. "So nobody really knows what kind of network she's engaged in, who she is, or where she's from."

"No. Sorry."

"Did she ever engage in violent crime?"

"Don't know. If she did, she covered her tracks. Wish I could be more helpful about it."

"No, you've been very helpful. I really appreciate that you called your contact in Arizona. If you think of anything more, please give me a call."

"Will do. Take care." He hung up and Chris put her feet up on her desk again, thinking. Was there a link between the El Paso killing Carl had told her about and Ramirez's murder? Seemed like similar MO's. Maybe the two killings weren't by the same person, but rather the same network. It wasn't unreasonable to presume that *La Catrina*'s network operated like a cartel all its own. The two murders could be hits. Which still left some questions about motive. She sighed. They needed to find Morales. She took her personal cell phone out of her pocket and dialed *Abuelita*. Maybe she'd finally managed to contact Inez Morales's mother.

CHRIS HEATED UP some green chile stew she'd had in her freezer and ate while standing at her kitchen island, going through her notes between bites. Did the same killer take care of both Ramirez and the unidentified man in El Paso Carl told her about? A contract killer? Part of the network? Was a shot to the crotch a calling card, too? She took a drink of Diet Sprite, since she was trying to cut back on caffeine in the evenings. Her cell phone rang and she smiled.

"Hey," she answered. "How was your day?"

"Entirely too long," Dayna said with a smile Chris could hear. "And yours?"

"The same. Where are you?"

"Home. Wishing you were here. Where are you?"

"Same. And same." She thought about Dayna, maybe sitting on her couch with a glass of wine, her hair down and a little smile playing at the corners of her mouth. A flush raced through her chest.

Dayna sighed. "I really wish you'd stay at K.C. and Sage's for a few days."

"I drove a different car and parked it down the block. Then I walked around the block the other way. If anybody's following me, they'll follow me to K.C.'s just as easily as they follow me here." She took another bite of stew. The thought of people following her pissed her off.

"Honey, you know how these people operate. If they find out your address, they'll post it."

"All the more reason to stay here. I don't want K.C.'s address posted, if they follow me there."

"You could use your place as a decoy or something. Talk to Jerry. See if they can put it under surveillance for a bit while you stay with K.C. and Sage." She sounded frustrated.

"Okay, look. I'll talk to Harper tomorrow, see what he thinks. Legal Eyes hasn't posted anything on us in a couple of days, so maybe they're getting bored with this particular case."

"We can hope." Her frustration was still evident in her tone.

"Hey, it'll be okay. They'll find something else to be pissed about.

That's how people like this work. They have to feed their audience, and if they've got nothing new and interesting about a particular topic, they post on something else."

"Or they find another angle. That's what I'm worried about."

Chris sipped her drink. She'd been thinking about that, too, but she didn't want to worry Dayna any more than she already was. "I'll talk to Harper and Jerry tomorrow, see if there's something maybe we could do to throw them off a bit. Maybe a press release sending me to St. Louis or something."

Dayna laughed. "St. Louis?"

"Or Flagstaff. Hell, Missoula. Some police workshop or whatever. Then Burgess can post about how taxpayer dollars are being spent sending cops out of state while illegal immigrants are running rampant through the streets. But at least he'll think I'm out of the state."

"Maybe you need a vacation for a few days. In San Diego. My sister could put you up."

"I would *love* a vacation. But it's not a vacation without you. So how about we plan one?"

She chuckled. "Don't try to change the subject with me, Gutierrez. Yes, we'll plan a vacation. But right now, I want you to know that I would greatly prefer that you stay at K.C. and Sage's for the next few days."

"Damn. Can't put anything over on you."

"No, you can't. Don't even try. So will you stay over there?"

"Let me talk to the guys. And Harper and I may be going to El Paso Saturday morning. We won't come back until Sunday, most likely, so that's another couple of days out of Burgess's spotlight. And hopefully, we'll have a definitive break in this damn case, and that'll take a little more hot air out of him. Christ. He's just a damn blogger. And here I am sneaking around."

"That's the power of social media, sweets. Now any weirdo with a computer can get all worked up about anything and everything and spread it across hundreds and thousands of readers. There's something to be said for going low-tech."

Chris laughed. "I feel much better now. Thank you."

"I thought you might. So how'd it go with Trish?"

She smiled. "Fine, actually. It was a little weird, maybe, but seemed okay. I told her to call me for coffee if she wanted to."

"How'd that feel?"

"Good. She said she didn't really feel the need to rehash the past, but I think she'd like to re-connect in the here and now."

"That seems doable. Are you okay with that?"

"Yeah." She traced a pattern in the wood that covered her kitchen island. "I'd like you to meet her."

"Why, Chris. People will talk. They'll say we're in love," she teased.

"Well, I am." She stopped tracing the pattern. "And I'd like people to know that."

Dayna was quiet for a few moments. "I think I just swooned."

"That's what you do to me practically every damn day. And I love that, too."

"Saying things like that only makes me want you more," she said in a particularly lascivious tone.

Heat shot down Chris's thighs. "Hold that thought for when I see you next."

"Oh, you have no idea the thoughts I have. Now that we've discussed that, I think I now want to talk about this vacation you mentioned. And also find out what you're wearing."

"Hmm. Isn't that a little forward, Counselor?"

"Never. Because I will guarantee that no matter what you're wearing, I will talk you out of it."

"Jesus. I have no doubt. So. Vacation first." She cleaned up her dinner dishes while they chatted, and warmth coursed through her veins, along with sparks that reminded her of the first time she'd spoken to Dayna Carson, and how she knew, that first night, that she wanted to learn a lot more about this woman.

An hour later, they hung up and Chris sat for a while in the living room, watching ESPN, wishing she was at Dayna's, in her bed and in her arms. At this rate, it might not be until next week that she'd see her. She sighed and flipped the channel to the local news. But no matter what it took to keep Dayna safe, she'd do it. She watched a little bit more of local programming, then went to bed, knowing she'd be up in a few hours, anyway, because that's how her sleep patterns worked when she wasn't with Dayna. Funny, how she always slept better when she was with her. Not that she wouldn't snap awake if something didn't feel right. It was just that Dayna made her feel accepted and wanted. And that made her relax. She smiled as she fell asleep, thoughts of a certain prosecuting attorney on her mind.

Four hours later, at two forty-nine, she woke up, registered the time, and got out of bed. She kept the heat turned low at night, but she ignored the chill through her T-shirt and boxers and went automatically to her front windows, covered by heavy drapes over venetian blinds. She moved one of the drapes aside and adjusted the slats of the blinds so she could see the street. Nothing that looked out of place. She couldn't quite see the unmarked car she'd driven, so she went back to her bedroom, pulled on a pair of sweats and a sweatshirt and slipped sneakers on over her bare feet.

She left the lights off and took the kitchen door into her car port and moved quickly to the opposite side, where she could take a position and peer down the street to her left, toward the vehicle, only her head showing. Maybe she was being too paranoid. Or maybe not. A car was parked across the street from the unmarked vehicle, and it wasn't one of the neighbors'. She carefully retreated and retrieved her binoculars from her hall closet then took up her post again in the car port.

Paranoid, she thought. I'm being overly paranoid. But she raised the binoculars and trained them on the unknown car. The dark played tricks on her vision and she lowered them then raised them again and swept the vehicle. There. She swept the vehicle again, thinking it might be a trick of the dark, though the streetlight at the far corner did offer a bit of clarity. No, there was definitely someone in the driver's seat. She trained the binoculars on the license plate, but couldn't make much of it out in the shadows.

Could just be a coincidence. Guy sitting in a car on this street wasn't completely unheard of in this neighborhood, since a couple of sketchy hotels and bars were just a few blocks away, on Central. Sometimes drunks made it onto the side streets and slept the alcohol off. A little safer in the residential neighborhoods than right out in front of a bar. And sometimes a john might bring a prostitute onto the side streets, this late.

She should probably check that out, she thought. Except she wasn't sure that was the case. And if this was somebody trying to stake her out and assumed she was in the house where the car was parked, she sure as hell didn't want to give him any tips about her actual address. So she watched a little longer, trying to determine if anyone else was in the vehicle. The windows weren't fogged up, so he might be alone. As she watched, she caught a glow from inside the vehicle. Dash lights. He'd started the engine. Probably cold. He'd probably been there a while.

She lowered the binoculars and pondered her next move. She could call dispatch and have somebody cruise by and question the guy. Chances were, though, that he'd start up and drive away as soon as he saw a cop car. No probable cause to pull him over, either. She didn't want Harper out here, either, because if the guy was trying to ascertain where she lived, Harper's presence might tip him off even more.

Or she could go back to bed, get up when it was first light, and get his tag number if he was still there and find out who the hell he was. If he was working for Burgess, he wasn't going to break into anybody's house. He was waiting to take photos. So how the hell had he managed to track her in the unmarked car? Fuck. Was she that sloppy? That bothered her more than the fact that the unmarked vehicle might be under surveillance. She watched for a few more minutes, but nothing else happened so she went back inside, set her alarm for quarter to five, and tried to get another hour or so of sleep.

# Chapter Seventeen

"INTERESTING," HARPER SAID over the phone. "Your watcher is Frank Rand, PI."

Chris poured herself a cup of coffee and leaned against her kitchen counter. "What else?"

"Former insurance adjuster. He's in his fifties. Looks like his specialty in investigations is cheating spouses and background checks."

"So he may not be staking me out. Maybe he's looking for someone else." She needed another hour of sleep, but knew she wouldn't get it. She'd called Harper right after she took down the guy's license plate, about a half-hour ago.

"Who lives in the house where you parked the unmarked?"

"Retired couple."

"Uh-huh. And in the house on the side he's parked on?"

She sighed. "Single college prof. Okay, he's looking for either me or another cop."

"My money's on you. So let's find out what our boy's up to. I'm sending a car over with a uniform. I'll drive separately. Think you can meet me on the next street over without Rand seeing you leave?"

"Yeah. The street behind my house."

"Here's how we'll play it. You and I are just following up on reports of a peeping Tom in the neighborhood who might or might not be tied to a possible shooting on Central. So of course, we have to question a gentleman in a car who a neighbor reported. Kind of suspicious, after all."

"Sounds good."

"See you in fifteen."

He hung up and Chris finished her coffee. "Fuck you, Burgess," she muttered as she washed the cup out. She was already dressed and ready to go, so she turned the coffee maker off, poured the coffee out, much to her chagrin, and set the house alarm before she let herself into the car port and unlocked the high wooden gate into her back yard. She pushed it closed, made sure the lock clicked, then crossed her yard toward one of the back corners. A few strides before she got there, she increased her speed and ran at the six-foot cinderblock wall that encircled her yard and jumped. Her palms hit the top of the wall and her momentum pushed her up enough to pull herself to the top, her hands braced. She swung her right leg over and dropped easily into her neighbor's back yard, part of the corner lot. There was no alley here, so houses just backed up to each other, separated by fences.

The neighbors whose yard she'd landed in weren't up yet, and their dog — a half-deaf schnauzer — wasn't out, either. She crossed their yard and easily swung herself over the four-foot chain link fence that separated their yard from the sidewalk. She was now on the street that ran at a right angle to hers. She walked briskly to the next street over that paralleled hers, and slowed to a stroll. She heard a car behind her and turned. Harper, in another unmarked police vehicle. He pulled up to the curb and she got in.

"Morning," he said, with his usual deadpan demeanor. He held a Styrofoam cup that had coffee in it.

"Yeah. Where's the other car?"

"A few minutes behind us."

"How the fuck did he track me?"

"Don't know. We'll find out. He's a PI. Probably has all kinds of tricks up his sleeve. Maybe even used subterfuge." He motioned at another Styrofoam cup of coffee in the battered cup holder. "That's yours."

She picked it up and sipped. Bad department coffee. But it warmed her up. "Thanks."

"Okay, here's Martin. We'll follow him."

A police car passed them and Harper pulled away from the curb. They both turned right, then right again onto Chris's street. Martin parked in front of the vehicle Chris had driven the night before and Harper pulled up in front of Rand's vehicle, facing the wrong direction. The driver had put both hands on his wheel and he stared at Harper and Chris. Officer Martin rapped on his window with his left hand, right hand on his gun.

"Let's go," Chris said. She got out of the car.

"Step out of the car, please," Martin said. Chris recognized him. He'd been on the force a few years. Solid cop.

"Certainly," Rand said, as he slowly did what Martin requested, keeping his hands visible. He was wearing jeans and a black pea coat over a dark blue flannel shirt. He stood about Chris's height. Another Midwestern-looking guy who appeared to keep himself in shape, even with the slight paunch at his waist. "Can I ask what this is about?"

"Put your hands on the hood of the car, sir," Martin said.

Rand did, and Martin quickly checked for weapons.

Chris moved her jacket so her badge, clipped to her belt, showed. "We've had reports of a peeping Tom in this neighborhood. We received a call that your car has been parked here for a while. Can we see some ID?"

"It's in my left coat pocket," Rand said. Martin stepped forward and removed a billfold, which he handed to Rand.

"Remove your license, sir," Martin said.

Rand did, and handed it and another ID card to Martin, who handed both to Chris.

Harper peered into the windows of Rand's car.

She looked the cards over. "Frank Rand. Private Investigator," she read, as if she didn't already know that. "Any particular reason you've been parked here for a couple of hours, Mr. Rand?"

"I'm working a case."

"And what case might that be?"

"I'm not at liberty to say. Confidentiality."

"That's a nice camera you've got, Mr. Rand," Harper said, gesturing at the window of the car. "What kind of case are you working?"

"I can't say."

"Insurance fraud? Husband stepping out on a wife? Photos would work for either of those scenarios. So which is it? Or do we need to escort you to the station for a little more questioning? Maybe you're taking dirty pictures of neighborhood women."

"No, that's not it. I swear."

"So why the camera?" Chris pressed.

He sighed, but kept his palms on the hood of the car. His hands must've been cold by now.

"Why the camera if you're not here to take photos?" she repeated.

"It's just a case I'm working. That's all."

"Yeah, we got that, Rand. What we're not getting is information that'll alleviate our suspicions as to what you're doing in this neighborhood," Harper said. "Wouldn't be the first time a PI went bad. Started using his work as a cover. That what you're up to?"

"No," he said, jerking his head toward Harper. "Look, my client is one of those guys who watchdogs city employees, makes sure our tax dollars are paying for what they're supposed to pay for."

"So you're staking out a city worker?" Harper said, sounding admirably skeptical. "Who?"

"Look—"

"No, *you* look." Chris fixed him with one of her cop glares and he dropped his gaze. "We have a call regarding a suspicious guy in a car that's been parked here for at least a couple of hours. We have complaints of a peeping Tom in the neighborhood and here you've got a nice big camera in your car and the best you can come up with is you're staking out a city employee? Officer Martin, I'd say we need to bring Mr. Rand in." She handed Rand's driver's license to Martin. "Run this."

"Okay, okay," Rand said before Martin could reply. "My client runs a watchdog blog. They keep an eye on city employees, look for stuff that's wasteful. That kind of thing."

"Uh-huh," Harper said. "Run his license, officer."

Martin nodded and took the license across the street to his vehicle.

And you're in this neighborhood because...?" Harper said to Rand.

"Before I answer, can I please move?"

"Go ahead." Harper gave him a nod and Rand turned so that his butt was against the front of the car. He slid his hands into this coat pockets gratefully.

"Okay, no disrespect. I'm supposed to get photos of a cop."

"So you're stalking a police officer." Chris's glare caused him to look away again.

"Look, it's a job. All he said was get photos."

"Mr. Rand, you're in a residential neighborhood. Are you trying to get pictures of this officer leaving a house?"

"I—uh—"

"You want an address of a private residence," she continued. "And then you'll pass that information along to your client who will most likely post that information publicly. You're deliberately putting a police officer's life in danger. And so is your client." And Rand apparently hadn't recognized her from the already extant photos Legal Eyes had. That played in her favor, that Legal Eyes didn't have better photographs.

"No, that's not—"

"Then what exactly does your client intend to do with this information, should you get it?"

He didn't respond.

Martin returned with Rand's license. "Keep your speed down, sir," he said as he handed it back to Rand.

"Yes, sir," Rand mumbled. He put the license back in his billfold.

"So you just took this job," Harper said. "Didn't ask much. Didn't think much about it, either, probably."

Rand shrugged. "Hey, a guy needs money now and again."

"Have you taken photos of this officer before?" Chris asked.

"No. I just started working this case a couple days ago."

She frowned. If he was telling the truth, he wasn't the one who took the photos of Chris and Harper at the station on Tuesday. Or he was a good liar. "What's the officer's name?"

He sighed. "Gutierrez. He's a detective."

Harper shot her a look, amusement in his eyes. That would explain why Rand hadn't recognized her.

"And this Gutierrez allegedly lives somewhere around here?"

"Maybe."

"So you're just...what?" Chris asked. "Going street to street until you find this officer and take pictures of him? Your client must have deep pockets."

"Look, I know how hard it is to get cops' addresses. I did some digging and I found a Christopher Gutierrez in this neighborhood. And anybody can tell that's an unmarked car." He pointed at the vehicle across the street. "I figured maybe the address I found was off and this might be it."

Harper kept a stone face but Martin was trying not to laugh. His lips twitched, but Rand didn't notice.

Chris handed him his PI license. "Mr. Rand, I'm going to strongly recommend that you ditch this client, whoever it is. Because I really don't think you want to be on the receiving end of a lawsuit from a police officer's family in event an address is made public and someone misuses that information."

He put the license into his coat pocket but didn't respond.

"That'd take a chunk out of your business," Harper said dryly. "Not to mention piss off every cop in the city."

Rand nodded. "Am I free to go?"

Harper gestured at his car. "Class dismissed."

Martin stood aside as Rand got into his vehicle, backed up, and pulled slowly away from the curb.

"That went well. What do you think, Mr. Gutierriez?"

Martin cleared his throat, fighting another laugh. "If you won't be needing my services any longer, I'll take off."

"We're good. Thanks," Chris said to him. "Oh, how many speeding tickets did you find on Rand?"

"Six in the last two years. Other than that, clean." He nodded at Harper and crossed the street to his patrol car.

Chris turned to Harper. "Got lucky. Burgess probably just told him to find Chris Gutierrez and didn't think to specify." She watched as Martin drove away.

"Good thing those photos of you on the blog weren't much good."

"And good thing I look kind of like a guy from a distance."

"And have a gender-neutral name."

She gave him a look. "Damn, Harper. You just used some PC language, there."

"Yeah. Happens sometimes." He rocked forward onto the balls of his feet, then back. He was wearing his usual work clothes: penny loafers, grey slacks, and a shirt and tie. Today's shirt was light blue and his tie was dark blue with maroon highlights. His trench coat completed his ensemble. "Here's what I think," he continued. "Stay away from your house for a few days. Rand may not be the brightest bulb in the box, but he will probably tell Burgess what happened and he might even describe us. Burgess'll probably blog it. You know, APD thugs messing with a fine, upstanding citizen who was doing the work of democracy." He gave her a dad look. "I think it'd be better for you to stay somewhere else. With people who have a car, in case something happens. I definitely don't think you should be driving an unmarked vehicle anywhere. Even that putz stumbled across it."

She slid her hands into her jacket pockets. "Rand still doesn't know who I am and Burgess won't make the connection that this is actually my neighborhood."

"Give me a break. Do you really want to take the chance that one of Burgess's dumb-asses won't come across a photo-op of you and your house?"

"Shit, Harper. Wherever I go, I'm inviting Legal Eyes to put somebody else at risk."

"It'll be a lot harder to find you if you're not driving an unmarked car back and forth to work from your house."

She started to say something else but he interrupted her.

"No, don't borrow anyone's car. If Burgess or his crew see you somewhere parking it, they'll take a photo of it and the plate and post that online. I'll drive you around for a few days. It's not a hardship."

She sighed, seeing his point but wrestling with being worried about putting K.C. and Sage in danger if she stayed with them. Rand demonstrated that Burgess didn't have the best help, after all. She glanced at the unmarked car. Except Rand might have busted her getting into the car that morning, had she not thought to check the street. Had she just left her house that morning to walk to her car, and didn't realize Rand's car had been there for a few hours, he just might have gotten his photo-op.

"Go get some stuff together," Harper said. "At least think about it. And if you decide to stay with friends, at least you'll be ready."

"All right," she conceded.

"I'll stay out here, keep an eye on things."

She walked up the block to her house, automatically looking for anything out of place. Burgess was becoming a bigger pain in the ass than she'd anticipated. Hopefully he'd find something else to target in the next few days.

"HE TOOK THAT well," Harper said as they left Lieutenant Jerry Torrez's office.

"It was the fact that Rand thought I was a guy. I think I want to know who this Christopher Gutierrez is who lives in my neighborhood. What are the odds?"

He grunted in Harper fashion. "I've got to make a bunch of calls. I'll check in with you in a few."

She nodded and returned to her cubicle, where she checked the Legal Eyes blog when she got to her desk. Mary Baca had posted something about Mexican drug cartels running rampant along the Arizona/Mexico border. She'd also managed to bring in worries about Middle Eastern terrorists entering the country illegally by coming over the Mexican border and endangering everybody. Because it's such a walk in the park, to cross the desert in that part of the country, Chris thought sarcastically.

She checked around on the site to see if there was anything new about APD, then went back to the post with the photos of her and Harper and checked the comments to see if there were any credible threats there from commenters. Fortunately not. Just the usual rants about how the police were probably in collusion with Mexican drug runners and some racist screed. No direct threats against APD.

"Hey, Gucchi," Harper said as he entered her cubicle and took the seat next to her desk. "Forgot to tell you, there were fingerprints on the Day of the Dead figures that weren't *Catrina*. All Ramirez's."

"Why am I not surprised? Not like the bad guys make it easy for us." She caught him up on her meeting with Graciela and her recent conversations with Carl and Dan.

"That's some good stuff," he said when she'd finished. "So you think Ramirez might've been a hit?"

"Not necessarily like the cartels do it. Maybe his murder was retaliation for something, and this *Catrina* or her network are responsible."

"Could explain the body Maestes was talking about, too. Doesn't take much to piss off a cartel and just because nobody knows for sure whether *La Catrina* traffics drugs or not doesn't mean she's not doing it."

"We really should go to El Paso tomorrow. I already gave Carl a heads up."

"Thought you'd never ask. I'll pick you up at seven. Where will you be?"

"I don't know yet."

He gave her a look.

"We just got in, Harper. Cut me some slack."

"What about K.C.'s?"

"That's an option. She offered."

"Take her up on it."

"Let me get on the same page with her and Dayna first."

"Dayna will agree."

She laughed, but didn't tell him that Dayna had already asked her to go over to K.C.'s. "How do you know?"

"I just know," he said in his dad tone. "So what's next on today's investigative agenda?"

"I'm waiting to hear back from my grandmother. I might be able to talk to Inez's mother this afternoon."

"That's a good lead. I'll drive you and play stakeout. If that lead doesn't pan out today, I'm sure we'll find some damn case to keep us busy until we leave tomorrow. I'll also see if anybody's got any news on Griego. Or anything else, for that matter."

"Can we get his phone records?"

"Trying. We'll see. The wheels of justice, you know..." He shrugged and stood. "There's always something to keep us occupied."

She smiled. "I sure hope so. I'd hate it if Randy Burgess thought we were just sitting around on our asses in here drinking shitty coffee and gossiping."

"Hell, we do that anyway. Okay, then." And he left her office. Chris worked on a couple of other reports, hoping *Abuelita* would call soon. An hour later, she did, and Chris went to find Harper to drive her to Old Town.

# Chapter Eighteen

CHRIS GAZED ACROSS the kitchen table at Juana Morales, whose features were tight with stress. She looked like she was in her fifties, but Chris suspected she was probably in her forties. The years had weighed on her, pressed her closer to the ground. She sat with hunched shoulders, fear and confusion in her expression. Her gray sweatshirt amplified her pallor. *Abuelita* set a cup of hot tea in front of her and Juana's fingers automatically embraced it. Her hair was pulled back in a tight ponytail, exposing a widow's peak that pointed at the bridge of her nose.

"*Señora*, I am very sorry to have to tell you these things," Chris said in Spanish. "But as you see, it's very important that I find out where Inez is."

"I told you, I have not seen her in over a week."

"Did you know she had gone to Las Cruces?"

Juana looked up at her, troubled. "No. She's always been headstrong and stubborn. She doesn't tell me everything."

But something like moving without a word bothered her, Chris saw. "Are you certain that you have not seen her more recently?"

She sat quietly, staring at her hands. Was she trying to remember or thinking up a lie?

"Yes, I'm sure. We may not see each other for a while, but she always calls maybe twice a week." She looked up at Chris. "Sometimes we don't get along. But she always calls. She has not called me for a week." Her eyes misted.

"We're trying to find her, *Señora*." Chris unfolded the photo of Griego. "Do you know this man?"

"That is Johnny Griego," she said. "Inez went to high school with him. They dated for a time."

"Are they still dating?" That was information Harper would appreciate. He could add it to the high school drama file.

"I don't think so." She shrugged. "They have a bit in the last couple of years. He means well, but he's not good marriage material. I told her that."

"What about this man?" She showed her the photo of Ramirez.

"Victor Ramirez," she said, with a faint layer of distaste.

"How well did Inez know him?"

"I don't know. She told me she was working on a project with him. She said she was the translator."

That was a lie she told Juana, Chris thought, because Victor spoke Spanish. "Did you ever talk to him?"

"No. I just saw him a couple of times. When Inez drove me places, sometimes she would stop and talk to him at the car place where he worked."

*Abuelita* set a cup of tea in front of Chris, along with a small ceramic container of honey and a spoon. Chris used the dipper in it to add honey to her cup. She held it over the tea, letting it fall into the liquid. She replaced the dipper and stirred the tea with the spoon. The smell of chamomile filled her nostrils.

"Was Inez involved with him?"

"I hope not. He had dead eyes. Like her father."

*Abuelita* shot a look at Chris.

"Is her father still alive?"

"I don't know and I don't care. Dead eyes. No soul," Juana continued. "Men like that, they are not good for women."

"Did Inez know her father?"

"No. I got away from him before she was born, and he never came looking. She is better off without him."

Another potential domestic abuse situation. If Juana was in the country illegally, did she leave Mexico to get away from Inez's father? Or was Inez's father American, and Juana met him after she'd already crossed the border? She changed the subject. "How did Inez meet Mr. Ramirez?"

"Victor worked with Johnny."

Chris sipped her tea. "Do you talk to Inez's cousins?"

"Not as often as I would like. They are in Juárez. My brother's daughters." She caught Chris's gaze, then, and her expression was wary, like a deer preparing to bolt.

"Have you heard from her cousin Marta at all? Perhaps Inez went to Mexico."

"I don't know if she did. Marta has not told me if Inez is there or not, or if Inez has called. This is why I worry." She lifted the cup to her lips with both hands.

"Do you know what kind of project Inez was working on with Mr. Ramirez?"

"No. She sometimes had to go to Las Cruces or El Paso, though. She did not tell me what she was doing. She worked hard at Smith's, and she was saving quite a bit, because she was able to help me with some money, though I never asked for it."

Maybe Morales was involved in Ramirez's human trafficking. It sounded likely. But if she killed him, what specifically had set her off?

"I must ask you a difficult question now," Chris said quietly. "What happened when Marta was attacked a few months ago?"

Juana set the cup down on the table with a clunk. *Abuelita* moved closer to her chair, holding a dish towel. She stared at Chris, a warning in her eyes.

"It might help us understand why Inez is missing. Perhaps Marta's attacker has also targeted Inez, and Inez is hiding, and trying to keep you safe by not staying here." She doubted that, but maybe it would help Juana feel better in some way.

"All I know is it was a man," Juana said. She dropped her hands to her lap and stared at her cup. "He went to her house and beat her and raped her."

*Abuelita* placed a hand on Juana's shoulder. Chris clenched then unclenched her teeth. She'd heard too many stories like this, and they always made her angry.

"Was it someone she knew?"

"She didn't say it was. She went to the hospital. Inez went to be with her."

"This man was not caught?"

"No."

"Could Marta describe him to me?"

*Abuelita*'s hand tightened on Juana's shoulder.

"I don't know." She stared at the table.

"One more thing, please. Did Inez ever mention anyone named 'Catrina' to you?"

She thought for a few moments. "No. But she didn't tell me everything."

Chris nodded. "Thank you for taking the time to speak with me. Could you please give Marta my number? Perhaps that incident has something to do with why Inez is missing." She took a business card out of her shirt pocket and pushed it across the table toward Juana. "And perhaps she has seen Inez."

Juana looked at the card, but she didn't take it. If she did take it, it would be after Chris left.

"Inez may have been one of the last people to see Victor Ramirez alive, *Señora*. It is very important that we find her."

"Did she have something to do with his death?"

"She may have. Or she may have seen what happened, and that puts her in danger."

A tear rolled down her cheek. "I have worked very hard, Detective, to create a life for Inez. She was a good student. I wanted her to go to college. I wanted her to find a nice man. I wanted many things for her. Now, I want only to know that she is all right. I can do nothing more for her."

Chris nodded. Juana washed her hands of Inez, because she brought too much trouble to her mother, and Juana could bear no more. *Abuelita* caught her eye and Chris got the message.

"Thank you, *Señora*. I'll let you know if we find her, and please let us know if you hear from her." She finished her tea, reached down and gave Rudolfo a scratch behind his ears, then stood. *Abuelita* followed her into the living room. Chris picked her jacket up from the arm of the sofa.

" '*Lita*, I need you to be on the watch for a few things." Chris told her quickly about the bloggers, and what their names were. *Abuelita* did not own a computer, which was in her favor. No accounts to hack, no information to be found floating around in the ether. "If they find out that I'm your granddaughter and they call you, don't talk to them. Find a way to get them off the phone quickly and then call me. If they come to your door, lock it and call me. If I can't come, I'll send another officer or Pete or Mike. And if you can't reach me or the boys, call Sage, K.C., or Dayna."

"You worry so much, *mi'ja*." She smiled and reached up to touch Chris's face.

She managed a smile. "These are not nice people. They will take things you say and twist them to cause trouble. They will try to take photographs and put them on their Website for everyone to see. And they don't like people with last names like Gutierrez or Garza or Montero." She used *Abuelita*'s last names for emphasis.

"There have always been people like that," she said. "But I will be careful."

"And make sure Juana stays in touch with you. Inez may bring more trouble."

*Abuelita* sighed. "Yes, she might. I worry more about that than these people you tell me about. I'll make sure she takes your card."

"Could you also ask her about a network along the border near El Paso led by *La Catrina*?

She gave her a look.

"I thought perhaps there are some things she might not want to discuss, like the border," Chris said.

She nodded and smiled. "I'll make sure she takes your card," she repeated. "Now go."

Chris hugged her and put her jacket on. "Lock the door after me."

"I always do."

Chris let herself out but waited on the porch until she heard the lock click before she went to the front gate, part of the picket fence *Abuelita* put up to keep animals off her front yard, and let herself out onto the sidewalk beyond. She turned right, toward the Rio Grande, and walked down the block to where Harper sat in the Buick, across the street. She got in and buckled up.

"See anything?" she asked.

"Nobody that looked like paparazzi. Not much traffic down this street during the day. What'd you find out?"

She updated him as he drove back to the station. When she finished, he nodded.

"That's some good drama there, Gucchi. So Griego and Morales have been on-again, off-again. Wonder if they're on or off right now."

"The mother didn't seem to think they're on."

"Doesn't mean Griego and Morales aren't doing the wild thing."

She stared at him then laughed.

"I'm a parent. I know that what moms want to believe and what's really going on don't always match." He shot her a grin. "Anyway, what's your take on the attack in Mexico?"

"I don't know. Maybe Morales really does want to bring Marta to the States. Luna said she has a little girl, after all. Maybe she was trying to hire Ramirez to do it. Or convince him to do it, if she was already working with him to bring people across the border."

"Huh. That's a good angle, too. Why would she dust him, then?"

"Maybe he took her money and asked for more, and he kept putting her off about bringing Marta over."

"Or maybe Morales is part of this *Catrina* network," he said, voicing another thought she had. "Maybe there was a hit on Ramirez."

"Maybe." She grimaced. "Too many damn maybes."

He didn't respond and Chris stared out the windshield, used to his silences. Harper had decided to take Fourth to Montaño and cut over. She liked this part of Albuquerque. Local businesses and houses lined the street, many faux- or actual adobe. Here, Spanish was nearly as common as English, as was a mixture of the two, and it made her wonder why anybody's immigration status was such a big issue for some people. New Mexico had Spanish speakers before English speakers. And all kinds of languages before that. Spanish speakers had been here since at least the 1530s, mixing with the Indian cultures and working to colonize them. A history of blood, peace, and everything in between.

Her father's side of the family arrived with some of the *conquistadores* in the late fifteenth century, at least 130 years before Mexico declared independence from Spain, and over 150 years before New Mexico ended up a territory of the United States. *Abuelita* and Grandpa Luis came to Albuquerque from Chihuahua after World War II, where he opened a grocery store that thrived for years until his death in the 1970s, when Chris was a little girl. They'd worked hard, raised two sons and two daughters, and created a network of friends and family that intertwined with older Hispanic roots and newer Anglo. Most people who crossed the border were looking to help their families back in Mexico. And like Chris's cousin had said on her last visit, if Mexico would fix its own problems, nobody would need to leave.

She quit thinking about that. Immigration policy was not her field. She just needed to know what laws were in place and what her role was in enforcing them. Harper pulled into the parking lot of the station and drove right up front so Chris could exit the car quickly and get inside. Everybody had an eye out for anybody with a camera near this station, she knew, but Harper wanted her to take extra precautions and his instincts hadn't been wrong yet. She grimaced. She'd call K.C.

THE MESSAGE LIGHT on Chris's desk phone glowed red when she and Harper returned to the station after grabbing some lunch. She listened to the one message. Ramirez's sister had called back, so she tossed her jacket onto her file cabinet and settled into her desk chair before she dialed. She hit record on the device she had hooked up to her phone line. It would help fill in the gaps in her notes later, if necessary. A woman picked up after the second ring.

"Hello?"

"Hi. This is Detective Chris Gutierrez, with Albuquerque Police. I'm trying to reach April Lancaster." She picked up her pen and prepared to write.

"That's me."

"Great. Do you have a few minutes?"

"Yes." She didn't sound enthused.

"I understand you didn't have much contact with your brother over the past few years—"

"No contact. I haven't seen him since high school," she said, sounding irritated. "I don't know anything about him or his life since then, so I don't think I can help you."

"That's certainly possible. But it's also possible that you might be able to shed some light on a few aspects of your brother's life that may have something to do with what happened to him."

She sighed, a little impatient.

"Can you tell me the kind of guy he was, in high school? Just a few things. What you remember."

Silence. Then, "Like what?"

"Was he popular in school? Have a lot of girlfriends? Did he play sports?"

She laughed, but it sounded forced. "He wasn't into sports and he didn't run in the popular crowd. He loved cars. A few girlfriends, but my brother had...problems."

Chris waited for her to elaborate. When she didn't, she poked at that. "What kinds of problems?"

"I don't know how to explain it."

"Try me."

"Anger issues," she said, like that should explain everything but instead left much more unanswered.

"Did he have particular targets for his anger?"

"My brother is dead. Why does this matter anymore?"

"Mrs. Lancaster, I'm very sorry if this is making you uncomfortable. But again, we're trying to get a broader picture of who your brother may have been, because that may lead us to who he associated with and hopefully, to the person or persons who killed him. I'll ask again. Did your brother take out his anger on anybody in particular?"

Another silence ensued and Chris could almost envision her, debating what to say or whether to say anything at all.

"Victor always had a mean streak," she finally said. "He took it out on me and my sister at first."

Bingo, Chris thought. "Was there anything going on that might have influenced him to act that way?"

She sighed again, but this time with resignation. "My father. He was not a good man to my mother, or to any of us. Victor was born with a mean streak, but my father made it worse, because that's the example he set, to treat women like trash. He'd beat Victor, too, if he thought my brother wasn't being man enough."

Chris was writing so fast her hand hurt. "I'm sorry you had to go through that."

"It is what it is," she said, trying to sound as if she'd moved past it though Chris knew she hadn't.

"Did your brother treat his girlfriends badly?"

"Not at first. But it would start after a while. The girls he left alone were the ones he'd have sex with but who didn't call him back. I think he decided that's all women were good for. He'd brag about that even before I left home after high school."

And those women probably didn't call him back because he'd raped them, Chris thought. "Did you ever hear any rumors from others about your brother and his girlfriends? About how he treated them?"

"Does that have something to do with his death?"

"Honestly, I don't know. But it might. We're looking at several different angles."

She didn't respond right away, perhaps considering her options again. "Some people talked," she said after a while. "They said he'd raped a girl at school when he was sixteen."

"What happened with that?"

"Nothing. The girl didn't tell her parents or any teachers. A friend of hers found out, and that's how the rumor started."

"Did you believe it?"

"Not at first. But the year before I graduated, I knew it was true. And I knew he did it more than once."

"Did anybody say anything?"

"You mean to police?"

"Yes. Or parents."

She made a noise in the back of her throat. "You must know how that goes, Detective. A girl dates a guy and things get a little exciting but the guy doesn't stop. And then she feels like it's her fault, because she thinks she must have done something to lead him on. So she doesn't say anything, and doesn't realize that she's been raped, but she knows something's not right."

She was speaking from experience, Chris guessed, and her chest tightened with anger.

"And some girls feel they can't tell their parents, because they know they'll get a beating from their fathers or their mothers will, because their fathers will blame the mothers that their daughter is a whore." The words fell like lead over the phone, hard and heavy with the weight of the past.

"And you think your brother did that to the girls he dated in high school?"

"I know he did. He got one of his friends to do it to me. He put something in a drink. I didn't know. I didn't feel right after I drank it. The last thing I remember was his friend on top of me and my brother watching and laughing."

Chris gritted her teeth. The bastard had trafficked his own sister. And God knows what else he did after she had passed out. That thought brought the taste of bile into her throat, and she knew the same thought had probably occurred to April, when she regained consciousness, however many years ago that was. She hoped it wasn't the case. And if it was, she hoped he hadn't told her, to spare her that, at least.

"My sister graduated the year before I did. She took me with her, and I lived with her while I finished high school," she said, voice shaky. "We didn't want to leave our mother there with our father, but my sister wanted to get me away from Victor." Her voice broke and Chris heard her softly blow her nose. "Sorry," she said after a few moments.

"No need to apologize. Thank you for telling me. What you've said may help us find whoever killed your brother."

"Do you think a woman did it?"

"We're considering all possibilities."

"If a woman did it because of something he did to her or because of something he did to someone she cared about, then I don't blame her. She did a lot of women a favor."

"I'll call you when we know more," Chris said, choosing not to address her statement. "I really appreciate that you called me back and that you were willing to talk with me. Please feel free to call me if you think of anything else."

"All right. Goodbye."

The finality of her statement ended the call more so than actually hanging up. Chris replaced the receiver carefully, as if afraid of further disturbing April Lancaster's past. Sometimes she hated parts of her job, and the boundaries she had to keep. When she was a counselor, she might have been able to offer more, even if it was just a conversation beyond the standard law enforcement professionalism. She rubbed her temples, and thought about April's statement, that she wouldn't blame her brother's killer if it was a woman, and if she was exacting revenge for herself or someone she cared about.

Love, money, revenge. Harper had said love and revenge could be related. Given what April had said, Chris wasn't so sure about that. She rubbed her head a little longer then typed up her notes while the details were still fresh. That done, she went through Ramirez's autopsy file more thoroughly. The bullet to his groin could have been a missed shot.

But she didn't think so. Ramirez's killer had gone to his house that night to dispatch him. The killer had done that, picked up the bullet casings, and left a calling card.

"Hey, Chris."

She looked up. Allen, one of the other detectives, stood in her doorway.

"Fax for you." He handed a few sheets of paper to her.

"Thanks." She gave him a smile.

"I'll leave you to it. You look like you're about to think a hole through your desk." He smiled back and left as she looked through the papers. Carl had sent her some information about the still-unidentified man who had been found last year in El Paso. He'd included a photo of the *Catrina* figure that had been found with him. It was similar to the one that had been found with Ramirez, but not completely. No surprise there, since so many different variations of Day of the Dead figures existed. The one found in El Paso had also been painted with ammo belts across her chest, a nod to the Mexican Revolution, the era in which Posada created his lithographs that ended up on many broadsides.

She studied the photo, which had a ruler next to it for scale, and compared it to the one found with Ramirez. Thousands of figures just like this circulated around Mexico and in American southwestern cities. But two of them had ended up with dead men, shot in similar ways. Maybe this alleged *Catrina* network had taken the unknown man out, and maybe they'd also killed Ramirez. Which meant that the killer in El Paso may not have had anything to do with Ramirez's killer, though they were tied together by a shadowy network that may or may not be headed by a woman who called herself *La Catrina*.

Her personal cell phone rang with a particular tone.

"Hey, *esa*. I was just going to call you."

"Of course you were," K.C. said. "Because Sage was sending out vibes compelling you to do that."

"Was that what that was?"

"Okay, not really. But Dayna called."

"Huh. Whatever for?" she asked, feigning innocence.

"Spare me, Detective Stubborn-ass. You will be staying with us for at least a couple of days, starting tonight. Sage has spoken. As have I. And Dayna."

"Three against one hardly seems fair."

"All is fair in love and war, *mujer*," she said imperiously. "We love you and some asshat is at war with you. So there you go. Two good reasons to stay with us for a bit."

She smiled. "All right."

K.C. started to say something, then stopped. "Wait. That was too easy. I had this whole speech planned. Dammit, Chris, you ruined my moment."

"Which one?"

"The one where my eloquence and the sheer brilliance of my arguments would completely convince you that this is what needs to happen, and for once in our long and storied relationship, you would agree with me, tell me I'm right, and show up for dinner with your stuff."

Chris laughed. "Jesus, Kase, that was speech enough right there."

"Did it work?"

"Yeah, though if you recall, I had already agreed to your plan."

"So the little speech part was icing, then. So can we expect you for dinner?"

"I don't know for sure when I'll be over, but I'll have Harper drop me off and we'll go from there. It'll probably be around dinner. Six, maybe seven."

"You're splendid," she said in an overblown British accent. "Call me or Sage if anything comes up. I've gotta run."

"I will. See you later. And thanks."

"Duh. You're family. Bye."

Chris hung up and leaned back in her chair, not completely convinced staying at K.C. and Sage's was a good idea. But given that she wasn't going to have a car, it was probably the best option, since she didn't want Dayna to be driving her around. Nor did she want Harper driving her to Dayna's. Even a guy like Frank Rand could probably follow an unmarked police car up to the North Valley. "Fuck," she muttered as her desk phone rang.

"Yo, Gucchi. Check Legal Eyes," Harper said when she answered.

"Shit. What now?" She reached for her mouse and pulled the site's URL out of her bookmarks menu. A new blog was up, and this one had the driver's license photo of Victor Ramirez that APD had released to the press. Somebody had captured it off an online video and created a screenshot. She read through the three paragraphs.

"Jesus fucking Christ," she said when she'd finished. "Who the fuck tipped them off that Ramirez might have been involved in human trafficking?"

"Good question. Maybe they hit up some of the people in the neighborhood."

She swore in Spanish. "I doubt Mrs. Marquez would. Maybe the woman across the street, with the little girl. She might have said something, depending on how they asked the question."

"Free speech," Harper said dryly. "Always so helpful when working a case like this."

She read the second paragraph again. "They're calling him a possible illegal. What the fuck? Everybody with a Hispanic last name is now considered undocumented?"

"To them, yeah. Look, let's go talk to the boss-man before he decides there's a leak."

She hung up and went to Harper's cubicle, thinking that she was really tired but she wanted to kick something.

# Chapter Nineteen

"I WANT YOU to stay at Kara's for a few days," Dayna said in a pleasant tone that left no room for argument.

"Your bossy side is hot," Chris teased.

"Chris," she said with her warning tone.

"Sorry. But it is."

Dayna started to say something else but Chris cut her off.

"Okay. I'll stay at Kara's. K.C. already called."

"Did she give you her speech?"

"Didn't have to."

"I see. So you talked to Harper?"

"Yeah. Something like that." She opted not to tell her about Frank Rand, since that would only make her worry more. Later, she would, once things calmed down. "And I'll be in El Paso tomorrow and tomorrow night, so that'll take some of the heat off."

"Thank you. What time are you leaving tomorrow?"

"Early. Harper's picking me up. And he said he'd drop me off tonight, too."

"Good. Hold on a second." She put Chris on hold for a few moments. "Okay, I have to go. But I'll call you when I'm done with this work dinner thing. And don't you dare change your mind and stay at your house tonight."

"I won't." She smiled.

"I mean it," she said in her stern lawyer voice.

"I know."

"Okay. Talk to you later. Bye, sweets."

"Bye." Chris hung up and rubbed her temples. She had called her brothers earlier and briefed them as well on Legal Eyes. Mike was ready to pay Burgess a special visit, but she convinced him that would play right into his hands about those awful, crime-prone brown people. With them in the loop too, at least she wouldn't worry about *Abuelita* while she was in El Paso.

"Yo," Harper said as he leaned on her cubicle wall. He didn't come into her space and instead looked at her from over the wall. "Nothing on the BOLO for Griego's truck yet. How the hell anybody can miss a truck like that, I don't know."

"Maybe he's got it stashed in a garage somewhere. A buddy in Cruces, I'm guessing."

He grunted. "Nothing on Morales, either. No address in Cruces. Maybe she's staying with friends."

"Maybe she's in Mexico."

He shrugged. "Could be. Maybe Griego is, too."

"Maybe. Anything on Griego's phone records?"

"Not yet. Hopefully we'll have those later tonight, maybe tomorrow morning."

She nodded. "We'll take them with us to El Paso."

"I'll see if they're ready before I come to get you. So what's the plan?"

"I think we should check the Mercado out. But I have a feeling we need to be at the Santa Fe Street Bridge around five. Not sure what we'll find, but it seems to me Ramirez picked up his cargo there then took it to the Mercado. I don't see the sense of waiting at the Mercado, since Griego might just take the cargo and start driving. Without Ramirez, he probably doesn't need to go to the Mercado."

"I like it. Did you check in with our compatriots in the jurisdiction?"

"Yeah. I called the department down there and let them know. Don't want to step on anybody's toes."

"Sounds good. Where are you staying tonight?" He said in his best dad voice.

"K.C.'s."

He smiled. "Bet Dayna had a say in that."

"Shut up, Harper."

His smile widened. "Not that I can't be convincing."

She gave him a glare, but he ignored it.

"I'll take you to K.C.'s, drop you off in the vicinity. You'll have to schlep your gear a couple blocks."

"Yeah, yeah."

He was still smiling as he moved away.

CHRIS SET HER duffle bag and daypack on the floor of Kara's living room, in the mother-in-law southwestern cottage behind K.C. and Sage's house. She looked around, a little surprised. For a flaky nature girl, Kara's taste in furniture and décor was urban hipster, which actually looked okay in the Mexican-style space. She'd put some colorful rugs down, since the entire guest house was Saltillo-tiled, and the colors were a nice contrast to the sleek earth tones of her furnishings.

She'd been in this apartment a few times when K.C. lived here two years ago. Then, Sage had lived in the big house with a roommate. Chris thought about that summer, when K.C.'s ex, Melissa, had asked her to come back to Albuquerque from Texas. Melissa's sister Megan had gotten herself tangled up with a guy who ran in neo-Nazi circles. She'd been a student at UNM, and living in the guest house before she'd disappeared. K.C. had helped Megan move after the shit finished hitting the fan, and then K.C. stuck around a while. Chris smiled, thinking about how hard K.C. had fallen for Sage.

"Hi."

Chris turned at Sage's voice, not surprised that she showed up right when she was thinking about her. Sage had some kind of mystical ju-ju, like *Abuelita*. "Hey. Just got here. Come on in." Kind of weird, she thought, to be inviting her into somebody else's space.

"I've got some decaf on," Sage said as she opened the security door and stepped in. "Have you had dinner?"

"Not really."

"Then K.C. and I will set you up with that, too." She was dressed in one of her gauzy skirts — this one turquoise — and a western-cut off-white blouse that hugged her form in ways Chris was sure left K.C. weak in the knees. She'd pulled her hair back into a ponytail, which drew attention to her cheekbones, sparkling brown eyes, and lips. Sage was a classic beauty wrapped in a western hippie-ish nature girl package.

"Thanks. And you look fabulous, as always," she said as Sage bounded over and pulled her into a hug.

"I see why Dayna keeps you around." She released her.

"That and my green chile lasagna."

"Both good reasons. Where's your car?"

"At the station. Harper dropped me off a couple blocks away. He'll pick me up tomorrow morning. We're going to El Paso. Back on Sunday."

She grinned. "Road trip with Harper. The fun never ends for you." Her expression shifted to serious. "How are you?"

She sighed. "Pissed that one asshole has made me feel like I shouldn't be at home. Or at Dayna's."

"He's got a big soapbox." She shrugged. "Consider this a staycation, except not at your house." She gestured at Chris's duffle bag. "Kara says to use whatever and do whatever."

Chris picked the bag up. "Good to know. Didn't want to mess up her chic furniture."

Sage laughed as Chris took the bag into the bedroom and placed it on the bed. Here, too, Kara displayed an urban hipster vibe. She favored greens and blues in this room, though.

"Towels are on the shelves in the bathroom," Sage called. "And she's got coffee and associated equipment for it on the counter in the kitchen." She appeared in the bedroom doorway. "K.C. put fresh half-and-half in the fridge."

"Then I am all set."

Sage gave her a look. "Come on. I don't like leaving bachelors for the evening unfed."

"Yes ma'am, Ms. Crandall."

Sage arched one elegant eyebrow, but flashed her a grin. Chris followed her out the front door and the few yards to the back steps of the big house. They entered a glassed-in mud room that doubled as a laundry room and crossed to the door that would take them into the kitchen. Sage had enchiladas cooking. Chris could smell them even from the mud room.

"Oh, my God. Is that dinner?" she asked as Sage opened the door to the kitchen.

"Of course. I knew you were coming."

"Maybe I'll just stay here a bit longer with you and K.C." She shut the door behind her.

"Fine with us. Since I know you're not so bad in a kitchen yourself." She shot her a look. "In more ways than one, I've heard."

Chris opened her mouth to say something, thought better of it, and coughed instead.

Sage smiled innocently. She had already put cups out, and she poured Chris one and handed it to her.

"Thanks." She sniffed. A hint of cinnamon and maybe vanilla. "Perfect." She poured a splash of half-and-half in and leaned back against the kitchen counter, still edged with its original chrome. She liked Sage and K.C.'s kitchen. The design was a mixture of its original 1940s flavor and modern upgrades. It all worked, somehow. "I'll call Kara and thank her, too."

"I already did. But I'm sure she'd love a call from you." She poured herself a cup of coffee and threw her a lascivious smile. "Kara told us before she left, and I quote, 'Chris is super hot'. She thinks you'll leave your hotness energy all over the house."

She groaned and a flush worked its way up her neck. "Not sure how I feel about K.C.'s sister saying that about me."

"Not to worry. K.C. agreed." Sage hid her smile behind her cup. "As did I. In other words, we are all in agreement about your hotness factor. I'm sure if we put the question to Dayna, she'll concur."

She laughed. "Did you tell Kara anything specific about what's going on?"

Sage gave her a "are you seriously asking me that" look.

"Never mind. Dumb question."

"It's the stress talking, I know," she said with another smile. "I told her you needed to stay here because of some shitty peripheral elements in a case you're working."

She laughed. "I like that. I'm going to incorporate that into my reports. Maybe we can have a whole new category on the form itself. Shitty peripheral elements."

"On a more serious note, what's Dayna's take?"

"She's pissed, too. And worried. The last thing either of us needs is some asshole with a camera catching us together. And not even in a compromising position."

Sage frowned, thinking. "Maybe you need a fake girlfriend."

She stared at her. "I'm not sure I'm following."

"Why not out yourself through the department?"

She waited for her to elaborate.

"On your terms. That way, it can't be used against you, if you're already out and the department knows." She set her cup down, more animated. "A fake something-or-other that says you're a liaison for LGBT officers or some shit like that and your bio could have a little notice about your partner. 'Detective Gutierrez lives in the South Valley with her agoraphobic partner of eight years and their retired police dogs, four cats, and parrot' or whatever the hell. Maybe even say you live in Belen. Even better. The asshats will spend days trying to find you there. Plus, it won't be this big, juicy gossip for them to break that the evil cop is also an evil lesbian because the department clearly knows about all her evilness."

"Agoraphobic?"

"That's why nobody sees her." She grinned.

She laughed. "Parrot?" she asked before she took another sip of coffee.

"You're clearly a complicated woman."

She almost spit her coffee out. Once she finished laughing, she set her cup down. "Damn, Sage. That could seriously work. Minus the parrot and agoraphobic partner. I'll run this by Harper and Jerry, see what they think."

"It'd be easy. Just be seen at some fake event. Hell, I could stage it for you and photograph it with a bunch of people, gay and otherwise. And you could get a couple of cops to come in uniform and it would look legit." She stopped. "And it doesn't even have to be an actual fake event. You could just have some former fake event plugged on a site somewhere. Or you could be announced as the new liaison to a committee forming to explore outreach to the LGBT community. Or whatever the fuck." Sage tended to swear more when she was excited about something.

Chris heard the front door open.

"Honey, I'm home," K.C. called from the living room.

"In here," Sage called back. "Hurry. We're plotting shit."

K.C. appeared in the doorway, wearing gray dress trousers, a red button-down shirt, and her nicer black leather jacket. She also wore black dress shoes in a guy's style, like the rest of her outfit.

"Well, don't you look all professional," Chris teased.

"I had another term in mind," Sage said as she looked her up and down.

"I learned from you," K.C. said to Chris and shrugged. "Besides, if anybody from the department comes by to make sure I'm actually teaching instead of throwing dance parties in the classroom, I can present like a real professor."

"What, the Ph.D. isn't proof enough?"

"Not for the bean counters." K.C. gave her a quick hug then pulled Sage into a full-on embrace with a long kiss.

Chris cleared her throat. "I'll just be out here." She picked up her coffee and made a show of pretending to go to the mud room.

"Sorry. Haven't seen the love of my life all day," K.C. said. "Not to suggest you're not the other love of my life." She made a show of waggling her eyebrows. "So what's up? What are we plotting?"

Sage filled her in on her idea while K.C. poured herself a cup of coffee. "I like it," she said as she added half-and-half. "Cut the fuckers off at the pass before they think they're all awesome by outing you. Plus, it throws them off Dayna's trail. You going to run it by Harper and the boss?"

"As a matter of fact, I am. I see Harper tomorrow morning, early. We have to go to El Paso to follow a lead. We'll have to figure out how to announce this without announcing it if Jerry goes for it."

"We could also just stage a photo of you at some gay event in town," Sage suggested. "And post it somewhere related to the department. Something that makes it obvious that you're not just there for show and that you actually are living in Gay Central with the rest of us, and that you're out."

"Chris Gutierrez. Not just a show dyke," K.C. said in a fake announcer's voice.

"Jesus," Chris said, laughing.

"You'd totally get best in show regardless," she continued.

"And on that note—" Chris poured herself more coffee. "How was your day, dear?"

"The usual. Whining, excuses, when can we get out of here. And that's just my colleagues."

Sage giggled.

"Seriously. Nobody is more uptight than academics. They put students to shame. At least students go out and party now and again."

Sage smiled and opened the oven to check the enchiladas. K.C. took plates out of the cabinet and walked them through the doorway to the space that served as a combined living room and dining room. The big Spanish-style table stood just off the kitchen. Chris took silverware out of the drawer and handed it to K.C. when she came back in. She then followed her with three glasses and set those on the table, too.

"You two having wine?" she asked before she went back into the kitchen.

"I believe so. There's an open bottle of white in the fridge. And Tazo tea, if you want some." K.C. was busy lighting the three pillar candles on the table, so Chris went to retrieve wine glasses and the bottle. She carried those out to the table and almost ran into Sage on her way back to the kitchen, who brushed past her with a smile, carrying a serving plate of enchiladas.

"Rice is in the oven," she said as she set the plate carefully on the table.

Chris removed the dish and carried it out to the table, where she set it on a ceramic tile next to the enchiladas. She returned to the kitchen to get the pitcher of water she'd seen earlier, with slices of lime floating in it, out of the fridge. She set it on the table.

K.C. had turned some music on. Some kind of worldbeat that sounded African.

"Oh, shit. The jicama. You two sit down," Sage commanded as she returned to the kitchen.

K.C. sat at the head and Chris took the seat to her right. She poured wine in K.C.'s glass then Sage's and set the bottle aside. K.C. poured water from the pitcher into the other glasses Chris had brought out.

"I love this about you," Chris said as she served enchiladas onto K.C.'s plate.

"What?" Sage set a plate of sliced jicama next to the enchiladas.

"Sit-down dinners. Maybe we should do this a couple times a month. The four of us."

"I'd like that." Sage sat down on K.C.'s left, across from Chris.

"We have an arrangement," K.C. said as she served herself some rice. "If we're both going to be home at the same time in the evening, we have a sit-down dinner. It's my turn to cook next time."

"That's so civilized." Chris finished dishing enchiladas onto her plate. She took a bite. "Oh," she said with pleasure. "Perfect. Clearly, I picked the best night to stay over. Seriously, Sage. Excellent. As always." She served herself some rice.

"John and I have been exchanging recipes. I took one he was using and tweaked it a little."

"The enchiladas have got sort of a *molé* thing going, but not quite."

"A culinary cop," K.C. said with a smile.

Sage giggled. "It's a less heavy *molé*. I'm experimenting. John's trying a version, too, and we'll compare notes."

"I'm glad my brother found his culinary side." Chris shot K.C. a mock glare and took another bite, savoring the melding of flavors. "And I'm really glad he's sharing it with you."

They continued chatting, and Chris relaxed into the conversation, glad once again that K.C. had found someone like Sage, whose mystical open-to-the-universe vibe served as a balance to the sometimes less flexible academic side K.C. wrestled with.

"I heard you had a blast from the past," Sage said, giving Chris one of her "do tell" looks.

"Yes. Trish called, and I'm sure K.C. told you that she has a client who was able to provide some information about a case."

"Trish was going to call you anyway."

Chris cut another bite of enchilada. "What do you mean?"

She shrugged. "She still had your phone number."

"So?"

K.C. poured herself a little more wine. "I don't know many people who keep their ex's phone number for two years after a break-up.

Maybe initially, because you have to do the ceremonial returning of each other's stuff, but two years?" She gave her a "just sayin'" look.

"Well, so what? Maybe she just wanted to touch base. Maybe she feels bad about the break-up."

"Maybe she still has a torch." K.C. set her glass down.

Chris looked at Sage for help.

"It's not unusual for some people to break up and one of the parties just doesn't want to completely let go," Sage said. "But it doesn't mean she's still attracted to you. After all, she hasn't called you before this."

"No, she hasn't."

"But she still feels there's unfinished business between the two of you. Could be something as simple as an apology. Is she the type to make amends?" Sage raised an eyebrow.

"Not that I know. And honestly, I was thinking about it, and I don't really think I knew her all that well at all. I think I thought I did. And I did think about something more serious with her. But she just couldn't deal with the cop thing. And clearly, she wasn't right for me." Trish had gotten close, but not close enough. Had Chris not been in law enforcement, chances were they'd probably still be a couple.

"She had issues with your cop self," K.C. said. "And I seriously doubt she was going to cut you any slack in that regard. Plus, being a cop is part of who you are. The only way it would have worked between you two is if you quit the force. And that just wasn't going to happen. You needed Dayna, who understands that about you."

"And thinks it's sexy," Sage said with a mischievous little grin.

"Well, who doesn't, besides Trish?" K.C. scoffed. "She's just in serious denial. What kind of lesbian doesn't like a woman cop?"

"The kind who don't like the work." Chris took another bite of her enchiladas. "Uniforms are one thing. The work's another."

"Okay, who doesn't like a seriously bad-ass hot woman like yourself?" K.C. teased. "Forget the damn uniform and the cop stuff. You're ultra smokin'."

"I'm—what? What am I?" Chris looked first at K.C. then Sage, who laughed.

"No argument here," Sage said. "Regardless, Trish clearly wasn't the right woman. But don't be surprised if she calls you sooner than you think."

"For what?"

"Coffee. And whatever business she wants to finish," K.C. responded.

"Maybe it's just closure. You and Melissa had to work through a little bit." Chris shrugged and took a drink of water. "Speaking of, how is Megan?"

Sage laughed. "Nice deflection. She's fine. She just called us a couple of days ago. She may be in town for Christmas. She says Oregon is great, but she really misses Albuquerque. And she asked about you."

"Good stuff, I hope."

"Please. Megan has a straight-girl crush on you. Always has." K.C. rolled her eyes, but she grinned. "Seriously, though. She's doing very well and is actually dating someone. Melissa assures me he's a cute, sweet sci-fi nerd and all her cousins have vetted him. He apparently thinks she's the coolest thing since video gaming."

"That's good news." Chris finished her enchiladas and took a few slices of jicama.

"Considering her history, yes. Although practically anybody would be a step up from her previous guy." K.C. picked up her wine glass. "Melissa will be at our Halloween party. And she's bringing a guest."

"Oh? Do we know who this guest is?"

"Her name is Sue," Sage answered. "From the sound of it, I don't think they've been dating very long."

"I'm not even going to ask how you know that," Chris said with a chuckle.

"She called the house to RSVP and I talked to her. It's in her voice. She's excited about her, but it struck me as fairly new."

Chris shot K.C. a look, who just shrugged with a helpless expression on her face. "I don't know who she is," K.C. said. "Not like Melissa calls me up to talk about her dating life. Only Megan's."

"But she does call you," Sage said.

"Sometimes. But never to talk about her own love life."

"And I doubt Trish will call Chris to talk about that, either." Sage picked up her glass and gave Chris a look. "But she will call you. More, now that the groundwork's in place."

Chris shrugged. "Fine. I won't be surprised when she does, since I've now consulted Sage the oracle."

K.C. laughed. "Anyway, did you tell *Abuelita* to call either one of us if she can't reach you? In case Burgess or his crew go sniffing around there. Though that may not happen, since her last name's different." K.C. reached for her wine glass.

"Yes. Pete and Mike know, too. And yes, so does Dayna. The contact list is ready to roll."

"Here's hoping we won't have to spring into action." She raised her glass, and Chris and Sage did the same. "And honey," K.C. continued, "that was seriously delicious. Beyond delicious. There isn't a category of word past that good enough to describe dinner."

"Thank you. We'll talk more about it later." She fixed K.C. with a gaze and Chris grinned.

"So what's Dayna up to tonight?" Sage asked.

"Work dinner." She missed her more than usual tonight, as if the change in her routine and an asshole blogger had somehow made their relationship long-distance.

"It's not permanent." Sage interrupted her thoughts. Or rather, intercepted them, as she often did. "Burgess and his merry band of buttheads will find someone else to go after soon enough."

"I'd love to nail him with something in the meantime."

K.C. stood and picked up her plate and Sage's. "Too bad it's not illegal to be an asshole."

"Hell, if it were, we'd have to build way more prisons." Chris started to get up to help but K.C. gave her a look.

"Relax." She added Chris's plate to the stack she'd collected and went into the kitchen.

Sage picked up her wine glass and took a sip, then fixed Chris with one of her assessing gazes. "You wear this new stage of your relationship well," she said, a little smile at the corners of her mouth.

"Oh? How does it look?"

"Grounded. And deep."

K.C. emerged from the kitchen and picked up the plate with the last of the enchiladas then retreated again, but she and Sage exchanged a charged look and Chris hoped that she and Dayna could sustain that kind of energy, as well. She thought about the other night and grinned.

"I like it," Chris said. "A lot."

"It shows." Sage smiled back.

K.C.'s cell phone rang in the kitchen. Chris heard her answer and she appeared a few moments later. "It's Kara." She handed her phone to Chris. "She wants to talk to you."

"Hi," Chris said when she put the phone to her ear. "Thanks for letting me crash at your place."

"No problem," came Kara's response. The last time Chris had seen her, she'd started growing her hair out again, and it made her look a little more like K.C.

"Eat whatever, drink whatever," Kara was saying. "Just wanted to make sure you knew that."

"I appreciate it. I don't know how long I'll need to stay—"

"It's cool. I won't be back for three weeks. You'll totally have everything under control way before then."

"Don't know about that, but I'll give it a shot."

"I have complete confidence in you. Okay. Back to Kase. Be safe."

"You, too." Chris handed the phone to K.C., who grinned and went back into the kitchen, chatting.

"K.C. is going to try to talk Kara out of dating my brother without actually mentioning his name," Sage said with a little twinkle in her eyes.

"I think Kara's got K.C. figured out, there." She leaned back in her chair. "How is that going, anyway?"

Sage smiled. "They talk. It's kind of cute, actually. She makes him laugh."

"Sounds like someone we both know." Chris picked up her water glass.

"She and K.C. do share a similar sense of humor. Must be a family thing. Though I've only met Joely a couple of times, she has a way with one-liners."

"Yeah, she does." Chris thought about K.C.'s other sister, who was teaching at a college in the Midwest. "So has River said anything interesting about Kara?"

"Not really. But he tends not to talk about stuff like that. They haven't gotten past the talking, because he can't get past feeling like he has to be on guard all the time to protect the women in his life. That's part of the damage my father left behind." She stared into her wine glass, then up at her again.

And it was part of the nuttiness they'd gone through a few months earlier in Farmington. Sage must have seen Chris's thoughts in her eyes.

"River's doing better after that. We all are, actually." She reached across the table and squeezed Chris's hand.

"I know. Maybe Kara will get him to come down off his mountain."

She shrugged. "I think Kara's good for him, even if they never progress past talking. He needs to meet women who don't have the same kinds of baggage he does."

"Because matching baggage is so last year," Chris said wryly, thinking about her own triggers and issues.

Sage laughed. "I certainly have a load of my own. Part of what I really love about K.C. is that she comes from such a different background than I do, and it makes her steady in her reactions to me and my issues. I had a hard time with that, in the beginning. I kept thinking I'd drive her away. But she stayed."

"She knows a good thing when she finds it, though it might take her a little bit to realize it." She smiled. "As you have discovered."

"Not unusual, for most people. We're all afraid, on some level, of being hurt and being alone and then we self-sabotage. I know I tried sometimes to drive her away, like I was testing her." She traced the rim of her glass with her fingertip. "She pointed it out, and I know it was hard for her to do, because her pattern is to bury herself in her work to avoid things."

"I'm familiar with that pattern."

"Yes, you are." She gave her a pointed look. "I suspect that's part of what drew you and K.C. together. We're attracted to something in other people that we're dealing with in ourselves."

"Or misery loves company." She grinned.

"Well, there's that." Sage smiled back.

Chris stared into the flames of one of the candles. She could hear K.C. talking animatedly in the kitchen. Sage could, too, because she smiled again, but in a softer way.

"She makes me feel safe. And she makes me laugh, Chris. Every day. And that is so very important to me, knowing that she has that side. I didn't grow up with much of that, especially when my father was around. And I sure as hell never felt completely safe as a child." She paused. "She grounds me in ways I never expected."

Chris smiled. "I am so glad you two found each other."

"And I'm so glad that you've been able to work through some things with Dayna. Because you found each other, too. Hang on to that."

"I plan to." She meant it, and it was so much easier to say those sorts of things, now. Because Dayna wanted the same things, and Chris felt it deep, all the way through, and it no longer unnerved her, no longer made her want to put up walls or build excuses about long-term.

Sage squeezed her hand again. "Trust the process." She stood. "Want another cup of decaf?"

"Yes, actually. One more cup for the road." She got up and collected a few of the glasses and followed Sage into the kitchen.

A half-hour later she was back at Kara's stretched out on the couch. She'd turned the TV on, but wasn't watching. Dayna's dinner should be over soon, she hoped. She sighed and checked her phone again, thinking she'd missed a call or a text from her. She hadn't. Then she debated going outside and canvassing the neighborhood on foot, to see if Burgess or his crew had managed to track her down. K.C. could loan her a baseball cap and a nondescript jacket so she wouldn't look like Detective Chris Gutierrez, but rather just a neighborhood pedestrian on the way home from one of the many restaurants on Central.

She threw that idea out. She needed to relax a bit. Maybe some of the stress from the day would ease up. So she unpacked a few things, including her clothes for the next day, then packed her daypack for El Paso. A few minutes later she channel-surfed, ended up on ESPN, and decided to go through her notes on the Ramirez case again. She flopped back down on the couch. There still wasn't a clear motive in Ramirez's death. Without that, it was a hell of a lot harder to pin a suspect, and the best bet they had was the missing Morales.

She went back through Ramirez's text log. Nothing that indicated what he was supposed to do in El Paso or how Griego was involved. Maybe Marta could provide some answers. The easiest way to talk to her, however, was if Juana convinced her to call. No guarantee of that, though. She was under no obligation to talk to an American cop.

"Fuck," she muttered. This whole thing felt like a dead end, and that would keep Burgess on her ass. She thought then about Sage's suggestion. That would at least defuse any potential gay-hunting he was into. And it would protect Dayna, if Chris was linked to somebody else, whether fictitious or not. She put her notes away because she was getting nowhere and maybe sleeping on it would help jog something loose. She went to the bathroom then returned to the couch for more channel surfing, decided that TV tonight sucked, and turned it off. She stared for a long time at the ceiling, different thoughts bouncing around her brain.

Dayna's ring sounded on her phone and she practically lunged for it.

"Hey," she answered, relieved and excited to hear from her. "How was dinner?"

"Long and boring. Nothing to report. Yours, I'm sure, was way better."

"Your company would have made it even more better."

Dayna laughed. " 'More better'? Is that even a phrase?"

"It is now. It's like 'way better'. Only more."

"I see. But I'm pretty sure that dinner with Sage and K.C. was probably as much fun as I envisioned it."

"Okay, maybe a little. But still. I wish you could've been there."

"Me, too. So when are you leaving for El Paso in the morning?"

"I'm meeting Harper a couple blocks away at seven." She glanced at the clock on Kara's cable box. It was nearly eight.

"Then maybe you should get some sleep."

She groaned. "Too restless. And I miss you. I feel like I'm a million miles away. If I had a car here, I'd drive up there just to see you."

"Is that all you'd do?" Dayna teased in a tone that always made Chris ache.

"No. And when I get a chance, I'll show you exactly what I'd do."

"A challenge," she practically purred. "I like that. So come on. Show me."

"No fair. I don't have a car."

"Details. Open the door."

Chris stared blankly at Kara's front door.

"Put out or shut up, Gutierrez," Dayna teased over the phone.

She stood, crossed the floor in three strides, and pulled the inner wooden door open and unlocked the security door. Dayna stood right outside smiling at her, wearing jeans, an old barn jacket, and a dark baseball cap. Chris stared at her.

"This is way better than Christmas," Chris said. "In fact, I don't even need Christmas, now."

"Don't you mean it's more better?" Dayna looked up at her, innocent.

"Oh, definitely." She stepped aside so she could come in and Chris locked up behind her, still holding her phone in one hand. Even in a coat that hid her form and a hat pulled low, Dayna turned her on.

"Wait," Chris ordered. "Cop stuff first. Explain." She tossed her phone onto the couch and fixed Dayna with a stare. God, she was hot. And everything she wanted, wrapped up in denim and flannel.

"K.C. and I engaged in subterfuge," Dayna said with a mischievous little smile. "She picked me up and brought me over after dinner. And for the record, Harper checked the area before I got here."

"What the fuck? Harper's in on this, too?"

She raised an eyebrow. "You have good friends. And a good cop partner. So," she said, hands on her hips. "What are you going to do about this, Detective? I distinctly recall you saying that you'd show me.

Or are you all talk and no action?" She put a flirtatious challenge on the last part of her question.

Chris studied her, security and cop things running through her mind, but those were quickly overtaken by other thoughts. Much more interesting and arousing thoughts. "I guess you'll have to judge for yourself." She slowly took Dayna's cap off and tossed it onto the couch. Then she ran her fingers just as slowly through her hair, and leaned down for a long, deep kiss. She pulled away, her fingers still in Dayna's hair, desire burning through her core.

"Damn," Dayna said. "That's enough to keep a girl warm at night."

Chris placed the fingers of her free hand against Dayna's lips, quieting further comment. "Take your coat off," she said in a low voice as she pulled her hands away.

Dayna regarded her, another little challenge in the heat of her expression.

"Take it off," Chris repeated, adding a little cop inflection to the order.

She let her coat slide down her arms onto the floor. She wore a faded untucked flannel shirt that brought out the blue of her eyes.

"Unbutton your shirt," Chris said softly. "Slowly."

A wicked smile quirked the corners of her mouth. She did, and revealed a black lace bra that accentuated all the right curves.

Chris's mouth almost went dry. "Take your shirt off," she said in a low voice.

It slipped from Dayna's shoulders to join her coat on the floor and Chris ran her fingertips down Dayna's bare arms, raising goosebumps on her skin. Her fingers traced the swell of her breasts, and Dayna shuddered. Heat raced from Chris's fingertips to her core.

"I am so turned on right now," Dayna said, looking up into Chris's eyes.

"Good. Don't move." Chris loved teasing her like this, loved that Dayna responded to her this way.

Dayna made a frustrated little noise, but kept her hands at her sides. Chris ran her fingers down Dayna's abdomen to the waistband of her jeans, which she slowly unbuttoned. Then she placed her hands on Dayna's hips and nuzzled her neck with her lips. She smelled hints of citrus and spice, and the ache at her core spread down her thighs.

"You are the sexiest woman I've ever seen," Chris said near her ear. "I thought that the first time I saw you." She gently nipped at the skin of Dayna's throat, which drew a soft moan and she smiled against her skin. "And I knew I had to find out who you were." She moved her hands to Dayna's breasts, and lightly stroked her nipples through the fabric of her bra.

"Jesus," Dayna murmured. She started to move her hands toward Chris.

"Not yet," she admonished with a little grin, and Dayna put her hands back at her sides with another little groan. Chris touched her lips to Dayna's shoulder and continued gently stroking her breasts.

Dayna tilted her head back and bit her lip. "You're driving me crazy," she said between gasps.

"Good." She ran her hands down her back, loving the feel of her warm skin and the muscles beneath. "The first time I touched your bare skin," she said against her neck, "was the first time I truly understood how amazing you are."

Dayna sighed and made another little noise deep in her throat, but kept her head back. Her breathing had sped up and her pulse pounded in her neck.

"I had already guessed," Chris continued, "because every time you kissed me before that made me feel things I'd never thought possible. But actually touching you the way I am now—" she moved her lips to Dayna's jaw, "was life-altering." She pulled her closer. "Still is." She held Dayna's gaze and again, Dayna started to move her hands but Chris shook her head and smiled.

"Ah, ah," she said and Dayna dropped her hands to her sides. Chris cupped her face and pulled her into another long, deep kiss and lost herself in Dayna's mouth and tongue. She could never get enough of her, would never want to, and the heat between them filled every corner of her heart.

"Tell me what you want," she said against Dayna's lips.

"All of you." Her breath was warm against Chris's mouth.

Chris smiled, heart pounding hard in her chest. "Done. Put your hands on me."

And Dayna obliged. She wrapped her arms around her and kissed her hard and moved against her in a way that turned her want to need and coals to flames and Chris held on tight, and surrendered to the delicious assault of Dayna's lips.

"Chris," she said softly after several long, exquisite minutes, "please take me to bed."

And Chris brushed her hair from her face, kissed her gently, and led her to the bedroom.

# Chapter Twenty

HER INTERNAL ALARM woke her up at five, according to the clock on the nightstand. She could see it from her position, which was naked against Dayna's back. She had to get up soon, so she could shower, get ready, and meet Harper a couple blocks away. But spooning Dayna after a night like the one they just had made that nearly impossible. Not fair, she thought. Not fair at all. She didn't know when she'd be able to spend another night with her. Damn asshole bloggers.

Dayna mumbled something and put her hand over Chris's, where it rested against her stomach. Chris pulled her closer, and held her like that until the clock read five-thirty. She sighed softly and kissed Dayna's shoulder before she gently extricated herself from the sheets and padded toward the bathroom, picking up the clothes she'd set out the night before from the top of the dresser.

Twenty minutes later, she emerged, showered and dressed in jeans and a dark tee underneath a navy-colored sweatshirt. Dayna was no longer in bed and the light on the nightstand was on. She smelled coffee and heard movement in the kitchen. Dayna always got up with her, no matter how early, and put coffee on. Dayna had told her she liked doing it, so she accepted it. Besides, Chris loved seeing her in the mornings, when she was fresh out of bed and wearing the previous night in her smile.

"Hi," she said when she went into the kitchen. Dayna turned from the counter. She had put on Chris's shirt from last night, which she'd only buttoned halfway up, and a pair of old shorts Chris had brought. Her hair fell in untamed waves around her shoulders and her eyes sparked with a familiar morning mischief and welcome. Chris's breath caught in her throat.

Dayna grinned. "You're staring."

"Yeah. I am. And it's the best view ever."

She gave her an air kiss and poured two cups of coffee out of the French press and put a splash of half-and-half into one cup and a bit more in the other. The one with less creamer she handed to Chris.

"I wish I didn't have to work on this case." Chris took a sip. Rich and smooth. Kara had good taste in coffee. But then, Dayna could make a great cup of coffee out of practically any brand or bean.

"I know. I wish you didn't have to, either." The unspoken, "because maybe this asshole blogger wouldn't be in the picture," hung at the end of her statement.

Chris moved closer and kissed her good morning. "Last night was unbelievable."

Dayna smiled up at her and set her cup on the counter. She then took Chris's cup from her and set that on the counter, too. "I was thinking the same thing." She slid her arms around Chris's neck. "I want a repeat. As soon as possible." And she pulled her into another long kiss that sparked Chris's nerve endings and sent heat surging down her thighs.

"Dammit, you and kitchens," Dayna said, breathing hard as she pulled away. "And every other fucking room. How is it that you turn me on even more now than when we first met?"

"I've revealed more of my charms." She released her, reluctantly, and picked up her coffee cup.

"Not to suggest I wasn't hot for you right off." Dayna gave her a little smirk and went to the fridge. "Bagel?"

"Yes, please. And hold up. You were hot for me right off?" Chris teased.

She didn't answer at first, as she sliced a bagel and put the two halves in the toaster on the counter. "I thought you were attractive, but I didn't get a good look at you until you handed me that beer at the conference." She pushed the lever on the toaster down then turned her gaze to Chris.

"And?" Chris prompted.

"And I thought you were hot. But somehow, you just keep getting hotter. I didn't think that was possible in the laws of physics."

"It must be. I have the same issue with you."

"Good. Because I have plans for you, Detective," she said, in a tone that always made Chris weak. She picked up her coffee cup and gave her another little smirk before she sipped.

"Do they involve kitchens?"

"Oh, yes. And a lot of other places."

Chris's work cell rang in the bedroom. It wasn't even six-thirty. She frowned and went to answer it. Harper's number.

"What's up?" she said.

"Yo. Slight change of plans. Griego's dead."

"Fuck. Where?"

"Highway Patrol found his truck in a pull-out off an I-10 exit ramp about twenty miles south of Cruces. He was in it, shot in the crotch and head. *Catrina* figure left in the cab."

She tensed even more. "When?"

"He was found about six this morning. Don't have an estimate on the time of death, but the trooper says the body felt pretty cold. Might have been there since the wee hours."

She pinched the bridge of her nose. "What's the plan?"

"I say we go down and have a look. Then we can still go see if anybody we know shows up at the Mercado and the bridge."

"All right. I'll meet you at Flying Star on Central in twenty."

"Okay, then."

He hung up and Chris glanced at the clock on the nightstand. Just past six-thirty. She returned to the kitchen, where Dayna had just plated her bagel. "Cream cheese okay?" she asked. "The hummus looked a little scary."

"Sure." She watched as Dayna smoothed cream cheese on the bagel with a knife then put it on a plate she had set on the counter. "I have to meet Harper soon."

"I figured. Still going to El Paso?"

"Yeah. I'll call you when I get a chance."

"I know."

Chris stared down into her eyes. "Thanks for coming over."

"My pleasure." She smiled and toyed with Chris's belt.

"And mine." Chris kissed her, a long, slow show of affection. A familiar heat spread down her thighs and she pulled away. "Sorry. Duty calls." She took the bagel and left the plate on the counter.

"Probably for the best. You know how I get around you and kitchens."

She chuckled and went to the living room, where she'd left her jacket and daypack. She holstered her pistol and made sure her jacket covered it, then slung the backpack over her shoulder.

"Be careful," Dayna said from the kitchen doorway.

Chris nodded and started for the front door then stopped and went over to her. She kissed her again, savoring the taste of her mouth. "Love you, Counselor," she said softly as she pulled away.

"I figured." Dayna gave her a cocky little grin. "It's mutual. Now go save the free world. I'll lock up."

She grinned back and let herself out of the house.

"WHY THE HELL would he come here?" Chris asked with frustration.

Harper looked over at her. He'd dressed down too, in jeans and a dark brown cable-knit sweater. They'd both tried to look like casual American tourists.

"Look at it," she continued, gesturing at Griego's pickup, which was roped off by crime scene tape and orange pylons. "Yeah, it's sort of off the exit ramp, but it's not like this truck isn't noticeable."

"It was dark." He shrugged. "Maybe he was meeting someone and got popped. His window was down, according to the trooper. Let's see what the local investigator says. They pulled Griego's cell phone." He grimaced. "At least we missed the press."

She didn't respond and instead surveyed the landscape, a canvas of grays, browns, and tans interrupted by tumbleweed and cactus. The Organ Mountains stood to the east, their peaks like ragged fangs jutting from the desert floor. A few small towns—some barely dots on a map—hugged I-10 between Cruces and El Paso. What were they not seeing?

"Maybe Morales did the deed," Harper said. He was standing at the truck, peering into the cab through the driver's side window. He didn't touch anything.

She joined him and stared into the cab, too. Blood stained the driver's seat between his legs. "How many shots in his head?"

Harper stepped back and changed his viewing angle. "Two, looks like. Small caliber, like with Ramirez."

"But shot in the head. Unlike Ramirez."

He didn't say anything.

"Hard angle to shoot him in the crotch if the perp is outside the vehicle," Chris noted. "Griego was driving."

"Yeah." Harper positioned himself near the front tire on the driver's side. "Griego must've had his window down. I'm not seeing any broken glass. She comes at him at this angle and shoots him in the head first, maybe? Then she gets closer and shoots him in the crotch."

"Why the crotch? He's already dead if the perp gets him in the head first. And it doesn't look like any shots missed." Like at Ramirez's. All the shots fired were found in Ramirez. No stray bullets in the walls, floor, ceiling, or furniture.

Harper rocked forward onto the balls of his feet, then back onto his heels. "Symbolism. Maybe Griego took some liberties, too." His tone was grim.

"Maybe. Or maybe his association with Ramirez was enough for somebody to do it. He may not have committed a sexual assault, but he probably let Ramirez get away with it and he probably helped Ramirez supply women for sex trafficking."

"Possible."

They both stared at the truck for a while.

"It'd be a bit easier if the perp's a leftie," Chris said. "Since he was shot from the front, that puts the gun hand closest to the truck." She envisioned Inez Morales approaching the truck, saying, "Hi," to Griego, and then opening fire. "I don't know, Harper. Morales has a history with Griego. Even if they weren't having sex anymore, they had longstanding ties. I'm thinking Morales wouldn't have been able to do it."

He stepped back from the truck. "If she did Ramirez, she could do Griego. Love or money, Gucchi. Sometimes both." He paused and studied the truck for another few seconds. "Another question might be whether he was coerced to drive out here. Maybe he gave the perp a ride."

"You don't think he met someone out here?"

"Nah. Why out here?" Harper said skeptically. "Who's going to say, hey, meet me at that exit near wherever the hell so we can talk."

"Somebody claiming car trouble?"

He grunted as if conceding her point.

"Or," she continued, "in your scenario, maybe someone came with him and directed him here. If he knew the shooter, and didn't suspect an issue, then he'd drive out here, no problem. But if the shooter coerced him, he or she would've made him drive. Easier to control."

"Plausible," he said.

She studied the blood. What had Griego done to deserve that? Had he assaulted a woman? Had he helped Ramirez traffic? Or was he just caught in the middle of something that got somebody else really spooked? Unlike Ramirez, he seemed to have a wider network of people who actually cared about him. Why did he get mixed up with a guy like Ramirez? She exhaled, thinking about the cops who had to deliver the news to those people. She knew what that was like, and it never got easy. She didn't envy them this task.

She exhaled through her teeth. "Where was the figure placed?"

"Don't know. We'll ask."

"If it's Morales," she posed, "what is she driving?"

He didn't answer and instead took a bunch of photos of the cab's interior with the camera he'd brought from Albuquerque.

"Maybe the shooter had a car stashed here. Dumps Griego and bails. Maybe the shooter told Griego that the car was off this exit, and could he or she get a ride."

He made a noncommittal noise.

"Any chance anybody saw anything?" Chris asked the state patrol officer who approached.

"We're checking the surrounding area," he said, all business. "The perp might have been a passenger in the vehicle."

Harper muttered something and took a few more photos. "The bullet trajectories don't seem to indicate that," he added after a couple more shots. "Shooter probably stood at the driver's side window. A passenger probably would've shot him while still a passenger."

The State Patrol guy just shrugged. He stood about three inches shorter than Chris, but he was broad across the shoulders and chest and looked like he could handle himself in a bad situation.

"Did you find any casings?" Chris asked.

"No."

She sighed. Nothing to run through the IBIS database. Whoever the shooter was, he or she was at least experienced enough to remember to collect casings. And not miss, at least not at close range.

"Hi," said another man who strode up to the truck. He was dressed in pressed gray trousers, a light blue shirt rolled up to the elbows, and a tie. "Steve Barnes. Investigator on this one."

"Chris Gutierrez, APD," she said. "This is Dale Harper, also APD."

Harper straightened. He was easily two of Barnes, who was so thin Chris worried he'd blow away in a high wind. He was balding on top, but other than that, he could have been anywhere between thirty and fifty. She put him at around forty.

"Good to meet you," Barnes said. "Can't tell you yet what Griego was doing for the past few days. His mom claims she hadn't seen him and had only talked to him last Sunday. We're checking out the other family members."

"You pull his phone calls? Texts?"

Barnes looked at Harper. "Yeah." He reached into his shirt pocket and removed a few pieces of folded paper. "Had my guy pull the last week, as you requested. When we get the last year, we'll send 'em along." He handed the papers to Harper, who unfolded them and started reading.

"Thanks," Chris said. "Anything on Inez Morales?"

"Looks like her number is included in the vic's texts. We're checking around to see if she was in the vic's company. My guys have her photo."

"You have a photo of the figure left in the cab?"

"Yep." He removed a smartphone from his back pocket and worked a couple of buttons. He handed the phone to her. "It was on his lap. This was taken after we sat Griego up straight so we could get a clearer shot of it. Coroner will be here soon."

The photo showed the figure lying across Griego's thighs, head pointed toward the passenger side. This one was a more traditional version of *Catrina*. She was dressed in a purple gown and matching bonnet. Her skeletal smile was visible in the photo, lending an extra macabre touch. She exchanged a look with Harper. The shooter had to open the driver's side door to put the figure on his lap.

"*La Catrina*," Barnes said.

"Yeah. What do you make of it?" She handed his phone back.

"Rumor has it there's a woman who calls herself that, runs various things over the border. She's supposedly on the Mexican side."

"Runs what? Drugs? People?"

He shrugged. "My money's on drugs, but nobody's been able to link anything to anybody who calls herself that. Or anybody in a network that has anything to do with her. I heard a few tales from INS about somebody calling herself 'Catrina' who helps women get across the border. A few murders since the early nineties. All men. Most unsolved."

She glanced over at Harper, who was writing in his notebook. To Barnes, she said, "Were figures like that left at the scenes of any of those other murders?"

"A few of them. Not all."

"Possible hits?"

"That's what I think. It's similar to what an organized mob or cartel might do. Specific MO, including a calling card. I doubt it's all the same person, though. After all, some of these murders date back to the early nineties. Probably not likely that the woman who calls herself *La Catrina* is still active in the game."

Chris didn't respond. She'd heard about women who had been Mexican drug lords in the early part of the twentieth century who were active well into the 1970s. Depending on when *La Catrina* got started, she might only be in her forties by now. And if she was part of a family network, she probably had lots of support to continue. At least Barnes seemed thorough and willing to help.

"Thanks. Appreciate it. We're headed to El Paso to follow a lead. Call either me or Harper if you get anything." She handed him one of her cards and Harper did the same. "Oh, hey, if anybody calls or texts Griego's phone, will you let one of us know ASAP?"

"Will do. You want a copy of the photo of the figure? I'll forward it from my phone."

"That'd be great. Thanks."

He slid the cards into his shirt pocket and pulled his billfold out of his back, extracted one of his cards, and handed it to Chris. "You're the one who broke the Henderson case," he said, looking up at her. "Good work on that. Carl Maestes is a buddy of mine. That case always bothered him, that he couldn't solve it before he went to El Paso."

"He told me."

"So what's going on with the guy arrested for that? Mumford?"

Chris shook her head. "Don't even get me started. He's been in custody since we arrested him this past spring. You know how these things play out. Could be years."

He laughed. "Don't I know it. Here's hoping we can get this one solved sooner rather than later. I'll be in touch as soon as we get evidence reports." He motioned at the truck.

"Yeah. Thanks again."

He gave her a curt nod and went to talk to someone who was probably a crime scene tech.

"Nice work, Gucchi," Harper said with a smile. "Grease the wheels."

"Whatever works." She turned and looked back toward the freeway. Griego had gone nearly to the end of the ramp, where he could have then made either a left- or right-hand turn. Right would've taken him into Vado and, farther west of that, La Mesa. Not much to the left. Probably ranching land and the southern border of White Sands. Fort Bliss lay farther east, and there was no reason Chris could think of that Griego would be headed out there. For that matter, why would he be going to either La Mesa or Vado?

"Anything in the texts?" she asked.

Harper handed her the printouts. "Yeah. Check out yesterday's."

"Huh," she said after a few moments. "Griego got a text yesterday afternoon saying that today's package will be available at the bridge. From a Mexican number."

"You think that's what Ramirez was supposed to pick up?"

"Yeah. But I don't think we're dealing with things, here. I think we're dealing with people."

He nodded and rocked forward onto the balls of his feet. "Which bridge?"

"Good question." She read through the rest of the texts, but nothing jumped out at her. The texts to and from Morales's number might help with a time line for Griego's last movements and Morales's whereabouts. At first glance, there was nothing incriminating, but they did demonstrate that Morales was alive. Or at least her phone was.

"Border Patrol and local cops have Morales's photo," she said. Not much else we can do, especially since we're not sure which bridge this package is coming in on. And we don't know if it's a car or a pedestrian."

"I'm guessing pedestrian," Harper said. "Walking across the border doesn't draw as much attention, right? Especially if the car's got Mexican plates. Walking, you just pay a quarter or whatever and pop over for some night life — it's Saturday, after all — then head back. Or sleep it off and head back the next day."

"I was leaning that way."

"What's your gut say?" He asked, rocking forward onto the balls of his feet then back onto his heels.

She read through the most recent texts again, but most looked like they were from friends, asking to get together for beer or a game. "I'm leaning toward the Santa Fe Bridge. It's not far from downtown clubs and bars. So pedestrians coming over on a Saturday at that bridge wouldn't get a second look beyond just checking a couple of things since they'd look like they were headed for some entertainment."

"I like it. So who are we looking for?"

"No clue."

He gave her a wry smile. "I like that about you, Gucchi. Tell it like it is."

"I could guess Morales, but who the hell knows who Griego and Ramirez were making deals with? And who knows whether the package is a person or thing?"

"You've got good instincts," he said.

"Hell, it could be somebody on the Mexican side wanting somebody to take a care package to a sick relative on this side."

"Oh, yeah. A guy like Ramirez was just playing postman."

She shrugged and handed the printouts back to him. "See if anything jumps out at you." She looked over toward the truck. "Hey, Barnes," she called.

He looked over at her from the passenger side of the truck.

"Could you find out if Griego knew anybody in this area? Maybe he was on his way to see somebody." Though she doubted it. The shooter scenario she and Harper had just discussed sat right with her.

"We'll check it out." Barnes gave her a wave of acknowledgement.

She looked over at Harper. "Thoughts?"

"We've got two dead guys, shot in similar ways, who knew each other. So far, they've got Britney Luna and Inez Morales in common.

Morales seems to be the stronger link between them. At this point, my money's on her as the shooter. If that's true, she's pissed about something because of the groin shots."

"Maybe a rape."

Harper rocked forward on the balls of his feet again. "That could be motive. Maybe Ramirez assaulted Morales, too."

"But why would she hang out with him, then? Why wouldn't she just kill him as soon as she found out where he was?"

He shrugged. "Stalking him, maybe. He clearly didn't recognize her if that's the case. If it is, maybe he assaulted her a while back."

That was possible. But still not something she was ready to buy.

"We need to talk to Morales's cousin," he said. "I'm going to see if we can get a lead on her. Let's just run her under the last name Morales, see what shakes out."

Chris didn't hold much hope for that. After all, there were probably hundreds of people with the surname Morales in Juárez. Without an address, they couldn't narrow it down. Their best bet was if Juana convinced Marta to call.

"Is it just me, or is this case really sucking?" she said.

Harper looked at her, the hint of a smile beneath his bland expression. "I'm going with the latter." He crossed the road to the stakeout car they'd come in, a late '90s nondescript Chevy Caprice the color of muddy water.

She followed him and he tossed her the keys. She caught them and went to the driver's side. They'd grab lunch in El Paso, see what they could find at Mercado Mayor, and then do surveillance at the Santa Fe Street Bridge. As she started the engine, she couldn't shake the feeling that they might be dealing with retaliation hits from an underground network. What that meant for this case, she didn't know yet, but if they couldn't solve it, chances were Burgess was going to become an even bigger pain in the ass.

# Chapter Twenty-one

CHRIS ALWAYS THOUGHT of El Paso as otherworldly in some ways, like maybe a view of Mars, if somebody from Earth went to colonize it. Especially when entering on I-10, which came in from the northwest. The craggy Franklin Mountains flowed into the city from the north, and divided it nearly in half. The western slopes formed a little bit of the Mesilla Valley of New Mexico while the eastern slopes joined up near El Paso's central business district, at the southern end of the mountain range.

Consequently, over the years, El Paso residents built their houses and suburbs right up those slopes, as far as they could get before the mountains steepened. And they expanded west and east across the Chihuahuan Desert, adding roads, suburbs, and strip malls to the dry soil. Juárez sprawled to the south, running right up to the Rio Grande on the Mexican side of the border just as El Paso's urban tide flowed right up to the opposite bank. Though the two cities often shared culture, history, and even families, it was visibly obvious which side of the border was better off. Here in El Paso, the divide between First and Third Worlds didn't seem so wide, and the view across the river from the south fueled the hopes of thousands, who just wanted to make more money than they'd ever see in a lifetime of work if they stayed.

She understood the lure. She could see it, driving into El Paso. And she had seen it first-hand, driving through Chihuahua with *Abuelita*, in the limitations that poverty and its relatives, crime and corruption, breed. El Paso was one of the safest cities in the U.S. and right across the border was a city wracked by violence as drug cartels warred over turf. Two different worlds, created by an arbitrarily set boundary after a war nobody remembered. Strange, how a line on a map could decide stability, opportunity, and possibility.

Harper had been making follow-up calls on the half-hour drive from the site where Griego's body was found. Chris half-listened as she drove, then thought about Dayna and the night before, which made heat spread through her torso, before it headed even lower.

"Our buddy Burgess is on somebody else's case, now," Harper said to her.

She snapped out of her reverie. "Whose?"

"Cop out of a substation. Apparently, he didn't check to make sure some Hispanic dude involved in an accident was legal."

She made a disgusted noise. "He doesn't have to. Burgess needs to go back to Arizona if he wants a 'papers please' law. Hopefully, they'll check *his* papers, too. And how the fuck would he even know what happened in a traffic situation?"

"He inferred. The accident was multi-vehicle on I-25 near I-40. A few people were injured, and it looks like Burgess just went for the Hispanic name in the report in the paper."

"Christ," she muttered.

"Wish we could nail him with something." Harper tapped his phone on his thigh. "He didn't even violate his probation in Arizona."

"Too bad. But give him some time." The guy was a loose cannon, and he was bound to get involved in some kind of altercation sooner or later. Hopefully, it would be very public and very obvious.

He grunted an agreement and remained silent as they entered downtown El Paso, which reminded Chris of Albuquerque in some ways. Neither city had towering skyscrapers, and both retained structures that had been built decades earlier, mixed with newer and more hip architecture that featured curves and lots of glass.

She parked near the Mercado Mayor, a large festively painted building, and found a Mexican restaurant for lunch. She ordered for both of them in Spanish, and when they'd finished, they walked to the Mercado. She didn't think they'd find anything or anybody useful to the investigation and two hours proved her right. She met Harper at the entrance.

"Nothing. Unless we don't know what we're looking for," he said. "This place is kind of dead," he added.

"Yeah. Not really a place where you'd want to run a covert op."

"Let's go work the bridge," he said in his noncommittal way, but Chris knew he didn't miss much.

She nodded and started to follow him outside, when she stopped. "Give me a minute." She turned around and went back to a shop that was still open, stocked with Mexican folk art and kitsch. The proprietor had decked it out for Day of the Dead, and a bin near the door contained several papier-mâché skeletons, about a foot long. She picked one up and took it to the counter, where a pleasant older woman rang up the purchase. Chris paid, thanked her in Spanish, and left, the skeleton in a plastic bag.

"Let's go," she told Harper, who was standing outside near the curb.

"Souvenir?" he asked sardonically.

"Hunch." She handed him the bag as they walked.

He glanced inside, smiled, and handed it back. "Perfect day for some recon."

She hoped he was right.

A STEADY STREAM of pedestrian traffic in both directions filled the bridge. It was nearly five, and Chris was tired and a little stiff from standing around for the past couple of hours. She'd texted Dayna earlier to check in, then called Carl and asked him to alert Border Patrol agents stationed at this port of entry about Inez Morales, and make sure they had her photo and were aware of the BOLO. She doubted Morales was in Mexico, but it was better to be over-prepared.

This was a long shot. Hell, beyond long shot. She adjusted her earpiece and stifled a yawn. They'd be here at least another hour, if anything was actually going to happen at this bridge on this night. With Greigo dead, the plans might be off.

She thought about that. Would the package show up with Griego out of the picture? Then again, had somebody tried to text him or call him? Neither she nor Harper had heard from Barnes, so probably not. Maybe whoever Griego was working with didn't know he was dead. And maybe, if Morales was in on this, she was going to try to...what? Pick up the package? Meet with whoever was on the other end of this deal? And if the package was a person and Griego didn't show up, what would happen then?

Too many damn questions. She adjusted the plastic bag with the Day of the Dead figurine in it under her left arm and strolled a few yards away from the pedestrian entrance to the bridge on her side. Car lanes separated one side from the other, packed like a parking lot on the narrower part of the bridge over the river, but then more lanes opened like a fan near the checkpoints as the bridge spread a little wider, and allowed seven to eight streams of cars to jockey for position before clearance into El Paso.

Beneath the bridge ran the Rio Grande between concrete embankments. She knew that sometimes, people from the Mexican side actually tried to cross the river here. They'd climb the high fence or maybe find a weak spot and bend the chain-link enough to crawl under. Then down the twenty feet or so of sloping cement to the water, across the water, then reverse the procedure on the northern side of the border. These attempts rarely succeeded and sometimes she wondered if they were diversionary tactics so somebody else could make a successful border-crossing elsewhere in the area.

She scanned the pedestrians emerging from the walkways, a mixture of old and young, some children. The clubbers were starting to arrive, she noticed. Groups of twenty-somethings, the women dressed in tight slacks or short skirts with high heels and the men in dress trousers or nice jeans and button-down shirts. Some wore Mexican-style pointed cowboy boots, and some had clearly put on extra cologne, because Chris caught whiffs of it as they passed, talking and laughing, mostly in Spanish. Nobody who looked uncertain, like they were supposed to meet someone.

"Fifteen minutes," came Harper's voice in her ear. "I'll hang back, but I'll keep a visual on you."

"Copy." She took the figurine out of the bag and stuffed the latter into the back pocket of her jeans. She had her sweatshirt on, since nights here could get a little cool, but she didn't need a jacket. She moved closer to the walkway that funneled people from Juárez to El Paso, and picked a vantage point where she wasn't obstructing the people emerging from it, but was visible.

She held the figurine by its legs so most of it could be seen, and moved a little closer to the walkway. This was a much longer shot than way past half court at the buzzer. And there was no guarantee that five o' clock was an agreed-upon time. Besides that, the "package" may have gotten held up at the checkpoint.

A half-hour passed. She surreptitiously clicked her lapel mic, which she'd attached to the collar of her T-shirt so it was mostly hidden by her sweatshirt and a pair of cheap sunglasses she'd hung on the sweatshirt's collar. She hoped passersby just thought she was adjusting her sunglasses.

"Nothing. You?"

"Nothing," came Harper's voice in her ear.

"Another half-hour, see if anything happens."

"Copy."

She moved a few yards, closer to the walkway entrance, mindful of the evening shadows. Not much daylight left. Fifteen minutes dragged past, and Saturday club-goer traffic had definitely picked up. Again, she scanned the people loitering near the entrance. Most she figured were waiting for friends or family from the Mexican side. Most had been there since her last scan. A few hadn't, though, so she checked those out. One of the women caught her attention.

Chris moved a little closer for a better view. Bingo. She clicked her mic. "Got a visual on Morales," she said as she pretended to mess with the sunglasses. "My eleven. Black sweater, black jeans."

"Got her. Plan?"

"Sit tight. She might be meeting the package."

"Copy."

She smoothed her sweatshirt and looked at her watch, then at the walkway, like she was waiting on someone, too. Morales glanced around nervously, then continued staring at the people coming down the concrete walkway toward them. In her left hand she held a Day of the Dead figurine. She looked around again, then moved a little closer to the entrance. She was practically in the flow of pedestrian traffic.

Chris followed, keeping about twenty feet between them. A few of the lights in the area had already come on as nightfall approached and a few local police officers stood nearby, more deterrent to trouble than actually necessary. Much later that night they'd probably have to break up a few drunken mishaps and altercations.

"Excuse me," said a young woman in Spanish to Chris's right. "My uncle said he'd send a driver. Is that you?" She gestured at the Day of the Dead figure Chris held. She was dressed in a baggy gray sweatshirt, jeans, and sneakers.

"*Sí.*" This young woman – the package – thought she was Morales.

"Now listen to me very carefully," she continued in Spanish. "I have an associate who will help ensure your safety."

She looked at Chris, suddenly fearful and confused.

"It's all right." She glanced toward Morales, who hadn't seen the exchange taking place nearby.

"I've got this," Harper said, appearing like magic at her side. He motioned with his chin at the young woman with Chris.

"We're police," Chris said to her in Spanish. "My name is Chris Gutierrez and this is Dale Harper. We need to ask you a few questions." To Harper, she said, "Flag down the nearest El Paso cop. Explain who we are and that this woman might have some information about our case." She didn't wait for his answer and instead handed him the figurine and beelined for Morales, trying not to attract her attention, moving as if she was simply trying to get closer to the walkway's entrance. She hoped the other woman wouldn't make a scene.

No such luck. She heard a commotion behind her and glanced back toward Harper. The woman was trying to get away from him. As she watched, he handcuffed her wrist to his. Several people were shouting at him in Spanish and a couple of El Paso cops were pushing through the growing crowd toward him and the young woman. She jerked her attention back to Morales, who was still standing near the entrance to the pedestrian walkway, watching the disturbance. Chris was close enough that even in the twilight's deepening shadows, she could see the mixture of puzzlement and wariness on her face.

Chris was just a few paces away from her when Morales suddenly focused on her and her eyes narrowed slightly. She started to move, up the walkway. Shit. Chris did not want to chase her into Mexico.

"Inez, stop. I have a message from your mother."

Morales hesitated, dropped the figure, then bolted straight into the crowds of people making their way down into El Paso.

Fuck. Chris followed, shouting in Spanish at people to move She wouldn't draw her gun here. Too many people, and for all she knew, somebody in the crowd might have a gun, too, and would start shooting back, even though she was shouting that she was police. People swore and yelled at her in Spanish as she bulled through the crowd, keeping her gaze locked on Morales's back. Fortunately, lights lined the bridge, and she couldn't merge with shadows. But she could definitely get lost in this crowd.

"Inez, stop!"

Morales hesitated, glanced back at her, then resumed her pace toward the checkpoint. Even in the flood of people, they were halfway there. Chris heard shouts behind her that sounded like law enforcement. Maybe Harper had gotten the El Paso police involved, which could be either good or bad. She somehow managed to increase her speed, but knocked hard into several people.

"Move! Police," she continued to shout. She was only a few paces behind Morales now. Just a few more—she lunged, and grabbed a handful of Morales's sweater. She locked her fingers in the fabric and hauled her badge out of her jacket pocket with her free hand. She held it up and the crowd fell back. Morales sank to her knees, panting.

"Stand up," Chris ordered. "There are too many people here. You could get hurt." She kept her grip on her sweater and pulled her to her feet. She put her badge back into her jacket pocket and did a quick search for weapons on Morales before she gently pushed her back toward El Paso when she didn't find any. She gripped Morales's sweater with one hand and held her badge up with the other, which helped part the crowd.

"Gucchi, you there?" Came Harper's voice in her ear.

"Yeah. I've got her. Heading back."

A uniformed El Paso cop was on her way up the walkway toward them, but she didn't have as difficult a time as Chris had. Probably the uniform. People moved out of her way immediately. A couple of catcalls accompanied her, and she shot glares in the direction they'd come from.

"Detective," she said with a nod. "I'm Corporal Bustos, here to escort you."

"Thanks."

Bustos kept her hand over her weapon and used her other arm to motion people out of the way. The walk back into El Paso wasn't nearly as difficult as the race up the bridge toward the checkpoint had been. Once they exited the walkway, Chris's escort motioned at a squad car parked nearby. Bustos opened the back passenger door and Chris finally released her hold on Morales's sweater. Her fingers tingled as she straightened them out.

"Ms. Morales, I'm Detective Chris Gutierrez with Albuquerque Police. I've been trying to reach you for several days. We have some questions about Victor Ramirez and Johnny Griego."

She didn't respond. The other cop caught Chris's eye with a "hate it when they do that" expression.

"Ms. Morales, we have reason to believe that you may have knowledge about at least one homicide. We need to take you in for questioning. I'm going to place you under arrest." She hated doing that, since they didn't have much on her, but Morales would walk if she didn't.

Still, Morales said nothing. The El Paso officer patted her down, and clicked the cuffs onto her wrists. She motioned at the open squad car door, placed her hand on Morales's head, and pushed her inside. Morales slumped onto the hard plastic seat. The officer closed the car's door as another El Paso police officer approached with Harper and the woman who had first come up to Chris. He'd uncuffed her, and she walked between him and the other cop, both of whom dwarfed her.

"Thanks, Corporal," Chris said to Bustos.

"Welcome to El Paso, huh?" The other El Paso cop said.

"Officer Mike Jeffries," Bustos said by way of introduction.

"Chris Gutierrez, APD."

"Dale Harper, APD," Harper said to Bustos. "So what've we got?" He asked.

"Morales in custody," Chris said. "Let's see if she'll talk to us. Can we use your facilities?"

"Absolutely." Bustos punctuated her statement with a nod.

"Great. Did you get any info from our other guest?" she asked Harper.

"She doesn't speak much English and she quit talking once Jeffries showed up."

"Give me a few minutes with her," Chris said.

Harper gave his "sure" shrug and Chris addressed the unknown woman in Spanish.

"I'm Chris Gutierrez with Albuquerque Police. I'd like to ask you a few questions."

She looked at her, fearful.

"Over here," Chris said, moving a few feet away from the squad car where Morales sat.

The woman followed her, pulling nervously on the hem of her jacket.

"Who were you trying to meet?"

She didn't answer.

"Please," Chris entreated. "We're trying to find the person responsible for at least one murder. You might have information that will help us."

She looked up at Chris, eyes wide. "Murder?"

"Yes. A man in Albuquerque. His name was Victor Ramirez. Do you know that name?"

She shook her head.

"What about the name Johnny Griego?"

"No."

Chris studied her. The myriad street lights provided plenty of light for her to see the other woman's features. If she was lying, she was a damn good actress.

"Did you ever hear of a man who called himself *el viento*?"

Her brow creased in puzzlement. "No."

"What about *La Catrina*?"

That got a reaction. A tightening around her mouth and a convulsive swallow.

"So you do know of someone called that?" Chris pushed.

She shrugged. "I have heard of her."

"Have you ever spoken to her?"

"No. Never," she said, adamant.

"Who were you supposed to meet tonight?"

"A woman," she said softly. "I—" she stopped and glanced over at the squad car again. "I thought it was you, because of the figure you carried."

"Was that some kind of signal?"

She nodded. "At first, I was supposed to meet a man, but I was told this morning that it would be a woman."

"Who told you?"

"Someone in Juárez."

"Who?"

"I don't know."

"How did they contact you?"

"Phone."

"Do you have the number?"

She nodded and dug into her purse and pulled out a cell phone. She found the number in her call log and handed it to her. Chris entered the number into her own phone and saved it. She gave the phone back. "Was it a man or a woman who spoke with you?" She put her phone in her jacket pocket.

"A woman. She said that I would meet another woman tonight in El Paso, who would help me."

"Help you with what?"

The woman stared down at her feet. When she spoke again, it was in a voice so low that Chris could barely hear it.

"Leave my husband."

"Why?"

She pulled the sleeves of her sweatshirt up, displaying a patchwork of bruises. "I have these all over. He doesn't hit my face, because that would be difficult to hide." She shook her arms and the sleeves slid down to cover them once again. "I have relatives in Phoenix. The woman I was supposed to meet was going to help me get there."

Chris stifled a frustrated, angry sigh. "What is your name?"

"Maria."

She looked over at Harper and said in English, "Give me your notepad." He walked it over, along with a pen, then retreated a few steps. Chris opened it to a blank sheet of paper and gave it to Maria. She switched back to Spanish. "Can you write your full name down, please? And your phone number?"

She complied, reluctantly, and gave the notepad and pen back.

"Do you live in Juárez?" Chris asked.

"My husband does."

She understood Maria's statement. Her home was no longer with her husband, and therefore, no longer Juárez. "Do you have somewhere in Juárez to stay for the next few days?"

Maria glanced at the walkway. "Yes."

Chris took one of her business cards out of her pocket and handed it to her. "Should you remember the names Victor Ramirez or Johnny

Griego, please call. My office line and my cell phone number are listed."

She took the card and slid it into her purse.

"It would be best for you to go back to Juárez right now," Chris said. "El Paso isn't my jurisdiction, but it is theirs." She gave a slight nod toward the squad car, where Jeffries and Bustos stood talking to Harper.

Maria nodded and clutched her purse against her chest. She turned and quickly walked away, toward the line of people headed back over the bridge, toward Mexico. Harper walked over.

"What did you get?"

"Pretty much nothing. She didn't know who she was meeting tonight. She said it was supposed to be a man, originally, but then she got a call this morning from a woman who told her she'd be meeting a woman."

"So her original meeting might have been with Ramirez or Griego?"

"Probably. She said the Day of the Dead figure was a signal. She thought I was the woman she was supposed to meet."

He rocked forward onto the balls of his feet, hands in his front pockets. "She didn't know she was supposed to meet Morales."

"No. Didn't react to either Ramirez's or Griego's names. Did react a bit to *La Catrina*, but probably because she's heard of her and maybe it was weird to her that some American cop who's not even from this area is asking her questions about that."

"Is she from Juárez?"

"For now. She claims she's trying to get away from an abusive husband. Said she has relatives in Phoenix."

"You want to track them down?"

"Don't think it'll be useful. However, the phone number of the woman she said called this morning might be. I did get that. Let's see who picks up." She took her business phone out of her back pocket and dialed the number. It rang four times and went to voicemail, which offered nothing but silence and a beep. Probably wouldn't pick up, since she was calling from an American number. She didn't leave a message. Didn't want to tip anybody off.

She shook her head at Harper. "The voicemail doesn't include a greeting."

"No surprise. Let's get Morales to Bustos's station, see if she'll talk."

She nodded, but watched the crowds of people streaming into El Paso for a night of reverie and maybe some shopping. Strange, how two cities could be so tightly bound and so similar in some ways yet so different in others. Cartel violence wracked Juárez, but rarely spilled over the border, because even the cartels knew they needed clear passage into the U.S. and forcing violence north was a sure way to put a damper on their illicit trade. So Mexicans experienced the brunt of the brutality and corruption. No easy answers here, where the border often blurred between those headed north and those who used to come south. She turned back to the squad car where Inez Morales sat. No easy answers anywhere.

"Detectives," Bustos said. "She wants to say something." She gestured with her head at the squad car where Morales sat. "To you, Gutierrez."

"I'm a little hurt," Harper said. "You get all the good stuff."

She gave him a look and went over to Bustos, who opened the back door. Chris leaned down a little so she could see Morales. "Yes?"

Morales turned her head and looked at her. "I did it. I killed Victor and Johnny."

# Chapter Twenty-two

"IF SHE DIDN'T do it, she was definitely an accessory," Harper said from the passenger seat. They'd finally left El Paso around three in the afternoon, the day after they'd arrested Morales, who had refused to talk to anybody and instead requested a lawyer.

"How would she even have known Griego was dead, after all? They just found him yesterday morning."

Chris nodded. "I know." She stared out the windshield as her headlights picked up the city limit sign of Socorro. It'd be fully dark before they got back to Albuquerque. She sped up a little.

"But?" Harper asked.

"But maybe that's all she was. An accessory."

He grunted. It sounded like "huh."

"It doesn't feel right. Why the hell would she just confess like that?"

"Because you collared her. Had she made it into Mexico, it'd be a different story. Her options ran out."

"Maybe." But something still didn't sit right about Morales's statement. She had refused to say anything more about the murders and instead only requested to be returned to Albuquerque for custody. That would take a while through bureaucratic channels as law enforcement sorted things out with Las Cruces and El Paso.

"Hell, Gucchi," Harper said after a while. "Doesn't feel right to me, either."

She smiled.

"But we can now say we have a suspect in custody, which might be useful to get certain parties off your back. Until we see how that shakes out, I'm going to strongly recommend that you stay a few more days with K.C."

"Okay, Dad."

"Yeah, if only it was that easy," he said. "So what's next?"

"Talk to Jerry, see what he wants us to do."

"You know he'll tell us to keep digging."

"Yeah," she agreed. "But we might be able to at least get a breather from public scrutiny with a suspect who's at the very least an accessory."

"Maybe we don't need to implement our preemptive Operation Gucchi's Gay after all. Burgess might just go bother somebody else now that Albuquerque's finest did their job to his standards."

"I don't know. Maybe we could out me as the former Christopher Gutierrez. That should make Burgess's head explode."

"At least you wouldn't have to change your name completely."

She grinned and they drove the rest of the way in silence. Harper dozed and Chris turned the police radio down a little. Why was she not completely buying Morales's confession? Maybe because she had refused to say anything more. Maybe Morales was savvy, and was waiting for a lawyer so she could cut some kind of deal. Or she was protecting someone. That sat in the back of her mind. Was Morales part of the *Catrina* network and she was willing to take the fall for someone else? She exited onto Lomas headed east, toward K.C.'s house.

"Maybe she's covering for somebody," Harper said.

"I was thinking that."

"Which means we have to find that person."

"I was thinking that, too."

"I love police work," he said sarcastically.

She turned from Girard onto Central Avenue. Though it was Sunday evening, people were out strolling through the Nob Hill arts and restaurant district and most parking places along the street were taken. She turned onto a side street and went a block south to Silver Avenue, where she found a spot. "Want to grab something to eat?"

"Nah. I'm going to head home. But be ready at Flying Star tomorrow at seven for your official ride to the station."

"All right." She popped the trunk and left the keys in the ignition and got out. Harper did, too, and went around to the driver's side as Chris retrieved her daypack and jacket out of the trunk. She closed it and set her backpack on top of it as she put her jacket on and arranged it to hide her gun. She slung her backpack over her shoulder and slapped the trunk so Harper would know he could drive away.

"See you tomorrow," Harper said to her out his window. "Get some sleep."

"Same to you." She tossed him a wave and crossed the street, headed back to Central. He pulled away from the curb and she took her phone out and dialed Dayna.

"Hey," Dayna said as she picked up. "Where are you?"

"Hi. Central. I'm going to Il Vicino to get something to go and take it over to K.C.'s."

"How'd everything go?"

"Okay. I'm just tired." She stopped walking so she could talk before she crossed Central. "And I miss you."

"I miss you, too. Any word on how long you'll need to stay at Kara's?"

She sighed. "Harper thinks another few days. I'll keep you posted. It's tied to developments in a case. Can't talk about it. Dammit."

Dayna laughed. "There's no danger ever of pillow talk from you, sweetie. I'm glad the CIA hasn't discovered this, because they'd recruit you for your incredible ability to keep secrets and then I'd never see you."

"Well, it kind of feels that way now. And if you keep making me feel the way you did Friday, you'll never get rid of me."

"That's my evil plan. Go grab some dinner and call me when you get to Kara's."

Chris smiled. "Okay. Catch you in a few. Bye." She signed off and crossed the street. Before she went in to the restaurant, she called K.C.

"Hey, *mujer*. Where are you?"

"Il Vicino," Chris said. "Have you guys had dinner?"

"Yes. But thanks for asking. And we have leftovers, in case you wanted to save your money."

"I think I'm wanting an Il Vicino calzone, *esa*."

"And I don't blame you. Who doesn't want one of those giant mounds of goodness? Go get one, and stop by the big house tonight if you want. We're just hanging out. We'll probably watch a movie a little later. Something that involves lots of car chases and cussing."

"So it was Sage's turn to pick?"

K.C. laughed. "Yeah. I'm guessing something like *Fast and Furious* nineteen or whatever number they're on."

She smiled. "I actually might like that. Let me put in an order. See you in a few."

"Excellent. Glad you're back. Bye."

She put her phone in her pocket and took a step toward the door.

"Chris."

She turned. "Hey, Trish. Wow. Twice in a few days I've seen you. I might actually start to think you're stalking me."

"I could say the same about you." Trish smiled up at her. She wore jeans and a jean jacket over a sweatshirt. She wore sporty well, too. "But I was going to call you. I heard from one of my Mexican contacts."

"Oh? Is it juicy?"

"Maybe." She glanced at the door to Il Vicino then back at Chris. "Have you had dinner?"

"No."

"I just ate, but if you want to eat here, I'll have a glass of wine and tell you what my contact said."

"You sure?"

"I wouldn't offer otherwise." Trish smiled again.

Chris shrugged. "Okay. Let's grab a table." They went in and found one toward the back. Trish hung her jacket on one of the chairs and they returned to the front counter to order and pay.

"I've got her glass of wine," Chris said to the cashier. She gestured at Trish.

He nodded.

"Thanks," Trish said. "Does this make me a paid informant?"

"If that's all it takes, sure."

Trish laughed and ordered, then went to the table they'd selected. Chris finished paying and joined her. The space, which mimicked a sleek European bistro, wasn't that big. It was a great place to have a beer and eat with friends or a date, so most people were focused on their tablemates and not the conversations of others. Chris put her backpack under the table against her feet. She kept her jacket on, but rolled up the sleeves. If Trish wondered why, she didn't ask.

"Hold on a sec," Chris said. She texted Dayna to let her know about the change in plans, then looked up as the server approached with their beverages. Chris put her phone away "Everything still good since I saw you...what? Two days ago?" she asked as she picked up her glass.

"Yes. You?"

"Yes." She took a drink, thinking that it was kind of weird, having dinner like this with her ex. It allowed more opportunities for personal talk, which she didn't want to deal with. Not tonight, and not with Trish.

"Okay, I called some people after you left on Friday," Trish said. Maybe she thought it was weird, too, and just wanted to get down to business. "Most didn't know much. One had heard vague rumors about a network run by someone who called herself 'Catrina,' but she hadn't had any clients who mentioned it."

"This person is on the Mexican side?"

"No. El Paso. Anyway, I heard back from a woman who works with battered women—also in El Paso—and she knew a lot more." She picked up her wine and sipped.

Chris waited.

"My contact said that the first time she heard about a network run by someone called *La Catrina,* was in the mid-nineties. But she said that people who have worked where she does longer than her said it started in the early nineties."

"Did the network just kind of appear or did it split off from another one? Maybe it was part of a cartel and this *Catrina* went her own way."

"I don't know. My contact didn't seem to think that. It was like one day it wasn't there, and then suddenly it was. I guess it makes sense that *La Catrina* would have been part of something else. You can't just build a network like that overnight."

Chris sat back. "Generally not, but if she'd already been operating on a smaller scale, it's possible that it just took a while for word to get out. She could be an organic, from the ground up leader."

"That's the other strange thing. Nobody knows who *La Catrina* is." She took another sip of wine. "It's possible for her to still be a leader. There are Mexican women who have been drug lords for decades, after all. But most of those women operate with other family members in their network and they run front businesses that at least have a veneer of legitimacy to cover the drug activity. *La Catrina* is a ghost. You'd think after all these years, somebody somewhere would have figured out who she was, like with the drug lords."

Chris nodded. "It is weird."

The server arrived with their order and left. Chris gratefully dug in.

"You sure you don't want anything?" she asked.

Trish shook her head. "I'm fine. Just had a huge dinner over at Nob Hill Bar and Grill." She watched Chris for a moment. "So my contact also told me that a few of her clients have dealt with *Catrina's* network. They all say the same thing. They had a phone number to call if there was an emergency that didn't involve Border Patrol or other law enforcement. Someone always showed up within an hour or two to help."

"Did they call if they were having trouble with men or possible sex trafficking?"

"Yes. Always. And they denied being mules for drugs."

"Doesn't mean they weren't." Chris took another bite and chewed. It was like a really good folded-over pepperoni pizza.

"My contact said that, too. And she did say that there are a few cases she's heard of where drugs made it over the border, but the mules were caught and claimed they were with *La Catrina*. I think we should just assume that there are probably drugs involved, but maybe not with some of the women who call the network for help."

"Sounds reasonable." Chris took a drink of club soda. "So did your contact say anything about *La Catrina's* involvement in murders?"

"Yes. But again, mostly rumors. A few bodies found here and there near the border that people say were killed by members of her network. Some accounts say there's a *Día de los Muertos* figure left behind."

"Were the bodies men or women?" Chris took another bite.

"She said all the bodies she knows about were men. She didn't know if any had been identified. If they were on the Mexican side, we might not ever know."

That was true. Chris finished up her calzone.

"One of the other things that I thought was interesting," Trish said, "was that the clients my contact worked with who had dealings with this network say that they got the impression that there wasn't a central leadership."

"Oh? So how did it function?"

"She's not sure. But from talking to her, and the way it sounds, it might be like how some of the guerrilla cells operated in El Salvador in the eighties. Sort of small, mobile cells that could carry out certain operations and then disband until the next time."

"Huh. Like how some of the environmental and animal rights groups operate. Leaderless resistance."

Trish looked at her appreciatively. "That's what I was thinking. At least, that's what it sounded like to me. And that might explain why it's been difficult to pinpoint a definitive leader."

"But even those groups have a propaganda arm. A public face that disclaims all responsibility for whatever actions leaderless cells take." She moved slightly so the server could take her plate. "*La Catrina* doesn't seem to have something like that. So if it's been operating all these years as an amorphous leaderless resistance, that says something about the commitment of its members."

Trish nodded and sipped her wine. "Most times, there's a core of committed, and then fringe players who might come and go and participate in some direct actions but not others. That might be how this particular network has been able to survive this long. A constant influx of new blood. Among that new blood are the next generation of the committed core, who then groom the next."

"Are there Americans in the network?"

"My contact says yes. Some of her clients commented on women who helped them who spoke Spanish, but could switch to American-accented English. I'm not sure we could call those women committed core members, but it seems that they're involved to a certain extent."

Chris stared at her half-empty glass. Something occurred to her. "Like volunteers for a battered women's shelter, maybe. They don't have to do something every day. Maybe not even every month. But they're on call for crises."

Trish nodded. "I was thinking that, too. Volunteers that mobilize quickly, perform a specific task, then drop off the radar. Not that they were ever on the radar, but you know what I mean."

She nodded.

"So is it hard for you, to have to find a murderer even though the victim was—um, not the best person?" Trish asked after a few moments.

"Nobody's squeaky clean." She caught Trish's gaze. "But yeah, there are a lot of screwed-up situations and there are lots of people who get away with terrible things. But vigilante justice isn't the best answer."

"But maybe sometimes it's an understandable answer."

"Maybe. Doesn't make it right. Two wrongs, after all, don't make something right."

Trish looked down at the table. "You know, I guess I never thought about the things you have to deal with as a cop." She looked up at Chris again. "Or how you have to put your personal feelings aside, even if the victim does awful things.

"Even assholes are sometimes victims," she said with a wry smile. "Doesn't matter how I might feel about who they are or what they might have done. But yes, sometimes it's difficult."

Trish finished her wine and set the glass down, though she toyed with its stem. "After what Graciela said about Victor Ramirez, I didn't feel sorry for him anymore. I felt sorry for any family or friends he might have had. Especially if they didn't know what he'd done or was involved in. But him?" She shook her head. "Not sorry. I think I feel kind of guilty about that."

"No need to. We all make choices. Some of us make really bad ones. Ramirez's caught up with him. And whoever killed him made a bad choice, too, because it's going to affect that person's life and the lives of his or her family and friends."

Trish sighed. "And on that note, thanks for the wine."

"You're welcome. Thanks for the conversation."

"I'll let you know if any of my other contacts have anything interesting to add." Trish stood and put her jacket on while Chris picked up her backpack and slung it to her shoulder. She pushed the sleeves of her own jacket down and followed Trish out of the restaurant.

"I enjoyed this," Trish said out on the sidewalk.

"Same here." Chris smiled down at her. "Catch you later and take care."

"You, too." She gently pulled her into a quick hug. "Bye," she said as she released her. She walked the few yards to the corner and crossed to the other side of Central before she walked east.

Chris watched her, thinking that she should have offered to walk her to her car. Would that violate ex-girlfriend protocol? Maybe. But then Trish stopped a half-block away and got into her car, parked along the curb, and pulled into traffic. Out of habit, Chris scanned the area before she headed to K.C.'s. Light from Nob Hill businesses spilled across the sidewalks, illuminating pedestrians as they strolled along Central, both sides, or stood talking outside of various establishments. A few were smoking. A lone woman stood almost directly across the street from her, talking on her phone. She started walking west and Chris stared at her. *Oh, hell no.*

The woman finished talking on the phone, but kept walking. She passed under a street light and Chris swore under her breath. Even across the four lanes of Central, she recognized Mary Baca. Had she managed to track Chris here? Doubtful. More likely, she happened to be hanging out in Nob Hill and probably didn't even know Chris was in the neighborhood. But if she had, that could be a problem. She might even have called someone like Frank Rand to continue surveillance. She swore again, this time in Spanish.

Her personal cell rang with a particular tone.

"Hi, Sage."

"Hi. We figured you might have decided to eat at the restaurant, but I had a popcorn fit and I'm at La Montanita to buy some to pop. Do you want a ride?"

"Yes, actually. Where are you parked?"

"Out back, right on the curb. I'm driving K.C.'s car."

"Perfect. I'm going to come in through the front. Are you in your car now?"

"No, but I'm about to be. What's up?"

"Fucking Mary Baca, that's what." Chris started walking east along Central.

"Shit. Where is she now?"

"Walking west on Central. I don't know for sure if she saw me, but I did see her on her phone right across from Il Vicino and I'm guessing that she might have."

"Fuck. And she might have called somebody else."

"Exactly. Have the passenger side open. If you see her—do you know what she looks like?"

"Yes. And if I see her or anybody who looks asshole-ish hanging around, I'll call you. Where are you?"

"About three minutes away. Hanging up now." Chris put the phone back in her jacket pocket and crossed Central at Carlisle. The natural foods co-op stood tucked in the corner of a little shopping area on the other side of Central. Usually the small parking area out front was full, and tonight was no exception. Sage had lucked out finding a spot right on the street out back.

Chris entered the store, cut through the produce section, and took the public stairs up to the back entrance. She could see K.C.'s Subaru through the double glass doors at the curb, parked a little to her left. Two guys dressed in baggy torn jeans and flannel shirts opened one of the doors to exit and Chris followed right behind them.

The passenger side door swung open just as she reached the car and she tossed her backpack into the back before she ducked into the front seat, pulled the door closed, and slumped down.

"Sorry about this," Chris said.

"Not your fault. Mary fucking Baca better hope she didn't see you tonight." Sage gave Chris's arm a squeeze and pulled away from the curb. "I'm going to drive around a little." She checked her rearview mirror. "Stay down."

"Do you say that to K.C.?"

She laughed. "What do you think?"

Chris grinned. "I think she'd better, when you do." She worked her phone out of her pocket and dialed Harper's number.

"Yo," he answered.

"Hey, heads up. I had dinner at Il Vicino tonight and woman on the scene Mary Baca was in the area."

"Where?"

"Across the street when I was leaving, about ten minutes ago. She was standing talking on the phone then walked west."

"Did she see you?"

"Don't know. She might have. She might have been calling for reinforcement spies with big cameras."

He grunted. "Maybe. Where are you now?"

"K.C.'s car." She told him what she'd just done.

"Sounds good. Guess we'll know in the next couple of days if she saw you or not. We'll talk to the boss-man tomorrow, see if we can release the news about our suspect. That might delay any planned posts about you having pizza. God forbid a cop wants to eat now and again." His tone was dry. "Got you covered, Gucchi."

"Thanks."

"Okay, then." He hung up and Chris sighed.

"I am really starting to hate the Internet," she said.

"People like Legal Eyes are why we can't have nice things." Sage turned left and drove on a straightaway for a few minutes. Then she turned left again.

"K.C.'s going to kill me. I've got you playing cop," Chris said.

"No, she's going to be pissed that she wasn't here to play, too." She smiled. "True." Then she fell silent. "So the reason I ate at the restaurant was because I ran into Trish outside."

"Oh?"

"She had just had dinner elsewhere and was going to her car. She said she had some more info from some of her contacts about the larger context of this case. So I bought her a glass of wine."

"Interesting. You haven't seen her in two years and now you've spoken to her three times and seen her twice in a week." Sage glanced in the rearview mirror again.

"I know. Weird."

Sage shrugged. "Maybe it's closure time. Or maybe you need something from her."

Chris frowned. "Need what? I'm perfectly happy, thank you."

She chuckled. "Not *that* kind of need. In a more cosmic sense. She's already provided information that helped with your case. Maybe that's why she's moved into your orbit again." She stopped at a light. "And maybe she needs something from you, too. In a cosmic sense." She flashed Chris a grin. "Not to suggest Dayna isn't capable of fulfilling your deepest cosmic needs."

A flush of embarrassment heated Chris's neck. "Okay. Moving along. Are you noticing if anyone's following us?"

She laughed. "I am in full notice mode and no, I'm not seeing anything to suggest that."

Chris sat up and stared out the back window for a bit while Sage drove. She relaxed. "Looks good. Let's head back."

A few minutes later Sage pulled up in front of the house she shared with K.C. and got out. "Looks clear," she said. She opened the back passenger side door behind Chris and took the bag of unpopped corn off the back seat. Chris scanned the area before she got out and retrieved her backpack. She waited while Sage locked the car up.

"You want to watch a movie with us?" Sage asked.

Had Chris not seen Mary Baca, she might have still been in the right frame of mind to hang out. But now, she just wanted to retreat into Kara's house, lock the doors, and draw the blinds. "I think I'm going to go call Dayna and crash. Maybe next time. But I will go in and say hi to Kase." She followed Sage into the house and twenty minutes later went out the back to Kara's. She unlocked both inner and outer doors and locked them behind her before she tossed her backpack onto the couch and sank down next to it. She speed-dialed Dayna.

"Hi," Dayna said, a velvety warmth in her voice that washed over Chris in a welcome wave.

"Hey. I really miss you."

"Same here. So how was your evening with your past?"

Chris half-laughed. "Got a story for you." She settled back into the cushions, and with Dayna's voice in her ear, the stress of her day fell away. By the time she crawled into bed, the only thing on her mind was Dayna.

# Chapter Twenty-three

CHRIS CHECKED THE Legal Eyes blog at her desk the next morning. Nothing about her or Il Vicino. The latest post was one of their standard "stop the illegals from overrunning the country" diatribes, with contact information of relevant members of congress and senators listed. They generally posted one or two a day, so she'd check back that afternoon. She picked up her coffee cup and went to Harper's office so they could go to the lieutenant's office together.

"Sorry we don't get to run Operation Out Gucchi." Harper said when they returned to his office. He sat down behind his desk and Chris took a chair on the other side.

"Part of the drawbacks, I guess, when you're not really closeted. Can't run dummy ops."

He shrugged. "I liked the fake girlfriend idea, though. Good red herring. So what do you think about Morales?"

"Still not sure. Yeah, she confessed, but I still think there's something we're missing. Not like she talked to us at all yesterday."

He leaned back. "Smart enough to lawyer up and wait for extradition. Let's think for a minute that she didn't pop Ramirez or Griego and she confessed to protect someone. Who would that be?"

"Someone she cares about."

"Or someone who threatened her."

"Possibly. What if she's part of the *Catrina* network? That's another reason to confess, to protect it. And if she is an accessory to the murders, she'll know enough details to make it plausible that she is the killer and she can just plead guilty and avoid a trial. *Catrina* never comes up, except in whatever terms she decides to describe the figure at the murder scenes, and she goes and does time."

"You don't think she'll rat out anybody else in the network?"

Chris shook her head. "Think about it. If she is part of the network, she knows the risks. They probably have a protocol to follow if someone gets caught. And if someone does talk, I'm guessing the network will find a way to take that person down, whether in prison or not."

He looked skeptical. "You think it has that kind of reach?"

"Sure. If they're running in conjunction with cartels and other illicit organizations along the border, they can contract someone to take somebody down in prison."

Her business cell rang and she picked it up off her desk and looked at it. "Unknown," she said to Harper before she answered and engaged her recording app. "Gutierrez."

"Is this the detective who spoke with Juana Morales?" asked a woman in Spanish.

"Yes," she responded, also in Spanish.

"My name is Marta Reyes. I am Inez Morales's cousin."

"Thank you for calling. May I ask you a few questions?" Chris reached for her pen and legal pad. Juana clearly took her business card after all and passed the numbers to her niece. She scribbled the name on the pad along with "Morales cousin" and held it up for Harper.

"Yes," Reyes said. "But I am calling to tell you that my cousin did not murder those men."

"Your cousin confessed."

"I know. She was trying to protect my sister."

Chris picked up her pen again. "Why?"

"Because my sister is the one who killed them."

*Fuck*. She wrote, "Says her sis killed G and R" and held up the tablet for Harper. He read it and groaned softly.

"Where is your sister now?"

"I'm not sure. She called me this morning and told me that Inez had been arrested in El Paso and that Inez was going to tell the police that she had killed Victor Ramirez and Johnny Griego."

Chris frowned. "How did your sister know that Inez was arrested?"

"She saw it happen."

"How?"

"She was on the Santa Fe Street Bridge, coming down to the American side and she saw Inez running through the crowd, back toward Mexico. She was caught and taken back down to the American side."

"What was your sister doing on the bridge?" Chris was writing so fast her hand hurt.

"She had a message for Inez."

"Inez told her she was at the bridge that night?"

"Yes. She was meeting someone else."

Chris put her pen down and flexed her fingers then picked it up again. "Who?"

Silence. Then, "An acquaintance."

"Name?"

"I don't know."

Chris doubted that. "What message did your sister want to give to Inez?"

"I don't know."

She doubted that, too. "Ms. Reyes, I can't help Inez if I don't have more information."

"My sister will call you."

"What's her name?"

The line went dead.

Chris checked the display. "She hung up on me."

"Kids today," Harper said. "No manners." He motioned at the legal pad on Chris's desk. "So our killer isn't Morales."

"We don't know that for sure. The cousin's name is Marta Reyes. She says her sister was at the bridge the other night when we collared Morales. Hell, for all we know, Reyes is trying to protect Morales and she made up this whole thing."

Harper grunted. "Okay, here's what we know. Morales has two cousins who are sisters, and she's close to them. One was assaulted—probably sexually—by parties unknown but it was a bad situation and Morales went to help her out. Probably the other cousin was there to help, too."

Something clicked. "Jesus. Maybe it was Ramirez." She looked over at him. "Maybe he was the guy who assaulted Reyes."

"Huh." He nodded. "I could see that. Motive for the sister to ice him."

"Shit, it's motive for Morales to kill him, too. And frankly, motive for Reyes."

"True. So we may be dealing with a family cover-up here, and everybody's trying to take the heat for everybody else."

"Not quite," Chris said. "Reyes is ratting out her own sister to save her cousin."

Harper leaned back in his chair. His head almost touched the cubicle wall.

"So what does that mean?" he asked. "The sister is odd man out? Morales wants to take a dive for Reyes, but Reyes isn't having that and rather than turn herself over—if she did it—she turns her sister over? That's cold."

"Love or money, Harper. You said it. Family love gone bad in this case, maybe."

"Okay, I'll buy it, but something's still not right. Reyes says her sister was at the bridge and saw Morales get arrested."

"Reyes said her sister was trying to get a message to Morales. Reyes claims she doesn't know what." Chris stood next to her desk, hands on her hips. She stared at the opposite cubicle wall, thinking.

"We don't know for sure that Reyes is telling the truth about her sister and the bridge," she said after a few moments. "It could have been Reyes on the bridge, waiting for Morales."

"Or that could have been Reyes you talked to after we got Morales in the car. Only she gave you a fake name," Harper said.

"I don't think so. The voice on the phone was different than hers. One way to find out." Chris used her business cell to call the number Maria had given her at the Santa Fe Street Bridge. A few rings and she was sent to voicemail where a woman's voice instructed the caller to leave a message for Maria.

She hung up. "The number Maria gave me at the bridge to contact her goes to voicemail for someone named Maria."

Harper grunted. "Okay, so where are we? One woman says she did it, one says another did, and that one we're not even sure is on the level."

"That's about right."

"And if a Mexican national committed the murders, that's a giant clusterfuck in terms of extradition. We have to bring the feds in."

Chris nodded and rubbed her forehead. She felt a headache coming on. "I'm beginning to really hate this case."

"Just now?" He grinned and stood. "Hell, you're late, Gucchi. So what's next?"

"You tell me. Morales is in limbo until she's extradited. I'm not going to stop that process because somebody called claiming to be her cousin and says Morales didn't do it. We need a bit more than that," she said with extra sarcasm. "I'll let Jerry know about it, see if he wants to hold off on the announcement about a suspect."

"Sounds good. I'm going to go back through everything. Check Griego's phone records again. See if anything sticks out."

"Here." Chris wrote two phone numbers on a sticky note and handed it to him. "The top number is Maria's and the bottom is the number she gave me that she said was used to tell her Griego wasn't coming."

"How'd she get it?"

"Call log."

"Kind of strange, don't you think, that a secret network wouldn't take precautions to do an ID block or something?" He rocked forward onto the balls of his feet.

"Maybe. But my guess is it's a burn phone, so it doesn't matter if the number shows up, since it'll be out of use soon."

He clicked his tongue against his teeth. "Maybe Griego called it before he got popped. Speaking of, the body should be back in Albuquerque tomorrow. We might get autopsy results this week. I'll call the Cruces office and see if the investigators found anything at the crime scene that'll lead us to a perp."

"All right. I'll go to Jerry's office right now. And stop by Tony's, see if he can get a fix on the number Marta called from."

"Okay, then." He left her cubicle and she rummaged in one of her desk drawers for the bottle of Tylenol she kept. She took a couple with her now-cold coffee, grimaced at the taste, and left to find the lieutenant. Yes, she was really hating this case.

"SINCE MORALES CONFESSED, she gets to be our suspect in custody," Chris said as she entered Harper's cubicle a little over a half-hour later. She took a seat across the desk from him. "But Jerry's not releasing her name or gender. 'Suspect in custody' is how he wants to play this. And they're not doing a formal press conference, so we don't have to hide."

"Good. When's the announcement?"

"Evening news."

He nodded. "It'll be interesting to see how Burgess plays it."

She snorted. "Conspiracy. He'll claim APD is only saying that in order to satisfy public opinion."

"Speaking of, nothing new yet on Legal Eyes. Still the post from this morning."

"Good. But remember, Baca didn't post those photos of us until a day or two after she took them. If she got photos of me at Il Vicino, she may still post them." And that put Chris's stomach in a knot, because she had been with Trish, and that would mean that Legal Eyes would target her, too. If the photos were any good. If they were as crappy as the ones of Chris and Harper, then it would be a lot harder to identify Trish.

"You're assuming Baca saw you. Did she have a camera?"

"Just her phone. And she was talking on it when I left."

He shrugged, a "there you have it" expression on his face.

"So have you found anything in Griego's phone records yet?"

"Yeah, actually. He called that number Maria gave you."

She leaned forward. "Interesting. When?"

"Once. Friday evening at six thirty-one. It lasted thirty seconds, so I'm guessing he left a message."

"Like maybe 'I'll see you in El Paso' or something?"

"Maybe." He leaned back and put his hands behind his head. "I had a hunch and I checked it with the text he got about the package waiting at the bridge. Same number."

"Even more interesting."

"Here's my new theory," he said. "Morales was in contact with Griego. But she's also somehow involved with the coyote network that Ramirez was dealing with. So she hooks up with him in Cruces, and they have to rendezvous south of the city with unknown party number three. Possibly the person with the Mexican number. That party shoots Griego."

Chris frowned. "Not bad. Or they were on their way to El Paso and Morales pulls a gun and forces Griego onto that exit ramp where party number three is waiting. Morales gets out of the truck, tells Griego to roll down his window, and party number three shoots him. Or Morales is the shooter."

Harper shrugged. "But if Morales acted alone, where was her car? She had to have transportation to get to El Paso. It's possible she called Griego and told him she had car trouble out there, and could he come and pick her up."

"That's good, too," Chris conceded. "Doesn't require a third party. She's parked on the ramp and maybe standing outside her car waiting for him. He pulls up and she's at his truck before he can get out, but he rolls down his window as she approaches and she shoots him." She stopped, thinking. "But it's still an awkward angle, especially if you're not that familiar with guns. Plus, it's dark out."

"She got really close."

"Fuck," Chris muttered. "This case is nuts." She stood. "I'm going to go back through my notes. We're missing something."

"I'll let you know if I get anything else."

"Same here." She returned to her office and spent the next hour reading through all the notes she had typed. She started to go back through her original written notes when her desk phone rang, an El Paso area code showing up in the viewer.

"Gutierrez," she answered.

"Detective. Eileen Bustos."

"Hey, Corporal. Call me Chris. Do you have something?"

"Eileen. And yeah, we do. We've located Morales's vehicle. Gray Ford Escort. It was parked on a residential street about a half-mile from the bridge. I'll fax you the registration info we got from the VIN. Got a pen? I'll run the VIN by you if you want to run your own search."

"Got one."

Bustos recited the letters and numbers slowly.

"Nice work. Can you somehow get the car back to us in Albuquerque?"

"Doing the paperwork and making arrangements."

"One of us will come down to accompany. Just let us know."

"Definitely. Got something else, too. You're going to like this. Found a nine mil Glock in the trunk. We've got it in evidence here, but we figured you'd need it for ballistics testing so we're holding it until the paperwork's done and we can turn it over. Here's the serial number so you can run it." She recited it and Chris wrote it down.

"That *is* some good news," Chris said. "Let me know when we can come down and pick it up."

"I will. And Morales still isn't talking with the exception of agreeing to extradition through her lawyer."

Chris pinched the bridge of her nose. "We're announcing on the evening news that there's a suspect in custody in El Paso. So you might get some calls from press after that."

"Are you releasing her name?"

"No. Not yet. Probably in a couple of days." Hell, by that time, they might have yet another suspect in custody who also had confessed.

"Thanks for the heads-up. I'll keep you posted," Bustos said.

"Appreciate it. Thanks for the call."

"Sure. Later."

Chris hung up and dialed Harper's desk. He answered and she filled him in on what Bustos had said.

"You think that's the gun used in the murders?"

"I'd like to. But if the killer was so careful about cleaning up casings, why not file the serial number off of it?"

"People make mistakes."

That was true, but it wasn't sitting right with her. "I don't even want to think about this for a few. I'm going to finish up some other reports and then I'll come back to this case. I need to let a few things sit."

"Good idea. Let me know when you're ready to head out."

Shit. She'd forgotten that she wasn't staying at her house. Another source of irritation. "Yeah."

"Okay, then." He hung up and Chris replaced the receiver and stared sightlessly at the papers and files on her desk. She rubbed her eyes with the heels of her palms.

"Fuck you, Burgess," she muttered. "And your fucking bullshit xenophobic crusade." She went to get another cup of coffee and then settled in for a few hours of getting caught up on other cases. Her desk phone rang an hour after she'd gotten coffee.

"Yeah, Tony. What've you got?" she answered.

"The number that called you was from a burn phone. Mexican number. No way to figure out where it was bought. You want the number?"

"Yeah."

He read it off and she wrote it down. It wasn't the number Maria had given her. "Thanks," she said.

"Sure." He hung up and Chris added the information to her call log with regard to the case and then to her notes. She then called the number back. It rang twice then bumped to voicemail, which consisted of no greeting. Just silence and then a beep.

"This message is for Marta Reyes," Chris said in Spanish. "Please call Chris Gutierrez in Albuquerque. You have the number." She hung up and went back to her other cases. She needed a new perspective on the Morales situation. And at some point, she would have to tell *Abuelita* what had happened. She imagined the press that would generate. Daughter of a most likely undocumented Mexican woman murders two American citizens. Her stomach clenched. Maybe a few hours away from it would help. But not yet. She called Tony back.

"Yeah."

"I need a vehicle registration check. Here's the VIN." She recited it and he repeated it back to her. "And I need a gun check. Here's the serial." She gave that to him and he repeated it, too.

"Okay. Give me a few," he said.

"Thanks." She went back to working on another report for another case, but kept checking the time for the evening news. At twenty to five, her desk phone rang. Tony's number showed up in the ID.

"Yeah," she answered.

"The car is registered to Inez Morales. Last known address is here in Albuquerque." He provided it and Chris wrote it down, though she knew it was the apartment Morales had shared with Britney Luna.

"The gun?"

"Legally purchased two years ago by Johnny Griego, who resided at—" he rustled around then read the address.

She recognized it as Griego's apartment. "Did he report it stolen?"

"I checked on that and nothing came up."

"Okay. Thanks."

"Yeah." He hung up.

She replaced the phone on its cradle and went to Harper's workspace. He kept a small portable television on his file cabinet, and he'd already turned it on.

"Tony ran the gun and the car," she said.

"And?"

"Griego's gun, legally purchased. Morales's car."

He leaned back. "Huh. So did she borrow it to pop Ramirez?"

"I don't think so. Griego seemed surprised when we told him Ramirez was dead. Maybe he loaned it to her for protection when she moved to Cruces. They'd had a thing, after all. Or so her mom says. Or she could have taken it out of his apartment on one of her visits. Especially if they were seeing each other off and on."

"Makes sense. Or she knew where it was and took it when he wasn't looking." He gestured at the television. "Let's see how bossman's message turned out." He turned his desk chair so he could watch and Chris pulled a chair from the front of his desk to the side he was on so she could see better. They sat through fifteen minutes of other local news and commercials before a photo of Monica Lewiston, department spokeswoman, appeared on the screen. Her statement about the arrest appeared in quotes next to the picture. A suspect had been arrested in Texas for the murders of Victor Ramirez and John Griego and more details would be forthcoming. The scene cut to footage of Ramirez's house roped off with crime scene tape the night of his murder, press and police milling around the periphery, then to a daylight shot of Griego's truck on the ramp. Troopers diverted traffic at the ramp's entrance and crime scene techs worked on the pickup. That must have been before she and Harper had arrived.

The news channel's Las Cruces reporter briefly re-capped the murders then the Albuquerque newscasters reappeared. One thanked the Cruces reporter, reiterated that more information would be available later, and they cut to another story.

"Not bad," Harper said. "That should keep Legal Eyes busy for the next couple of days. They'll probably be calling us to demand more information."

"No doubt." Chris moved her chair back to its original position. "Let me do a few more things before we head out," she said, thinking that the newscast might flush Marta out or, better, her mysterious sister.

He grunted something in response and she went back to her desk. The announcement took some heat off them, but it also left her uneasy, because of Marta's refutation of her cousin's confession. If Morales didn't commit either murder, then what the hell made her decide to take the heat for both crimes? She faced life in prison. Who or what was worth that? She picked up the photo of the *Catrina* figure found with Ramirez and compared it to the photo on her phone of the figure found with Griego. Both *Catrina,* but different incarnations of her. Did that mean anything to the shooter? Or maybe shooters. Were there two separate killers? She put the photo of the figure found with Ramirez back in the file.

Two separate killers. She mulled that for a while. But if the gun found in Morales's car could be tied to both murders, which two did the deeds? She looked at the time on her computer desktop. Nearly six, so she called K.C., who picked up almost immediately.

"Hey, *mujer*. When can we expect you tonight? Or are you going to stay at the station?"

"Hey. No, I can't take much more of this place today. I'm leaving in about five minutes. Do you want me to pick anything up for dinner?"

"Hell, no. We've got you covered. Just come in. We'll be fully clothed and behaving staidly."

Chris laughed. "What's the point, then?"

"Tease. Good thing I know that about you." She paused. "You sound tired."

"Yeah, I am. Very."

"Saw the news. Guess the trip to El Paso panned out."

"Yes and no. Things I can't talk about."

K.C. made a sympathetic noise. "Well, come on over when you get here. At least let us feed you."

She smiled. "I'm on my way."

"Good. Bye."

"Bye." She glanced across the room to Harper's cubicle and saw that he was on his way over to hers, so she texted Dayna to let her know she was on her way to K.C.'s and she'd call her a little later. She looked up at Harper, who was standing in her doorway.

"Yo, Gucchi. I'm hungry and tired of this place. Can we go, now?" He tried to sound plaintive, like a kid asking his mom if they could finally leave some boring adult meeting.

"Fuck, yes." She organized her paperwork, closed programs on her computer and logged out, then shut her desk lamp off.

"Let's get an extra hour of sleep. I think we earned it. I'll pick you up tomorrow morning at eight at Flying Star unless something comes up," he said as she grabbed her jacket and backpack.

"Please don't say that, Harper. You'll jinx us."

He gave her a wry smile and followed her out of the station.

# Chapter Twenty-four

HER WORK CELL phone was ringing. Chris dragged herself out of sleep and automatically reached for it, mind already scrolling through several possibilities. It was the ring tone that deployed for unknown or unrecognized numbers. Who the hell was calling her at this hour on her work cell? She glanced at Kara's clock. The glowing blue numbers read 1:34.

She cleared her throat before she answered. "Gutierrez." She somehow remembered to engage the app to record the conversation.

"Inez Morales did not kill those men," said a woman's voice in Spanish.

Chris sat up, fully awake. "Who is this?" she answered in Spanish as she reached with her free hand to turn on the bedside lamp.

"Someone who knows the truth."

"You're going to have to do better than that." She got out of bed and crossed the floor to her backpack, where she'd stashed a notepad and pen.

"Inez did not do it."

"I'm sorry, but a nameless voice on a phone is not going to change the fact that she confessed." She didn't recognize the voice, but guessed it might be Marta Reyes's sister. She sat down on the bed and used the nightstand as a writing surface. "Tell me who you are and I'll try to help Inez if what you're saying is true."

"I'm the person who killed Ramirez and Griego."

"I don't believe you." She goaded the caller, trying to get more information.

"I used an American gun, a Glock nine millimeter. Easy enough to get. I shot Ramirez twice in the chest, then once in the crotch, then twice more in the chest. I used that order on him because usually when I shoot a man who is standing up in the crotch first, the man bends over and I don't get a clear shot at his chest. I left *La Catrina* with him." She recited it like she might have been reading from a shopping list.

"Where did you put the figure?"

"On his chest."

"Inez could have told you that," Chris prodded.

"She doesn't have the stomach to do that part of the work."

The work? This was sounding more and more like an organized hit.

"She is good at the set-up," the voice continued dispassionately, "but I am the shooter. Inez waited in the car in Albuquerque when I killed Ramirez. She does not know the details because she didn't go into the house. Then we had to find Griego. She made contact with him, and they agreed to continue with a pick-up for Ramirez." She stopped and when she continued, there was something like pride in her voice.

"Inez is very good at the set-up," she repeated. "She called Griego and told him she had car trouble. She waited in the car then, too, hiding in the back seat. I stood outside. We look a bit alike, she and I. He rolled his window down when I walked over to his truck. I shot him in the head first, then the crotch. The angle was difficult to do the crotch shot first. I had to get closer to the vehicle and he would have seen that I was not Inez by then, so I had to take the head shots first. I left *La Catrina* there, too."

"Where?"

"On his lap."

Chris scrawled the details as fast as her hand would let her. "Why exactly did either you or Inez kill them?"

"Detective," she said with pronounced patience, "Inez did not kill them. I did. And they died because that is what was decided. Ramirez hurt many, many women. Those he did not hurt directly he gave to men who did. We tried to take care of this a few years ago, but *el viento* — that is what he liked to call himself — left El Paso for Albuquerque, and he was very careful when he made trips back to the border because someone warned him that we were seeking justice. And then we decided to go to him, because of what he did to Marta."

Chris heard a shrug in the voice, and an undertone as cold and hard as a gun barrel. This was a woman who could do what she described. Who else was involved? "What did he do?" she asked, though she already knew. Her suspicions about the assault had been confirmed.

"He raped and beat her. That is why we shoot the crotch. A good message, no?"

She ignored the last bit. "I thought he was avoiding the border. Was Marta in the States when it happened?"

"No. He went to Juárez because he wanted to send us a message. We had disrupted a few of his dealings."

"And Griego?" Chris asked.

"He helped Ramirez traffic women and he profited from it. We warned him. We always warn them first. But some don't want to repent."

Vigilantes. Chris wrote the word and underlined it. "What is your name?" She didn't expect the caller to give it, but she asked anyway.

Pause. "*La Catrina.*"

Her pen hovered over the paper. "That would mean you're nearly fifty or older, depending on how long the *Catrina* network has been active. And you don't sound fifty. Especially if you're Marta's sister."

"*Catrina* never grows old, Detective. And she never dies. There have been many of us over the years. We are all *Catrina*. When I am gone, there will be others."

A self-perpetuating network. Like what Trish had suggested. Loose cells, maybe a core leadership somewhere that brought others in, but no true hierarchy. "How many?"

"Too many to count over the years. None of us truly knows. That is what keeps us effective."

"Who was the first *Catrina*?"

"No one knows for certain. *Catrina* has always operated that way."

And no doubt that was something else that kept it effective. She shifted topics. "Will you turn yourself in for the murders of Victor Ramirez and Johnny Griego?"

"I am not American, Detective. It is not so simple."

"If you agree to turn yourself in, you can be prosecuted in Mexico. You won't have to leave your country." And as long as the process was to get that kind of prosecution in accordance with international agreements, at least it would get under way. The thought of the real murderer—if the caller was telling the truth—getting away with the crime galled her. No matter how much work she had to do to prepare for a prosecution like this, it was better than knowing a perpetrator had walked.

"If I don't, what will happen to Inez?"

"She's confessed. She'll get a hearing and if she sticks to her confession, she'll be sentenced."

"She doesn't know the details of the crimes," the caller said flatly. "It can be proven that she was not the one who killed them."

"If she continues to keep silent, no amount of questioning will change her situation."

Silence. Finally, after a few moments, the caller spoke. "I will call you again, Detective." And she hung up.

Chris finished scrawling down what had been said, as close as she could remember, then stared into space. After a few minutes, she called Harper.

"Yo. You okay?" he answered, voice graveled with sleep.

"Yeah. Fine. Just got a phone call on my work cell. I think it was Reyes's sister. There may be some new complications in the Morales case. Wanted to talk it through with you while it's still fresh."

"Give me a minute."

She leaned back against Kara's headboard while Harper did whatever he was doing. Why couldn't shit ever be simple? Just this once?

"Okay," Harper said. "Hit me."

Chris picked up her notepad. "Might be a long night, Harper."

"Won't be the first time."

So true. She sighed and told him what she remembered. By the time she was able to try to go back to sleep, it was past three in the morning.

"FUCK," CHRIS MUTTERED as she glared at her computer screen and the photo on the Legal Eyes blog. Her desk phone rang. She checked the ID. Harper.

"You seen Legal Eyes?"

"Yeah," she answered. "I'm looking at it now."

"On the plus side, Baca seems to think you're with whoever that is in the picture. It'll take the heat off Dayna."

"Thanks, Harper," she said sarcastically. "I feel so much better, now."

"It's a shitty photo," he said. "You can barely tell that's you. And if they hadn't posted other shitty photos of you, it could be anyone. Even a guy. As for the other woman — that was Trish at the restaurant with you, right?"

"Yes."

"She doesn't look anything like Dayna. And they did give you credit for having a suspect in custody."

"And they turned it into some kind of near-porn. 'APD detective bags suspect and then a babe.' Are you fucking kidding me?"

"Could've been worse."

"Fuck," she said again, though he was right about that and the photo, which was blurry and shadowed because she and Trish had been standing in the doorway of Il Vicino, but like a lot of gossip rag blogs, a red circle had been drawn around Chris's head and Trish's and that had been enlarged and placed to the side, as if to titillate viewers with this lesbian embrace. It was when Trish had hugged Chris goodbye outside the restaurant.

"Let's go see the boss man," Harper said. "You can run last night's phone call by him, too."

"Yeah, I was going to. Be right there." She hung up and swore again, this time in Spanish. A half-hour later she was back at her desk. Jerry wanted to see her and Harper again after another meeting, so she figured she'd catch up on some phone calls. She texted Dayna and asked her to give her a call ASAP. Then she dialed Trish. Seemed a bit more professional to do that than text her with something like this. Her stomach knotted. Trish was not going to be pleased that cop stuff might have created a problem for her.

"Hi," Trish answered. "What's going on?"

"Hey. Am I interrupting anything?"

"No. Just doing some paperwork. I have a meeting in twenty minutes, though."

"This won't take that long." Might as well get right to it. "An asshole anti-immigrant blogger posted a photo of us when we were at Il Vicino the other night."

"A photo? Of what?"

"Us hugging outside the restaurant."

Pause. "What's the blog?"

"Legal Eyes. Just do a search on that."

She laughed, a reaction so far from what Chris had expected that she didn't know what to say.

"Oh, for Christ's sake," Trish said. "Who posted it? Randy or Mary?"

"Mary," Chris said, still surprised. "I saw her that night after you walked away. She was across the street talking on her phone."

"And using it for pictures, obviously. I haven't been following them as much over the past few months. So they're going after APD more?"

"Yeah. Me in particular."

"Randy has an issue with gay people, as I'm sure you know. Not to suggest you're advertising, but he probably assumes all women on the police force are lesbians. Plus, you're a detective, and working on possible high-profile cases."

"So you're saying I should be honored that Legal Eyes is stalking me?"

She laughed again. "Sorry. I shouldn't make light of it, but it is kind of funny because they're so predictable. He targeted us earlier this year. I started taking coffee out to Mary in the parking lot, she was staking us out so much."

"You didn't."

"I sure as hell did," she said with a little giggle and Chris remembered Trish's scrappy side. She'd liked that about her.

"What did she say?"

"She was actually polite and would thank me. She'd drink it, too. After a while—must've been two straight weeks—she stopped coming around. Randy came a couple of times during business hours and tried to basically bulldoze his way into the back offices."

"Why?"

"Looking for 'illegals', I'm sure," she said, putting extra sarcastic emphasis on the term. "I guess he figured he could be a one-man deportation station. He did call INS, but all our paperwork is in order and all our clients are in the system to varying degrees. Some are in legal limbo, but they have a record that tracks that, so there's really nothing for INS to do, since none of our clients have committed crimes and they have some form of representation."

"Sounds like something he'd do," Chris said. "Do you have your computer on? Go have a look at the blog."

"I have my iPad. Let's see..." A few moments passed and Chris assumed she was entering the blog's URL. "Well, that's a really bad photo. How do they even know it's you?"

"Baca knows who I am."

"But it was dark, even with the street and restaurant lights. And you said she was across the street."

"She probably walked past the restaurant at some point, looked in, and saw us there then decided to stake us out."

"Then why didn't she put my name down, too? She knows who I

am. That would've been an even better story," Trish said. "Lesbian cop hanging out with one of those pro-immigrant social workers."

She was right. That would have been a much better story. "Maybe she didn't get a good look at you. Your back was to the front windows. And you got up to go wash your hands. Or the server could've blocked her view." Or she just happened to recognize Chris from across the street.

"It had to be something like that." She paused. "At least they gave you credit for having a suspect in custody in the Ramirez murder. And I guess it's kind of a compliment, that they think I'm a babe."

Chris didn't respond.

"Are you out with the department?" Trish asked after a few seconds.

"For the most part. I'm sure there are a few who didn't know before this. I don't hide it, but I don't run around broadcasting, either."

"So this isn't going to cause problems with your bosses?"

"No. I just talked to them this morning about it."

"That's good news. Even a few years ago, this really could have done some damage. Thank God for small miracles."

"True." She hesitated. "I'm really sorry about this. I didn't want anyone else to get dragged into the Legal Eyes issue with me."

"You didn't do it on purpose. And it's not like anyone can tell that's me in the picture. I doubt that'll change. And honestly, it's kind of funny. They're obviously trying to out you and they inadvertently get a photo of you with an ex. If you're seeing someone, she can rest easy about getting outed, too. I don't mind being your cover, Chris." She laughed again and Chris relaxed.

"Funny story about that, actually. K.C. and her partner suggested I plant something gay in public — me doing cop stuff outreach at an LGBT event — to derail Burgess in that regard. We talked about setting me up with a fake girlfriend. Kind of a 'look, over there!' thing."

"See? This could actually work in your favor in some respects. And on that note, I have to go. Thanks for letting me know. I'll catch you later."

"All right. Bye." Chris hung up and set her phone on her desk. Maybe that was Trish's cosmic purpose. A gay cover. She chuckled and picked her phone up to check for texts. Then she called Tony on her desk phone to run a check on the phone number Marta's sister had called her from the night before. She was pretty sure that was who the caller was. She then used her business cell to call the number Tony had provided that was possibly the number Marta was using and left another message. On another hunch, she called the number Maria had given her at the bridge. Straight to voicemail, like the last time. She left a message in Spanish, asking for someone to please return her call. She didn't say she was with APD.

She thought then about Inez Morales, and the things she was

clearly willing to do to protect people who considered themselves a vigilante force that inflicted their own ideas about justice onto people they thought deserved it. Did Morales think about her mother at all, about what her arrest and possible conviction could do to her mother's position in the United States if she was undocumented? Or was she that much a believer in whatever ideologies the *Catrina* network pushed?

Chris had seen the kinds of violence that women suffered and sometimes died from, often at the hands of the men in their homes and families. A cycle that could pass from one generation to the next, like a virus, infecting the lives of children and their children, until the entire family tree bore rotted limbs. She could understand, maybe a little, why some women might join *La Catrina*, especially in a country like Mexico, where law enforcement often rode herd with corruption. She had read the reports about the hundreds of women found dead in the desert around Juárez, brutalized, tortured, raped. Two decades' worth, the bodies piling up with international condemnation, and still women suffered. Was it any wonder that a vigilante group was operating in that area, trying to provide protection for the living and justice for the dead?

She remembered what Ramirez's sister had said, about how she wouldn't blame her brother's killer if it was a woman, because she'd done a lot of women a favor. Chris could almost sympathize with that perspective, but she was a law enforcement officer, and it was her duty to find the person or persons responsible for the murders in this case, and every other case. No matter what she thought about the victims or what they had done in life, there were rules and responsibilities that she had sworn to meet. Even the worst person in life could be victimized in a crime. And it was her job to find their killers, too. But when she thought about Inez Morales again, and how small and deflated she'd looked in Bustos's squad car, and when she thought about women like Graciela and a network along the border that helped women find some kind of freedom from abuse and violence, she wondered if she was really doing anybody any favors.

She glanced at the time on her computer screen. Time to meet with Jerry and Harper again. She stood, put both her phones on silent mode, and headed to Jerry's office.

# Chapter Twenty-five

"SHOULD WE DRIVE or fly to El Paso tomorrow?" Harper asked as they left Jerry's office.

"Let's just drive. Probably cheaper, though in this case it's a little bit more of a pain in the ass."

He grunted in agreement. "I'll pick you up at seven at our usual rendezvous."

"Legal Eyes will think you and I are seeing each other, the number of times we've been at Flying Star over the past few days."

"That would mess up their Gucchi gay narrative," he said wryly. He stopped at the entrance to his office. "I'm going to call Joey, see if she has time to talk to us today about the Morales case. You know how DAs and prosecutors are about being in the loop." He gave her a sly little grin. "And I know how you love visiting prosecutors."

She gave him a look. "Nice, Harper. Just wait until you start seeing someone."

"How do you know I'm not?"

"I'm a detective. It's my job to know exactly what's going on in your love life."

His smile widened to a grin.

"And if you're done riding my ass about *my* love life, I'll let Bustos and Morales's attorney know we're coming down to try to talk to Morales again."

His grin remained, but she ignored it.

"Let me know what Joey says," she said over her shoulder as she headed back to her own office.

"Yep."

She went back to her desk and checked her phone again, almost compulsively. Dayna had texted earlier that she'd try to call her around lunch, but she had meetings all day and it might be later. Chris sighed. Maybe she'd get lucky and see Dayna later in the day at the prosecutors' offices. She dialed the number for Morales's attorney and got his assistant, who put her through. Yes, he could meet them on short notice at the jail and would one be okay? It would, see you then and thank you. Chris signed off politely and dialed Bustos, who picked up on the first ring.

"Bustos."

"Hey, Eileen. Chris Gutierrez, APD. Harper and I need to come down and try to interview Morales again. Got some new info that might be pertinent."

"Sounds good. You flying in? I can arrange to have you picked up."

"No, we're driving. We'll be there around twelve-thirty. Her lawyer's meeting us at one."

"Couple of masochists, aren't you?" she said with a laugh. "Fine. Just come by. I'll give everybody a heads-up and let Morales know."

"Thanks. Has anybody besides her lawyer been in contact with her?"

"Not that I know of. I'll check to see if anybody's come by for visiting hours."

"That'd be great. Could you give me a call either way?"

"Yes."

"Excellent. Thanks. Catch you later." Chris signed off and rubbed her forehead. She had the kind of headache you get from lack of sleep and stress.

"Yo," Harper said from her doorway. "Saddle up. Joey can see us in thirty minutes. Meet me in the lobby. I'll bring the car around."

"Okay." She took her jacket off the file cabinets and shrugged into it. Then she drained the last of her coffee from earlier. Nearly cold, but she needed a caffeine boost. She texted Dayna that she'd be at the DA's building for a meeting with Joey and did she have time to chat. She almost laughed out loud because she had to set up an appointment with her partner to talk for a few minutes. And then she stopped for a moment. Partner. She kind of liked how that felt, rolling around in her brain. A lot. She put both her work and personal cells into the inside pocket of her blazer and went to meet Harper.

Twenty minutes later, they stood outside Joey's office. Harper was rocking forward and back on the balls of his feet and Chris leaned against the wall, listening to the low, almost soothing rhythm of voices emanating from the open doors of various judicial staff. She heard somebody's cell phone ring down the hall, to the tune of "Bad to the Bone." One of her phones buzzed with a text message. She took both out of her pocket to check them. The message was on her personal cell and she smiled. Dayna, telling her to stop by her office when she and Harper were done meeting with Joey. She texted a quick affirmative and put the phone back in her pocket when one of Joey's staff stepped into the corridor.

"Detectives?"

They both looked at her.

"I'm sorry, but Joey's other meeting is running a little late. It'll be another half-hour or so. Can I get you anything?"

"No, thanks," Harper and Chris said almost at the same time.

"Well, let me know if that changes. We've got some water and pop and coffee in the back."

"Thanks," Chris said, giving her a smile. The staff member went back through the open doorway into Joey Trujillo's reception area.

"Looks like you have a little free time," Harper said. "I'm sure there's another attorney around here you could talk to, kill some time."

"You know, I'm not sure how I feel about you playing matchmaker."

He shrugged. "Don't need to. You're already hooked. I'm just helping ensure you stay hooked."

"Nice. Is this where I get the ball-and-chain speech?"

He grinned. "Not yet. But let me know when you want that one. I use a Navy buddy of mine's version."

She smiled. "I'm sure it's convincing."

"Yep. Be back in a few. I'll go get us some coffee downstairs at the coffee cart. That stuff's pretty strong."

"Thanks, Harper."

He nodded and walked down the corridor toward the elevator. Chris walked the opposite direction and turned right down another corridor. She stood outside Dayna's office door, which was partially ajar, and knocked.

"Come in," came Dayna's voice, and it sent little ricochets of delight down her spine.

She pushed the door open. "Hi."

Dayna looked up in surprise. "Hi. I thought you were meeting with Joey." She got up and came around her desk to stand directly in front of Chris.

"Her meeting went over. Another thirty minutes, maybe. Harper went to get the good coffee downstairs." She refrained from touching her, as she always did when in Dayna's professional environment, but it was always difficult. And today, Dayna wore a black broomstick skirt, a loose white blouse unbuttoned enough to show the silver chain around her neck, and a beautifully tooled concho belt. Her hair was pulled back loosely, held in place with a southwestern-style silver comb, and she'd put on her blue-framed glasses, that brought out her eyes.

"God, you look good," Chris said.

Dayna smiled. "I might say the same about you."

"And you know I love it when you wear your cowboy boots."

She raised her eyebrows and moved past Chris to shut her office door. Then she turned and gave Chris one of her looks that could melt metal. "Come here."

Chris gratefully moved into Dayna's embrace, and allowed herself a few moments of bliss, surrounded by her smell and the feel of her body.

"I miss you," Dayna said. "When can I see you again?"

"Not tonight. Sorry. Harper and I have to go back to El Paso tomorrow morning. Hopefully, we won't have to stay the night." She pressed her lips against Dayna's forehead.

Dayna pulled away and studied her face. "You look really tired," she said, concern etched in her expression.

"I am."

She cupped Chris's cheek with her hand. "Promise me you'll get some rest before you travel tomorrow."

"Barring anything that requires my attention, yes." She gave her a wan smile. "Love this job."

Dayna chuckled. "I know. But I want to make sure you're as okay as you can be." She leaned in and kissed her, a long, sweet melding of mouths that sent waves of affection and connection through Chris's chest.

"Damn," Chris said as Dayna pulled away. "Can you do that again?"

"I'd love to. But I won't be able to stop, and you've got a meeting coming up and so do I." She gave her a wicked little smile. "As much as I would love to put my office couch to much better use, it wouldn't do either of us any favors." She glanced over at it then back at Chris. "But don't think I'm not sorely tempted."

Chris gave an exaggerated sigh. "Fine. Business, then."

"Before pleasure. So what's up? The ASAP you included in your text this morning suggested there might be something you want to tell me."

"There is. Legal Eyes posted another photo."

"Of?"

"Me at Il Vicino the other night. I'm guessing it was Mary Baca who took it. She posted a photo of Trish giving me a goodbye hug."

Dayna raised an eyebrow. "Let's have a look." She went back to her desk and typed in the URL on her browser. She stared at the screen. "It's fortunately a really bad picture. If I didn't know you, I wouldn't be able to say that's you. And I can't tell who that is you're with." She looked up at Chris. "Did you tell Trish?"

"Yes."

"What was her reaction?"

"She's had dealings with Legal Eyes in the past. They've targeted Faith Social Services. She doesn't think Mary got a very good view of either of us in the restaurant, because Mary knows her and would have included her name in the story if that was the case. She asked if it would cause problems at work for me. I told her no. Then she thought it was sort of funny that Legal Eyes outed me, unknowingly, with an ex."

"I think the same thing. It sort of fulfills Sage's plan of creating a whole other girlfriend to throw them off the trail."

"Trish did say she didn't mind being cover for me, especially since you can't really tell who I'm with in the photo."

"And from the comments, it doesn't seem anybody's all that interested in the gay thing. Lots of anti-cop statements, though. Oh, here's an anti-gay one. According to this commenter, you're a sinner, sweetie."

"Duh."

Dayna laughed. "I can tell you're spending a lot of time around K.C." She got up from her desk and pulled Chris against her. "So what does this latest blog mean?"

"Jerry thinks that with a suspect in custody, Legal Eyes will focus on something else. Of course, they'll keep waiting for more information, but with the wheels of justice turning as slow as they do, they'll have to find other stories to drive readership."

"I actually feel a little better with Trish as cover." She pulled back and gave Chris a little grin. "As long as I'm your undercover."

She laughed. "Always, Counselor." She gave her a kiss. "I have to go. I'll call you later."

"I know. Check in as you can. You know I worry when you're not sleeping much."

She smiled. "Pencil me in later this week?"

Dayna pretended to think. "I'll check. See what's available. I can probably spare an hour or two." She winked. "Be safe out there, sweets."

"You, too," Chris said. She paused at the door. "I really miss you."

"Then I'm definitely penciling you in."

She laughed. "Later." She went back into the corridor and left the door ajar, as Dayna liked to do when she was in her office to let people know she was in. Harper stood outside Joey's reception area when she approached. He wordlessly handed her a cup of coffee. She took a sip. Very strong, not much cream.

"Thanks."

He nodded.

The same staff member who had spoken with them earlier appeared in the doorway. "Okay," she said. "Joey's ready."

Chris followed Harper into the DA's office. Hopefully, they'd be out of here in under an hour.

"HEY," CHRIS SAID when Tony picked up. "What'd you get on that phone number I gave you this morning?"

"Nothing. Sorry. Another Mexican burn phone."

She'd figured that. "Oh, well. Thanks for trying."

"Sure." He hung up and Chris rubbed her eyes. The meeting with Joey had taken forty-five minutes and then she and Harper had grabbed some lunch and come back to the office. She had to return a call from Bustos and then she wanted to finish up a couple of other reports on other cases before Harper drove her back to K.C. and Sage's.

She called Bustos on her business cell.

"Hey," Bustos said when she picked up. She'd apparently recognized Chris's number.

"What's up?"

"Checked the visitor log. Nobody's come in to see Morales except her lawyer."

"Any calls?"

"She made one to a local cell phone when she was booked. She asked whoever it was to get her a lawyer."

That explained the attorney, but Chris wondered who the local contact was. "Has she been acting strangely?"

"No reports of that. You want me to check? What am I looking for?"

"I don't know. Does she socialize with anybody else there? And how's her demeanor?"

"You worried about a suicide attempt?"

"I wouldn't rule it out." Especially if Morales had really been thinking about what a confession to two murders might do to her and her mother.

"All right. I'll call you when I find anything out."

"Thanks. I'll buy you dinner tomorrow."

She laughed. "Hell, a cup of coffee will be fine."

"You got it. Bye." She hung up and set to work on her reports. By five, she had finished both. Her desk phone rang. Harper.

"You ready?" he said when she picked up. "I need to get some sleep before our road trip."

"Yeah. Be right there." She shut everything down, put a few files into her briefcase, then grabbed her blazer. Harper dropped her off closer to Lomas and Carlisle this time, away from the Central Avenue shopping and entertainment area of Nob Hill. It was already dark, but she took side streets through the residential area to K.C.'s house, about a ten-minute walk from where he'd left her. Maybe after this trip to El Paso, if they could get Morales to describe the crime scene and determine for certain whether she could conceivably have committed the murders, APD could release her name to the press and Legal Eyes could go back to bashing immigrants instead of her and the department.

She liked this time of day in the fall, when the air stilled with night and sound carried across rooftops. A dog barked somewhere to her left and a child's shout and laughter followed. At least one person was grilling out, because she smelled the kind of smoke that accompanies charcoal briquettes, and the tang of meat. An SUV pulled into a driveway across the street from her and its driver got out, a man who looked like he was getting home from work, since he carried a bag that looked big enough for a laptop. He went into the house through the front door and the porch light went on. Chris relaxed a little, though she did another scan of the street as she walked.

Nothing seemed out of the ordinary, and a few minutes later, she turned left onto K.C.'s street then left again onto the walkway between K.C.'s house and the neighbor's fence that led to Kara's. As she went inside to drop her stuff off, her business cell rang. She set her briefcase down and pulled the phone out of her pocket. Bustos.

"Hey. Got anything?"

"Not really. Asked around. Morales seems as fine as anybody who's being detained waiting for transport. She talks to people, takes her showers, and she's eating. No indications that she's suicidal."

"Is she hanging out with anybody in particular?"

"Not really. She keeps to herself, which a lot of the newbies do when they're brought in. We've got a few female gang members waiting for trial, and they can be difficult when someone initially comes in. She's steered clear of them, though. Plus, word gets out what you're in for, so maybe they're impressed."

"I guess that's good news for Morales."

Bustos laughed, a short bark of a sound. "Yeah. If you're being detained, make sure it's for something like that. Keeps people off your back."

"Or something. Well, thanks. Appreciate it."

"No problem. Give me a call when you guys get in. I'll try to swing by."

"Will do. Later." She hung up and hoped the only other phone call she'd have to deal with before she went to bed was Dayna's.

"Hey," K.C. said through the security door.

"*Esa*. Just got in."

"We know. Figured you'd be wiped out, so we've got pizza."

Chris grinned. "I love you both. Let me get organized and I'll be right over."

"Excellent." She hesitated. "Okay if I come in for a minute?"

"Sure."

K.C. opened the door and stepped inside. She wore faded jeans, a plain gray sweatshirt and a pair of black Converse sneakers.

"That's a good look on you," Chris said. "Let me match it." She went into the bedroom and changed into her favorite jeans, an old hoodie, and old sneakers.

"I presume you've seen the really shitty picture on Legal Eyes?" K.C. said from the other room.

"Yeah. I already talked to Dayna and called Trish. Jerry knows, too," she said as she laced her shoes.

"What do you think?"

Chris came back into the living room and picked her briefcase up off the floor and put it on the couch. "Fortunately, you can't really tell who Trish is. And you can barely claim that's me."

"I agree. Bad composition, poor focus. Sage was appalled. You know how she is about photography."

Chris chuckled. "And it actually falls right into Sage's plan, doesn't it? A fake girlfriend might provide some cover for Dayna. Plus, it doesn't really out me, since I'm not closeted. And fortunately, I've got support at work."

"Which makes a huge damn difference in something like this." She studied Chris for a moment. "So how are you?"

"Tired."

"I can see that. I'm guessing it's not just physical."

"Sage is rubbing off on you."

"Nah. I just know you that well."

"I'll tell you more when I can, *esa*. You know that." She squeezed K.C.'s shoulder. "I'm just really tired and not up for talking much right now."

"Yeah, I can tell. Come on and get some pizza. Hell, bring it back here and then go to bed. I'm sure Sage and I will be able to figure something out to pass the time until we see you again."

Chris laughed and followed K.C. outside.

# Chapter Twenty-six

"YOU STILL THINKING Morales didn't do it?" Harper asked. He kept his eyes on the road as he drove, one hand on the wheel, the other holding a to-go cup of coffee.

"Maybe. The caller knew the details of the murder scenes, but Morales could've told her." Chris stared out the windshield as the landscape whipped past, stretches of desert grays and browns veined with arroyos and speckled with hills. To the east—the driver's side of the car—the Rio Grande followed them south, and beyond that, the Manzano Mountains blocked a view of the horizon. A structure or town occasionally broke the rhythm of the geography, but often in harmony with the contours of the land.

"I'm not feeling her as the shooter," he said after a while. "Accomplice, sure. But from your description of your caller the other night, I'd probably go with her as the shooter."

"I'm thinking that, too. But if the caller is the shooter, what the fuck can we do about it? She said she's not American, we don't have a name, a phone number, anything that'll ID her. And it's not like Mexican authorities are going to drop anything and help us find her." She picked up the to-go cup of coffee and took a sip. Still warm. "Shit, *La Catrina*'s been operating down there for at least two decades. Not like Mexican officials have been overly concerned about it."

"Reyes could be a key. She said her sister did it."

Chris made a disgusted noise. "For all we know, her sister told her to say that. Hell, for all we know, Morales is the shooter and this is just part of a plan to cast enough doubt on the confession that she won't be charged with murder. That's what I'd do, if I was running with a secret border network and one of ours got nailed by the cops."

"So you'd try to protect someone in your network." Harper took a drink from his cup and adjusted his position slightly. "Would that be cost effective?"

She looked over at him. "What do you mean?"

"If the *Catrina* network operates like you suspect—with leaderless cells—chances are people in it understand that if something screws up, you're on your own. You mentioned that yourself already."

Chris thought about that. "Point taken." Something else dawned on her. "Maybe it depends on what your position is in the network."

"Everybody's expendable in a situation like that," he said. "There's no real leadership. There might be a hierarchy, but the whole thing is designed to operate no matter who gets taken into custody or who dies. You join something like that, you'd better get that through your skull quick. And if you don't play by the code..." He shrugged. "Like a gang.

You're in for life."

Because you know too much, she thought. "If Morales isn't the shooter, why did Reyes's sister—or whoever she is—call me claiming she's the shooter and that she's with *Catrina*? Why would she reveal that much about the network?"

"She doesn't think we can catch her. Hell, there's a good track record of that going on with this network. If they're getting busted, it's on the Mexican side."

"Unless they keep quiet about it. Morales hasn't said anything about *Catrina*. Only the caller did. Why would she set Morales up like that?"

"Good question."

Chris stared out the window again for a few minutes. She thought about the gun in Morales's car. Why would she put the murder weapon there? If she was the shooter, she'd been careful enough to remove the casings from each scene. Including a dark highway. And she just tosses the murder weapon in her trunk?

"Morales is being set up," she announced. She looked over at Harper. "Reyes's sister and the network. They're making sure she takes the fall for this. That's why the gun was in her car without the serial numbers filed off. Shit, for all we know, the ballistics tests may come back negative. That might not even be the gun used to kill either of the vics."

"But why bother? She already confessed. There's no point to setting her up for it."

"True." Chris chewed her lip. What was she not seeing? She replayed parts of the conversation she'd had with Reyes's sister the other night. "Expendable," she said softly. Jesus. That was it. She picked up her business cell from the seat next to her and called Bustos, who didn't pick up.

"Hey, Eileen. Chris Gutierriez here. Harper and I are on our way down. Can you give me a call back as soon as you can? I need to ask you a couple of questions." She hung up and stared out the window again, tapping the phone against her leg, willing Harper to speed up a little though he was already driving over the limit. The minutes crawled past. She dialed Carl Maestes, who did pick up.

"Hey, *esa*. How goes it?"

"Hi, Carl. Listen, can you give me a number of someone to talk to at the jail? I want to check on one of the detainees."

"Do you know what floor?"

"One of the women's."

"All right, hold on."

She took her pen and notepad out of her jacket pocket while she waited.

"Okay, call this number. It's a direct line to the box on one of the women's floors." He gave it to her and she wrote it down.

"Thanks. Talk to you later."

"*No hay problemo.*" He hung up and Chris dialed the number he'd given her.

No answer. Not even a voicemail. She hung up.

"What are you thinking?" Harper asked.

"I don't know. I have a gut feeling."

He didn't respond, but she felt the car speed up.

"What if this *is* a set-up," she said after a few more minutes, "and it's also—"

Her phone rang.

"Hey, Eileen. Thanks for—"

"Chris, bad news. Morales is dead."

She gripped the phone so hard her hand hurt. "When?"

"This morning. Fight at a neighboring table in the rec area. Couple of hardcores got into it. I don't know all the details, but she sustained a head injury. Where are you?"

"About thirty minutes north of Cruces. We'll be there in an hour."

"All right." Bustos hesitated. "Sorry," she said before she hung up.

Chris looked over at Harper. "Morales is dead."

He didn't say anything for a few seconds. Then, "What the hell?"

She told him what Bustos had said.

"What's your take?"

"My gut says it's a hit, made not to look like one." She tapped the glass on her phone with her fingertip, trying to calm her nerves. "Like you said. A network like that can't risk members talking. They set her up, so it would look probable that she killed Ramirez and Griego. And then they took her out." She thought about Morales, sitting in Bustos's squad car just a few days ago. A twenty-something, pretty young woman. How did she get mixed up with *Catrina*? Was it one wrong turn? Or several? Did she believe she was doing something for the greater good?

"Could be just an accident."

"I know. And I'll take that into consideration. But something's not right about this whole thing."

"Yeah, but think about it. What's the likelihood that *Catrina* has somebody in the downtown facility in El Paso? That's a stretch."

"They could have paid someone."

He made a noncommittal grunt. "Rein it in, Gucchi. Let's see where the evidence takes us."

He was right and she knew it. But her instincts were telling her otherwise. "Fuck," she said.

"Yeah," Harper said quietly. "That about sums it up."

CHRIS SAT ACROSS from Lieutenant Jerry Torrez Thursday morning. She and Harper had spent Wednesday in El Paso anyway, getting whatever information they could about Morales's death. She studied his desk, and for the hundredth time, thought that it was as organized as Harper's, no doubt something Jerry had picked up in the military, too. It had carried over to his personal habits, as well. He still wore his hair—now streaked with gray—short and he never looked rattled or rumpled. He was like a panther, Chris had decided a few years back. All coiled muscle and purpose but with a veneer of calm. He leaned back in his chair and regarded first her, then Harper.

"Sounds like a FUBAR situation."

Harper nodded. "El Paso's conducting the investigation into her death."

"But all it'll probably show is that she was collateral damage in a fight." He glanced at Chris for confirmation.

She nodded.

"What's your take?" he asked her.

"It could be a random act. I'll concede that."

"But?"

She leaned forward. "I'm still leaning hit, but I doubt I can prove it. I sure as hell can't prove it with what I've got now."

He gave her a wry smile. "I appreciate that about you, Gutierrez. You don't get ahead of yourself." He raised his hand when she started to say something. "You've got good instincts, but that doesn't go anywhere in court."

She nodded again.

"So basically we've got evidence that definitively links Morales to the murders of Ramirez and Griego," Jerry said. "We've got a gun that will probably match ballistics in both, we've got a confession. We've got a lot of good circumstantial that will put her at both scenes."

"And we've got a confession from someone else who gave us details about the scenes that haven't made the press," Harper added.

Jerry shrugged. "Morales could've told somebody that. And why would anybody confess after somebody already took responsibility for it?"

"To throw a serious monkey wrench into any investigation," Harper suggested.

"The caller said she wasn't American." Jerry looked at Chris for confirmation.

"Yeah," she said. "And she's part of the *Catrina* network. She said Morales was the set-up person in the murders, and that she was good at it, but didn't have the stomach to be the shooter."

"We can't prove this other person did it, because Morales can't tell us what she knows about the crime scenes." Jerry picked up a pen and tapped it idly on his desk. "I'm guessing Morales was in on the murders in some way. If she didn't do them, she knew about them and helped in some way. We probably could have nailed her as an accomplice and maybe even gotten some help from Mexican authorities regarding this other person who called you." He looked at Chris. "We can announce that the confessed killer of Ramirez and Griego died in an altercation with other prisoners in detention. That's the best we can do."

She bit back a response.

"I know," he said. "I know it bites. But two calls from Mexico saying Morales didn't do it can't prove she didn't."

She clenched her teeth.

"We'll back-burner it," he said, as if he was trying to placate her. "Won't close it down completely. We'll run ballistics on the gun, go over the car. We'll keep the investigation as active as we can. Who's Morales's next-of-kin?"

Harper glanced at Chris.

"A cousin," she said. "Marta Reyes. She's based in Juárez." And she hoped fervently that Marta had decided to contact Inez's mother with the news.

"That what Morales indicated when she was processed?" Jerry asked.

"Yes."

"Let El Paso know to call us about what Reyes wants with regard to Morales's personal effects."

"Already done." She leaned back, stiff with stress and exhaustion. "They've already been in contact with her."

"I haven't gotten the official word yet," Jerry said. "Once they give me the go-ahead, we'll release her name."

Chris hoped Juana Morales didn't watch much TV.

"Anything else?" Jerry asked them both. Neither responded, so he motioned at the door. "Keep me posted if anything changes. Nice work."

Harper pushed his big frame out of the chair and Chris followed him.

"Gutierrez," Jerry said. "Hold up."

Harper gave her a sympathetic look before he walked down the corridor.

She turned and looked at Jerry, knowing that he was probably going to give her a pep talk, which would only grate on her nerves more because it wasn't going to change anything about this case.

"Close the door."

She did, and stood with her back to it.

"You and Harper did some damn fine work on this. I know you've got your instincts about who's responsible, and I'd put money on it that you're right. And maybe things could be different if we weren't dealing with a possible suspect in another country."

In other words, our hands are tied. We've got no solid evidence that Morales didn't do it, no solid evidence that anybody else did. Chris kept quiet so that she didn't snap her frustration at him.

"We've got a confessed killer and good circumstantial that backs up that confession. We've got no strong evidence to suggest otherwise besides a 'she said, she said' kind of thing." He gave her a long, measured look. "We don't know for sure that Morales didn't do it."

"I know."

"And we might not ever know if she died in an accident or a hit. El Paso will cooperate with us as best they can. Let their investigators do their work."

"Yes, sir."

He gave her a nod of dismissal and as she opened the door, he added, "Take a couple of days off. Oh, and I think it's okay for you to go home, now. We'll be releasing Morales's name probably this evening. That'll give Burgess something else to chase after."

She looked back over her shoulder. "Thanks." Then she closed his door and went back to her office where she returned a few phone calls that dealt with other matters before she worked on her reports regarding Ramirez, Griego, and Morales. When she finished, she leaned back in her chair and stared at the ceiling for a while, and allowed herself to think about Morales and Marta Reyes and her sister, the woman who claimed she'd come to New Mexico and left two men dead. She'd already transferred the recordings of the calls from her phone to her computer and sent them to Tony, who'd get them saved for evidence. But she'd saved copies for herself on her hard drive and she'd listened to them twice already that morning. And heard nothing new. Nothing that would lead her to the caller who claimed she'd done the killings.

Why had Reyes even bothered to call her and tell her Morales hadn't done it? And why had Reyes's sister done the same thing? If they were going to kill Morales anyway, what was the point in throwing her that bone? Why not just let people think Morales had done it, and then get rid of her? That would have looked like an unfortunate accident, and the confessed killer of two Albuquerque men was now dead. No trial, no prison, saves taxpayers lots of money. Burgess would approve.

She leaned forward and clicked on her Web browser to check the Legal Eyes blog. Nothing about her today or yesterday. That was a relief. Instead, Burgess was reporting live from the Arizona-Mexico border, claiming that some rancher had accosted border jumpers speaking Arabic. She read through it. The rancher actually hadn't been that close to the "illegals," as Burgess said, and couldn't be sure it was Arabic. Might just have been Spanish. Or, Chris thought, Nahuatl.

She doubted Legal Eyes would go after APD for what happened to Morales in El Paso once that news broke. Most likely, Burgess would grouse about the incompetence of the El Paso police and then dig around trying to find more information about Morales. Which might then lead them to Juana. Chris pinched the bridge of her nose. And Juana was most likely undocumented. "Fucking mess," she muttered.

Her personal cell rang with a distinctive tone and she smiled.

*Abuelita* always knew when something was bothering her.

"*Hola*," she answered. "How are you?"

"I am well, though I fear you are not."

"Oh? Why do you think that?"

"Because I heard bad news," *Abuelita* said. "News that I am sure you already know."

"What's wrong?" She sat straight up, thinking something had happened to someone in the family.

"Juana Morales was just here. She said her niece had called her about Inez."

Chris sank back into her chair, partially relieved that Marta had let Juana know. "I'm sorry, 'Lita. Inez did not put Juana as her next-of-kin. That makes it difficult for the police to let her know what happened." She phrased it delicately, because she suspected that Inez had been trying to protect her mother's identity and probable immigration status should anything happen to her.

"I understand. I know why you could not say."

"What happened is tragic. She was a young woman who made some bad choices."

"Marta told Juana why Inez had been arrested," *Abuelita* said, in her "I had a feeling so-and-so was headed down the wrong path" tone.

"What did she say?"

"That Inez had confessed she killed that man in the neighborhood and another man in Las Cruces."

"Did she say anything else about it?"

"No. But Juana doesn't think Inez would have been able to do those things. Inez was a follower, not someone who could take such action."

Chris heard a clinking, as if *Abuelita* was stirring tea. "Maybe those men did something bad to Inez," she said. "Or someone else that Inez cared about." Inez must have known Ramirez had assaulted Marta, who was like a sister to her. How was she able to string him along like that until she killed him? Or until Marta's sister killed him? Did the network tell her not to, until they had a plan in place?

"Many things are possible, *mija*. And some things are perhaps not for us to know."

She forced her irritation down and glanced at the Legal Eyes blog. "I need you to take a message to Juana for me. Do you remember when I told you about those people who write bad things about immigrants?"

"Yes."

"When the press releases Inez's name, those people will probably try to find out more about her. They may find Juana, and they may write bad things about her. They may also contact INS."

*Abuelita* didn't respond right away, but Chris heard more clinking.

"No need to worry," she finally said. "Juana is leaving."

"Oh?"

"She's going back to Mexico." *Abuelita* made a tsking sound, something she did when Rudolfo was chewing on an object he wasn't supposed to. Usually one of her house slippers.

"What will she do for work?"

"She says Marta has some extra money and they can move somewhere safer than Juárez and open a little store."

Chris sat back. Extra money. All of a sudden, Marta has extra money to bring Juana back to Mexico. Maybe a bunch of cash from a dead man's house in Albuquerque? "Did Juana mention Marta's sister?"

"No. But she has never spoken much about her."

"When is Juana leaving?"

"Soon."

Chris sighed. That could mean tonight or next week.

"*Mija*," *Abuelita* said after a few long moments, "Inez was not your responsibility."

"Yes, she was." She thought again about her, sitting in the back of Bustos's patrol car, deflated.

"No, she was not. Her choices placed her in those circumstances. Had you not been so good at what you do, she may have gone on to make more bad choices," she said, a note of pride in her voice.

Chris smiled in spite of her mood.

"And those choices could have caused pain for even more people."

Including Inez's own family. "Please express my condolences to Juana," Chris said after a few moments

"I already have, because I know it is what you would have wanted. Now go. I think Dayna misses you."

Chris heard a sly note in the comment and she chuckled. "I think you know too much."

"Or perhaps I simply remember how it is to be young."

"I'll come by this weekend."

"I am fine, *mija*. There are others in your life who require your attention. Besides, your mother is coming over and we're cooking again for another church event."

"Do you need help?"

"No, but I'm sure your mother will if you stop by." She giggled. "Especially if you bring Dayna."

"Troublemaker," Chris said, laughing along with her.

"It would serve her well, to see the happiness Dayna brings her daughter. But I think you and Dayna could use a couple of days together, uninterrupted. I will talk to you next week. Bye."

Still smiling, Chris signed off and hung up. She leaned back and shut her eyes, the weight of the past couple of weeks dragging at her.

"Yo."

She opened her eyes. Harper stood in the doorway to her cubicle.

"Yeah?"

He came in and sat down. "I had this case once," he said. "Two punks. They blamed each other for a young woman's overdose. One said he was visiting his girlfriend on the other side of the city. The other said he was out with friends. The evidence pointed to somebody injecting her. These two punks were a couple of her known associates." He shrugged. "We showed up at one's house to ask him some questions and he bolted. When I caught him, he kept saying it was the other guy who put the drugs in her. When we caught up with the other one, he said it was the first guy."

"So which one was it?"

He gave her a sardonic smile. "Don't know for sure."

"Why not?"

"The one who said he was with his girlfriend got popped a week later and the girlfriend couldn't remember for sure which night he had been there." He shook his head. "She wasn't the brightest bulb in the box. Plus, she used, too. Meanwhile, the other punk disappeared. No trace. Every trail went cold and that poor girl's family never really got any closure because we couldn't say for sure who had injected the drugs in her or why. Evidence suggested it was the guy who disappeared, though. Just could never prove it."

She glanced at the Morales folders on her desk then back at him. "Is this one of your dad ways of trying to make me feel better?"

He grinned. "Yep. Did it work?"

She chuckled. "Yeah, in a weird way. A little."

"I figured I couldn't do any worse than Jerry."

"I think yours is better, actually."

"Point is," he said, "sometimes we don't get to finish these cases with a neat little package and a pretty little bow. We do the best we can to get the bad guys off the streets, and make sure their victims get justice. Even if they're punks. Most of the time, we get our man. Or woman," he corrected himself. "But sometimes, as they say, shit happens. Doesn't matter how or why or who did it, if anybody. It happens, and there's not a lot we can do about it."

"I know that here." She tapped her head. "But I haven't gotten the message here." She tapped her chest.

He nodded. "Yeah. I know that feeling." He stood. "News is on in a few minutes. Boss man got the all-clear from El Paso. They're releasing Morales's name. And I'll bet Jerry said you could go home once that's done."

"Yeah. I'm more than happy about that." She glanced at the Legal Eyes blog again. Once they had this news, they'd be off and running to find out more about the confessed killer of Victor Ramirez and Johnny Griego. That should be all over their blog tomorrow and probably the next couple of days. Which meant that tomorrow after work, she'd drive her own damn car to her own damn house. The thought made her feel a bit better. She got up from her desk and followed Harper to his office.

"SO THE CASE isn't really closed." K.C. took a bottle of beer out of the fridge and handed it to Chris.

"I don't know. There's some closure, but maybe not a closing. Technically, it's sort of open but not really. Especially if the real killers are Mexican citizens. If we could find them — and that's a big if — Mexico doesn't have to turn them over. They can try them in a Mexican court. God knows how long that would go on or even if we have enough evidence to make anything stick." She twisted the cap off the bottle and set it on the counter, frustration still gnawing at a little corner of her gut.

K.C. touched her bottle to Chris's. "Happy Friday."

"Yeah."

K.C. gave her a look. "Hey. You ran that case all the way down to Mexico, *esa*. And then you cracked some crazy secret border network and ended up with a pretty good idea who else might be involved. I'd say that's a hell of a finish, given what you had to work with."

Chris shrugged and took a sip of beer. "Maybe."

"I know what you're thinking."

"Oh? Is Sage finally rubbing off on you?"

"Please. I've known you over ten years, *mujer*. You're pissed at yourself because you somehow feel what happened to Morales is your fault, and that you somehow failed because you didn't go to El Paso and bust every door down and then go into Mexico and do the same thing in Juárez. If only you'd checked three million houses, you're thinking, the case would totally be closed and you'd for sure have the culprits and maybe Morales would be alive and well, would see the error of her ways, and admit that it was the people you dragged out of the secret network in Juárez who actually did it and she was just the accomplice." She took a breath. "Am I close?"

Chris grinned. "So you might have a point. And that's why I keep you around. Your amazing speeches."

"That and she looks damn good in jeans," Sage said as she entered from the living room. "Especially those." She gave K.C. a lascivious look and Chris laughed as K.C. flushed.

"River says hi to everybody," Sage said as she gave Chris a quick hug. "I might just have convinced him to come visit for Thanksgiving." She picked up her half-empty beer bottle from the counter.

"That would be great," Chris said. "I've pretty much got my mom convinced she needs to let John and me do the dinner at my house. You two are invited. So are River and Kara, if she's not off doing whatever it is she does these days."

"Cool," K.C. said. "Honey?" She looked at Sage for confirmation.

"Can I help cook?" Sage asked Chris.

"Absolutely. John would love that. He'll be here the weekend before to start getting ready."

"Monster Gutierrez blow-out." K.C. practically chortled. "Drinks?"

Chris nodded. "The usual. Beer and wine. Stuff for the kids."

"I'll handle that. You know how I am."

"Excellent."

"Yes, it is," Sage said. "And we can run some interference for you with your mom."

Chris groaned. "You had to bring that up."

"Just what I was thinking." K.C. took another swallow of beer. "Though I doubt we'll need to. Once Dayna turns on the charm, mere mortals can't withstand it." She looked over at Sage. "Kind of like you," she said with a smile.

Sage pecked her on the cheek. "I noticed your car out front," she said to Chris. "Does this mean that Burgess the butthead has found someone else to mess with?"

"We can hope. Legal Eyes was all over the Morales story today after we released her name on the news. Burgess didn't even mention APD. Harper predicted he'd rag on El Paso PD for somehow allowing Morales to die in custody. He was right." She took a swig and shrugged. "Burgess might actually go down to El Paso. He was just in Arizona, so clearly he likes to take his anti-immigrant circus on the road."

"Nothing about you specifically since they allegedly outed you?" Sage asked.

"Nope. And that apparently didn't go over how he planned. Nobody seemed to give a shit. We got no calls, no complaints." Though she did get teased by her fellow law enforcement officers.

"The times, they are a'changin'," K.C. said.

Chris nodded. "In some ways, yeah. Thank God."

"Hello," came Dayna's voice from the front door and Chris's nerve endings sparked.

"In the kitchen," Sage hollered back. "Hot women and cold beer."

Chris heard Dayna laugh as the front door closed. She set her beer on the counter and went to meet her halfway between the front door and the kitchen, where she pulled her close and kissed her, long and deep.

"Damn," Dayna said when Chris stopped after a few more. "I missed you, too."

"Here's what I'm thinking. Let's eat dinner with Sage and K.C.," Chris said softly. "Then I'm going to follow you home."

"Mmm. And?" She brushed her fingertips over Chris's lips, sending a delightful wave of chills down her spine.

"Wait and see."

"You're a tease, Gutierrez."

"And?"

"Just pointing it out." Dayna leaned in and kissed her, then pulled her toward the kitchen. "Hey, Sage," she called. "I've got a hot woman. How about that cold beer?"

"Comin' right up," K.C. answered as they entered the kitchen.

Chris laced her fingers with Dayna's and the last two weeks fell away in the warmth of Dayna's hand and the sound of her voice.

"We were thinking somewhere close," K.C. said as she handed a beer to Dayna. "Sage made reservations at Scalo for a half-hour from now. Sound good?"

"Perfect," Dayna said. "I haven't eaten there in a while."

"Plus, Italian is kind of sexy food." K.C. grinned. "Not that either of you needs any help in that area."

Dayna laughed.

"It's good to see you," Sage said as she gave Dayna a hug. "Give me a few minutes. I need to change."

K.C. looked down at her jeans and baggy sweater. "Yeah, I guess I should probably wear something else, since we're having sexy food and all. Back in a minute. I'm sure you two will find something to entertain yourselves." She gave Chris an innocent look and followed Sage out of the kitchen.

Dayna set her bottle on the counter and looked up at Chris. "How are you?"

"Fine, now."

"I know you can't talk much about it, but if you need to talk around it..."

"I'm not sure how I feel about it, actually. I think I'm okay, but if I'm not, I'll tell you."

Dayna squeezed her hand and Chris pulled her into another hug, and breathed her in, let the essence of Dayna both soothe and arouse her in a wholly delicious contradiction.

"I'm going to take Monday off," Dayna said after a few moments.

"Yeah?" Chris looked at her, surprised and pleased. "Did you have something in mind?"

"Let's go somewhere. It doesn't have to be far. A couple hours of driving or so. Just somewhere away." She stroked Chris's cheek.

"I'll go anywhere with you."

"So my plan worked." Dayna ran her lips along Chris's jaw.

She groaned in pleasure. "Which one?"

"The one where you fall madly in love with me and follow me to the ends of the Earth."

"That was your plan? I thought it was mine."

Dayna chuckled. "But did it work?"

"Completely."

"Hey, you two," K.C. called from the living room. "Dinner awaits."

Dayna smiled up at Chris. "You're mine after this, Detective," she said with a low growl that made Chris ache.

"Hell, I'm yours regardless, Counselor."

"Hold that thought," Dayna said as she kissed her.

"I plan to hold a lot more than that," she said as she followed Dayna out of the kitchen. For as long as she possibly could.

## More Andi Marquette titles

## *Land of Entrapment*

K.C. Fontero left New Mexico in the wake of a bitter break-up to take an academic fellowship in Texas. With a doctorate in sociology and expertise in white supremacist groups, she's on her way to an academic career. But a plea for help from her ex, Melissa, brings K.C. back to Albuquerque to find Melissa's troubled younger sister. Megan has disappeared with her white supremacist boyfriend. K.C. knows she has the expertise to track the mysterious group, and she knows she'll be doing a public service to uncover it. What she doesn't know is how far into her past she'll have to go to find both Megan and herself and the deeper she digs into the group, the greater the danger she faces.

ISBN 978-1-935053-02-6

## *State of Denial*

Albuquerque Police Detective Chris Gutierrez is not having a "Thank God It's Friday" kind of day. Not only is she on the scene of a murdered young man, buried near the Rio Grande, but she also has to put up with the other detective assigned to the case, the homophobic and sexist Dale Harper.

As if things weren't uncomfortable enough between the two detectives, they soon find out that the young victim was gay, and the trail leads Chris and Harper to another unsolved murder whose victim was also a gay youth. Soon, their suspect is a popular minister at a local mega-church who has spent years working with ex-gay groups. Enlisting the research skills, networks, and expertise of sociologist and long-time best friend K.C. Fontero, Chris works to build the case against Mumford, all too aware what mistakes in such a potentially explosive and high-profile investigation could cost her and the police department.

As Chris strives to prove the case and make an arrest before anyone else dies, she must also face her growing feelings for attorney Dayna Carson. The dangerous nature of police work and Chris's own reticence about romantic relationships are destined to collide. Struggling with her attraction to Dayna and the complexity of a difficult case, Chris is drawn into an ominous and potentially deadly game of cat-and-mouse with a man who harbors dark secrets and who will kill to protect them. Will Chris outsmart a diabolical murderer — or become another victim?

ISBN 978-1-935053-09-5

## *The Ties That Bind*

When the *Albuquerque Journal* reports that a white man was found dead along a remote stretch of road on the Navajo Reservation in northwestern New Mexico, UNM sociology professor K.C. Fontero thinks she might be able to use the case as an example of culture and jurisdiction in one of her classes. But it's soon apparent that this dead man has something to do with a mysterious letter that River Crandall, brother of K.C.'s partner Sage, recently received from the siblings' estranged father, Bill. What does the letter and Bill Crandall's link to a natural gas drilling company have to do with the dead man? And why would Bill try to contact his son and daughter now, after a decade of silence? From the streets of Albuquerque to the gas fields of northwestern New Mexico and the vast expanse of the Navajo Reservation, K.C. and Sage try to unravel the secrets of a dead man while Sage confronts a past she thought she'd left behind. But someone or something wants to keep those secrets buried, and as K.C. soon discovers, sometimes beliefs of one culture jump the boundaries of another, and challenge her logical and analytical mindset, threatening to drive a wedge into the relationship she's building with Sage.

Joined by K.C.'s younger sister Kara and Sage's brother River and aided by best friend and police detective Chris Gutierrez and Chris's partner Dayna Carson, K.C. and Sage are drawn into the life of a dead man, the embittered past of an estranged father, and dark, inexplicable forces whose origins are rooted in Navajo culture and traditions. Whatever happened out there along that road is inextricably linked to Sage and River, and K.C. knows that in order to help them, she has to change her very way of thinking or she could lose the woman who's come to mean the most in her life.

ISBN 1-935053- 23-1

# Other Quest Titles You Might Enjoy:

## *Murder and the Hurdy Gurdy Girl*
### by Kate McLachlan

It's 1897, and Susan Bantry is on the run from the law. She ends up in Needles Eye, Idaho, where she works in a hurdy gurdy as a dancing girl.

Jo Erin, Susan's childhood friend, is the cross-dressing Pinkerton agent sent to track Susan down. Before she can complete the job, a mining war breaks out and interferes with Jo Erin's plans. Complicating matters even further are the feelings that resurface between Susan and Jo Erin, as events from their past come back to haunt them.

ISBN 978-1-61929-126-3


## *The Chameleon*
### by Brenda Adcock

Six years ago Detective Christine Shaw left her happy life and a good job in Texas to follow her libido to New York City. She's still a cop, but her stewardess girlfriend has flown the coop and Chris hasn't been able to fill the void. Everything in her life begins to change when she and her partner are assigned to a high profile case.

The murder of Broadway star Elaine Barrie propels Chris into a whole new world. A fan of the murdered actress since she was a teenager, Chris isn't prepared for the secrets she uncovers during their investigation, including her attraction to the daughter of her number one suspect.

Was the victim any of the personalities witnesses describe, or was the real person a chameleon, satisfying the expectations of each person she met?

ISBN 978-1-61929-102-7

## *Now You See Me*
### by S. Y. Thompson

Corporate attorney, Erin Donovan, has nothing on her mind except representing her clients to the best of her ability. One fateful day, she shows an irritating new client, Carson Tierney, around the tenth floor space of her own building and her life takes off in an unforeseen direction.

Carson is an awe-inspiring woman by anyone's standards. Possessing genius-level intelligence that has allowed her to become a self- made millionaire from her computer software company, Carson still has a dark secret that could be her undoing.

When the two are thrust together, in a high-rise office building, to escape a deadly killer while a blizzard rages outside, they have no one to count on but themselves. So begins an unexpected yet tender romance. Unchecked love and desire isn't in their future, however. The murderer is still out there and he's coming for them. Will Carson's street-wise skills protect them both as Erin attempts to discover the killer's identity just as relentlessly as he is seeking their demise?

ISBN 978-1-61929-112-6

## *Jump the Gun*
### by Lori L. Lake

Dez Reilly and Jaylynn Savage are happy together. They have both advanced in their jobs with Jaylynn a Field Training Officer and Dez a patrol sergeant. Dez is now trying to decide what direction to go with her career: To SWAT? Or to investigations? Or does she settle for patrol supervision which she is heartily tired of? With some family complications, a murder of one of their own, and the hunt for a dangerous killer, the girls have their hands full.?

ISBN 978-1-935053-50-7

# OTHER QUEST PUBLICATIONS

| | | |
|---|---|---|
| Brenda Adcock | Pipeline | 978-1-932300-64-2 |
| Brenda Adcock | Redress of Grievances | 978-1-932300-86-4 |
| Brenda Adcock | Tunnel Vision | 978-1-935053-19-4 |
| Brenda Adcock | The Chameleon | 978-1-61929-102-7 |
| Sharon G. Clark | Into the Mist | 978-1-935053-34-7 |
| Michele Coffman | Veiled Conspiracy | 978-1-935053-38-5 |
| Blayne Cooper | Cobb Island | 978-1-932300-67-3 |
| Blayne Cooper | Echoes From The Mist | 978-1-932300-68-0 |
| Cleo Dare | Cognate | 978-1-935053-25-5 |
| Cleo Dare | Faultless | 978-1-61929-064-8 |
| Cleo Dare | Hanging Offense | 978-1-935053-11-8 |
| Lori L. Lake | A Very Public Eye | 978-1-61929-076-1 |
| Lori L. Lake | Buyer's Remorse | 978-1-61929-001-3 |
| Lori L. Lake | Gun Shy | 978-1-932300-56-7 |
| Lori L. Lake | Have Gun We'll Travel | 1-932300-33-3 |
| Lori L. Lake | Jump the Gun | 978-1-935053-50-7 |
| Lori L. Lake | Under the Gun | 978-1-932300-57-4 |
| Helen M. Macpherson | Colder Than Ice | 1-932300-29-5 |
| Linda Morganstein | Harpies' Feast | 978-1-935053-43-9 |
| Linda Morganstein | On A Silver Platter | 978-1-935053-51-4 |
| Linda Morganstein | Ordinary Furies | 978-1-935053-47-7 |
| Andi Marquette | Land of Entrapment | 978-1-935053-02-6 |
| Andi Marquette | State of Denial | 978-1-935053-09-5 |
| Andi Marquette | The Ties That Bind | 978-1-935053-23-1 |
| Andi Marquette | Day of the Dead | 978-1-61929-146-1 |
| Kate McLachlan | Hearts, Dead and Alive | 978-1-61929-017-4 |
| Kate McLachlan | Murder and the Hurdy Gurdy Girl | 978-1-61929-126-3 |
| Kate McLachlan | Rescue At Inspiration Point | 978-1-61929-005-1 |
| Kate McLachlan | Rip Van Dyke | 978-1-935053-29-3 |
| Keith Pyeatt | Struck | 978-1-935053-17-0 |
| Rick R. Reed | Deadly Vision | 978-1-932300-96-3 |
| Rick R. Reed | IM | 978-1-932300-79-6 |
| Damian Serbu | Secrets In the Attic | 978-1-935053-33-0 |
| Damian Serbu | The Vampire's Angel | 978-1-935053-22-4 |
| Damian Serbu | The Vampire's Quest | 978-1-61929-013-6 |
| Damian Serbu | The Vampire's Witch | 978-1-61929-104-1 |
| S. Y. Thompson | Now You See Me | 978-1-61929-112-6 |
| Mary Vermillion | Death By Discount | 978-1-61929-047-1 |
| Mary Vermillion | Murder By Mascot | 978-1-61929-048-8 |
| Mary Vermillion | Seminal Murder | 978-1-61929-049-5 |

## About the Author

Andi Marquette was born in New Mexico and grew up in Colorado. She completed a couple of academic degrees in anthropology and returned to New Mexico, where she decided a doctorate in history was somehow a good idea. She completed it before realizing that maybe she should have joined the circus, or at least a traveling Gypsy troupe. Oh, well. She fell into editing sometime around 1993 and has been obsessed with words ever since, which may or may not be a good thing. She currently resides in Colorado, where she edits, writes, and cultivates a strange obsession with New Mexico chile.

## VISIT US ONLINE AT
### www.regalcrest.biz

### At the Regal Crest Website You'll Find

- The latest news about forthcoming titles and new releases

- Our complete backlist of romance, mystery, thriller and adventure titles

- Information about your favorite authors

- Current bestsellers

- Media tearsheets to print and take with you when you shop

- Which books are also available as eBooks.

Regal Crest print titles are available from all progressive booksellers including numerous sources online. Our distributors are Bella Distribution and Ingram.

CPSIA information can be obtained at www.ICGtesting.com
Printed in the USA
LVOW12s1100290913

354573LV00002B/87/P